PRAISE FOR C.L. TAYLOR

'This masterfully woven story comes together in a thrilling and unexpected climax. I could not put it down.'
Fiona Cummins

'Wonderfully devious, clever cliffhangers and utterly addictive.'
John Marrs

'She's done it again . . . what a brilliant read *Strangers* is.'
Cass Green

'*Strangers* is her best yet. Expertly woven and so pacy – my heart was banging at the end!'
Holly Seddon

'This is REALLY good. Read it in a day.'
Jane Fallon

'Stayed up to finish *Strangers*, unable to put it down. It's her best one yet. A joy to read, full of living, breathing characters, a compelling plot, humour and a killer twist.'
Mark Edwards

'Clever, surprising and nuanced – C.L. Taylor is at the top of her game.'
Gillian McAllister

'Brilliant characters and a jaw-dropping denouement. I swear I hardly breathed for the last 100 pages. This one is going to be HUGE in 2020.'
Claire Allan

'Clever and unsettling, with a brilliant cast of characters, I am sure this is going to be another huge success.'
Rachel Abbott

'A deep and dark tale of three individuals whose lives collide with such force, I'm sure I was holding my breath near to the end. Utterly sinister and compelling.'
Mel Sherratt

'Claustrophobic and compelling.'
Karin Slaughter

'A masterclass in character. Clear to see why she's a million-copy seller.'
Sarah Pinborough

'Highly original – kept me utterly enthralled.'
Liz Nugent

'Twisted, unbearably tense, and a shock ending.'
C.J. Tudor

'Has a delicious sense of foreboding from the first page, and a final, agonizing twist. Loved it.'
Fiona Barton

'Fans of C.L. Taylor are in for a treat.'
Clare Mackintosh

'Claustrophobic, tense and thrilling, a thrill-ride of a novel that keeps you guessing.'
Elizabeth Haynes

'A gripping and disturbing psychological thriller.'
Lucy Clarke

'Pacy, well written, and anxiety-inducing.'
Lisa Hall

'A compulsive read.'
Emma Kavanagh

'Kept me guessing till the end.'
Sun

'Haunting and heart-stoppingly creepy, *The Lie* is a gripping rollercoaster of suspense.'
Sunday Express

'A rollercoaster with multiple twists.'
Daily Mail

'Packed with twists and turns, this brilliantly tense thriller will get your blood pumping.'
Fabulous Magazine

'A real page-turner . . . creepy, horrifying and twisty. Intriguing, scary and extremely gripping.'
Julie Cohen

'A compelling, addictive and wonderfully written tale. Can't recommend it enough.'
Louise Douglas

See what bloggers are saying about C.L. TAYLOR . . .

'I devoured *Strangers*. Twisty and clever, utterly compelling characters and a superb edge-of-the-seat finale.'
Liz Barnsley, *Liz Loves Books*

'My eyes were simply glued to the page, I couldn't tear them away!'
The Bookworm's Fantasy

'An intriguing and stirring tale, overflowing with family drama.'
Lovereading.co.uk

'Astoundingly written, *The Missing* pulls you in from the very first page and doesn't let you go until the final full stop.'
Bibliophile Book Club

'Imaginative, compelling and shocking –
The Fear is a highly engrossing read.'
The Book Review Café

'*The Fear* is a dark tale of revenge and just when you think you know where the story's going,
the author takes you by surprise!'
Portobello Book Blog

'[*The Missing*] inspired such a mixture of emotions in me and made me realise how truly talented you have to be to even attempt a psychological suspense of this calibre.'
My Chestnut Reading Tree

'Tense and gripping with a dark, ominous feeling that seeps through the very clever writing . . . all praise to C.L. Taylor.'
Anne Cater, *Random Things Through My Letterbox*

'C.L. Taylor has done it again, with another compelling masterpiece.'
Rachel's Random Reads

'In a crowded landscape of so-called domestic noir thrillers, most of which rely on clever twists and big reveals, [*The Missing*] stands out for its subtle and thoughtful analysis of the fallout from a loss in the family.'
Crime Fiction Lover

'When I had finished, I felt like someone had ripped my heart out and wrung it out like a dish cloth.'
By the Letter Book Reviews

'*The Fear* is a gripping, fast-paced read.'
The Book Whisperer

'*The Missing* has such a big, juicy storyline and is a dream read if you like books that will keep you guessing and take on plenty of twists and turns.'
Bookaholic Confessions

'Incredibly thrilling and utterly unpredictable! A must read!'
Aggie's Books

'A gripping story.'
Bibliomaniac

'It's the first time I have cried whilst reading. The last chapter [of *The Missing*] was heart-breaking and uplifting at the same time.'
The Coffee and Kindle

'Another hit from C.L. Taylor . . . so cleverly written and so absorbing that I completely forgot about everything else while reading it. Unmissable.'
Alba in Book Land

C.L. Taylor is a *Sunday Times* bestselling author. Her psychological thrillers have sold over a million copies in the UK alone, been translated into over twenty languages, and optioned for television. Her 2019 novel, *Sleep*, was a Richard and Judy pick. C.L. Taylor lives in Bristol with her partner and son.

By the same author:

The Accident
The Lie
The Missing
The Escape
The Fear
Sleep

For Young Adults
The Treatment

C.L. TAYLOR

Strangers

avon.

Published by AVON
A division of HarperCollins*Publishers* Ltd
1 London Bridge Street
London SE1 9GF

www.harpercollins.co.uk

A Hardback Original 2020

First published in Great Britain by HarperCollins*Publishers* 2020

A catalogue copy of this book is available from the British Library.

ISBN: 978-0-00-822246-8 (HB)
ISBN: 978-0-00-822107-2 (TPB)

This novel is entirely a work of fiction.
The names, characters and incidents portrayed in it are
the work of the author's imagination. Any resemblance to
actual persons, living or dead, events or localities is
entirely coincidental.

Typeset in Sabon LT Std 11.25/14.5 pt by Palimpsest Book Production Limited,
Falkirk, Stirlingshire

Printed and bound in Great Britain by CPI Group (UK) Ltd, Croydon CR0 4YY

MIX
Paper from
responsible sources
FSC™ C007454

This book is produced from independently certified FSC™ paper
to ensure responsible forest management.

For more information visit: www.harpercollins.co.uk/green

To Kellie Turner
My favourite Aussie

Chapter 1

Alice

Alice Fletcher has never seen a dead body before. She always imagined they'd look peaceful: their skin slackened, their muscles softened and their mouths settled, not into a smile exactly, but a loose, contented line. Alice Fletcher was wrong. The body lying motionless at her feet looks nothing like the soothing mental image she's been carrying around with her for the last forty-six years; the mouth is open, the jaw is hinged into a silent scream and the glassy, lifeless eyes are staring into the distance, somewhere beyond the toes of her sensible court shoes.

Alice isn't aware of the frantic pounding of her heart, the heavy-duty lino beneath her feet or the steel-grey shutter that separates her from the rest of the world. Nor is she conscious of the people around her. She doesn't notice when the tall hulking woman to her left takes a step closer. She doesn't see the sweat patches under the armpits of Ursula's pale blue sweatshirt or the way her hands are shaking, one fingernail torn away leaving behind a raggedy nail bed, tinged with blood. She isn't aware of Gareth's laboured breathing or the bruise blooming on his jaw.

An anguished scream from across the shop snaps Alice back into herself. There are other sounds too: whispering, sobbing and 'Oh God, oh God' repeated over and over again. And then there's the pain, the deep, nauseating ache that radiates up her arm and across her shoulder to her neck. Alice clutches at her arm, her fingers sliding over the warm, wet polyester sleeve of her blouse. But it's not the blood that makes her stomach lurch and her legs weaken. There's a dead body at her feet and her nightmare isn't over yet.

'I need my phone,' she mutters. 'I have to find my phone.'

'Where are you going?' Ursula shouts as Alice stumbles away and the frantic wail of a siren drifts through the open window. 'The police are coming. What do we tell them when they get here?'

Alice turns slowly, her gaze returning to the corpse. She looks at it for a second, two, three, then draws an exhausted, raggedy breath and raises her eyes.

'We say it was self-defence.'

Chapter 2

@realmadwife:
Massive police presence in the centre of Bristol.
What's going on?

@DiddleyBopDee:
Probably a road rage incident. The traffic is
MENTAL.

@PeterCrussell:
I follow BBC Radio Bristol and they haven't mentioned
anything.

@realmadwife:
That doesn't mean there's nothing going on, Peter. It
just means we haven't been told about it yet.

@pauldunphy:
Everyone's a conspiracist. Ring the police if you're so
worried.

@realmadwife:
I think they've got enough to deal with, don't you?
Anyway, thanks for butting in with your 'helpful' advice.

@onthecliffedge:
I bet the Harbourside Murderer is pleased.

@lisaharte101:
About what?

@onthecliffedge:
That we're talking about something else for a change.
Ha. Ha.

@lisaharte101:
Seriously? People have died and you're laughing?

@cris_matthiesen:
There's no such thing as the Harbourside Murderer. It's
an urban legend.

@snugbookshop:
Really? So how did three people just disappear then?
Answer me that . . .

Chapter 3

Alice

ONE WEEK EARLIER

Monday

It's the beginning of March but a bead of sweat winds its way down Alice's spine as she unbuttons her damp coat and slides it off her shoulders. There's a small round wooden table in front of her and a print of a dog sitting next to a gramophone on the wall but Alice isn't interested in what she can see. She's listening: for the tinkle of the bell above the door and the squeak of shoes on the sticky pub floor. But there's no one creeping up behind her. The pub is silent apart from the tap-tapping of a man at his laptop on the other side of the room, the murmured voices of two old blokes at the bar and the clink of glasses as the dishwasher opens. She takes a steadying breath then flings the coat over the back of a chair and sits down on the padded corner seat, shuffling around the table so she's facing the door. Her pulse slows.

Alice likes predictability. All-day delivery slots make her tense and just the thought of someone sneaking up on her, covering her eyes and shouting, 'Guess who?' is enough to bring her out in hives. The day she turned thirty-nine she texted all her friends telling them that under no circumstances were they to arrange a surprise party for her fortieth. It was probably the worst thing she could have done. Her phone didn't stop pinging with threats to hire village halls, to swipe her spare house keys, to collude with Peter. One so-called friend had even tormented her with the promise of a male stripper.

She shudders at the thought and takes a sip of her lemonade. As it turned out there was no surprise party for her fortieth and, although she'd felt nervous stepping into the restaurant her friend Lynne had booked, there was no stripper either. It was a lovely evening, surrounded by good friends and full of laughter. Peter had been on his best behaviour all evening and, even though she'd girded herself for unpleasantness in the taxi on the way home, he hadn't started a fight.

Her mobile vibrates on the table and she snatches it up, certain it's Michael, cancelling their date. But it's just Lynne, her best friend and workmate at Mirage Fashions, asking her how it's going. She taps out a reply, keeping one eye on the door. It's tipping down with rain outside and people are running past the pub, heads down, their faces obscured by heavy hoods and damp brollies.

He's not here yet and I'm shitting myself. I don't know why I agreed to this. Actually I do. Emily!

She inserts a rolling eyes emoticon at the end of the text, then deletes it. Her twenty-year-old daughter didn't force her into using Tinder. But Emily certainly dropped a lot of hints:

'It's been two years since Dad left . . .'

'I can't remember the last time you went on a date.'

'You're forty-six, not eighty-six. You don't have to spend the rest of your life alone.'

'Doesn't it get lonely? Spending the weekends on your own?'

She'd answered all of her daughter's comments with a sharp comeback but when she tried to respond to the last question the words dried in her mouth. Returning to her empty two-bedroom flat wasn't so bad in the week when her daughter was there. Besides, she was so tired after spending eight hours a day on her feet, smiling at customers and rallying her staff, that all she wanted to do was sink onto the sofa and lose herself in a documentary or some terrible reality TV show. But on a Sunday, when her daughter disappeared off to her boyfriend Adam's place, the flat seemed to swell and Alice seemed to shrink. As she walked from room to room, looking for something to do, she felt like a marble rolling through a maze. And on the rare occasions when she spoke – to herself or to the television – her voice seemed to bounce off the walls. It was almost a relief to wake up on Monday and get ready for work.

She stares at her phone, pushing down the wave of self-pity that threatens to engulf her and deletes the part about her daughter. She presses send and, a couple of seconds later, the phone vibrates with a reply.

Leave! Meet me for a coffee and a sandwich! Kaisha can cover for me.

It's a tempting offer but there's no way she's going to let her nerves stop her from meeting Michael. She decided, on 31st December, as she whirled around Lynne's living room with her hands in the air and her head thrown back as eighties hits pounded at her eardrums, that the new year would see a more assertive Alice. She'd learned through bitter experience that when you sit back and wait for what life throws at you, you mostly get covered in shit.

She glances at her watch. 1.10 p.m. She only gets an hour

for lunch and even if Michael walks through the door right now they'll only be able to spend forty minutes together before she has to leave. An old man's boozer with a sticky floor, tobacco-stained walls and choice of two soft drinks – 'Coke or lemonade, that's your lot' – wouldn't have been her ideal venue for a first date but he said it was his favourite pub and that they'd easily get a table because it wasn't busy at lunchtime. She'd given him the benefit of the doubt. He was new to Bristol and probably hadn't had chance to visit any of the nicer places yet. Either that or he has low standards. She smiles ruefully to herself, then pushes the thought away.

The bell above the door tinkles and a man in a black waterproof jacket walks in. Alice's stomach hollows as he pauses, his gaze flitting from the blonde bloke with the laptop to the two older gents at the bar. She fights the urge to slip down in her seat and slither under the table. Assertive Alice wouldn't do that, she tells herself as she straightens her spine and fixes a smile to her face. Assertive Alice *does not* hide. Instead she casts an eye over the man at the door. Michael's shorter than she imagined, five foot eight or nine to her five foot four, but he's better-looking than his photos (her daughter warned her that the opposite was more likely to be true). His thick dark hair is peppered with grey at the temples and he's very masculine-looking with his heavy brow, wide jaw and strong nose, the tip pinked from the cold. There's a tautness to his expression but it vanishes as he turns his head and his eyes flick towards her. His lips twitch at the edges. It's not a *smile* per se, more a flash of recognition, and as he ambles across the carpet towards her the pit in her stomach fills with self-doubt. He doesn't fancy her. She can see it in his face.

'Alice!' As Michael nears her table he half-falls, half-lunges in her direction and lands a cold kiss on her cheek. 'Sorry I'm late!'

'It's fine,' she lies, shifting across the padded bench to make room for him as he unceremoniously plonks himself next to her rather than taking the seat opposite. 'But I can't stay long. I need to get back to work.'

'You've got time for a quick drink, though . . .' His brow furrows as he takes in the near-empty glass on the table in front of her. 'Gin and tonic is it?'

'Lemonade.'

'Have a gin and tonic!' Still in his wet coat he heaves himself back onto his feet. 'You can't let me drink alone.'

'I'm working! I don't want a—'

But Michael is already halfway to the bar. As he signals to the bored-looking twenty-something barman Alice picks up her phone.

He's here, she texts Lynne. *He's a bit . . . exuberant . . . but he's nice-looking.*

She stares at the phone, waiting for a reply, then quickly drops it into her bag as her date returns from the bar, two glasses in his hands.

If that's gin I'm not drinking it, she thinks, warily eyeing the clear liquid and slice of lemon in one of the glasses.

'Lemonade.' He slides it across the table, his eyes not meeting hers.

She takes a sip to check – definitely lemonade – then sets it back down and takes a better look at Michael, or at least the part of his face that isn't hidden behind the rim of his pint glass. Up close his skin is grey and dry, spidered with red thread veins and dotted with age spots. His thick hair is dull and brittle and his nails are gnarly and split. She sniffs subtly, silently drawing his scent into her nostrils. Booze. And something worse: unwashed clothes. He senses her watching him and sets down his pint, swivelling his bloodshot eyes in her direction.

He's drunk, Alice realises. He's turned up to our first date drunk.

Perhaps he's nervous, she thinks, trying desperately to reconcile the glassy-eyed man to her right with the witty, clever man she exchanged dozens of messages with. It's after one o'clock, technically the afternoon. Maybe he had a glass of wine with his lunch to calm himself down and one swiftly became two, or three.

'Cheers! Here's to meeting at last.' He holds out his drink and clinks it, slightly too heavily, against hers. Lemonade slops over the glass and wets the cuff of her sleeve. 'I wasn't sure you'd come.'

'Why's that?'

'Catfish. You don't know who you're talking to on the internet half the time.' His words aren't slurred but they're louder than they need to be, given there's barely a foot between them. Definitely nervous, Alice tells herself.

'Have you been catfished before?' she asks.

He gives her a long, lingering look, his gaze drifting from eyes to her mouth. It rests there a fraction too long, making her feel so self-conscious she presses her lips together, pulling them between her teeth.

'I've met a lot of people who can't be trusted, but you seem different.' He pauses. 'Are you?'

Alice runs her hands up and down the skirt of the dress she changed into in the staff toilets at work. Nervous or not, this is too much, this intensity. She thought they'd make small talk, then segue into chat about their interests, their families and their plans for the future. She thought he'd be as light-hearted and jokey as he'd been in his messages.

She forces a laugh. 'I don't think I'd have got the manager's job if I was untrustworthy.'

'That's not what I mean and you know it.' He presses a heavy hand over hers. 'Are you someone *I* can trust?'

Alice glances at the bar but the near-teenager is too engrossed in his phone to notice the look she shoots in his direction and the two older men have their backs turned to her. But someone has noticed her anguish. The man with the laptop on the opposite side of the pub has stopped typing and is looking at her with concern. She raises her eyebrows at him, signally what she's not sure, but he doesn't move from his seat. Instead his attention returns to his screen and he hunches over, typing furiously. He wasn't watching her at all, he was staring into space.

'I asked you a question,' Michael says. 'Are you someone I can trust?'

Alice keeps her gaze firmly fixed forward. 'Yes,' she says from between her teeth. 'Of course I am.'

She tugs her hand away from beneath his sweating palm but he's quicker than she is and he pins her hand to the light cotton material of her skirt.

'Look at me. Look at me, Alice.'

No, shouts the voice in her head. I don't want to.

There's a part of her that wants to shout at him to take his heavy, clammy hand off hers. He's drunk but he must be able to see how uncomfortable she is, how rigid she has suddenly become. But there's another part of her, a bigger part, that doesn't want to cause a scene or risk angering him. He's not sexually abusing her. He hasn't touched her boobs or her bum. But that doesn't make it okay. Hot angry tears prick at her eyes. Of all the men on Tinder, she chose him. It's like she's got a sign on her head: *complete walkover seeks utter arsehole. Decent men need not apply.* Well she's not going to let him see her cry.

'Excuse me.' She stands abruptly, yanking her hand from his, grabs her handbag, shifts to her left and rounds the table. Out of the corner of her eye she spots laptop man packing up his things. 'I'm just going to use the ladies.'

Irritation flares on Michael's face. 'You're doing a runner.'

'No, I'm not.'

But I will, she thinks. When I get back.

'I'll get you a drink,' Michael calls after her as she hurries across the pub, following the sign to the toilets. 'Might make you a bit less uptight!'

Alice's pulse pounds in her ears as she throws open the door to the ladies' loo and stalks over to the sink. She grips the cold, ceramic sides and folds over herself, her eyes screwed shut, breathing rapidly through her nose.

'Arsehole,' she says, lifting her head, staring into the eyes of her tear-stained reflection. 'Stupid bloody arsehole.'

She steps into the nearest cubicle, grabs a handful of cheap, rough toilet paper and blows her nose. She flushes it, grabs another handful and returns to the sink. She blots the tears that roll down her cheeks, cutting pale rivulets through the thick foundation that mask her freckles. As she takes a deep, steadying breath, an image of her ex-husband flickers in her brain – curled up on the sofa with his new wife and her burgeoning baby bump – and fresh tears replace the ones she wiped away.

'Stop it,' she says to her reflection. 'Alice, stop it! You've got a nice flat, a lovely daughter, a good job and great friends. You don't need this shit.'

She roots around in her handbag for her concealer and powder and does her best to cover the redness on her nose, then replaces the eyeliner that disappeared down her cheeks. She doesn't want to give Michael the satisfaction of knowing that he made her cry.

'It'll do,' she tells herself and snaps her handbag shut.

She steels herself before she opens the toilet door. She'll go back to the table. She'll pick up her coat, say a cursory, 'It was nice to meet you,' and she'll walk out of the pub with her head held high.

'Right,' she says to herself, then she turns the handle, opens the door and steps out of the ladies' toilets.

'Hello, Alice.'

Michael is standing at the end of the narrow corridor, blocking her route back to the bar. As his eyes meet hers, her heart stills its frantic thumping. It pauses between beats.

A slow smile forms on Michael's lips. 'Did you get lost?'

'No. Why?' There's a quiver in her voice that she's never heard before.

'I thought maybe you were waiting for me to join you.'

'I'm sorry?'

He shrugs, his dark anorak shifting on his shoulders and Alice's stomach lurches. Clenched in his right hand is her coat.

'You only had to ask.' He leers at her. 'If you wanted a quickie. I'm all for a bit of . . . fun.'

'I have to go back to work.' She steps towards him, gesturing for her coat.

There's a pause as Michael considers the request, then he lifts her coat and holds it out towards her. She reaches for it, limp with relief. Her fingertips graze the shiny material and she fixes her mouth into a tight smile as she mentally prepares the last words she'll ever say to him.

It was nice to meet you.

No, it wasn't. How about, *I really must get back to work. Bye then.*

Or maybe just: *Goodbye.*

She raises her eyes to his, the word forming between her lips, then gasps in shock as the coat is ripped from her curled fingers.

Michael holds it behind his back. His smile widens.

'Kiss goodbye?'

She stares at him, too stunned to speak.

'I had to take half a day off work to meet you. And I bought you a drink.'

Her incredulity morphs into anger. He took the morning off work to get pissed and shelled out for half a lemonade and he thinks that entitles him to a kiss? What century does he live in? What planet?

'My coat.' This time her voice doesn't betray her. Every ounce of anger she feels is compressed into the two words.

He shakes his head then leans forward, lips pursed. Alice reaches round him, squeezing half her body between him and the wall, and grabs at the coat, dangling from his hands. 'Just fucking give it to me!'

The air is knocked from her lungs as Michael lunges to the side, his elbow connecting with the small hollow between her collarbones. She stumbles backwards, the crown of her head hitting the wall as her handbag tumbles to the ground.

'Don't swear at me.' His breath is sour, his eyes glassy. '*Never* swear at me.'

Alice presses a hand to her throat, sucking in air, her brain empty. She is vaguely aware of the soft squeak of a door opening and a dark shape in her peripheral vision but all she can do is stare up into the sweaty, open-pored face of the man whose right hand is clamped around her right shoulder, his fingers digging into the soft tissue beneath the hard bone. Michael lowers his face to hers, his dry cracked lips parting, as he draws closer.

He's going to kiss me.

His wet, red tongue quivers against his bottom lip, saliva glistening on its tip. The revulsion that courses through her body makes her dazed brain spark back to life.

He's NOT going to kiss me.

Her knee whips through the air then stops suddenly as it finds its target. Michael throws his head back and roars as he falls away, hands clasped between his legs.

Alice doesn't wait for him to recover. Instead she stoops down, snatches up her bag and her coat, and she runs.

A male voice follows her as she bursts out of the pub, shouting, telling her to stop, to wait. She hears footsteps behind her, pounding the cobbled street as she heads for the Meads, but she doesn't look back.

Chapter 4

Gareth

It's the sudden movement across the top left screen that catches Gareth's eye. Someone is speeding across the shopping centre, running hell for leather. He snatches up his radio, his thumb primed over the talk button. Someone moving that fast can only mean one thing – shoplifter. He pushes a button on the control desk, zooming in on the sprinter, then his eyes widen as she comes into focus. He knows this woman. She works in the ladies' fashion boutique on the first floor. He's watched her open up in the morning and close up at night. Given the fact she's always the first one to arrive and the last one to leave he's pretty sure she's the manager. She's short, not much more than five foot, with vivid red hair that she wears curled up in a bun on the back of her head.

He jolts in his seat as a hand darts across the screen, grasping for the red-haired woman. Male fingers latch around her shoulder. Gareth zooms out to see a tall blonde man in a beige jacket with a black laptop bag slung across his body, then lifts his radio to his mouth.

'Alpha Charlie Zero. Anyone available on the first floor? Red-haired IC1 female being assaulted by a blond-haired IC1 male. Just outside Superdrug. Over.'

He takes his thumb off the button and stands up to get a better look at the screen. The shop manager looks terrified: her hands are up by her mouth, her eyes are wide with fright and she's backing away from the man. He's got something in his hand and he's waving it in her direction. Gareth's radio crackles.

'Bravo Golf Seven,' says Liam, one of his security guards. 'I've spotted them. En route. Over.'

As Gareth watches, the guard sprints across the expanse and inserts himself between the man and woman. Gareth holds his breath, waiting to see what Liam will do next. He's already had one warning for aggressively apprehending a shoplifter, on top of another for the state of his uniform. One more and he's out.

Gareth pans back in so he can see everyone's faces. The tall blonde man is shaking his head, holding up his hands as though in surrender. He opens his right hand and looks from Liam to the red-haired woman. There's a small, black purse on his palm. The woman stares at it in surprise then opens her handbag and rummages around inside. Her lips move as she looks back at the man with the laptop and, not for the first time, Gareth wishes he could hear what was being said. He continues to watch as the woman takes the purse out of the blonde man's hand then scurries away in the direction of Mirage Ladies Fashions.

Gareth's radio crackles to life.

'Bravo Golf Seven,' Liam says. 'Incident under control. No assault took place. IC1 male was returning a purse to IC1 female. Apparently she dropped it during a scuffle in the Evening Star pub on Broad Street. Over.'

Gareth raises his eyebrows. 'Received. What do you mean by scuffle? Over.'

'Not entirely sure. Sounds like she was assaulted but fought back. Not by the IC1, someone else. Over.'

'Is she pressing charges? Over.'

'I asked her that and she said no. Over.'

Gareth runs a hand across his face. He wishes he could go down and chat to her, to see if she's okay and counsel her about pressing charges. But he can't. He can't leave the CCTV office when he's manning it alone, not even for five minutes. At 2 p.m. he'll swap with one of the other guards, currently on patrol. Until then he's got to stay where he is.

'All right,' he says into his radio. 'Don't forget to write it up and file it. Over and out.'

He wheels himself over to the side of the desk and enters the details of the incident into the database, then rolls back to the centre of the desk. He looks from screen to screen, watching mothers pushing babies in prams, dads carrying young children on their shoulders, toddlers having tantrums, two elderly ladies walking arm in arm, a small group of teenagers on the skive from school, a single bloke, a single woman, people frowning, laughing, chatting and deliberating. It's not a large shopping centre – two floors (three if you count the level where the CCTV office is situated) containing about forty shops. But hundreds of people go in and out of the Meads every day, and he watches them – looking for signs of trouble, for shoplifters and vandals, for the infirm and unwell, for missing children and frantic parents, for accidents waiting to happen (or accidents that already have). Even when he's on patrol people rarely look him in the eye. The other guards moan about their families – how their wives nag, how their kids fight, and how the dog's shat behind the sofa again. But in the same breath they'll tell him what a bloody good mum their missus is, how their kids were 'star of the week' at school, and how the dog's learned a new trick.

Gareth's just got his mum. He lives in the same house he was born in. You could blindfold him and spin him around and he could still find his way from the living room to his bedroom without stepping on the loose nail in the stairs or the squeaky plank in the hall.

His mum used to wake him up in the morning with a sharp tap on the door and a cup of tea on his bedside table. He can't remember the last time she did that. Before Dad left maybe? These days it's him doing the waking up: knocking softly at her door, opening it a crack, holding his breath, looking at the small shape of her shrouded by the duvet, watching for the rise and fall of her chest.

The thought makes him dig in his back pocket for his mobile. It's 1.40 p.m. and, sure enough, there's a text from his mum's carer Sally.

All good. Mum seems coherent today. She was telling me all about your dad and how he won the biggest marrow competition at some fair. I've left her with a sandwich and Bargain Hunt *on the TV. Yvonne arrived before I left.*

Yvonne is his mum's other carer. Gareth hits reply and slides his thumb over the screen.

Any visitors today?

There's a pause then,

That man from the church popped in.

Gareth grimaces. William Mackesy, the local Spiritualist Church leader, aka the biggest fraud that ever lived. He taps out a reply: *What did he want?*

A text pings back: *He just wanted to say hello but he did mention something to your mum that freaked her out a bit.*

What's that?

I'm not sure I should tell you.

18

STRANGERS

Tell me!

There's another pause then Gareth's phone pings again.

He said he's been receiving messages from the other side for you and that you should be careful. There's someone close by who means you harm.

Chapter 5

Ursula

Ursula steps from foot to foot as she fumbles her key into the lock.

'Come on, come on, come on!'

The key doesn't turn so she wiggles the handle. To her surprise the door opens. It's the middle of the day and both of her flat-mates are at work. There's a distinct possibility that she might be about to interrupt a burglar clearing out the house, but Ursula doesn't care. She bursts into the hallway, slams the front door shut with a kick of her foot and speeds up the stairs to the bathroom. At the sight of the white porcelain her pelvic muscles weaken, she lets out a little squeal of alarm and yanks down her jogging bottoms. She needs to use the toilet, leave the house and get back in the van as quickly as possible. The traffic was terrible at Temple Meads and she's already running seven minutes behind schedule. Much more and she won't complete her delivery round on time.

'Ahhhh.' She sighs with relief as her bottom hits the seat. As she reaches for the toilet roll there's a sharp knock at the bathroom door that makes her jump.

'Ursula, it's Charlotte. Can I have a word in the living room when you're done?'

Charlotte? What's she doing at home? Ursula pulls up her pants and jogging bottoms, washes her hands and reaches for her pink hand towel. But it's not on the top rung of the metal wall radiator. Matt's black towel is on the next rung down and Charlotte's grey towel beneath that, but hers isn't there. She looks down at the tiled floor then peers behind the sink. It's definitely gone. As she casts her eye around the small bathroom she notices other missing items – her toothbrush and toothpaste, her shower gel, her shampoo and conditioner, her body cream and her contact lens solution and pot. Charlotte and Matt's things are still in their usual places so it's not as though one of them went on a cleaning rampage – something Matt is very fond of doing ridiculously early on a Sunday morning, Ursula's only day off. So why move her things? Glancing at her watch, she hurries across the landing, throws open the door to her bedroom and steps inside. Then immediately steps back out again. She's in the wrong room, maybe even the wrong house . . .

'Charlotte!' She hurries down the stairs and through the open door of the lounge. She stops short and gawps at the enormous pile of cardboard boxes crowding the middle of the room.

'We're very sorry, Ursula.'

She jolts at Matt's voice. He's sitting on the sofa behind the mountain of cardboard, his fingers entwined with Charlotte's.

'Sorry? Sorry about wh—'

The pieces slot, Tetris-like, into shape. They've packed up all her stuff. That's why her bedroom has been stripped bare and none of her things are in the bathroom. That's why Charlotte zipped back into her room without saying good morning when they passed on the landing a little after seven. It's why Matt cheerily offered her a cup of coffee when she came downstairs. They planned this. They let her think they were going to work and then they let themselves into her room and they moved her out.

'You've been through my things,' she says, goose bumps prickling beneath the thick cotton of her hoody. 'My personal things.'

'Not just *your* things, Ursula.' Matt tugs his hand from Charlotte's and stands up. At a little under six foot he has to tilt his chin up to make eye contact with Ursula but there's no fear on his face (despite her size). Instead he looks determined, and more than a little pissed off.

'We knew it was you.' Unlike Matt's steady tone, Charlotte's voice is tight and screechy with emotion. 'We tried to give you the benefit of the doubt. We made allowances for you, Ursula. We even told you that if you returned our things we'd say no more about it but—'

'You took her granny's wedding ring,' Matt says. 'That had huge sentimental value to Charlotte. Didn't it, Char?'

Charlotte nods, her eyes shining with tears. Ursula's throat tightens. She didn't know it was her granny's ring or that it had sentimental value. The little ceramic dish had been in the bathroom for what felt like forever. There wasn't much in it – some hair bands, toothbrush heads, the knob that had come unscrewed from the cupboard, and a slim gold band with a slit that broke its perfect circle. It had glinted at her in the early morning sun and she'd picked it up and put it in her pocket. She barely even noticed herself doing it. She'd been thinking about Nathan at the time.

'I'm sorry,' she says now. 'I meant to put it back.'

'Like you meant to put my watch back,' Matt says, 'and Char's mug and my pen and her scarf and my photo frame and . . .' He shakes his head. 'I'd be here all day if I listed it all. We found it, by the way, all our stuff, and some things that belong to our friends. Friends who stayed over on the sofa believing that their belongings would be safe in our house.'

Ursula swallows. She hadn't meant to take the fancy shower gel from the bathroom, or the book from the arm of the sofa, or the umbrella from the hook in the hall. She'd wanted to return them – she always wanted to return the things she took – but the friends never stayed long enough for her to sneak their valuables back into their bags. Unfortunately there'd been no way she could return Charlotte's ring to the dish after she'd practically torn the bathroom apart looking for it.

'There was other stuff we found in your room too,' Charlotte says. 'Clothes, jewellery, knick-knacks with price tags attached. Matt said we should go to the police but I don't want you to go to prison. I just want . . . I just want . . .' Her voice breaks and she sobs.

'Please, Charlotte,' Ursula begs. 'Please don't do this. I'll change. I promise. You can't kick me out. I've got no money and nowhere else to go.'

'You could stay with your mum.'

'I can't. Even if she wanted me there I couldn't afford the flight to Spain and there's no one, literally no one else in Bristol I can stay with.'

'Nathan's mum then.'

'No.' Ursula shakes her head violently, tears pricking at her eyes. 'Please, Charlotte. Let's talk about this. Let's sit down this evening, have a glass of wine and sort it out.'

'I can't.' Charlotte shakes her head miserably. 'I'm sorry but I really can't.'

Matt presses a hand to his girlfriend's shoulder and gives it a consoling squeeze. 'I'm sorry, Ursula. We just want you out.'

Fat tears drop onto the piece of paper in Ursula's hands. The back of the van is crammed with her belongings, the engine is running and she's nearly forty-five minutes behind schedule, but she can't bring herself to release the handbrake and pull away.

She managed to hold it together until Matt held out his hand. When she went to shake it he snatched it away.

'Your house keys.'

Hot tears welled in her eyes as she unclipped two keys from her keyring and dropped them into his palm.

'Where do I go?' The words scratched at her throat. 'I've got nowhere to live.'

Other than Charlotte and Matt, she doesn't really know anyone in Bristol. There's Bob, the guy who drops round her packages every morning, but other than a brusque 'hello' they've never actually spoken. Her boss Jackie is nice but she's married with two kids and won't have space. And Ursula isn't in touch with anyone from her previous job as a primary school teacher. Her thoughts flit from the present to the past, to a bench outside Banco Lounge, six pints lined up on the table, male laughter and the sun making her squint. Nathan is beside her, as small, round and hairy as a bear, his rotund tummy wedged between his lap and the top of the table. His friends . . . she searches their sepia faces and plucks names from the air. Andy. 'Randy Andy', Nathan called him. Joe. Tom. Harry. Even if she could get in touch and they had a spare room, they wouldn't want her to move in. They blame her for what happened, even if they've never come out and said it. It's why she deliberately lost touch with them. When she lost Nathan half her world disappeared too.

She swipes a hand over her eyes, dampening the sleeve of the Long Tall Sally hoody she bought on eBay, and focuses on the image on her phone. It's a photograph Charlotte just texted her of an advert in a shop window. She can see the grey shape of Charlotte reflected in it. Something twangs in Ursula's heart. She'd assumed that Matt was the driving force behind getting her out of the house. She never completely warmed to him, despite sharing a home for over half a year. He'd given her a strange, narrow-eyed look, and wrinkled his nose – just the tiniest amount but enough for her to notice – when Charlotte introduced them for the first time.

'My boyfriend, Matt!' Charlotte's face glowed with pride, before a flash of apprehension dulled it as she glanced at Ursula, looking – hoping – for approval.

They were living together – Charlotte and Ursula, best friends since secondary school – in the two-bedroom terraced house that Charlotte had bought with her inheritance money when her father died. They were happy – happyish – and then Matt moved in and everything changed. All the little routines they'd established – late night sofa chats, girls' night in, cinema on Sunday – gradually disappeared and Ursula began to spend more and more time alone in her room. Three was most certainly a crowd.

House share available now.

She reads the first line of the handwritten advert.

William Street. Decent-sized double room with bed, wardrobe and chest of drawers available for clean, tidy, non-smoker employed person (m or f). Shared use of kitchen. Live-in landlord. Parking available. £350 pcm including bills. No pets, couples or benefits.

A telephone number is listed below the description.

Ursula glances back at the house she called home for nearly two years and spots movement at the far left of the living room window, Roman blinds that suddenly close.

She looks back at the advert. William Street is still in Totterdown, just a few roads away. If she stays in the neighbourhood she'll get to keep her round and she likes her clients and the safe familiarity of the local roads. The rent is very reasonable too. It's a whole hundred pounds less than she's been paying Charlotte.

She dials the number, her heart flip-flopping in her chest. She mustn't get her hopes up. The room's bound to have gone, or else it's tiny and dirty, or the landlord's a weirdo. If she doesn't – or can't – take it she'll have to find a hotel for the night, something she can barely afford when she's earning seventy pence for every parcel she delivers. And she can't take tomorrow off work to go round letting agents; she simply can't afford it.

As the number dials out she raises her eyes to the ceiling of her white van and says a quick prayer.

If this pans out I'll never steal anything again. I promise.

And this time I'll keep it, she adds as an afterthought.

'Hello?' a pleasant male voice says into her left ear.

'Hello, I'm calling about the room. My name's Ursula Andrews and—'

'Like the Bond girl?'

She fakes a laugh, the number of times she's heard that. 'No, that was Ursula Andress, she's like eighty or something. I'm thirty-two years old. I don't smoke and I'm very neat . . . well . . . quite neat. I'm a courier. I wasn't always one. I used to be a primary school teacher . . . Sorry, I'm waffling. Anyway, I need to take in my deliveries every morning but they wouldn't get in your way and—'

Warm laughter interrupts her. 'You sound nervous, Ursula. Take a breath.'

He sounds posh, which makes her more nervous, but she does as she's told and fills her lungs with the warm cab air then exhales shakily. 'Sorry.'

'No need to be sorry. The room's still available if you'd like to see it.'

'Is it? Brilliant. When could I move in?'

There's a pause, then, 'Are you free to see it now?'

'Yes! No.' Her heart sinks as she remembers the thirty-odd parcels squeezed up against her belongings in the back of the van. 'I've got to finish my round first, but I could be with you about sixish. Is that too late? I do really want it. I'm very keen and, as I said, I'm very reliable and tidy and—'

More laughter. She's not entirely sure if he's laughing at her or with her. 'You haven't seen it yet. You might hate it.'

'I'm sure I won't. It sounds perfect.'

'Listen, no one else has booked in to see it today and, if anyone does ring, I won't make any decisions until after you've come round. Okay?'

'Okay.' A warm wave of optimism courses through her. She's not going to end up penniless or on the streets. Everything is going to be okay.

'All right then,' says the male voice. 'I'll see you about sixish. I'm number fifteen by the way.'

'I'll be there. Oh.' A thought hits her. 'One more question before I go.'

'Shoot.'

'I didn't catch your name.'

'It's Edward.'

'Edward what?'

There's a pause, then Edward laughs lightly. 'Goodbye, Ursula. Looking forward to seeing you soon.'

Chapter 6

Alice

Alice catches Lynne staring at her as they sort through the rail of rejected clothes outside the changing rooms and pile them over their arms, preparing to return them to the racks.

'What?'

'You're amazing. You know that?'

Alice laughs. If Peter had been as ready with the compliments they might still be married. Actually, no, they wouldn't. Nothing would have allowed her to forgive him for his infidelity, but she might have left the relationship with a tiny amount of self-confidence.

'Why am I amazing?'

Lynne lugs a heavy coat off the hanger and loops it over her arm. 'Most normal people would have gone home after what happened to you.'

'So I'm not normal then? Cheers.'

Now it's Lynne's turn to laugh. 'You know what I mean. I'd

have been straight under my duvet. Or . . .' she gives her a sideways glance '. . . at the police station. Are you sure you don't want to report him? I don't want to go on at you but—'

Alice sighs. That was what Simon said – the man who'd nearly given her a heart attack by running after her all the way from the pub to the mall with her dropped purse. He'd seen the whole thing and was willing to make a statement to the police. She'd said no, she just wanted to forget it, but her decision has been rankling at her ever since. What if she wasn't the first woman Michael abused on a date? What if there were dozens of other women he'd creeped out and hurt? She realised she was going to have to report what happened but now she had no way of getting in touch with Simon, the only witness. She'd gone back to the shop without getting his details, desperate to put the whole episode behind her.

'Oh, crap.' She swears softly under her breath, causing Lynne to look round. It's not long until they close and a customer has just wandered in.

'It's her.' Lynne sidles up beside her and hisses in her ear. 'The one I told you about.'

Alice watches the customer as she drifts from rack to rack, trailing her fingers over the clothes. She's the tallest woman Alice has ever seen – at least six foot three or four – with wide shoulders, a weighty physique and a large face with a broad forehead that her fine fringe draws attention to rather than hides. She's dressed casually, in jogging bottoms, trainers and a lumpy wool coat.

'Last time she was in she took a size eight skirt,' Lynne hisses. 'One of the new lot of stock – the ugly blue floral design none of us like. And she's at least a size twenty-four.'

Alice's gaze flicks towards the door where Larry, their sixty-something security guard, is staring longingly out towards the concourse. Probably desperate to get home.

'Did he catch her?' she asks Lynne, already knowing the answer.

'He didn't even notice and there was nothing on the CCTV.'

Alice sighs softly. Chances are the woman's stealing to order – probably has a list as long as her arm. The regular shoplifters are known to every manager in the Meads. They're all banned but it doesn't stop them from chancing it if Larry's distracted and the staff are busy. But this woman isn't on the printout Alice has got pinned up in the back of the shop.

'But she definitely took it?'

'Yeah. I saw her stuffing it into her jacket, but I had a customer kicking up a fuss about a button coming off a pair of trousers she'd bought two months ago. The next time I looked up, Godzilla over there had disappeared. So had the skirt.'

Alice watches as the tall woman drifts towards the back of the store where they keep the handbags and jewellery.

'You cash up,' she tells Lynne. 'I'll tell her we're about to close.'

She follows the shoplifter across the store, dawdling at the racks en route, sorting the sizes into order as she keeps an eye on her. It doesn't seem as though the woman's looking for anything in particular but there's a strange, tense air about her as though she's holding her breath or she's primed for a fight. It reminds Alice of her daughter and the way the air in the house changes when she gets back from work. There's no point talking to Emily for at least half an hour after she comes in. Alice has to wait for her to stomp along to her room, get changed, stomp back down again to the kitchen, open the cupboard, uncork the rioja and glug a sizeable measure into a glass. Then they *both* relax.

'Excuse me?' The tall woman with the fringe appears beside Alice, making her jump. She looms rather than stands, her shoulders curved inwards, her head slightly bowed. The blue/grey eyeliner under her lower lashes is smudged and there's a faint tint of pink lipstick on her top lip.

'Yes?' Alice tries to read her body language. Most shoplifters are harmless – they want to get in and out without being spotted. But there's another, more dangerous, breed: feisty and desperate women who'll threaten anyone who gets too close with a dirty syringe. This woman doesn't look like a druggy but there's an edgy vibe to her that puts Alice on her guard.

'There's a man over there who's trying to get your attention.' The shoplifter raises a long arm and points over Alice's head.

Standing near the cash desk, shifting awkwardly from side to side with an enormous bouquet of flowers in his hands, is Simon. Lynne, still behind the counter, catches Alice's eye and pulls a face as if to say, 'What the fuck?'

'Excuse me.' Alice abandons the shoplifter and hurries across the shop towards Simon. He clears his throat as she draws closer, the base of his neck flushed red.

'I . . . um . . . sorry, this is probably a bit weird but I . . . er . . . I've been wrestling with what happened earlier. I can't help but feel that I should have stepped in or done something and I really didn't help matters by chasing you down the street so um . . .' He thrusts the bouquet of lilies and roses at her. 'These are to say sorry. For what you went through and me . . .' he clears his throat again '. . . being a bit crap.'

'It wasn't your fault.' Alice feels herself flush as she takes the flowers. She buries her face in the blooms, sniffing to give herself a couple of seconds thinking time. She can't remember the last time someone gave her flowers. Peter was never much of a romantic; she was lucky to get a card on Valentine's Day and she'd always receive something functional and lacking in romance on her birthday.

'My . . . um . . .' Simon taps the cellophane wrapper. 'I wrote my number on the florist's card. Just in case you changed your mind about talking to the police.'

'Thank you.' Alice raises her eyes to meet his. 'You really didn't have to do this. But it's very kind of you.'

He smiles awkwardly, one side of his mouth lifting more than the other. He's not an attractive man per se – it's not just his mouth that's asymmetrical; there's something about the balance of his face that's a little bit off – but his grey eyes are soft and warm and his voice is deep and melodic.

'Okay then.' He shrugs and half-turns to go.

'I'll be in touch,' Alice says.

Simon stops walking and looks back at her, surprise registering on his pale, freckled face.

'About the police,' she clarifies. 'I'm going to ring them when I get home.'

'Of course.' He gives a small sharp nod, his eyes flicking towards the hulking woman who slips between him and Larry and trots out of the shop, arms folded tightly over her bulky coat.

'Oh shit,' Lynne breathes from behind Alice. 'She's nicked something else.'

Chapter 7

Gareth

Gareth is still fizzing with irritation as he parks up outside the house he shares with his mother. How dare William Mackesy scare his mum with a message like that? She suffers from dementia – something Mackesy knows perfectly well – and a comment about Gareth being in danger could easily make her have one of her turns. It wouldn't just be a momentary upset either; she could be unsettled for days. It was a ridiculous thing to say. Of course he's at risk from harm. He's a security guard: there's always the possibility that someone he apprehends could be carrying a weapon. Hell, just the other day he read about an ASDA guard stabbed in the arm and leg trying to stop a shoplifter.

Bloody William Mackesy with his weasely little face, dark, shiny ball-bearing eyes and balding comb-over. He's only met the man twice – once when he accompanied his mum to one of the 'services' at the church and once when he returned home from work to find him sitting in his armchair and drinking out of his mug. Gareth's mother Joan, a book-keeper pre-retirement, had always pooh-poohed religion but she'd been talked into going to the spiritualist church by a friend (some time before she developed dementia). She'd find some comfort, the friend said, in knowing there was an afterlife, even if she didn't get a message. Gareth tried to talk his mum out of it but somehow found himself going along too.

It was mostly women in the small, packed room, their coats and bags gathered onto their laps, their eyes fixed on the slight, slim man who stalked back and forth at the front of the room, pausing whenever he received a message 'from the other side', one hand pressed to the side of his head, his eyes raised to the polystyrene ceiling tiles. Gareth had braced himself for a miserable experience, for the weight of sadness and loss to pin him to his plastic seat, but there was a palpable excitement in the room. All the attendees were sitting up straight in their chairs, alert and ready, desperate for a message from their loved ones.

'I've got a man here,' William Mackesy announced, his gaze sweeping the audience, 'and he's shivering.'

Sitting beside him, Gareth's mum gasped softly and Mackesy zoomed in on her like a heat-seeking missile dressed in shiny Littlewoods trousers.

'I'm so cold.' He rubbed his hands up and down his arms, shivering dramatically. 'That's what he's telling me. I'm so, so cold.'

Joan nodded, lips pressed tightly together.

'I'm getting a . . . Marvin . . .' Joan gently slumped. 'No . . . no, that's someone else trying to come through. Wait your turn please, Marvin!' The audience tittered. 'Now I'm hearing from a Jeffery . . .' Gareth felt his mum stiffen at the 'J' sound. William Mackesy obviously noticed too. 'Or is it John . . . yes, it's John. A John and he's . . .' he tilted his head to one side '. . . he's calling for you. He's asking you to help him. Is that ringing any bells, love?'

His mother's croaked, heartbroken 'yes' was so painful it was all Gareth could do not to storm up the aisle and punch Mackesy straight in the face. Instead he reached for his mum's hand, squeezed it and stared at the floor. An excruciating minute or two later, Mackesy finally moved on to someone else.

'Do you think it was really him?' his mother whispered when they filed out of the room forty-five minutes later. 'Do you think it was Dad?'

'There's no way Dad would send you a message via a cock like that,' Gareth wanted to reply. Instead he said, 'If it brings you peace, Mum.'

She gave him a long look. 'I won't find peace until I see him again.'

As Gareth gets out of his car and opens the gate his thoughts switch from William Mackesy to his dad. It's been twenty years since he went missing whilst hiking on Scafell Pike. A huge search and rescue effort was mounted but his dad was never found. They'd always assumed, and the police had agreed, that his dad had suffered some kind of accident while hiking alone on the mountain, and his body had fallen or rolled somewhere he couldn't be spotted by the search and rescue helicopter or the on-foot search teams. When the police interviewed Gareth and his mother and they'd asked about his dad's mental health his mum was quick to dismiss suicide as a possibility. They were a happy family and John was enjoying his retirement. He had a sturdy constitution – physically and mentally – and rarely visited the doctor.

Gareth agreed. His had been a happy childhood, without the arguments and stony silences that seemed to punctuate so many of his friends' memories. Life became more difficult when Gareth entered his teens. Almost overnight he seemed to morph from 'my little man' to 'you don't know what side your bread is buttered'. Looking back now he understands why his dad had such a heavy hand when it came to school and homework – he wanted Gareth to achieve more than he had – but it still stings, remembering his father walking out of the kitchen in silence when Gareth's O Level results arrived. Years later his dad made no secret of the fact that he was bitterly disappointed with Gareth's decision to become a security guard. 'A job for a failed policeman,' was how he dismissed it. But Gareth wasn't a failed policeman. He was a man who'd failed to get into the police. Regardless of the distinction, the criticism was still there and it hurt.

He glances up, sensing movement at one of the windows in the house next door. He catches a glimpse of Georgia, the thirteen-year-old who lives with her mum Kath, but the curtain is drawn swiftly across the window before he can raise his hand in hello.

Gareth sniffs as he steps into the dark hallway and turns on the light. An eggy, carbon smell floods his nostrils. What's she burnt this time?

'Mum!' he calls as he runs towards the kitchen, but there's no sign of his dumpy mother in her sheepskin slippers and Dad's oversized navy-blue cardigan in the tiny smoke-filled kitchen. There's a pan holding two incinerated boiled eggs smouldering on a gas ring. Covering his mouth with his sleeve, Gareth grabs a tea towel from the drawer, yanks the billowing saucepan off the cooker top, and drops it into the sink. It fizzes against the cold metal as he throws open the back door and turns on the extractor fan.

'Mum!' He pushes through the living room door. 'You know you nearly burnt the house down!'

His mother, sitting in complete darkness save for the flickering television in the corner of the room, turns and looks at his feet. 'You've still got your work boots on. Take them off; you're traipsing mud into the fitted carpets.'

Gareth unlaces his boots and places them by the front door.

'Can't you smell that?' he asks as he walks back in and pulls the cord on the standard lamp behind his armchair. 'That burning smell?'

His mum wrinkles her nose. 'Maybe, a little bit. Are next door having a bonfire?'

'No, Mum.' He pulls the curtains shut. 'You just incinerated two boiled eggs and nearly burnt the house down.'

'Oh dear.' She moves to stand up but Gareth waves her back down.

'It's fine. I've sorted it. But I think you're going to have to stop cooking, Mum. This is the third time it's happened.'

'But I like cooking.'

'Then we'll cook together.'

'But . . .' she glances at the clock '. . . you always get home so late and I was hungry.'

'Didn't Yvonne make a snack before she left?'

'Who?'

'Yvonne, your carer. She texted me to say you'd had fruitcake and an apple. And Sally made you a sandwich for lunch.'

'Did she?' His mum waves a dismissive hand in his direction. 'Stop talking please. I'm trying to watch *EastEnders* and you're spoiling it.'

As Gareth settles back into his armchair he thinks guiltily of the fifteen minutes he spent parked up in McDonald's car park enjoying a Veggie Deluxe burger and large fries, washed down with a vanilla milkshake. He's going to have to give that up and get home earlier to cook supper for his mum. Not that he knows one end of a saucepan from the other. He's going to have to get some recipe books and teach himself. Or maybe he could ask someone to teach him. He thinks idly of Kath next door and the nice smells that emanate from her kitchen when he's out in the back garden hanging up his work shirts. He imagines a different life, making dinner with her after work. He'd chop and she'd organise. They'd talk about their days and they'd laugh about the stupid stuff they'd seen or heard and then—

Out of the corner of his eye he spots something unusual on

the side table and snatches it up. It's a postcard, of a man and woman dancing cheek to cheek. It's all very 1950s. He's in an army uniform and she's got bright red lips and hair that's smooth and rolled around her face. He flips it over, reaches into his pocket for his reading glasses then peers at the familiar handwriting on the back. There's his mother's name and address on the right and five words on the left.

I love you, Joan.
John
x

He smiles to himself at the simple romantic gesture and places it back on the table. Sally or Yvonne have obviously been through Mum's memory box with her again, encouraging her to chat about her life. They must have forgotten to pack it all away. He gets up and retrieves the large wooden box from the dresser on the right of the TV then settles back in the armchair and opens the lid.

'Mum,' he says as he picks up the postcard, 'how do you fancy scrambled eggs on toast, or maybe—'

He breaks off, frowning at the stamp in the corner of the postcard. It shows a Christmas scene but there's something about the image that doesn't look right. There's a bright red post box with a bustling snowy shopping scene behind it but it's not that that catches his eye. It's the postwoman in a neon orange reflective jacket crouching down to retrieve the mail. A postwoman? In a reflective jacket? It's far too modern an image for when his mum and dad were courting. He holds the postcard at arm's length, squinting to make out the date in the blurred mark beside the wavy grey lines that cover the left side of the stamp. He turns to stare at his mother.

His father went missing twenty years ago and the postmark shows yesterday's date.

Chapter 8

@sammypammy99:
OMG. Apparently another man went missing on the Harbourside.

@NotMobiledriver:
Yeah, I heard. Just disappeared around 3 a.m.

@sammypammy99:
Probably drunk, coming out of a club and fell into the water.

@MotobkeBob:
Clubbing on a Monday?

@elbowframe15:
People do do that you know.

@MotobkeBob:
Not if they're over thirty.

@elbowframe15:
Well I'm over thirty and I've been known to go clubbing after a work do on a weekday.

@dopeydons:
Poor bloke. I'm guessing they'll be fishing him out of the water in a few days.

@lisaharte101:
Fishing him out of the water? Nice. Imagine it was your son or brother who was missing?

@sammypammy99:
Actually the first man to go missing hasn't been found yet.

@gemzy9:
OMG. We're all assuming they fell in the Avon but what if a serial killer's hiding them in his basement or something?

@MotobkeBob:
Yeah, because that's likely.

Chapter 9

Ursula

Ursula parks up outside number fifteen William Street, flips down the sun visor and scrutinises her refection in the mirror. Her cheeks are flushed, her eye make-up is a little smudged and her bottom lip is chapped but she looks presentable. Presentable-ish. She rakes her fingers through her fringe then sniffs at her armpits and wrinkles her nose. She takes a deodorant can from the glovebox and applies it liberally. 5.58 p.m. Time to meet her new landlord.

After Charlotte and Matt kicked her out she burned through her deliveries, forgoing chats with her regulars to try and make up time. A visit to the shopping centre was the carrot at the end of her shift and, after she'd delivered her last parcel, she'd driven to the Meads with her shoulders hunched, a pain in her chest and her forearms knotted tight.

Don't, said a voice in the back of her head. Don't do it. It's what got you in this mess in the first place. But her legs had ignored the frantic pleading of her mind and carried her out of the car park, across the forecourt and through the glass doors of Mirage Fashions. The shop was empty apart from two assistants and the bored-looking security guard. That made it risky, more risky than normal, but she didn't turn back. Instead she headed towards the back of the shop as adrenaline coursed through her, quickening her reflexes and sweeping her anxiety away. There was no plan, no item she particularly wanted or needed, but the urge to steal crawled from her forearms to her fingertips, like ants under her skin. She'd feel better once she'd taken something, when it was in her hand or under her jacket or shoved deep into her bag; the tension knotting her shoulders would vanish and she'd be able to breathe deeply again. She searched the rows of clothes like a magpie, her heart thumping in her chest. She felt a spark of irritation as the shop manager drew closer, pretending to sort one of the racks.

Spotting the man with the bunch of flowers, gesturing for her to get the shop manager's attention, had been a godsend. The moment the manager set off across the store, Ursula had whipped the sparkly dress from the hanger and shoved it into her jacket. The security guard hadn't given her so much as a second look as she'd marched through the glass double doors. Her high had lasted for all of the four or five minutes it took her to leave the Meads, enter the car park and open the door to her van. Then the shame set in and her mind filled with noise: discordant voices shouting over each other, telling her she was fat, a failure, unlovable, unliked and unwanted.

'You're a freak.'

'What's the weather like up there, Mount Ursula?'

'You scared the children. You need to get help.'

'You'll never amount to anything.'

She shoved the dress under the passenger seat, squishing it up against cutlery she'd stolen from restaurants, plastic pot plants she taken from McDonald's, a cushion she'd nabbed from a café, make-up she'd swiped from Debenhams and lots and lots of clothes and jewellery with the tags still on. Then she started the engine, pressed play on her CD player and blasted out George Michael, turning the volume louder and louder until her eardrums throbbed.

Now, she opens the door to the van, walks up the path to the small terraced house in Totterdown and knocks on the door. Unlike the other houses on the narrow, car-lined street there's no light on beyond the bay window and no television screen flickering from between the gaps in the blinds. Ursula raises her eyes to the first floor. No light on in the bedroom either. She checks her watch. 6.03 p.m.

She knocks again, then jolts as the door is wrenched open, leaving her curled fist hanging in the air. Even with the step up into the house the man in the doorway is still several inches shorter than her. His gaze flicks from her face to her battered trainers and then back again and she braces herself for the inevitable comment about her height.

'Edward.' He holds out a slim hand. His eyes seem to bore into her from behind his round, wire-framed specs. 'You must be Ursula.'

She returns the handshake, noting the man's neatly clipped nails. He doesn't look like she imagined from their brief phone call. She thought he'd be tall and angular like Benedict Cumberbatch, but he's actually very small and slight. His is the physique of a thirteen-year-old boy but there's a ruggedness to his skin and a peppering to his temples that suggests he's at least mid-thirties. His accent, and polo shirt and chinos, suggest he's posh, but the hall carpet by his feet is thin and worn, and when he turns on the light only one bulb in the overhead fixture comes on.

'Lovely to meet you,' she says.

Edward doesn't immediately respond, instead he continues to stare up at her. The intensity in his eyes, small and bright behind his Harry Potter glasses, makes her shift from foot to foot. But then he smiles and Ursula feels the tension in her belly melt away.

'Do come in,' Edward says. 'I'll give you the tour.'

He leads her into the living room first and switches on the light. There's nothing unusual about the rooms. Nothing remarkable either. There's a shabby two-seater sofa covered with a multi-coloured ethnic throw that looks like it was rescued from a student bedroom in the 1990s, a forty-inch TV in the corner of the room, a large brown leather armchair and a gilt mirror above the fireplace. There are no prints on the walls, no books, no ornaments, nothing to give the room any character apart from a dartboard on the wall opposite the doorway. Edward catches her looking at it.

'I like darts.'

She raises her eyebrows. 'Obviously.'

A memory creeps into Ursula's head, of Nathan standing beside her in the pub, pointing across the room and shaking with laughter at the three darts she managed to embed in the wall.

'I'm a courier,' she says as she follows Edward to the galley kitchen. It's so cramped she has to remain in the doorway while he points out the oven, sink, microwave and recycling bins and explains that he does his washing at a local laundrette because there's no space for a machine. Like the living room it's a bland, characterless space. There's a wooden knife block with six gleaming stainless steel handles and a yellow-white kettle that looks like it's seen better days. The only splash of colour is a portable red digital radio, the news reporter gravely explaining how another man had gone missing near the Harbourside.

'I can't remember if I already told you this,' Ursula adds, 'but

I get a delivery of parcels every morning, at about 6 a.m. It's my round for the day. Would that be a problem?'

Edward glances in her direction but his gaze doesn't rest on her face, instead it drifts past her, towards the front door. He frowns as though considering the request. 'Where would you keep them?'

'In the living room.' Ursula mentally kicks herself. She should have given herself enough time to make a good impression on him before mentioning this. 'But only for an hour or so, until I load the van.' She pauses, trying to read the troubled look in his eyes. 'It's going to be a problem, isn't it? I can tell by the look on your face.'

'No, no.' His gaze sweeps past her to the knife block. He straightens the breadknife by a millimetre or so then wipes his hands on his chinos. 'I don't get up until 7.30 a.m. so if they're out of the house by then it won't be a problem.'

'What do you do,' she asks him, 'for a living?'

'I get by,' he says in a manner that lets Ursula know that the subject is closed.

The voice on the radio stops speaking and the tinny beats of a pop song fill the room. It's loud, louder than most people listen to the radio in their homes, but Ursula doesn't care; when a good track comes on she cranks the volume right up in her van.

'I like this song,' she says, then immediately wonders why. She doesn't like this sort of thing – a trembling female voice, screeching about a man who did her wrong. She likes George Michael, Mariah Carey, Whitney Houston, ABBA and early Madonna. She was too young to enjoy the music when it first came out but there's something about 80s hits that appeals to her. They're cosy and safe.

'Do you listen to the radio?' Edward asks.

'Not much.' She shrugs. 'I prefer CDs. But I listen to Ken

Bruce's pop quiz sometimes, to test myself. I never score very highly though.'

He wrinkles his nose disapprovingly. 'Well don't get any ideas, about changing the station. I like it to stay on all the time. No turning it off. No fiddling with the volume.'

'No problem. Oh. What's through there?' Ursula touches the door to her left. There are three doors in the kitchen: one at the far end that leads to a boxy garden, the door to the hall that was propped open, and this one. 'Downstairs loo is it?'

'No.' Something in his expression shifts. 'The basement.'

'Oh. Cool. Good for storage. You wouldn't believe the amount of stuff I've got in the van. I could—'

Edward crosses the kitchen and lays a hand on the door. 'I'm afraid the basement is off limits.' He smiles tightly. 'Although you're very welcome to make full use of the kitchen, the living room, the bathroom and the garden.'

'Great.' Ursula flashes a fake smile in his direction as a knot forms in her stomach. She can already predict how this living arrangement will work out. She'll be told off for leaving coffee mugs in the living room and smearing toothpaste onto the sink. On the other hand – she glances around the minimalistic space – there's nothing to steal.

She sniffs, subtly. There's a weird smell in the kitchen that she can't place. The counters and oven top are thoroughly scrubbed but there's a distinctly musty tang to the air.

'Upstairs next,' Edward says and she flattens herself up against the hall wall to let him past.

Any doubts Ursula might have had about living with Edward disappear the second he opens the door to her potential bedroom. She'd anticipated the room being poky but it's absolutely enormous. Well, maybe not enormous, but it's much bigger than the little box room she had at Charlotte's house and there's a double bed, wardrobe, chest of drawers with a small flat screen television on the top and a comfy-looking armchair in the corner. Not to mention the picture window that stretches across one wall. The curtains are drawn back and the sun is an orange streak across the sky but she can imagine the room being flooded with light earlier in the day. She'd never need to venture down to the lounge with a room like this.

'It's £350 including bills, right?' she asks, perching on the bed and running her hands over the spotless mattress.

One side of Edward's mouth twitches up into a lopsided smile. 'Plus deposit.'

Ursula's smile slips. In her excitement she hadn't even considered the prospect of a deposit. If he asks for three months' rent in advance she's screwed.

'How much would that be?' she asks, tightening her grip on the mattress.

'Call it £500 all in.'

'So . . .' She tries to remember the last time she checked her bank balance. It would be tight and she'd have to live on beans on toast for the rest of the month but it's just about doable. 'One month's rent in advance and £150 deposit?'

'That's right.'

She considers her options. There's no doubt that Edward is a little on the eccentric side but then again she's not exactly normal and he hasn't asked for a reference – something Charlotte might struggle to provide. If she takes the room she'll be absolutely skint until next payday but at least she won't have to shell out for a hotel. She gazes around the room, taking it all in, weighing it up, then lets out a little 'ooh' of surprise as she notices something unusual about the door. There's a huge great hole, stuffed with tissue paper, just under the handle.

'There's no lock.'

'No.'

'Why not?'

'I had to break in.'

'Why?'

Edward doesn't shift his gaze from the door. 'I'd fit a new lock,' he says quietly. 'If you'd like the room. You are . . . female after all.'

'Well, yes.' She frowns.

'Like I said, there are other interested parties but I did promise you first refusal so it's up to you.'

'I'll take it,' she says before she can change her mind. She's got some packing tape in her bag. She'll plaster over the toilet roll stuffed hole before she goes to bed, and put the chair in front of the door. It's not the right height to jam under the handle but the floor's wooden; she'd hear it moving. And besides, she's a good eight inches taller than Edward and at least eight or nine stone heavier. Unless he's a knife-wielding maniac she can fight him off.

I won't need to fight him off. She catches the dark thread of her thoughts and mentally shakes herself. He's a bit odd but that doesn't mean he's a psycho. I'm a bit odd and I'm perfectly well balanced. Well, a little bit off-balance, but harmless. Mostly.

'Excellent.' Edward nods curtly. 'If you could furnish me with the £500 we can discuss a move-in date.'

Ursula's heart sinks. 'Oh. I was hoping I could move in tonight.'

'Tonight?'

'Yes . . . I . . . um. I . . . er . . . I've got all my belongings in my van outside.'

'You've got nowhere else to stay?'

'No.' She says a little prayer, not to God – she's already broken her promise to him about not stealing again – or the universe, but to the only person who ever really loved her. If you're there, if you're listening, please help me out.

Edward gives her a long look over the top of his rimless

glasses and she braces herself for the inevitable 'no, sorry', but then he gives a faint shrug.

'I don't see why not. If you can get the money tonight I'll give you a hand getting your stuff out of your van.'

'Thank you.' Ursula practically bounces to her feet. 'I'll do that now. Give me five minutes to find a bank and I'll be right back. Oh.' She pauses, halfway across the room. 'I think I can only get £200 out of the bank today.'

'That's all right,' Edward says. 'You can write me a cheque for the other three hundred. It's not as if you can do a runner.' His eyes glint behind his glasses. 'After all, I know where you live.'

Chapter 10

Alice

Alice closes the door, rests her back against it for a few seconds, then heads into the kitchen where her daughter Emily is sitting at the table, glass of red wine in hand. There's a scarlet smudge around her lips and the bottle is half empty.

'You okay?' Emily asks as Alice sits down and helps herself to a glass. 'You didn't shut the living room door properly, by the way.'

'So you heard everything?'

Emily shrugs. 'Pretty much. He sounds like a freak. What did the police say?'

'I have to go in to give an official statement, and they're going to speak to Michael.'

'And the other guy?' She nods towards the bouquet of flowers, still in their cellophane wrapper, on the kitchen counter.

'Simon? He needs to give a statement too. I gave them his number and . . .'

But Emily has stopped listening. She's tapping away at her phone with both thumbs, her brow furrowed, her lips set in a tight, hard line. It's the same expression she had as a child when she thought some kind of injustice had occurred – a friend took her toy or Alice announced it was bedtime.

'Everything okay with you, love?'

'Fine.' Emily reaches for her wine glass and takes a long swig.

'How's work?' Her daughter's been working as a receptionist for a property maintenance company in the centre of town for the last year and she knows she finds it boring.

'Crap. Sooner I get a new job the better.'

'And Adam?'

'Adam's a cock.'

Alice raises her eyebrows. Emily and Adam have been together for about eighteen months and it isn't the most harmonious of relationships; even the start was rocky. Adam was dating Laila, one of Emily's friends and there was some 'confusion' over when that relationship ended and his relationship with Emily began. The two girls had a massive falling-out and Laila successfully managed to convince most of their friends that Emily was a bitch. The experience threw Emily and Adam together in a way that Alice didn't find particularly healthy but there was no talking her daughter into slowing things down. Suddenly it was 'Adam this' and 'Adam that' and she barely saw her for weeks on end. About three months in, Adam finished things with Emily out of the blue and Alice nursed her daughter through the toughest break-up she'd ever experienced – cuddling her on the sofa, making her endless cups of tea as Emily poured her heart out. And then Adam reappeared. He'd made a mistake, he said, he'd freaked out at the speed things were progressing but he wanted to give it another go. Emily, who'd heard from one of her few friends that Adam had been cheating on her, was sceptical but her love hadn't faded and he didn't have to work very hard to talk her into taking him back. Then things returned to normal – three or four nights spent at home during the week then every weekend doing whatever it was Adam wanted to do.

It had hurt Alice's heart, seeing her vibrant, confident daughter shrink into Adam's pocket, fitting herself into the tiny girlfriend-shaped space in his life. *Did she learn that from me?* she wondered. Had Emily watched her kowtow to Peter's demands, putting his happiness before her own? Or perhaps she thought she hadn't been compliant enough and that's why he'd left?

'What's Adam done?' she asks as her daughter's phone bleeps with a reply.

Emily shakes her head, her lips stubbornly pressed together as she recommences her attack on her phone's keypad.

'Ems . . .'

'Leave it, Mum. You wouldn't understand.'

Sighing, Alice gets up and begins unwrapping the flowers. If there's one thing Emily has inherited from her it's her stubbornness. She wouldn't have opened up to her mother at that age either. She steps on the pedal bin and drops the cellophane inside then takes the white card that was stapled to one corner from out of her pocket. There's something about the scrawled message – *Sorry, Simon* – with his number written underneath that stops her from throwing it away too. Simon went to so much trouble to check she was okay; the least she can do is let him know she spoke to the police.

She slips her phone out of her work trousers and taps out a message.

Thank you again for the flowers, you really shouldn't have. I've spoken to the police and they took your number. They said they'd like you to go in to give a statement.

She pauses, unsure what else to add, so ends the message with her first name, presses send and drops the card, along with the cellophane, into the bin. As she fills a vase with water a stern

52

voice on the radio cuts through the tinny pop song and announces that it's eight o'clock and time for the news. Alice half-listens as she trims the ends of the flowers and arranges the stems in the vase. More political upheaval, an ageing celebrity has died and . . . her ears prick up at the mention of Bristol, unusual given the fact that, thanks to Emily, the digital radio is permanently tuned in to Radio 1. A young man has gone missing after a night out, last seen walking along Bristol Harbourside. Forty-eight hours have passed since he was last seen. Alice sighs softly, thinking of the anguish his poor parents must be going through. The number of twenty-somethings who've died after getting drunk, getting separated from their friends, stumbling home alone and falling into the river Avon . . . She's lost count of the number of times she's drummed it into Emily to make sure she always leaves a club with a friend. Not that she goes out with her friends very often. It's all Adam, Adam, Adam.

Her daughter's shriek makes her turn sharply. Emily's on the phone, her mobile pressed to her ear and the fingers of her other hand curled around the wine bottle as she tips it into her glass. 'No, Adam. I won't calm down. You fucking *know* how I feel about Laila and I know for a *fact* that she was there last night. Don't you dare lie about—'

A question forms on Alice's lips but Emily angrily waves her away. Sighing, Alice leaves the kitchen, the vase of flowers in her hands. As she sets it down on a window ledge in the living room her phone vibrates in her pocket. It's a message from Lynne:

How did it go with the police?

Alice taps out a reply: *I need to go in to give an official statement.*

A couple of seconds later Lynne texts again.

Are you ok? Have you heard from Michael?

No, she types back. *Haven't heard a thing. Thank goodness.*

With the sound of her daughter's raised voice drifting through from the kitchen Alice shuts all the curtains. She turns on the TV and sits on the sofa then gets up to adjust the curtains again. She sits down again and flicks through the channels, watches a few seconds of a property programme about homes abroad, then checks her phone. No reply from Lynne. No reply from Simon either. She feels unsettled after speaking to the police. Maybe she needs another glass of wine, take the edge off her nerves. That's if Emily hasn't finished the bottle. Her phone bleeps as she crossed the living room.

It's a text from Simon:

Police rang me. I told them everything I can remember and said I'll go in tomorrow. I hope it helps. How are you doing?

I'm okay, she taps out. *How are you?*

She rereads her reply then deletes it and tries again:

Thanks so much. I am feeling a bit unsettled but

For a second time she deletes what she's written. Why is she deliberating over every word? She didn't agonise over the reply she sent to Lynne.

Thank you, she types. *I really appreciate you doing that. I'll be honest. I'm quite freaked out by what happened but the way you reacted has reassured me that not all men are drunken, dangerous arseholes. Need a drink (or two).*

Send.

As she steps out of the living room her daughter bursts out of the kitchen, phone still clamped to her ear. She grabs her coat from the stand and snatches her keys off the sideboard.

'You're not driving, are you?' Alice asks, horrified. 'You've had the best part of a bottle of wine to drink and—'

'I've booked a taxi to Adam's. Don't stress.'

And then Emily is gone, the silence she leaves behind pulsing in Alice's ears. Sighing, she heads into the kitchen and picks up the empty bottle of red wine from the kitchen table and drops it into the recycling bin. The only booze left is a small bottle of

Bombay Sapphire gin that Lynne gave her for Christmas. She pours out a large measure, adds a splash of tonic, then heads into the living room. As she settles back onto the sofa her phone bleeps again. Two new messages, one from Lynne and one from Simon:

Have you seen that new reality show on Channel 4? OMG. Makes me SO glad I'm not in my twenties again.

Alice skips over Lynne's message to get to Simon's.

Ah, I have my arsehole moments that's for sure but I'd never do what that guy did. If you hadn't dropped your purse I would have lamped him one myself, that's for sure. What are you drinking? I'm on the gin.

Alice smiles.

I'm on the gin too. Bombay Sapphire.

Her phone beeps.

I'm an Adnams Copper fan myself.

Alice taps the Chrome app on her phone and googles 'Adnams Copper'. She gives a little laugh.

An artisan gin! Get you. Hipster!

She takes a sip of her drink. A second or two later her phone bleeps again:

Hipster?! How very dare you. I'll have you know that a) I don't have a beard, b) I can't stand craft ale and c) my thighs are far too chunky for skinny jeans. Although I have been known to crochet a cabbage and stew my own pickle juice.

Alice laughs loudly. *What the hell's pickle juice?*

You know how Peter Parker was bitten by a spider and became Spiderman? Pickle juice is like that but for hipsters. It gives us superpowers.

She takes another sip of her gin as she composes her reply in her head. There's something hugely enjoyable about bantering with him like this – batting silly comments back and forth without second-guessing herself.

As her phone vibrates again she glances down at it. Her fixed smile fades. Someone called 'Ann Friend' just sent her a Facebook friend request with a message. She clicks it.

Whatever you do, don't trust Simon.

What? She clicks on Ann Friend's profile. The photo is a black square and there's nothing in the cover photo space either. No friends, no information. Just the name – *Ann Friend*. It has to be Michael, lashing out and angry because she called the police. Anger bubbles in her belly as she taps out a reply.

Leave me alone, Michael. I'll be passing that message on to the police and any other message that you decide to send me. Don't EVER contact me again.

Hand shaking, she sets her phone down on the table and reaches for her glass. She knocks back the last of the gin then refills it. As she raises it to her mouth her phone bleeps with a new message. It's from Ann Friend again.

Who is Michael?

Chapter 11

Gareth

Gareth waits for the familiar dum-dum-dum music that signals the end of *EastEnders* then crouches beside his mum's chair. She leans away from him, startled by his proximity.

'What are you doing?'

He holds out the postcard, showing her the image of the dancing couple. 'When did this arrive?'

His mother looks vaguely in the direction of the card and squints. 'What is it?'

'It's a postcard, Mum. Put your glasses on.'

She reaches a hand over to the side table, her hand spidering over the surface until her fingertips find the rough tapestry of her glasses case. She snaps it open then places her specs on the end of her nose. She holds the card at arm's length.

'Isn't that lovely, a postcard from your dad.'

Gareth frowns, trying to read her face. The gaps between her lucidity and her dementia have been growing and he's not entirely sure which state she's in now. The latter probably, if she thinks the postcard is 'lovely'. At a guess she's firmly caught in the first fifteen years of her marriage when his dad was in the navy and would be away from home for months at the time. Gareth knows from bitter experience that breaking the news that his dad is missing presumed dead would lead to an outpouring of grief so wretched and terrible it would take him until bedtime, or beyond, to calm her down.

'Do you know when it arrived?' he asks. 'The postcard?'

His mum shrugs and flips it over to look at the image. 'It's lovely, isn't it? Reminds me of Lauren Bacall and Humphrey Bogart.'

'Mum, when did the postcard arrive?'

'I don't know. I've never seen it before. Lovely, though.' She dismisses the card with a wave of her hand and looks up at her son. 'I'm hungry. I should probably think about putting the dinner on.'

Standing in the kitchen, slopping singed scrambled eggs onto two pieces of toast, Gareth presses a hand to the centre of his chest. He fishes a crumpled packet of antacids from his pocket and pops two into his mouth. Bloody junk food, bloody stress. He looks down at his belly, sitting on top of his belt like a fleshy bowling ball hidden behind straining shirt buttons. It's the only part of his body that's carrying any weight; his arms and legs are still as lithe as they were when he was younger and competed in cross-country races, going out to run several times a week. He smooths a hand over the curve of his stomach. His dad, who prided himself in staying in shape, would be appalled at the way his son has let himself go. Gareth's gaze flits towards the postcard, lying beside the cooker, the location on the postmark too smudged to read.

Maybe, he thinks, as he carefully places the supper tray on

his mum's lap, apologising as she warily regards the burnt offering, his dad wasn't as content in his early retirement as he let everyone believe. Maybe he never had any intention of going anywhere near Scafell Pike and had simply packed up his navy rucksack, his walking poles and his anorak and walked out of their lives without looking back. It was a gutless move if so, and something Gareth can't reconcile with the principled man he grew up with. To abandon him, a twenty-seven-year-old man at the time, would be one thing, but to vanish without saying goodbye to the woman who'd loved him for so many years? He can't, won't, let himself believe that his dad would stoop so low.

As his mum picks up her knife and fork Gareth slopes back into the kitchen, a fist pressed against his sternum, acid still burning deep in his chest. He pops another two antacids into his mouth and picks up the postcard, tracing one finger over his dad's familiar handwriting. How well did he know him, really? Could his dad have been one of those men with another family, a secret life he'd kept hidden for years? Might he be gay or transsexual? He could have struggled with his true identity and chosen to vanish rather than out himself and cause his wife pain. For nearly twenty years Gareth has grieved his father's disappearance, believing with more and more certainty with each year that passed that the man he'd loved and respected was dead.

Back in February, when a national newspaper broke the news that the Missing Persons Bureau were sharing images of unidentified people and their belongings on a public access website, he spent a gruelling evening searching through the records of all the men on their database. By the time he went to bed he felt hollow, as though each death, each unclaimed, unknown man, had carved a piece out of his soul. There were so many suicides – hanged, struck by trains, found in rivers. One man, whose almost skeletal remains were found hanging from a tree in the woods near a golf club, had been there for approximately three months, the website said. His identity was still unknown. How was that possible? For no one in the world to care where you were?

Gareth barely slept a wink that night.

He wants to believe that his dad is still alive but it seems so unlikely. The police searched for him. They discovered he'd taken the train from Bristol to Penrith, hired a car and then booked into a hotel at the base of Scafell Pike. If it was all an elaborate ruse to escape from family life he'd laid the trail well. Then again, he was an ex-military man. But if he had sent the postcard, why do it now, after twenty years? He must be nearly eighty. Was he looking back on his life and regretting his disappearance? Or perhaps he was dying? Maybe he'd been told to put his affairs in order and that included saying sorry to his wife. Although he hadn't actually said sorry, had he? Just that he loved her.

Gareth runs the hot tap, squirts washing-up liquid into the tub in the sink, then plunges the pan with its burnt, eggy stains into the water. As he scrubs, he gazes out of the window. Apart from two lines of solar-powered fairy lights – strung up to celebrate his mother's 79th birthday with a small garden party last year – that cast a wan light onto the peeling paint of the shed, the garden is in darkness. His mum loves that garden; on a sunny day she'll sit outside for hours watching the birds in the trees. But it's not the garden that Gareth's looking at. He's looking beyond the reach of his small world, out into Bristol and the lights that flicker and twinkle in the distance. Is his dad out there? Is he thinking about them? Has he reached out in the secret hope that he'll be found? Gareth's gaze flicks again towards the postcard and the pain in his chest radiates through his body.

I love you, Joan.

His dad hasn't mentioned him at all.

Chapter 12

Alice

For the last hour Alice has been holed away in the back office of Mirage Fashions, rearranging the rotas to fit around childcare issues, holidays and doctor's appointments and now her head is pounding and she feels breathless in the tiny room. She stretches her arms above her head then stands up, stamping the life back into her legs. She hasn't finished but she needs to get back out on the shop floor and check how everyone's getting on before she breaks for lunch.

As she walks through the staff changing room she glances at her coat, hanging on the rack that runs the length of one wall. She's strict with her staff when it comes to checking their mobile phones at work – only ever on official break times – but the urge to see if there have been any new messages is more than she can bear. Keeping one eye on the door, she fumbles her phone out of her bag. Nothing. No new messages from 'Ann Friend' and nothing from Simon either.

Last night, after she received the 'who is Michael?' message, she rang the number of the detective she'd spoken to earlier.

'This is Alice Fletcher,' she said, when DC Mitchell's phone went straight to voicemail. 'I spoke to you a couple of hours ago about an assault a man named Michael Easton carried out on me in the Evening Star pub. Well, I've just had a Facebook message from someone calling themselves Ann Friend saying that I shouldn't trust Simon, the man who witnessed the assault. I thought it might be Michael so I replied saying I'd go to the police. The next message I received said: "Who is Michael?" He's obviously playing games with me and I wanted to tell you just in case . . .' just in case anything happens to me, she thought but couldn't bring herself to say '. . . Just in case it might be evidence. Anyway, thank you. Goodbye.'

There was a voicemail from DC Mitchell waiting for her at 8 a.m. telling her to come in and make a statement. Alice rang Lynne, telling her she'd need her to open up, then made her way to the station. After she'd finished relaying what had happened to the detective, a blonde woman in her thirties with sharp, inquisitive blue eyes, she was reassured that she was right to report the messages and to keep a record of any other contact, sightings or occurrences that frightened or upset her. Three hours later, DC Mitchell left a message on Alice's phone. Michael Easton had been interviewed and admitted assaulting her. He'd been given a caution and released.

Alice didn't know whether to be upset that Michael hadn't been locked up or relieved that he'd admitted to the assault. But she wasn't going to spend the rest of her life looking over her shoulder, being startled by her own shadow, because some wanker had shoved her into a wall. If he got in touch again she'd tell him exactly where to get off.

Now she tucks her phone back into her bag, then presses a

hand to her grumbling belly. Lynne's already had her lunchbreak so she'll be eating in Costa alone.

Alice pushes open the door to Costa, takes three or four steps across the coffee shop then freezes in her tracks. Sitting at the far end of the room with headphones jammed over his ears and a book in his hands is Simon. Keeping her eyes on him, Alice moves between the tables and reaches into the sandwich cabinet.

'A latte please,' she says to the barista as she places a char-grilled chicken and pesto sandwich on the counter, 'and this.' She fishes a bottle of water out of a chiller cabinet. 'And this.' She adds a chocolate muffin.

She pays, then moves to the end of the counter, Simon temporarily out of sight as she waits for her hot drink. Her heart is fluttering in her chest and she feels jittery and excited, like she did as a schoolgirl when she'd spot her crush, Jim Seymour, walking down the corridor towards her. Simon must work locally to spend his lunchbreak in Costa, she thinks. Or maybe, says a little voice in the back of her head, maybe he came here for lunch today in the hope that he'd run into you.

She carries her lunch to a free table near the window and chooses a chair between the glass-walled shop front and the counter. This way she can see the door *and* Simon. Normally she'd sit with her back to a solid wall like he has but everyone else seems to have had the same idea and there are no such tables free. She takes a sip of her coffee and unwraps her sandwich. Someone's left a newspaper on her table, the headline, 'Hunt for Missing Man Continues', splashed across the front page alongside the image of a laughing young man. Instinctively Alice thinks about Emily and how easily someone else's heartbreak could be her own. She pushes the thought away and steals a glance at Simon. She holds her gaze for a second, two, willing him to look up from his book, simultaneously excited and terrified. It's one thing to share jokey text banter at home with a gin and tonic in her hand, and another to run into him in the middle of the day, sober, in her work uniform. She pats at her hair, smoothing it away from her face and runs her fingers through the ends. Why didn't she refresh her lipstick before she left for lunch?

She takes a bite of her sandwich, steals another look at Simon, then reaches into her bag for her phone. She grins to herself as her thumbs move over the keys.

If I drank pickle juice I'd be more likely to turn into a villain than a superhero.

She presses send then peers from between her fingers to watch for Simon's reaction. A second or two later he lays down his book and picks up his phone. Alice feels a jolt of pleasure as a smile creeps onto his lips. He's not going to answer, she tells herself. He'll want to get back to his book instead. But she's wrong; his thumbs move over the screen, then Alice's phone bleeps.

What would your villain name be?

Gin-Face. Like Two-Face but with better skin, and smelling faintly of juniper berries.

She isn't sure if she's imagining it or not but she's pretty sure she catches the sound of a soft chuckle from across the room.

And what powers would Gin-Face have? he messages back.

Alice's grin widens. *Invisibility.*

She presses send then, before Simon has time to reply she fires off another text.

Enjoying your book?

His jaw drops, then he looks up, his gaze sweeping the room. As their eyes meet he throws back his head and laughs. He raises a hand in hello then bends back over his phone. As Alice reaches for her latte her phone pings again.

Want to join me or shall we continue to text and pretend we're not both in the same café?

Smiling, Alice gathers up her things and makes her way towards him.

'Well, fancy seeing you here,' he says as she draws closer. 'Are you stalking me?'

She laughs. 'I could ask you the same thing seeing as I actually work here.'

'True, true. So you're a Batman fan then?' he asks and all the awkwardness Alice is holding in her chest slips away as they segue into a discussion about Ben Affleck, Christian Bale or Michael Keaton and who made the best Batman. As Simon talks – all expressive hands and bright eyes – she takes in the details of his face: his nose, the bridge bending towards his left eye, permanently skewed by a rugby ball, an accident or a fist, his grey eyes framed with dark blonde eyebrows, his wide, pale lips and the hint of ginger stubble on his jaw. The difference between his face when he talks, and when he listens, is extraordinary. It's as though a light goes on behind his eyes when he speaks. It's not that he's not interested in what Alice has to say – he listens intently, his eyes never leaving hers – but he seems to find real joy in expressing himself. And he does it so well.

'Has anyone told you what an amazing voice you've got?' she blurts, before she can stop herself.

Simon laughs. 'That might have been mentioned before.'

'Has it?' She feels a flush of embarrassment and averts her gaze. As she does she notices the woman sitting at the table to their right. She's around Alice's age, dressed in jeans and a pale pink jumper, with shoulder-length brown hair and greying roots. She's got a book in her hands and a coffee in front of her and she's openly gawping at Simon. Alice looks away. It seems she's not the only one who finds Simon attractive.

'Yeah, anyway.' He moves a hand through the air, as though swiping the topic away. 'Tell me more about you.' His gaze flickers towards her left hand. 'I'm guessing you're not married?'

'Divorced.'

'Great!' His response is so enthusiastic, so unchecked, that now it's Simon's turn to colour. He looks away and clears his throat. When he looks back at her something inside Alice lurches. He likes her, she can see it in his eyes. And, even more terrifying given what she went through the day before, she likes him too.

'You?' she asks.

He shakes his head. 'Never been married.'

'Right.'

There's a beat as they continue to look at each other, neither of them saying a word. It is as though the volume has been turned down in the café. The chatter, the hiss of the coffee machines and the mewling of babies – Alice can't hear any of it, just her pulse, pounding in her ears

'So . . .' Simon smiles. 'This is nice, isn't it?'

Alice nods, not trusting herself to speak.

'I'd like to do it again.'

She clears her throat lightly. 'Me too.'

'Is tonight too soon?'

'For what?'

They both laugh.

'Dinner? There's a really nice restaurant I know where . . .'

As Simon describes his favourite restaurant Alice tunes out, distracted by the woman at the other table. She's put her book down and has turned in her seat so she's facing them. She's tapping her fingertips on her thighs and she's staring openly at Simon. There's a weird expression on her face – excitement mixed with nerves – and a strange energy emanating from her, as though she might jump out of her seat at any second.

Simon hasn't noticed her; he's still staring at Alice with an expectant look on his face. He wasn't joking about taking her out to dinner. He genuinely wants to see her again, but it's all happening so quickly – the first meeting, the flowers, the lunch and now an invitation out to dinner – that there's a part of her that wants to put her foot on the brake. Particularly after what happened yesterday. But Simon's not Michael – her gut instinct tells her that they're very different men – and she's so tired of being cautious and scared. She needs to be brave.

'Yes,' she says. 'I'd love to go to dinner with you.' She's just about to ask him what time when she's interrupted by her mobile bleeping. 'One second, sorry.' As she takes her phone out of her bag she inhales sharply. It's 2.17 p.m. She's late back for work.

Where are you? Lynne's text asks. *Everything ok? Fancy the cinema later?*

Sorry, she texts back. *I've got a night in with Emily planned.*

She cringes at the lie but she can't tell her best friend about dinner with Simon or she'll have to explain that she ran into him at Costa. Lynne would insist on analysing every detail to death and she can't face the third degree, not when she's got so much else on her mind.

'You all right?' Simon asks as she gathers up her partially eaten sandwich, the edges dry and curling.

'Yes, yes. Just um . . . I didn't realise what time it was. I'm late for work.'

'Oh God, sorry. Shall I text you later, about going out for dinner?'

'Yes,' she says, as she pushes her chair away from the table. 'That would be lovely.'

As Alice and Simon get up, so does the woman at the other table. She bounds across the two metres or so that separate them and touches Simon on the arm. He reacts as though he was prodded with a knife rather than a finger and turns sharply, knocking against a passing barista.

'Simon?' the woman says as he stares at her with undisguised horror. 'It is you, isn't it? I've so missed—'

He shakes his head sharply. 'You've confused me with someone else.'

'No, I don't think I have. I've been—'

The rest of her sentence is lost as Simon says to Alice, 'Let's get you back to work,' then he takes her by the arm and half-guides, half-pulls her down the narrow corridor between the other diners. Alice glances back as he opens the door. The other woman is still standing by the table, watching them go, her arms spread wide and a look of incredulity on her face.

Chapter 13

Ursula

Tuesday

Ursula flicks the Vs at Charlotte and Matt's house as she drives past in her van. She's starting to suspect that it was a blessing in disguise, them kicking her out. Edward, her new landlord, wasn't awake when she got up and she'd leisurely nosed at his bathroom belongings as she brushed her teeth. Her fingers had closed over a small nailbrush next to a metal pair of clippers in the back of the bathroom cabinet. She scrubbed her fingernails in the sink, then, before she knew what she was doing, slipped the nailbrush into her pyjama bottom pocket. She ran her fingertips over the bristles as she left the bathroom, then stopped at her bedroom door and reluctantly turned back. Edward might not miss this nailbrush today, he might not even realise it was missing for weeks, but at some point he'd want it. She had to return it.

Afterwards she headed down to the kitchen with the small box of groceries that Charlotte and Matt had so 'helpfully' packed up for her. She put on the kettle then glanced at the radio, blaring out Stevie Wonder's 'Superstition'. Smirking to herself, she wondered what Ed would do if she changed the station. She moved a finger towards the retune button, then snatched her hand away, turning the movement into an elaborate dance move. She didn't really care what radio station her landlord listened to, as long as it played music. As the kettle bubbled she slotted two pieces of bread into the toaster and looked through the cupboards. Edward's minimalism ran to his food choices too – half a dozen tins of baked beans, the same of baked beans with sausages, seven tins of tomatoes, seven cans of sardines, a half-kilo bag of pasta and the same of rice. That was it. There wasn't a single vegetable in the fridge, just a four-litre bottle of milk, some Flora Light and several bottles of Actimel. It was only when she investigated the drawer beneath the cutlery drawer that she found something of interest. Lying flat on the base of the drawer, beneath a roll of duct tape, a box of nails and a screwdriver kit, was a thick wodge of paper, stapled together. She lifted out the tape, nails and screwdriver, then hooked her nails under the edge of the document and picked it up. She scanned the first few lines: 'Tenancy Agreement between Mr Edward Bennett and Mrs Maureen O'Shea . . .' So *that* was why Edward hadn't given her a contract to sign. He was subletting her room; something explicitly forbidden in the agreement. She raised her eyebrows. She wasn't the only member of the household with a secret. Always useful to know.

She turned her attention to the locked door to the basement next. She jiggled the handle up and down several times, pulled on it, then peered into the dark keyhole.

'Hello!' she shouted into the tiny space, her lips grazing the cold brass fixture. 'Is there anyone in there?'

She fell silent, listening for an answer, then laughed nervously. If there was someone in there and they shouted back, she'd shit her pants.

There was no way that Edward was keeping a person locked up in the basement. Strange landlord, locked basement, lone female flatmate hunting around. It was like something out of a Sunday night ITV drama. At best he was keeping something expensive down there. At worst it was a dumping ground for all his unwanted junk. She hadn't spotted any keys during her search and if there was something expensive in the basement Edward probably wouldn't let them out of his sight.

Now Ursula sings along to 'Holiday' by Madonna as she navigates the narrow streets of South Bristol, parking up outside identikit terraced houses and rummaging around in the back of her van for parcels. She's met with smiles of delight, surprise and relief at every door she knocks on. Apart from one. It hasn't opened once in the eleven months that Ursula has been doing this round. She rings the bell, then looks expectantly at the nearest panel of the bay window. There's a light on in the living room and some kind of kid's show on the TV, but there's no one sitting on the sofa and no small child crawling around on the rug. The parcel in Ursula's hands is from a clothing store and there's a man's name written above the address: Paul Wilson. She doesn't visit this address more than once or twice a month but the parcels are always for him, never for the flustered, pink-cheeked woman who takes them in through the living room window rather than open the front door. But there's no sign of her now. Ursula glances at her watch then rings the doorbell again. A non-delivery means she won't get paid and she'll have to try again tomorrow which will cost her in petrol and time. Perhaps the woman's gone out? But she's always in, no matter what time of day Ursula arrives.

'Hello?' She tries tapping on the windowpane then crouches

down and peers through the letter box. There's washing hanging on the radiator in the hall and a row of shoes – male, female and toddler sized – along the skirting board. There's no door to the kitchen and she can see into that too – to the messy worktops covered with pots, pans, plastic containers and what looks a large pile of vegetable peelings.

Sighing, she turns to go. It's a wasted visit and 70p lost. As she reaches the gate a tapping sound makes her turn. The home-owner is at the window, the baby in her arms and a frantic expression on her face.

It's an unusual way of delivering parcels, through a window, and the first time it happened Ursula had assumed that maybe the woman didn't want to leave her child alone on the floor of the living room to answer the door, or maybe she felt it was quicker. Lots of Ursula's customers have little quirks – there's the weird man on Hawthorne Street who always asks her if she'd like to come in to use the loo, the elderly lady on Redcatch Road who always mentions the weather, and the young couple on Bushy Park who always race to answer the door first. The second time this customer opened the window to her, Ursula asked whether the door was broken and received no reply.

'Sorry,' the woman pushes the window open and jiggles the baby onto her hip as she reaches a hand out for the parcel. 'I was in the toilet.'

It's the first time the woman has ever spoken directly to her. She normally opens the window, reaches for the parcel, signs the electronic tracker and then disappears out of view.

'No problem.' Ursula smiles at the child that's gawping at her with large, startled blue eyes that match the woman's. 'Out of curiosity, why do you never answer the door?'

'I'm . . . I'm . . .' The customer's gaze flits from Ursula to the house opposite and then to the cars parked up on the street. The base of her throat flushes red.

'Agoraphobic?' Ursula ventures. 'You don't like going out?'

'No.' The woman shakes her head sharply. 'No . . . no, I don't.'

'Food shopping must take a while if they have to hand each item to you through the window.'

The blush at the base of the woman's throat deepens. 'I . . . I don't . . . my husband does the food shopping. He brings it home with him after work.'

There's something about the woman with her wide, frantic eyes, twitchy hand gestures and her habit of shifting from foot to foot as she speaks as though her skin is pulled too tightly over her body that strikes a chord with Ursula. There's something about her awkwardness that she can identify with.

'Is your husband very understanding?' she asks. 'About your condition? It must be very hard, especially with a little one.' She gestures towards the child. Her soft grunts have become pained whines and she twists and thrashes in her mother's arms.

'If I could just have the parcel?' The woman presses her shoulder up against the windowpane and waggles her hand. 'She's due a nap.'

'Of course.'

There's an awkward dance between Ursula and her customer as the parcel is tugged and pushed through the small gap in the window. Ursula waits while the woman juggles the heavy package with one hand, using her knee to carefully guide it onto the sofa, then slips the electronic parcel tracker through the window.

'You can sign it with your fingernail,' she says, even though the woman has signed for multiple parcels before. She waits for the woman to look up, to smile tightly as she normally does, but, as she lifts her finger from the screen, her gaze remains lowered. She continues to stare at nothing for a second, maybe two, after Ursula has pulled the device back through the open window, then without stopping to pick up the parcel she turns and walks across the living room and out of the door.

'Bye!' Ursula stares after her, then swears under her breath as her phone vibrates in the little leather pouch attached to her belt.

Please don't let it be bad news, she thinks as she unsnaps the popper on the pouch and pulls out her mobile. She's only had one customer complaint to the office in the eleven months she's been doing the job and even then the damaged parcel wasn't her fault; it was battered when Bob delivered it.

But it's not a message from the office informing her there's been a complaint. It's not from the office at all. It's from Edward, her landlord-cum-flatmate.

While I am happy for you to use the items of crockery and cutlery in the kitchen, may I kindly remind you that my personal possessions are not for shared use. I wouldn't dream of touching any of your belongings (unless I were cleaning and even then I'd ask you to remove such items before I began). Please extend me the same courtesy. You really DON'T want to fall out with me about this. E.

Ursula raises her eyebrows as she rereads the message. It's a bit of an overreaction considering all she did was use his nail-brush, and she doesn't like the threatening tone. And how does he know that she used it anyway? Unless he's got spy cameras rigged up in the bathroom? A shiver runs up her spine. As soon as she gets back she's going to check.

Chapter 14

Gareth

Gareth is in the CCTV room, scanning the screens, when he spots his dad. But that's not his first thought. What goes through his mind is, that man's moving very slowly. The other shoppers appear to be zooming past him. He's walking against the tide, his white-grey hair contrasting against the white, pink, brown skin tones of the people moving towards the camera rather than away. Gareth zooms in. There is nothing remarkable about the man. He's average height, his age-bleached hair thinning at the crown to reveal a pink scalp, and his olive-green Gortex-style jacket is slightly too large for his shoulders. But there's something about his stance that makes Gareth sit up taller in his chair. The man might be in his seventies or eighties but there's no curve to his back or stoop to his head. He's standing erect, shoulders back, neck long, head still. It's the posture of a private on parade or a sailor standing to attention in front of a senior officer. *That's* when he thinks of his dad, of the postcard lying on the sideboard at home, of the neatly looping writing and *I love you, Joan.*

Gareth's heart pounds against his ribs. Could it be him? Could his dad have shown up at the Meads looking for his son? Is that why he's standing to attention on a walkway, staring intently into a shop? Does he want to reconnect with Gareth before he makes his way home? Does he want to soften the shock? Frantically, Gareth looks from screen to screen, searching for a better angle of the man who may or may not be his dad, but none of the cameras are situated in a position where they can zoom in on the man's face. The best he can find is a quarter profile. He zooms in, examining the shape of the man's nose, the heaviness of his brow and the curve of his chin. Is it him? It's been twenty years and his dad will have aged, but there are enough similarities to make Gareth jump to his feet.

He looks from the screen to the door, then at his radio, lying on the desk. He could ask one of the other guards to apprehend the man and ask him who he is but what if he lies? What if his dad isn't ready to be reunited with his family yet? What if the confrontation makes him go back underground? He can't take that risk. He has to look the man in the face himself. Even after twenty years he'd know his dad. There are some things time can't steal.

He picks up his radio. Strictly speaking, the control room should be manned at all times – he could count on the fingers of one hand the number of times he's abandoned his post for more than a three-minute toilet break over the last thirteen years – but there is no way he can ask for one of his colleagues to take over. They'd ask questions, questions he isn't entirely sure he wants to answer, not yet. As far as everyone else knows, his dad is dead. He decides to go for it. He'll sprint down the steps, run across the first-floor walkway, take a look at the man and, if it isn't his dad, he'll run back again. He'd be away from his desk for less than four minutes. Three minutes tops. And if it *is* his dad? Then he won't care how long he's away from his desk.

He glances at his watch as he leaves the office, then he speeds down the stairs.

He's gone. Gareth stands outside Mirage Fashions and turns in a full circle but there's no sign of the man who was standing there just minutes ago. He's completely disappeared. Gareth runs the length of the upper floor, searching the escalators and peering over the barriers into the lower floor. Several white- and grey-haired men catch his eye but there's no sign of the one he saw on the screen. He runs back towards Mirage Fashions and through the open door. Larry, their security guard, is on the other side of the shop. He raises a hand in hello but Gareth doesn't acknowledge the gesture. He's too busy scanning the shop for any sign of his dad. Maybe he's popped into one of the other shops on the first floor? He turns sharply then grunts as a shoulder connects with his chest. It's the red-haired shop manager from yesterday, the one who was running hell for leather across the ground floor.

'Sorry,' he says automatically, looking down at her. Her cheeks are flushed and there's a light sheen of sweat on her forehead and above her top lip. 'I wasn't looking where I was going.'

'No, I'm sorry.' She flashes him a smile. 'I think I barged into you. I'm late back from lunch!'

There's a brief moment of awkwardness as they both step in the same direction to allow the other to pass, then Gareth holds out an arm. 'After you.'

The woman gives him a quick nod and steps into the store. Gareth glances at his watch. He's been away from the control desk for six minutes. His radio, attached to his belt, hasn't crackled once but that's doesn't mean there haven't been any issues. He hasn't got time to search the other shops for his dad. He needs to get back to the CCTV room before anyone realises he's been away.

He takes off again, his heart pounding in his chest and his lungs aching as he runs across the walkway and up the stairs to his office. He walks the last couple of steps, dragging himself up with the handrail with one hand and swiping the sweat from his brow with the other. He pauses at the top step and sighs. Standing with his back to the locked CCTV room door with his arms crossed over his chest and a smug look on his face is another security guard. Liam Dunford, Gareth's subordinate and a little sneak of a man.

'Been for a run?' Liam asks, struggling to hide his delight; Gareth Filer, head honcho and chief bollocker has abandoned his desk and broken a fundamental rule of security.

'Don't even go there,' Gareth says. 'There was an emergency.'

Liam cocks his head. 'Oh yeah? I didn't hear anything on the radio.'

'That's because it was nothing to do with you.'

'I thought emergencies went out to all staff.'

'Well this one didn't.'

'What was it? This emergency that required you to break protocol and leave the CCTV gallery?' Liam unfolds his arms and rests a palm on the wall. Everything about his body language says: *I am a sneaky little shit.*

'Like I told you.' Irritation burns like indigestion in Gareth's chest, but he tries to ignore it. If he bites, Liam has won and Liam is *not* going to win. 'It's none of your business.'

'Fine.' He shrugs. 'I'll ask Mark Whiting then. I've been meaning to chat to him for a while.'

Mark Whiting is the Meads' general manager, and Gareth's boss. He's only been in post for a year and Gareth can't stand the bloke. He's been cost-cutting left, right and centre and doesn't give a shit if that means they're understaffed or risking potential health and safety nightmares. In the last year alone he's sacked three cleaners, two security guards and a caretaker. He's made it very clear that he thinks his predecessor made a mistake by promoting Gareth and that his salary isn't justified. If Whiting had his way there wouldn't be a supervisor role at all and all guards would report to him.

'About what?' Gareth asks.

'A pay rise.' The slight bend in Liam's raised right eyebrow conveys his demand as clearly as if he'd said it aloud: give me cash or I'll tell the manager of the shopping centre that you just committed a sackable offence.

'Why aren't you on the shop floor?' Gareth counters. Liam's had two warnings. One more for deserting his post without permission would seal his fate.

'I'm on my break.' There's the smirk again. 'So I thought I'd come and get my holiday form signed.' He reaches into his pocket and pulls out a folded piece of paper.

'Fine.' On shaking legs, Gareth ascends the last step and approaches the door to his office. The two men lock eyes and Gareth's throat dries up. He's seen this before, in David Attenborough documentaries: the young buck rearing up, challenging the older herd leader when he's old and tired. If he asks Liam to move then he's showing his weakness. But if he shoves him out of the way then he's lost his job.

They face off, Gareth staring up at the taller, leaner man for what feels like an age but can only be a couple of seconds, before finally Liam steps to the side, gesturing for him to pass with a wide sweep of his hand. Gritting his teeth, Gareth keys in the code and opens the door. He turns and reaches out a hand for Liam's holiday form then, without inviting him in, rests it against the wall and scribbles his signature on the bottom.

'I'll enter it into the system.'

'And the pay rise?'

'What pay rise?'

Liam's smile reappears. 'Five hundred quid should help me forget what I saw. I'll give you until tomorrow to work out the details. See you then . . .' He pauses. 'Boss.'

The first mouthful of the burger is the best, it always is. Every stress, every worry and every niggling thought disappears as Gareth closes his eyes and chews. Gareth knows he'll hate himself later but, right now, he doesn't care. It's his favourite part of the day and the anticipation begins to build a good hour before he finishes his shift. It's just him, two McDonald's Veggie Deluxe burgers, a large fries and a vanilla milkshake. He doesn't even put the radio on in the car because he wants nothing, *nothing*, to detract from the glorious moment he opens the paper bag, unwraps his burger and takes the first bite. As he chews, eyes closed, he doesn't think about his mum and whether she's burning the house down. He doesn't think about the bored-sounding copper he spoke to that morning about his missing dad. He doesn't think about the texts he received from his mum's two carers – Sally and Yvonne – saying they don't know anything about a postcard. He doesn't think about the man who may or may not have been his dad. And he certainly doesn't think about Liam Dunford, the slimy little snake.

He takes another bite, and another, barely chewing in his desperation to get the burger into his stomach as quickly as he can so he can start on the second one. He likes it, the sensation of his stomach growing fuller and fuller, of it straining to contain all the food. It makes him feel settled and content, safe and warm. But with every mouthful of the second burger Gareth hates himself a little bit more. Not just for shovelling empty, dirty calories he doesn't need into his mouth or because he should have pushed that copper to transfer him to someone who could actually help, but because the situation he's found himself in with Liam is his own bloody fault. Not once in twenty-five years working in security has he jeopardised the safety of the shoppers. Not once.

What an absolute loser.

And now he's being blackmailed by a snot of a man who doesn't deserve the epaulettes on his shirt.

Goddamnit.

Gareth shoves the half-eaten burger back into the brown paper bag, crumples it, and tosses it into the passenger seat footwell. Then he slumps over the steering wheel with his head in his hands. His dad was right. He is a disappointment. And the worst thing is the person he's let down the most is himself.

Pull yourself together, Gareth tells himself as he pushes open the garden gate and walks up the pathway to his front door. For Mum if no one else. Out of the corner of his eye he sees Kath peering around her front door, frantically waving her hand. Normally he loves their chats – there's something infectious about her friendly, easy-going manner – but he's not in the mood for a conversation today and he tries to ignore her, hoping that if he doesn't make eye contact she'll simply go away. But Kath calls out his name, forcing him to acknowledge her.

'Sorry to bother you.' She opens the door wider, revealing a pink and white unicorn onesie, the horned hood hanging over her face. Coupled with the grime music that's being played at full volume somewhere in the house, it feels to Gareth as though he's just stepped into a surreal urban play. Kath clocks his raised eyebrows and offers him a wide grin. 'Nice, isn't it? Primark. I'll get you one the next time I pop in if you want.'

'No thanks.' Gareth glances towards his own house. The

curtains are closed but he can see the light of the television flickering through a tiny gap. 'What can I do you for, Kath?'

'It's your mum,' she starts, then, reacting to the look of panic on his face, quickly adds, 'she's fine. I was just wondering if it was her birthday, that's all.'

Kath's always been fond of Joan but, since she lost her own mother, she actively asks after his mum and often pops round in the day if she can.

Gareth mentally flicks through the significant dates in his memory – there aren't many – and shakes his head. 'No. It's not until 11th November. Why do you ask?'

'She had some lovely flowers delivered today and I . . .' Kath does an embarrassed little jig with her shoulders ' . . . I wondered what they were for.'

Kath's a beautician who works from home doing things to women's eyelashes and brows; Gareth isn't quite sure what. It's not unusual for him to return from work to find one of her customers parked up outside his house, but he rarely grumbles. It's worth the inconvenience of having to park around the corner knowing that Kath's available to pop in and check up on his mum if he gives her a ring.

'I gave her a knock,' Kath adds, 'to ask if it was her birthday – I'd have nipped to Marks for a cake and a card if it was – but she wasn't sure. She—' She breaks off to shout up the stairs. 'Georgia! Turn that racket down. I can't hear myself think.'

There's no answer and no pause in the relentless thump, thump, thump of the music. Kath takes a deep breath as though readying herself for a full volume shout. Instead she sighs, steps out of the house and pulls the door shut behind her.

'Sorry about that, Gareth. Normally I'd be straight up there but she's having a tough time of it at school at the moment. What was I saying?'

'That Mum didn't know if it was her birthday or not.'

Kath frowns, or at least Gareth thinks she does because there's no movement or creasing of any sort on her forehead, but there's a studied look in her eyes as she gazes past him towards the closed curtains of his living room. 'She's getting worse, isn't she?'

'Yeah.' His gaze drops to his shoes. Her next appointment with the consultant is in two weeks' time and he's already dreading it. He's not sure he'll be able to cope with her reaction if the consultant insists on moving her into a home.

'Well you know I'm always here,' Kath says. 'If you need me to pop in, or take her somewhere in the car, you just say the word. Okay?'

Gareth looks at her, standing on her doorstep in her bare feet in her ridiculously fluffy outfit and, for the first time all day, he smiles.

'Thank you,' he says as he takes his door key out of his pocket. 'Thanks, Kath, that means a lot.'

Gareth sniffs the air as he opens the front door, then sags with relief. Whatever his mum has done today she hasn't burnt anything to a cinder. His note – DANGER! DO NOT COOK, MUM! – taped above the cooker must have done the job. He slips off his shoes and hangs up his jacket then pokes his head around the living room door. His mum is sitting, as usual, in her favourite armchair directly in front of the TV.

'Gerbera,' she says, in answer to the quiz show host's question, then clenches her fist in delight as the correct answer – *her* answer – turns green at the bottom of the screen.

'Hello, love.' She turns to look at Gareth. 'How was work?'

'Yeah good.' He bends to kiss her on the cheek. 'How was your . . .' He turns his head, the bright yellows and oranges of a floral arrangement on the bookshelf catching his eye. 'Kath said someone sent you flowers.'

'Did they?' His mum turns to look. 'Oh, aren't they pretty. Yellow roses are my favourite. Who are they from, Gareth?'

He crosses the room, guts churning, and not just because of all the junk food he ate. He can't remember the last time someone sent his mum flowers. He's given her plenty – for Mother's Day and her birthday at least – but he can't remember her ever being given any by someone else, not since his dad disappeared. He plucks at the white envelope that's been stapled to the edge of the wrapping and opens it.

Could they be from his dad, he wonders as he carefully eases out the small card. First a postcard, then flowers, is he paving the way for his return? No, Gareth tells himself. They're not from his dad. His dad's dead. He's never coming home.

'Oh for God's sake!' His shout is so loud that his mum lets out a little cry of distress.

'Sorry, sorry.' He rushes to her side and presses a hand to her shoulder. 'I didn't mean to scare you. I'm sorry. I'll get you a cup of tea.'

He rushes out of the room before she can reply. The flowers aren't from his dad at all. They're from William Mackesy, thanking his mum for her kind donation to the church.

Chapter 15

Alice

'Tonight?' Emily looks aghast. 'You agreed that you'd go out with him tonight?'

'Yes, Emily, I did.' Alice looks at her daughter in the mirror as she applies red lipstick. 'He asked me out at lunchtime and we're going out for dinner. There's plenty of food in the fridge. You're not going to starve.'

Her daughter perches on the edge of her bed. 'It's not that, and I'm not bothered about being home on my own. You just . . . you're playing it all wrong, Mum. He's going to think you're desperate.'

'How is saying yes to dinner desperate?'

'Because you agreed to go tonight. You should have told him you have plans.'

'But I haven't.'

'He doesn't need to know that.'

'So I should have lied? Great way to start a relationship.'

'Oh my God, Mum!' Emily's exasperation fills the room. 'It's a first date. You're not going to marry the guy. Relationship!' She shakes her head. 'God, you are *so* out of touch.'

'But I like him and I *want* to go out for dinner with him. Besides, I'm too old to play games.'

'It's not *games*, you just want to look like you have a full and active life. Men don't respect you if you drop everything to see them.'

'And that's what you do with Adam is it?'

Emily stiffens. 'What's that supposed to mean?'

Alice turns to look at her daughter. 'Sweetheart, I know you're trying to help me out, and I appreciate that, but your own relationship isn't exactly healthy.'

'My relationship's fine.'

'Is it? Because from where I'm sitting you seem really unhappy.' She gestures at the glass of wine in her daughter's hand. 'I can't remember the last time you didn't come home and have a drink.'

'It's just a glass of wine.'

'*A* glass?'

'One glass. Two glasses. I'm not an alcoholic, Mum, if that's what you're implying.'

'I'm not implying anything, love.' She gets up from the dressing table stool and crosses the room. 'But it's not normal, the screaming rows you and Adam have.'

Emily shuffles away from her as she sits down on the bed; the soft curves of her face have hardened. She says something under her breath that Alice doesn't catch.

'Sorry, what was that?'

'I said, I'm not a doormat. Just because you shut up and put up with Dad's shit it doesn't mean I have to do the same. If Adam's out of order, I tell him. That's why we row, because, unlike you, I'm not afraid to speak up.'

The ferocity of her daughter's accusation hits Alice in the

chest like a cannonball and she recoils, one hand pressed between her breasts. Is that what her daughter really thinks of her? That she's a doormat? That Peter cheated on her because she didn't speak up? She stares at Emily, her gaze flicking from her hard blue eyes to the tight line of her lips. She did everything in her power to give her daughter a happy, stable upbringing. She worked a part-time job so they could walk to school together every morning and back home at a quarter past three. She gave up her own little pleasures – weekly nights out with the girls, good quality make-up and getting her hair dyed professionally – to ensure that Emily could have violin lessons, go to ballet and learn how to swim. She read her a story every night, cooked her fresh food and told her she loved her and was proud of her at every available opportunity. She did everything she could to win at parenting but it wasn't enough, she's still failed.

'Mum,' Emily says as Alice stands, smooths out the creases in her skirt and walks out of the bedroom. 'Mum, I'm sorry. Mum! Say something. I'm sorry, Mum.'

Simon smiles and raises a hand in greeting as Alice crosses the busy Indian restaurant.

'Sorry,' she says as she draws close enough for him to hear her through the babble of conversation and the clatter of pots and pans drifting through from the kitchen. 'I couldn't find a parking space.'

She had meant to order a taxi so she could drink but after her argument with Emily she grabbed her coat, bag and car keys and walked straight out of the house. Hot, angry tears pricked at her eyes as she started the engine of her ten-year-old Golf. There was no way she was going to turn up to her date with smudged eye make-up and a red nose so she pushed the conversation to the back of her mind and instead ran through everything she had to do at work the next day.

'No worries at all,' Simon says, half-rising from his seat as she pulls back her chair. 'I'm just glad that you're here.'

As he looks at her, his eyes as warm and welcoming as his smile, Alice feels her shoulders relax, just the tiniest bit. And as she sits down at the table and reaches for the menu a voice in the back of her head says, Oh fuck off, Emily. What do you know?

'So,' she says, looking at him over the menu, 'what was that all about earlier?'

Simon frowns.

'The woman,' Alice clarifies. 'In Costa.'

'Oh.' He sits back in his chair and runs a hand through his hair. 'Dunno. Mistaken identity, I guess.'

'Really? She seemed pretty sure that she knew you.'

'Well I didn't know her.' He laughs tightly. 'What can I say? I must have one of those faces.'

'You looked freaked out.'

'Wouldn't you if someone leapt out at you?'

Alice studies his face. She barely knows the man, but she can't shake the feeling there's something he's not telling her. There's an undercurrent of unease beneath his denial but she's not going to push it. Maybe he feels embarrassed for jumping the way he did, or for the fact he shepherded her out of Costa at speed. He didn't say a word to her as they left the coffee shop. He just raised a hand and said, 'I'll text you about dinner.' And then he was off. He didn't look back until he reached the escalator, but then his gaze rested on the door to Costa and not on her.

'So,' Simon says. 'Have you decided what you're having yet?'

'Lamb bhuna I think.'

'Good choice. You know my dad once had an accident eating a curry?'

'Really?'

'Yeah. He slipped into a korma.'

Alice laughs and the awkwardness she's been feeling slips away. Simon keeps up the terrible curry jokes for another few minutes, then they slip into comfortable conversation, one topic morphing easily into the next. They laugh a lot and by the time Alice's lamb bhuna is placed in front of her, her cheeks are hurting from smiling so much.

'So,' she asks, as she stabs her fork into a hunk of meat, 'you still haven't told me what you do for a living.'

Simon dabs at his mouth with his napkin. 'Haven't I? That's because it's not very interesting.'

'Well, I'm interested. Go on, tell me. I won't judge. Or yawn.'

Simon laughs. 'I just, um . . .' His gaze flicks away from her, to the door of the restaurant as the bell chimes and an older couple walk in. 'I . . . it's really very boring. Just insurance . . . stuff.'

Alice fakes a yawn, her eyes on Simon, waiting for a laugh. When it doesn't come she says, 'Sorry, I'm being rude. What kind of insurance?'

'Just, um . . . financial, for companies, institutions. Like I said, really very boring.' He swipes a hand dismissively through the air. It's the third or fourth time Alice has noticed him do that and it's always when she asks him something he doesn't want to answer.

She takes the hint. 'Okay, so, where do you live?'

He runs a hand over the back of his neck, his eyes still on the door. Alice turns her head to look but it's closed. No one's just come in.

'St George's,' he says. 'I've got a little three-bed house.'

She starts to tell him that she lives in a two-bedroom flat in Kingswood with her daughter Emily, then realises she's already told him that. She shifts in her chair, suddenly uncomfortable. Simon definitely struggles with direct questions. He can riff for ages about books and films, holidays and politics, but whenever she broaches anything remotely personal he clams up.

'Are you okay?' she asks.

'Yeah, sure.' His smile returns. 'I'm having a really good night. You?'

'Yeah,' she says, but there's an invisible question mark that hangs in the air.

'What's up?' he asks.

I need to know what you're hiding, she thinks but doesn't say.

'Have you ever been in prison?' It feels unlikely but it might explain why he's so reticent about talking about himself.

Simon laughs – a loud, incredulous bark. 'What? No! Of course not.'

Alice changes tack. Why else would someone warn her off him?

'Have you ever cheated on anyone?' she asks.

This time his answer isn't quite so immediate and his gaze drops to the table. 'No. Unless you count a kiss. I was a student, my girlfriend was back in our hometown and I got drunk at a house party. Actually that is cheating, isn't it? So yes, but it was a long time ago.' There's a pause, then, 'Anything else? I've got the feeling you've got a checklist hidden away under the table and you're working your way through. Do you need my shoe size too? They're massive by the way.' The edges of his mouth lift into a smile.

Alice smiles too but it doesn't reach all the way to her eyes. He thinks she's a weirdo, bombarding him with questions, and she can't say she blames him. She *is* being unusually full-on. She's going to have to mention it, isn't she? The Facebook message that warned her not to trust him. She was convinced that Michael was behind it but the reaction of the woman in Costa made her rethink that theory. How would Michael know

Simon's name? As far as she knows, Simon didn't stop to check on Michael; he picked up her purse and ran after her, following her all the way to the Meads. And she's watched enough episodes of *Line of Duty* to know that offenders aren't told the name of witnesses by the police.

'Simon,' she says cautiously, 'can you think of anyone who'd want to put me off you?'

'Weird question.'

'I know.' She raises her eyebrows to let him know she'd still like an answer.

He reaches for his beer and takes a sip, his eyes not meeting hers. Alice waits, fighting the urge to fill the silence with an apology or an explanation. Simon takes another sip, longer this time, then sets his glass down on the table.

'No, not really. Although my ex-girlfriend isn't my biggest fan. I'm not going to call Flora a psycho because the sort of men who call their exes that are normally pretty dodgy themselves but . . . well, let's just say that relationship didn't end well.'

'In what way?'

'We were engaged, six months away from getting married. The venue had been booked, the dress had been bought, invitations had been sent out, the whole lot. And I, um . . . I called it off.'

'You cancelled the wedding?'

'I ended the relationship. She was a lovely girl, woman,' he corrects himself quickly, 'the best. But I knew it wasn't right. Spending the rest of our lives together would have been a mistake.'

'I'm guessing she didn't take it well?'

He laughs ruefully. 'You could say that. I'd been feeling that things weren't right for a while but I put off saying anything. I thought they might sort themselves out but they . . . um . . . they didn't . . . and when I went to the fitting for my suit I couldn't do it. I couldn't even put it on. Anyway, God . . .' he

91

runs his hands over his face and sighs heavily '. . . why are we even talking about this?'

'Look at this.' Alice pushes her mobile across the table towards him.

Simon picks it up and looks at the screen. His eyes flick from left to right as he reads the Facebook message from Ann Friend.

'Who is this?' He looks at her, her phone still in his hand.

'I don't know. I thought it might be Michael, the man from the pub, but there's no way he could know your name unless . . . unless you told him?'

'No.' Simon shakes his head. 'I didn't speak to the guy.' He reaches into his jacket and pulls out his own mobile. He checks it, then puts it back in his pocket.

'Don't you think it's creepy?' Alice asks.

There's that look again, blankness behind the impenetrable grey of his irises. 'A bit. I'd ignore it if I were you. If you'll excuse me.' He gets up. 'I just need to make a quick call.'

'Sure.'

Weird, Alice thinks as Simon leaves the restaurant with his phone in his hand, suddenly having to make a phone call after she showed him the message. Should she ask him who he was speaking to when he comes back or would that look too obsessive? No, she decides as she reaches for her glass, better to say nothing and see what he says. As she takes a sip of water her phone vibrates on the table. It's a text from Emily.

I'm sorry, Mum. I didn't mean to insult you. I hope you're having fun with Simon. You deserve to be happy. SORRY, SORRY, SORRY. I LOVE YOU. Xx

Alice smiles as she taps out a reply:

I love you too. You mean the world to me. xx

As she sits back in her chair she looks longingly at Simon's pint glass. Maybe she should ask the waiter for a small glass of red. She'd still be under the limit and it would take the edge off her nerves. As she raises her hand to attract a waiter's attention her phone bleeps again.

Hello! How's your night in with Emily going? There's sod all on the telly. Anything good on Netflix?

Lynne. Shit. She'd completely forgotten about the lie she'd told to get out of going to the cinema. She loves Lynne to bits but sometimes hanging out with her can be exhausting; their conversations go round in circles – picking over old relationships, gossiping about the staff in the other shops, gossiping about the staff in their own shop (although Alice tries very hard not to), and discussing various health woes. It's good to have a bit of time apart every now and then. But she should have been honest with her.

I'm such a dick, she thinks as she taps out a text:

Actually, I'm having dinner with Simon. It was a last minute thing. She cringes at the lie then continues, *It's not going well. I don't think there will be a second date. Cinema tomorrow night instead? You can choose. xx*

She presses send before she can second-guess herself then glances up as the bell at the front door tinkles and someone walks in. It's Simon, all ruffled blonde hair and broad shoulders but with the stooped posture of a man who feels uncomfortable with his height.

Alice's phone bleeps with a reply from Lynne.

No way, how exciting! Sorry it's not going well though. Give me the goss tomorrow. Yes definitely to cinema. x

'You're still here,' Simon says, as he shuffles, rather than strides, up to Alice. He doesn't sit down. Instead he hovers beside the table, unsure, his hands in his pockets.

'Of course I am.' She turns her body towards him. 'Why would I leave?'

Alice walks through the dark streets of Bristol, her arm looped through Simon's. There's something about the way her arm fits into the crook of his and the light pressure of her coat sleeve on his that feels right, even if she has to take two steps for each one of his. The mood lightened after Simon returned from making his phone call. Alice pushed Ann Friend's message to the back of her brain and she and Simon both laughed a lot over dessert. After he paid for dinner he said he'd walk her back to her car. It wouldn't be right, he said, letting her navigate the back streets of Bristol alone, not when it was so late. In any other circumstances she would have laughed and said she was perfectly capable of finding her car alone but she was touched by the gesture and besides, it would make the date last that little bit longer. And perhaps there would be a second date after all.

As they pass the NCP car park, Simon makes a soft little snort of disapproval. 'Full. Still. At nearly 11 p.m. on a Tuesday night. Honestly, the council really needs to sort out the parking situation. Not to mention the bloody roadworks.'

'I know,' Alice says, then, with nothing more to add to the discussion, adds, 'we're not far away now. I'm just round this corner.'

As they turn the corner into the dark alleyway, her heart flutters a little. Will he kiss her goodnight at the car? It must be at least twenty years since—

Simon sighs heavily. 'Yours isn't the white Golf is it?'

'Yes. Why?' Alice peers into the gloom and immediately spots the issue. A parking ticket, inside a clear plastic sleeve, tucked under the windscreen wiper. She swears under her breath, then unhooks her arm from Simon's and stalks up to the parking sign on the opposite side of the narrow street.

'It says here that parking is free after . . . oh.' She closes her eyes in frustration and inhales sharply through her nose. In her desperation to get to the restaurant as quickly as possible she'd only glanced at the sign, seeing what she wanted to see and not what it actually said.

'Alice,' Simon calls out. There's a note of urgency in the way he says her name. 'You need to look at this.'

She glances across the street, to the last place she saw him, a few feet from her car. But he's not there.

'Simon?' She looks towards the end of the alley and the traffic rushing past. There's no one in the other direction either. There are no shops open for him to have slipped into, no pub door- ways for him to shelter in. He's completely disappeared.

'Simon!' She heads back towards the main street but a flash of light somewhere between her car and the wall makes her pause. She turns, waiting for it to happen again, then squeaks in surprise as Simon pops up from behind the car. He's got his mobile in his hand, the light from the torch app flashing across the alleyway.

'Alice.' He beckons her over.

'What is it?' she asks as she draws closer, but Simon doesn't answer. Instead he crouches down and slowly sweeps the light of his phone across the driver-side door.

It takes her a couple of seconds to make sense of the jagged scratches in the paintwork but the longer she looks, the clearer it becomes. Three words.

YOU'RE NOT LISTENING.

Chapter 16

Ursula

Definitely no spy cameras in the bathroom. Ursula looked every-where – twice – and then searched her room. It's 11.05 p.m. and she's lying back on her bed, a book in her lap and head-phones clamped to her ears. She can't settle, and not just because of nail brush-gate. It's been a good day in a lot of ways – she delivered all but two of her parcels, nothing hugely stressful happened and she didn't steal anything. But she can't stop thinking about the woman at number six. Was she telling the truth? About being agoraphobic? Ursula moves her book onto the bedside table, then swings her legs off the bed and stands up. She stretches, fingertips nearly grazing the textured ceiling, and wanders over to the window. A name has been scratched into the thick gloss paint on the sill: Nick.

She runs a fingernail over it, wondering how many people lived in her room before her, then pulls back the curtains and looks outside. Unlike Charlotte's house with its incredible view of Bristol's twinkling lights, there's nothing of interest at the rear of Ed's – just a matchbox-sized patio with various dead plants in tubs and the backs of other people's houses. She presses her palms against the glass and raises her gaze. No stars, just a sliver of moon, peeping out of a murky grey-black sky. It's one of the things she misses most about her old life: being able to see the stars. She and Nathan would travel up to the Lake District every opportunity they had. They'd camp out and lie on their backs outside their tent, gazing up at the inky black sky, making up stories about the shapes they could see in the stars.

Ursula presses a hand to her chest, suddenly struggling to breathe. The radiators are pumping out heat and the room feels stiflingly hot. She fiddles with the latch on the old window then, as the painted sill cracks and groans, gives it a shove. It swings open, then BANG, the wind grabs it and slams it against the side of the house.

'Fuck!' She says under her breath as she leans out of the window, hair wrapping around her face as she reaches for the metal arm. 'Fuck, fuck, fuck.'

She tenses as she pulls the arm towards her, anticipating a shattered pane or a bloody great hole where the glass used to be, but the window is still intact. As she sighs with relief there's a bang from somewhere else in the house that makes her bedroom door shudder on its hinges.

She stares across the room, listening. Did Ed just come home and slam the front door? He wasn't in when she got back a little after seven o'clock. The TV in the living room was off and cool to the touch, and she couldn't hear anything when she listened at his bedroom door. She went into the bathroom, half-expecting to see police tape festooned around his stuff, but everything was as it had been that morning, including the nail brush on the shelf. She stood for a while, staring at it, trying to work out how he'd known she'd touched it. It was lined up with his other toiletries, each item about an inch apart, all labels facing forward. Had she just chucked it back in? She couldn't remember.

When her stomach rumbled noisily she headed down to the kitchen and made beans on toast topped with grated cheese. She ate it standing up, shovelling forkfuls into her mouth as she leaned over the counter. She was already in Ed's bad books and she didn't want to make things worse by dropping a rogue bean down the side of the sofa. Afterwards, she quickly washed the dish and the pot she'd used, put them away and scurried back to her room. She's been listening out for Ed ever since. He hasn't responded to her *Sorry, it won't happen again* text and, in Ursula's mind, that can only mean he hasn't forgiven her.

She moves across her room and listens at the door for the sound of footsteps, the clank of pans or the squeak of the stairs. Nothing. The house is still silent. She puts a hand on the handle and slowly eases the door open. She steps out onto the landing and peers down the stairs. The front door is shut and the only coat on the peg is hers. So Ed hasn't come home. But what was the noise?

She turns as something catches her eye. There's a small piece of paper wedged in the floor, in a gap between two of the planks directly outside Edward's room. She crosses the landing and stoops down to pick it up. It's a photo clipped out of a newspaper, a full headshot of a smiling man. On the other side is part of an article about new building regulations in Bristol. There's something about the man's face that looks vaguely familiar but she can't place his name. The clipping wasn't on the landing when she got home; she would have noticed it when she went into the bathroom. Did the wind blow it out from Edward's room? She drops to her knees. It's a Victorian house and there are gaps under a lot of the doors. She presses her cheek against a cold wooden board, screws up her right eye, and peers under Edward's bedroom door. She can't make out much, mostly the floorboards of his room, but there is something else. More pieces of paper. The bang she heard must have been Edward's window. By opening hers she caused a draught and the wind scattered his collection of newspaper clippings all over the floor. Shit. She gets to her feet and tries the handle to his door. Locked.

She crouches down and slides the photo she found under the door, but the man's smiling face doesn't make it all the way back into Edward's room. She isn't sure *why* she can't bring herself to push him all the way inside; maybe it's the little voice in her head telling her that it's not normal to cut out photos of people from newspapers, or maybe she's curious to find out what Ed will do when he realises it's missing. Either way, she plucks it back up, carries it to her room, tucks it under her pillow and lies down on her bed. She glances at the door and the mess of parcel tape covering the missing lock and makes a mental note to ask Ed when he's going to replace it, then promptly falls asleep.

The sound of creaking wood infiltrates Ursula's dream. She's on a beach, looking for Nathan, and the noise makes her turn towards the sea. She looks for a rowing boat, oars dipping and turning, gently bobbing on the waves. But there's nothing there. Just miles of sea that fade into a dull grey sky.

'Nathan!' she calls. 'Nathan, where are you?' But her shout is drowned out by the creak, creak, creak of the wood. She turns towards the dunes, looking for whoever, or whatever, is making the noise. But there's no one in the dunes either, just long blades of grass that curve and bend in the wind.

That way, it seems to whisper as it points in the direction of her house. He went that way.

'He's not there,' she tells the grass but as she waits for its answer the blades fade and swirl, drifting and twisting and then vanishing completely. Her eyes flicker open and she blinks, still trapped in the arms of the dream. There's a length of dark material a metre or so from her head. She stares at it, wondering why there's a curtain on the beach, then jolts at the sound of a creaking floorboard.

There's someone in her room; a dark shape, a man, standing next to her chest of drawers, going through her stuff. Ed. He's so absorbed in what he's doing that he hasn't noticed that she's awake. Her lips part, but terror has stolen her voice and all she can do is watch as he moves silently from the chest of drawers to the pile of clothes draped over the chair in the corner of the room. She forgot to prop it up against the door before she fell asleep. Edward keeps his back to her as he picks up her sweatshirt and wriggles a hand into the pocket. He discards it, then picks up her jogging bottoms and does the same. Her heart pounds, urging her to run. But Ursula can't move. She's barely breathing. So instead of running she pretends to be asleep.

I'll scream, she tells herself as she closes her eyes and sweat prickles on her temples. I'll fight. If he so much as touches me I *will* fight back. She mentally scans her room, searching it for weapons to use in self-defence. There's an umbrella propped up against the chest of drawers, the tip hard and pointed. But even as she wills herself to open her eyes, get off the bed and grab the umbrella, she can't move. She feels like a shop mannequin tipped onto its side: rigid, cold and immobile.

A floorboard creaks, then there's silence. She hears Edward breathing, a short, sharp snort of irritation. Then there's a soft click and the room falls silent again. She waits, her damp T-shirt clinging to her back, the muscles in her arms and legs aching. What if Edward closed the door to trick her into thinking he'd gone? What if, right now, he's standing beside her and when she opens her eyes his face is millimetres from hers?

I have to open my eyes, she tells herself. I WILL open my eyes. In three . . . two . . . one . . .

Her eyelids fly open and she throws her hands up by her face but there's no one to protect herself from, no slight figure with dusty blonde hair and intense eyes standing beside her bed. She flips over and looks towards the door. Closed. He's definitely gone . . . unless . . .

An image flashes into her mind, of a woman in an episode of *Luther*, swinging her legs over the side of her bed only to have her ankles grabbed by a man hiding beneath it. Ursula lies very still, holding her breath, listening for sounds of life in the room. Logically she knows it's unlikely that Edward slid under her bed without making a sound. But what if he did? What if the click she heard wasn't the bedroom door closing but the blade of a Stanley knife being extended?

She stares up at the ceiling, listening, skin prickling and her heart thumping against her ribs, forcing her to take a breath. Did Edward just hear that – the gasp of air entering her lungs? Is he smiling up at the springs, his hand gripping the knife?

Ursula, stop it! she tells herself.

Girding herself, she sits up sharply. She imagines Edward, beneath her, sucking in his breath as the springs sag towards him.

He's not under there, she tells herself but a louder voice tells her to run. You can get to the door faster than he can wriggle out from under the bed.

He's not under there. The click you heard was the door.

I don't . . .

CHECK UNDER THE BED!

As adrenaline surges through her, she grips the edge of the bed and peers underneath. Her imagination fills the dark space beneath and she sees Edward's face, leering out at her, the glint of a blade in his hand. Then he vanishes. Other than a few dust balls and a scrunched tissue, there's nothing, and no one, there. She collapses back against the pillows and runs her hands over her face. She feels sick. Her heart's still pounding so much she can feel it in her throat. She knew it was a risk, moving in with a stranger and taking a room with no lock on the door, but she'd convinced herself she was safe. She hit six foot three the year she turned sixteen and for half her life she's towered over almost every man she's met. She's never clutched her keys between her fingers when walking home from a pub alone late at night. She's never had a man press up against her in a crowded train or crossed the street when a man was walking behind her. Charlotte was aghast when they discussed it once and Ursula had looked at her blankly and said, 'Why would I do that?' She hadn't been brought up to be afraid of men. Her six foot six father had drummed it into her from an early age that she should be proud of her height, not an apologist for it; that she should walk with her shoulders back and her head held high. She's lost count of the number of men who've jumped when they turn from a bar, pints in their hands, to see her standing behind them, waiting to be served. She's been ridiculed and laughed at, pointed at and mocked.

Regret courses through her as she reruns what just happened. Why did she pretend to be asleep? Why didn't she just sit up in bed and scream at him to get out? She was passive, a victim, *letting* him invade her room, allowing him to be the one in control. She hears her dad's voice in her head, bellowing over her thoughts. 'No one has the right to make you feel inferior, Ursula. No one should make you apologise for the space you take up or the person you are. You are many things, my dear, but you are not weak and you are certainly not an apologist. Stop slouching, stop crying and push your shoulders back and raise your chin. You are Ursula Andrews; be proud of who you are.'

STRANGERS

A sudden spike of rage slices through her. This isn't about her and how she should have acted or reacted. It's about him. How *dare* he go into her room while she was sleeping and sift through her personal belongings? How dare *he* make her feel so afraid!

She reaches under her pillow and pulls out the newspaper clipping she rescued from the landing earlier, then crosses the room to the window and pulls back the curtain. It's 6.02 a.m. and the sky outside is marbled with orange and pink.

'Who are you?' she whispers to the black-and-white image.

The man in the photograph says nothing. He stares up at her, all big grin and mischievous eyes. Whoever he was, or is, he's important to Ed. Ursula looks back at her heavily taped bedroom door. The sensible thing to do now would be to pack up her stuff and move out. If Charlotte were in the same situation she'd rather forgo the £500 rent and deposit she'll never get back and spend the rest of her life living in the back of the van than spend another night under Edward's roof. But Ursula is not Charlotte. Whatever it is that her landlord's up to, she's going to find out. She is Ursula Andrews and no one gets to make her feel small.

Chapter 17

Gareth

As Gareth marches up the broad driveway that leads to an impressive detached Georgian-style house, he presses a hand to his stomach, not because he's nervous but because he hasn't had breakfast yet. He lifts the heavy brass knocker on William Mackesy's door. He tried ringing the man several times last night after he found the note on the flowers, but there was no reply and there's no way Gareth can do a full day at work without answers. He'd been a fool to think his dad might still be alive, that he was wandering through the Meads looking for his son, when all along it was obvious who was behind the postcard. Bloody William Mackesy. Not content with extorting money from the desperate and the grieving, now he was branching out and sending postcards from the dead. It was an idiotic thing to do. No one with healthy neurons would ever believe a dead

104

relative had magicked words onto a card then floated it into a postbox, and even his own mother, with her protein-coated cells and her withered synapses, thought the card was from a living person. Was Mackesy trying to befuddle her to work his way into her will somehow? His visits certainly seemed to have increased in frequency recently, if Sally's reports were anything to go by.

Bang

Gareth brings the knocker down hard.

Bang

Bang

He steels himself, pushing back his shoulders and drawing himself up to his full five foot seven. Dogs – at least two or three – respond by barking frantically. The sound has a strange echoey quality. Gareth has never been to William Mackesy's house before but it didn't take much to persuade the church secretary to hand over his address. After all, hadn't Joan made such a generous donation?

'Hello?' The door opens to reveal a man not much taller than Gareth with thinning grey hair, wire-framed glasses and a face that wouldn't be out of place on an ageing game show host. 'Oh.' He looks Gareth up and down, struggling to place him.

'I'm Joan Filer's son,' Gareth says. 'We met briefly at one of your . . . events . . . about a year ago.'

'Joan's son. Oh, of course!' Mackesy holds out his right hand. 'To what do I owe this unexpected early visit . . . er . . .?'

Gareth doesn't tell him his name, nor does he shake the proffered hand. Instead he nods his head towards the cavernous hallway behind Mackesy and says, 'I'd like to come in if I could.'

The older man's eyes widen and he glances behind him. 'One second. I'll just shut the dogs in the utility room.'

And the door closes in Gareth's face.

*

'So . . .' William Mackesy says, his elbows on the mahogany desk that separates him from Gareth, an expression of utmost compassion on his face (faked, Gareth thinks bitterly). 'What can I do you for?'

They're in his office, a large book-lined room, twice the size of Gareth's bedroom with a massive computer screen on the desk, various expensive-looking ornaments dotted around and an enormous pot-plant-cum-tree in the corner of the room.

'Two things,' Gareth says. 'Firstly, I would appreciate it if you didn't tell my mother upsetting messages from . . .' he forms quotation marks with his fingers '. . . the other side.'

Mackesy shakes his head lightly. 'I'm not sure I understand.'

'You told her that someone close to me would cause me . . .' Gareth falters as an image of Liam Dunford, propped up against the wall outside his office with a smug look on his face, pops into his head. If by 'close' Mackesy had meant proximity then maybe he wasn't a million miles off target with his little prophecy. No. Gareth dismisses the thought. Pure coincidence.

'Anyway,' he continues. 'Stop telling her things that might upset or worry her. She's not well.'

Mackesy holds out his hands, palms out. 'I only tell people what the departed tell me, but I take your point.'

Gareth reaches into his pocket and slides the white card that was attached to his mother's flowers across the desk. 'The other thing I wanted to talk to you about is this.'

Mackesy picks up the card, nods, then looks back at him. 'I sent your mother flowers to thank her for her donation. Is there a problem?'

'That depends on how big the donation was.'

The other man shrugs. 'I'm not sure I can tell you off the top of my head. Sheila, my wife, deals with that side of things. Our parishioners are so . . . so very generous. We receive a lot of help. We couldn't keep the church going without it.'

106

Can't tell you off the top of my head my arse. Gareth grits his teeth. William Mackesy is lying. He knows exactly how much Joan donated, he just doesn't want to tell him. Gareth's mum had no idea what he was talking about when he asked her about it and he hasn't got power of attorney over her affairs which means he can't legally access her bank account. She still receives a paper statement every month but the last one arrived three weeks ago so he'll have to wait another seven days if he wants to take a look at her outgoings.

'Do a lot of your *parishioners* suffer from dementia then?' he asks, his hands curled into fists beneath the desk.

'I'm sorry.' Mackesy tilts his head to one side. 'I'm not sure what you're implying.'

'Aren't you? Well let me spell it out for you then. Somehow you've managed to wheedle money out of my mum. As soon as I get hold of her bank statement I'm going to the police.'

Gareth waits, expectantly and slightly gleefully, for a reaction, for horror to register on the other man's face and for his hands to fly up in repentance. Instead his continues to sit stock-still, the only movement in his entire body the slight arch of one eyebrow.

'Is that so?'

'Yes, it is. I think they might be interested to know that you're sending vulnerable older people postcards from their dead relatives in an effort to extort money from them.'

Now Mackesy reacts. He recoils, pulling his hands away from the desk, more of the whites of his eyes visible beneath the glint of his glasses.

'What postcards?'

'This one.' Gareth reaches into his coat pocket and pulls out the postcard. He slides it across the desk so it sits alongside the florist's card.

Mackesy snatches it up, his brow creasing as he reads it, then flips it over. 'Who's John?'

Gareth laughs lightly. 'John? My dad. The one that talks to you and tells you how cold he is?'

'Oh . . . well . . .' Mackesy looks from the postcard to Gareth. 'Yes, of course but . . . but your dad's dead.'

'Yes. He is. Which makes what you're doing really bloody twisted.'

'I didn't send this.'

'Are you sure about that? Because it's a bit of a coincidence that it arrived on Monday and your flowers thanking Mum for her donation arrived yesterday.'

'Quite sure.' Mackesy tosses the postcard onto the table then shoves it towards Gareth. 'Whoever sent that to your mother it's got nothing to do with me. Ask Sheila. I've been in Brighton for a Mind, Body and Spirit Fayre since last Friday. You're lucky to catch me. I only got home forty-five minutes ago. Want me to call her? She keeps my diary. She could show it to you if you'd like.'

'Don't bother,' Gareth snaps. 'I've heard enough bullshit for one day.'

Brighton or not, he could still have sent the postcard. Or Sheila could. With the postmark partly smudged there's no way of knowing where it was sent. Gareth flexes his fingers and runs his damp palms up and down the cheap material of his work trousers. Every cell in his body is screaming at him to stand up, lean over the table, grab Mackesy by the collar and drive his fist straight into his smug face, but he can't get out of his chair. He can't do anything but stare at the man he despises and will all the shit in the world to come crashing down over his shiny, comb-over head.

'If that's everything,' Mackesy says, standing up. He walks around the desk and heads for the door. At one point he's so close that Gareth could shoot out a hand and grab him. But he doesn't. Instead he stands up, pulls back his shoulders and follows him out into the hall, the sound of whining, barking dogs drifting from somewhere in the depths of the house. As Mackesy opens the front door, standing back to allow him through, Gareth pauses and turns to face him.

'Leave my mum alone. Don't call her, don't drop in and if you take another penny of her money, then I'll . . .' He tails off. 'Just leave her alone. Okay?'

As he steps through the door he hears Mackesy say his name under his breath and turns sharply. 'What was that?'

The other man presses a hand to the side of his head and narrows his eyes, staring off into the distance. 'Yes . . .' he says. 'Okay. Yes.'

For a moment Gareth has no idea what's going on, then it's all he can do not to roll his eyes. Mackesy's communing with the dead. Of course he is.

'He's proud of you.' Mackesy looks him straight in the eye. 'Your dad. He wanted me to tell you.'

Gareth takes a deep breath and stares at the grey clouds rolling over head. A cold breeze whips at the thin cotton of his shirt and he shivers. The air smells different, sweet and earthy, he needs to get back to his car before it starts to rain.

'Did you hear me?' Mackesy shouts after him as he jogs back down the driveway. 'He's proud of you, your dad. He said it was important that you knew that.'

'Fraud!' Gareth shouts, not slowing his pace as the first spots of rain land on his nose and cheeks. If he ever had any doubt about William Mackesy's abilities, he certainly doesn't now.

Chapter 18

Alice

YOU'RE NOT LISTENING.

The three words have been going round and round Alice's head all morning. It wasn't a horrible dream; 'YOU'RE NOT LISTENING' was still scratched into the side of the car when she left the house in the morning and it'll still be there when she gets home. She rang DC Mitchell last night with Simon beside her, an arm over her shoulder, pulling her close. But the call went straight to voicemail so she left a message and rang 101 instead. She was told they wouldn't be sending anyone out to investigate but to take a photo and they'd file a crime report. When she told them that she'd previously reported an assault and creepy messages to DC Mitchell they said they'd pass on the details of the vandalism. Alice did as she was told, blinking as the flash on her phone camera lit up the side of the car, then looked at Simon, unsure what to do next.

'You don't want to get in, do you?' he said, sensing her hesitation.

Alice shook her head.

'I'd offer to drive but I'm over the limit.'

'No, it's fine.'

'It's not though, is it?' He squeezed her shoulder. 'Want me to come with you? I could get a taxi home from yours.'

She couldn't say yes fast enough.

Neither of them said very much on the journey back to Kingswood. Alice tried, half-heartedly, to strike up conversation a couple of times but she was so distracted she barely heard a word Simon said in reply. By the time she parked the car outside her flat a strange, stultifying atmosphere had settled between them, all the joy and excitement of earlier in the evening a distant memory. Simon followed her into the silent flat, Emily long gone, and hovered in the kitchen as she made coffee. Even with her back turned Alice could feel his presence in the room. He filled so much of the tiny space and she wasn't used to having a man in the house. Simon obviously felt as uncomfortable as she did; she could see him out of the corner of her eye as she filled the kettle, shifting his weight from one foot to the other, crossing and uncrossing his arms. He barely had more than two or three sips of coffee before his phone vibrated with a call. His taxi had arrived.

There was another awkward moment at the door where she didn't know whether to hug him goodbye or just wave. Simon made the decision for her. He stooped down, kissed her lightly on the cheek and said, 'I'll be in touch.' The four words reverberated around her mind as she pulled the door shut and returned to the kitchen. I'll be in touch. It was the sort of thing James Malone, her area manager, said after a visit. It was a polite goodbye, not the sort of thing you said at the end of a date.

Alice's heart was heavy as she tipped Simon's coffee into the sink and washed up his mug. When she went to bed fifteen minutes later she was certain she'd never see him again.

Over lunch Lynne nibbles at the corner of her sandwich and taps at her phone as Alice complains that she hasn't heard from Simon since he left her house the previous night.

Lynne looks up sharply. 'Seriously? You've got to fork out a couple of hundred quid to sort out your car and you're stressing about him?'

'But what if he got home and his ex was waiting for him?'

'What, with an axe?'

'It's not funny.'

'To be honest, Alice, if he has got a psycho ex you're better off out of it.'

'I'm worried about him.'

'Worry about yourself for a change.' Lynne sighs heavily. 'Jesus. It's like Peter all over again.'

'How is it like Peter?'

'You're putting a man first instead of yourself.'

'It's nothing like what happened with Peter!' Indignation burns in Alice's chest. If anyone should be on her side it should be Lynne.

'Look.' Lynne sets down her sandwich. 'What if Simon's not as innocent as he appears? It's all a bit Disney, isn't it? The knight in shining armour rescuing you from your attacker and then—'

'Simon didn't rescue me. I'm the one that kneed Michael in the bollocks, remember?'

'Okay, fine, but Simon chased after you with your purse, then he appears at work with a bunch of flowers, then he's magically in the café that you choose for lunch. He's everywhere you go.'

'Turning up at work and Costa isn't everywhere.'

'If you say so.'

'What? Why are you looking at me like that?'

'Because there's something dodgy going on. Someone warns you off him and then scratches your car and instead of doing what anyone normal would do and run a mile you're all over him.'

'I'm not all over him. I just want to make sure he got home safely.'

'You're sucked in.'

'By what?'

'The scam. It's all a big ruse. He and Michael are working together to extort money from lonely women.'

'I'm not lone—'

'Hear me out! Michael plays the bad guy, Simon's the knight in shining armour. You turn to Simon because Michael's scaring you, then the next thing you know Simon's asking you for money. He's wheedling his way into your life, Alice. He's seen your flat and where you work, he knows loads about you, and you know next to nothing about him. Admit it, I'm right.'

'Lynne this is ridiculous.' Alice snatches up her sandwich and takes a big bite. 'Honestly, you've come up with some random shit in your time but this is . . .' She puffs out her cheeks to illustrate her point.

'All right then,' her best friend replies, a note of irritation in her voice. 'Don't believe me, but I think there's something dodgy about him, and this story about his psycho ex fiancée seems a little bit too neat to me. He'll be in touch with you. Guarantee it. He's just making you sweat a bit so he doesn't look too keen. But he'll text you. I bet you a tenner.'

Alice sets her phone on the table, suddenly uncomfortable with it in her hand. She stares at it. There's a part of her that wants it to vibrate with a new text message from Simon. And a part that really doesn't.

'Lynne,' she says. 'Do you think—'

The phone judders on the table, making her jump. She snatches it up and reads the text message that's flashed up on the screen.

'Well?' Lynne asks.

'He wants me to go to the cinema with him tomorrow.'

'What did I tell you?' Lynne holds out a hand. 'That'll be ten pounds please.'

Chapter 19

Ursula

Ursula works the drill in short bursts. Drrrrrrr. Stop. Drrrrr. Stop. The motion makes the soft flesh on the backs of her arms wobble and her teeth vibrate. She stops, listens, turns her head towards the stairs, then begins again. When she woke up that morning, a little after 5 a.m., she got out of bed and drove her van several streets away, then she rang in sick, leaving a message on her boss's answerphone. She felt bad lying but it was the first time she'd rung in sick and she wouldn't have done it unless it was absolutely necessary. Afterwards, she returned to the house and spent the next couple of hours lying in her bed, waiting for Edward's footsteps to reverberate on the landing outside. Only when she heard the front door bang shut did she let herself relax. In order to carry out her plan Edward *had* to go to work not knowing that she was still home.

She pauses her drilling to swipe the back of her hand across her forehead. It was like someone hit fast forward on her day the moment Edward left the house. She dressed quickly, cleaned her teeth in record time (making sure not to touch any of Ed's belongings), pulled on her trainers, then jumped into her van. She flew around B&Q, list in one hand, basket in the other, and paid with cash to avoid bank card faff. Then she jumped back in the van, unlocked the house, double-checked that Edward wasn't in and set to work. It's an expense she hadn't budgeted for – the drill, chain, screws, latch and padlock – but she'd rather eat the stale crackers in the back of her cupboard than spend another night in a room without a lock. Working out how to fit the lock to the outside of the door and the chain to the inside wasn't a problem – a quick visit to YouTube on her phone sorted that out. Neither is using the drill; her dad taught her how to put together a flatpack chest of drawers with an electric screwdriver when she was eleven, then progressed her DIY knowledge to a drill when she turned twelve. What will be harder will be tracing the man in the black-and-white photo. With no laptop, and no working camera on her phone, she can't do a Google image search. She's going to have to use a library computer instead.

She finishes the job as quickly as she can, twisting the screws into place then giving first the chain, then the padlock, a hefty tug to check that they hold. She nods, pleased with her work, then deposits her tools in the bottom of her wardrobe and closes and padlocks her bedroom door.

Knowle library is surprisingly quiet and Ursula joins a queue to speak to the librarian, hovering behind a woman who can't borrow any more books for her child because the last lot were overdue. The librarian, a tall, thin man with grey hair and a neat beard, unlocks the woman's account, then looks up at Ursula and offers her a quick smile.

'How can I help you?'

She gestures at the bank of computers across the room. They're all being used, apart from one. 'Hello, can I borrow a computer please? I need to use a scanner.'

The man pulls an apologetic face. 'You're very welcome to use a computer but the scanner's broken, I'm afraid. We're waiting for a technician to come and take a look at it.'

'Oh no.' She touches the left pocket of her jogging bottoms where the newspaper clipping is being kept flat and smooth between two pieces of cardboard cut from an empty box of Weetabix. 'Is he coming in today?'

The librarian shakes his head. 'He's not due until tomorrow, I'm afraid. You could try the central library. What is it you want to scan? Phone cameras are pretty good these days. Could you take a photo instead?'

Ursula shakes her head. 'My lens is all scratched up. Any photo I take is so grainy and blurred it looks as though it was taken in the 1970s, and I need to run it through Google Images.'

The librarian laughs. 'Ah. Well, if you're after a good quality replication I'd say a scanner is your best bet.'

Ursula considers her options. To get into the centre of town she could either take a bus or she could walk back to her house and use the van. A bus would be cheaper but would probably mean hanging around a stop for twenty minutes and the same on the way home. Taking her van would be quicker. She presses a hand to her belly as it tightens with excitement. She could go to the Meads shopping centre before she visits the library. Maybe pop into Mirage Fashions.

She never used to go into the city centre and did most of her shopping online. But then she had a breakdown at work, a month after Nathan died. She was teaching her Reception class in a tiny village school on the outskirts of Bristol. She was introducing the children to some new phonics and hadn't noticed the window cleaner strolling through the playground until he was right up against the glass. She saw a knife, not a squeegee, in his hand and she screamed at the children to run. And as they shrieked and froze and stared at her in horror, she curled up in a ball under her desk and sobbed with fear. The headteacher was understanding. She told Ursula to go home, that it had been a mistake returning to work so soon, that she should see her GP and talk to him about PTSD. But Ursula didn't go back to the empty house that was no longer a home and she didn't take herself off to the doctor's surgery. Instead she got in her car and she drove. She can't remember why she went into the centre of town, or how long she walked before she drifted into the Meads. But she can remember the numbness in her chest and the feeling that something inside her had died. She remembers the row of jewellery at the back of the shop and the sharp edges of a pendant under the pad of her thumb. She remembers walking out with it in the clutch of her palm, staring at the security guard, daring him to stop her. But he didn't. How could he? She was invisible. She didn't exist.

Instinctively, she reaches into the right-hand pocket of her jogging bottoms and fingers the polished brass door knob that caught her eye in B&Q earlier. It was so bulbous and smooth in the palm of her hand, cool and calming, that it found itself in her pocket before she even knew what she was doing.

'Before I go.' She reaches into her other pocket and carefully extracts the newspaper clipping. 'Do you know who this is?' She holds it out towards the librarian, then snatches it away from his grasping fingers. 'Sorry, I don't want it to get crumpled.'

The librarian drops his hand and sits forward in his seat to get a better look. Ursula searches his face for any sign of recognition then sighs in disappointment as he shakes his head.

'I don't recognise him. Should I?'

'I don't know. That's why I need the scanner.'

'Oh well. Good luck.'

'Thanks for your help.' She flashes him a smile in goodbye.

She cuts through Subway, thinking about the blank look on the librarian's face as he looked at the newspaper clipping. He can't be famous, the man in the photo, or he'd have recognised him. So why did she feel a frisson of familiarity when she first looked at it? Well, she'll find out who he is soon enough. She just needs to get to her van and—

She squeals in surprise as someone walks straight into her, then yelps as her chest sings with pain. One look at the brown stain on her white T-shirt, the aghast expression on the face of the woman standing in front of her, empty cardboard cup in one hand and mobile phone in the other, makes her realise immediately why she feels as though someone just set fire to her chest.

'I'm so sorry. I'm so, so sorry.' The woman waves her hands around desperately, her gaze flicking from Ursula to the shocked faces of the customers on the tables either side of them. 'Let me . . . let me . . .'

'Here!' Another woman, with a toddler in a pushchair, leaps up with a wad of napkins in her hand.

'Pull the material away from your skin!' someone else calls. 'Or it'll burn.'

'No, don't!' A man further down the room stands up from his chair. 'It'll pull the skin from your body. You need to splash yourself with cold water.'

With everyone still shouting, and ignoring the employee in his green polo shirt and stripy apron rushing towards her, Ursula turns and runs out of the shop.

She winces as the cold water of the shower hits her skin. She didn't immediately run home. She headed for the toilets near

Iceland first and splashed her T-shirt until it, and the floor, were sodden. Then she fastened her coat over her chest and speed-walked to the house, gritting her teeth as the wet material rubbed against her skin. Her chest is pinkened and sore to the touch but not badly burnt. As she steps out of the shower she gingerly wraps her towel around her body and steps out onto the landing.

'Woah!' She freezes, pressing a hand to her chest. Edward is standing outside her room. The door is ajar, the padlock hanging from the latch. She didn't think to lock it when she hurried into the shower.

'Ursula.'

She winces as she peels her hand from her damaged skin, then, suddenly feeling exposed in a towel that only reaches part way down her thighs, steps back into the bathroom and peers out at him. He's dressed casually in jeans, boots and a navy-blue crew-neck jumper, the sleeves pushed up to his elbows. She's not sure why but she imagined he'd go to work in a suit. Not that she knows what he does for a job. The one and only time she asked him what he did for a living he was so prickly and evasive she resolved not to ask again.

'What are you doing home?' she asks, annoyed with herself for the note of distress in her voice.

'I live here.' He arches an eyebrow.

'But you left this morning?'

'And I've come home between shifts. Just like I do every day, not that you'd know. Why aren't you on your round?'

'Day off,' she lies.

'It's not Sunday.'

'I booked an extra day.'

'I see.' His gaze shifts towards the door of her bedroom, the padlock hanging open. 'It appears you've been busy.'

'I . . . um . . . I thought I'd save you a job.'

'Did you now?' His tight smile doesn't reach his eyes. 'You

do realise that, officially, you've caused damage to the fixtures and fittings. I could withhold your deposit and kick you out.'

The threat isn't entirely unexpected. Ursula knew as she set to work on her door that it would probably infuriate her landlord, particularly given his fondness for walking uninvited into her room, but she has a weapon of her own in her arsenal. It's the secret she discovered in one of the kitchen drawers on her first morning in the house – his contract with the real owner.

'You could do that,' she says, tightening her grip on the bathroom door. 'But as you're breaking your tenancy agreement by subletting my room that probably wouldn't be the best idea.'

Edward's face remains impassive apart from the tiniest upwards twitch of his eyebrows. It's the smallest of movements but enough for Ursula to register his surprise. Check, she thinks, the memory of her one and only chess victory against Nathan flashing through her mind. But does Edward have checkmate?

She waits, heart pounding, for his next move. Despite her height and weight advantage, she's dressed in a towel with no weapon to hand and nowhere to retreat other than the bathroom. Edward might be small and slight, but he's an unknown quantity – he could be a complete psychopath for all she knows – and there's no correlation between size and aggression.

The air between them grows thick with anticipation as Edward keeps his beady eyes fixed on Ursula, his hands hanging loosely at his sides and the toe of one boot tap-tapping on the wooden floor.

You could always sleep in the van, the little voice in the back of her head whispers urgently. An apology rises in her throat. She wants to say something to break the terrible tension but a bigger part of her refuses to back down. She hasn't actually done anything wrong.

As Edward steps towards her she braces herself. If he lunges she'll pull back into the bathroom and slam the door in his face. But her landlord doesn't lunge anywhere. He walks straight past to his room, then reaches into his pocket for his key. He slots it into the lock, then turns back to look at her.

'I like you, Ursula.' Something glitters in his eyes that she can't quite read. Mischief? Danger? Amusement? She can't be sure. 'You keep me on my toes.'

Before she can respond he slips into his room. He disappears inside and pulls the door closed with the quietest of clicks.

Ursula slides the safety chain across her bedroom door, then slumps onto the bed, not caring as her towel untucks from her chest and puddles around her naked body. Her hands, resting by her sides, are shaking so much she has to press them between her knees to still them. She fights to control her breathing, inhaling for four counts, holding for seven, then exhaling for eight until her pulse gradually slows and she slumps forward over her knees, closing her eyes as she hugs her legs to her body.

What are you doing? Nathan's voice is as clear in her head as if he were sitting next to her. *It's not safe, Albi.*

She smiles at his use of her pet name – Albi, Nathan's very own 'big bird'. She's not heard that nickname for a *very* long time.

Yeah well, she answers him back, *we all know what happens if I just walk away.*

This isn't your battle.

Everything's my battle now, Nath.

She gets up, carries the towel over to her laundry basket, drops it inside, then stoops to pick up her coffee-sodden T-shirt and jogging bottoms. She drops the T-shirt into the laundry basket then, reflexively, searches the pockets of her jogging bottoms for tissues, change or pens and drops them into the basket too. As she crosses the room to her chest of drawers something rankles at her, making her pause: something about the jogging bottoms. She returns to the laundry basket and fishes them out. Something's missing from the pockets. Her keys? No, they're still on the chest of drawers where she left them. Her work ID? No, that's right next to the keys. What then? The photo! It was definitely in her pocket when she got home. She remembers because she checked that it didn't have coffee on it.

She searches through the soft, fleecy pockets again. Nothing. Nothing on the floor either, or on the bed. Nothing on or under the chest of drawers. Nothing in the laundry basket. Nothing caught up in the folds of her damp T-shirt. She searches the room from top to bottom, then wraps her dressing gown around her and slides back the security chain on her door. She hurries into the bathroom and scans the top of the toilet cistern, the sink, the floor, even the shower, then walks the length of the corridor, scanning each gap between the boards. But it's not there. She turns slowly and stares at the closed door to her landlord's room. The small scrap of newspaper, carefully pressed between two thin pieces of cardboard, didn't just disappear. Edward took it back.

Chapter 20

Gareth

His mum is asleep in the armchair when Gareth gets home, the TV booming out the seven o'clock news. He stands in the doorway, watching for the rise and fall of her chest. He can't remember when he started doing that, checking that his mum was asleep rather than . . . the alternative. Was it after the official dementia diagnosis and he realised that both of their lives had swerved, roughly and painfully, onto a new course? Or was it before that? He hadn't ever thought of his mum as old before. She always had so much energy, always visiting this person or that, forever baking and cleaning, gardening and shopping. Maybe he'd started to worry about her around the same time he'd looked in the mirror one morning and hadn't recognised the tired, lined man staring back at him. Ageing didn't creep up on him, he didn't notice a wrinkle here and a dark spot there. It was as though he looked in the mirror one day and, BAM, he was stunned by what he saw. Nothing could have prepared him for the shock of acknowledging the jowly, tired man it had taken him forty-eight years to become. He started growing his goatee the very next day.

As he watches his mum sleep he thinks about his dad, about the mental image he's been carrying around for the last twenty years. His dad at fifty-seven, his hair more grey than brown, with a lined, sagginess to his face that hadn't been there in his forties. Just ten years older than Gareth is now. Until the other day, he'd never imagined him as an old man. And now he was struggling to concentrate at work. Even though he was convinced that Mackesy was behind the postcards he couldn't stop himself abandoning whatever he was doing and zooming in every time he spotted a male with white-grey hair amongst the shoppers. But none of the men were wearing an olive-green jacket. None of them had a military posture. And none of them were his dad.

He scans the living room, looking for anything out of place, and his gaze rests on the vase of flowers on top of the sideboard. Mackesy's flowers. Sighing, he leaves the room and heads upstairs. He had a thought earlier, while he was at work, about the donation his mum had made. He'd jumped to the conclusion that she'd taken money out of her account to give Mackesy, but how could she? She'd never signed up for internet banking, her branch was in the centre of Bristol and she hadn't used a bus in years. She didn't send Sally or Yvonne out to get her some money either; he texted them both to check. He opens the door to his mum's room then drops down to his knees and reaches around under the bed.

For as long as he can remember his mum's kept money in an old shoebox; to make sure she has enough at hand to pay tradesmen in cash or to slip into a birthday card. He counted it before he employed Sally and Yvonne three years ago, just in case either of them had sticky fingers. There was £220. He's checked it sporadically since and there's never been any less. He grunts as he pulls out the shoebox, then opens the lid and takes out the wad of cash, held together with an elastic band. He counts it quickly, his forefinger slipping over the notes – £140. So his mum gave Mackesy £80. He blows out his cheeks. It's not as much as he feared but he was right to confront the man. The bunch of flowers he sent her had to have cost at least £40. Why do that unless he was buttering her up to donate more? Gareth puts the lid back on the box and slides it back under the bed. He's told Sally and Yvonne that they're not to let Mackesy in again and if he forces his way in they're to call the police.

He feels a bit lighter as he walks back down the stairs and wanders into the living room. His mum's still asleep and the TV's still blaring away. He reaches for the remote control on the side table beside her and inches the sound down bit by bit (too quickly and she'll wake), then puts the remote back. He's just about to head through to the kitchen to start making dinner when he notices something lying on the floor to the left of the armchair, something rectangular and white, centimetres from his mum's loose fingers. He crouches down to pick it up then sways on the spot, darkness clouding his vision as he stands up too quickly. It's a postcard, in the same neat cursive as the last one.

To my darling Joan
We will be together again. Very, very soon.
I love you,
John.

And this time there's no stamp.

Chapter 21

Gareth

Thursday

Gareth is standing on the top rung of the stepladder, one hand pressed against the outside wall of his house, the other gripping a drill, when someone shouts his name. He turns, carefully, to see Kath and Georgia leaving their house; Kath looks lovely in a black pencil skirt, grey jumper and low heels, while Georgia's in her school uniform with a bag clutched to her chest and a scowl on her face. In an alternate universe, the one where he and Kath are an item, he'd probably tell her to put her feet up for a bit while he gave Georgia a lift to school on his way to work.

But this is his reality, so he smiles instead. 'Good morning!'

'Your peephole's a bit high, isn't it?' Kath points to the hole Gareth's drilled above his front door.

He gestures at the small black camera on the top step of the ladder. 'CCTV.'

'Ooh.' She looks mildly impressed, as though he's just announced that he's getting a new car or an extension, then her expression changes. 'You haven't . . .' she glances at Georgia, who's turned away and is fiddling with her phone '. . . you haven't been burgled, have you?

'No, no. Nothing like that. I've been meaning to put it up for a while. Mum's not getting any better.'

'Has she been going on walkabout then?'

Walkabout. The word sounds vaguely ridiculous to Gareth's ears. It reminds him of a book he read at school about a brother and sister who survived a plane crash in the Australian outback and then wandered around aimlessly, looking for help. His mother has never walked aimlessly anywhere. She's always strode, Margaret Thatcher-like, swinging her handbag at her side. Even now, in the grip of dementia, she still moves with purpose through the house even if, once she enters a new room, she frequently forgets what she's doing there. He's had multiple conversations with her since her diagnosis, about how she shouldn't go out unless accompanied by Sally, Yvonne or himself, but she refuses to listen.

'No one's going to keep me a prisoner in my own home.' It was a dictat, rather than a discussion, the last time he brought it up.

There's only a small snatch of time – two or three hours tops – when she's alone in the house each day and, while she's unlikely to stray much further than the corner shop and post office at the end of the road, he finds himself holding his breath as he walks up the path and looks for the flicker of the television in the front room and the familiar shape of his mother in her favourite chair.

It hadn't occurred to him that the CCTV camera could keep an eye on her movements but now Kath's mentioned it it's definitely a bonus. His primary motivation is to catch Mackesy in the act of leaving another postcard. The first one was posted but the second one was almost certainly hand-delivered; it had to be, considering there was no stamp.

'She's allowed to go out,' he says to Kath, then immediately regrets his sharp tone as her chin drops and she mutters, 'Of course she is.'

He's tired, that's why he's being so prickly. He barely slept last night for worrying about his mum and the situation at work. He came up with a plan for dealing with Dunford as he paced his room a little after midnight but now he's not sure if he can go through with it. It seemed like such a good idea at the time, but when he woke, and cool dawn light crept through the curtains, so did chest-crushing doubt.

'I don't often see you two leaving together,' Gareth says, forcing a bright tone. 'Getting a lift in are you, Georgia?'

'We've got a meeting with her head of year.' Kath silently mouths the word 'bullying'.

Georgia's bent head and slumped shoulders reminds Gareth of himself as a teen. He can still remember waking up with a feeling of dread in his stomach and having to force his legs to walk through the school gates at the start of the day. He tries to think of something encouraging he can say but nothing that crosses his mind – they will stop eventually, I stood up to my bullies and won, I was bullied but I'm really successful now – is true. Instead he flashes the young girl what he hopes is an expression of empathy but suspects looks more like a gurn.

'I'll let you get off!' He nods at Kath and raises a hand in goodbye. He's already made the hole as big as it needs to be to feed the CCTV cable through to the camera but he picks up his drill anyway. It's weighty and powerful and as he pulls the trigger he idly imagines the drill bit whirring its way through the centre of Liam Dunford's forehead.

*

I can do this, Gareth tells himself as he keys in the code to the cramped, airless room that serves as a bag and coat drop for the security staff – a toilet cubicle at one end, benches under the coat hooks and absolutely nothing else. When he started at the Meads thirteen years ago one wall housed a row of metal lockers, the sort you'd find in a swimming pool changing room, but they were ripped out at the end of last year because they were so damaged they'd become a health and safety hazard. Replacement lockers have been ordered but, in the interim, the guards have no choice but to hang up their belongings and hope their colleagues don't have sticky fingers. There was a discussion about whether to install a CCTV camera in the room but it was ruled out because of the cost and disruption it would cause. At the time, Gareth was pissed off with management but now, as he surveys the row of largely black, grey and tan coats and jackets in front of him, he's quietly grateful.

Liam was waiting when he arrived at work, standing outside the CCTV office at the top of the stairs.

'Today's the day.' He grinned at Gareth, revealing the penny-edge gap between his front teeth.

'The day for what?'

'That you give me a pay rise.'

'You know I can't do that. It's set by head office. I can't just magically award you extra cash. It's just not possible.'

Liam coughs. 'Who said anything about getting head office involved? Like I said yesterday, five hundred pounds should be enough to give me a touch of amnesia.'

Gareth shifted his weight to one side and leaned against the wall, arms crossed over his chest. 'You're blackmailing me.'

'That's an unpleasant word. I prefer to think of it as two colleagues helping each other out. You don't end up in the shit and I get a bit of cash to put towards my next holiday. We both win.' Gareth laughed, a low, incredulous rumble. What planet was Liam living on, thinking he'd just hand over that kind of money? It was ridiculous. He glanced over his shoulder to check that no one more senior was walking up the stairs, then looked back at the man. 'If you think I'm giving you anything, you can get fucked.'

'Harsh, really harsh. Well, I guess you'll need every penny you've got when Mark sacks you. You know he's looking for any excuse. You said as much too the other week. Didn't you, Gaz?'

Gareth unfolded his arms and pulled himself up to his full height. He was a good four or five inches shorter than the other man and had to raise his chin to look at him. He clenched his hands into fists and drew back his shoulders.

'Like I said, get fucked.'

'Is that all you've got? Good luck on the breadline!' Liam raised a dismissive hand. 'There's a food bank in Bedminster if your mum gets hungry.'

As Liam sauntered down the stairs, rage surged through Gareth like nothing he had ever felt before. It was as though a fire had been lit in the base of his brain. It spread rapidly, travelling down to his throat, his arms, his torso, his legs and he leapt forwards, hands reaching for Liam's shoulders. He wanted to shove him and watch him tumble down the stairs. He wanted him to shut the fuck up. He wanted him gone. Dead.

But as his fingertips grazed the thick fabric of Liam's jacket the fire in him was damped down by a new thought. If you go to prison, what will happen to Mum? He snatched back his arms, feet see-sawing on the edge of the top step as he fought to keep his balance and Liam Dunford, completely oblivious to his sliding-doors fate, continued on down the stairs.

A bead of sweat dribbles down Gareth's back and settles under the thick elastic waistband of his jockey shorts as he surveys the row of bags and jackets. He pulls on a pair of latex gloves.

Theft. Ironically, the offence most sacked security guards commit. That and brutality, but Liam's been on his best behaviour recently and there isn't time to wait for him to screw up again. No, what Gareth needs to do is transfer some of the valuables from the other guards' bags into Liam's sports holdall, then sit back and wait for the drama to unfold. He knows Liam will point the finger in his direction as soon as the crime is discovered but he's pretty sure some of the other guards will back him up. Or at least he hopes they will. Old Larry who does the security for Mirage Fashions can't stand Liam but he's not sure how Adrian, Jakub and Hafeez feel. He knows Adrian's been for beers with Liam before.

Gareth twists his hands together, his palms sweating beneath the latex. He can't do it. He can't bring himself to rifle through his colleagues' belongings. It's not the kind of thing he does. He's not a vengeful man. He's not deceitful. There isn't much he prides himself on, but he's always been a man of integrity. 'Upstanding' – that's the word his mum would use to describe him. Gareth Filer, a good, upstanding man. He can't fit Liam up. That's not who he is.

Sighing, he peels off his gloves and chucks them into the bin in the corner, then he heads for the CCTV room to ring his boss. A man of integrity indeed. Why couldn't he have been born an arsehole instead?

Chapter 22

Alice

Alice is sitting on a hard plastic chair in the staff changing room chewing on her sandwich and grimacing at the combination of soggy bread and briny tinned tuna (it's two days until pay day and it's all she's got left in the house). Her mobile vibrates on the table in front of her and the jingly jangly tones of Abba's 'Dancing Queen' fill the air.

'Hello?' She frantically swallows back the last of her mouthful then promptly has a huge coughing fit as it goes down the wrong way. She reaches for her water bottle and takes a swig. 'Sorry, I was just having my lunch.'

'I could ring back later if it's a bad time.' There's a note of impatience in DC Mitchell's voice.

'No, no. It's fine. I can talk.'

'Great. I just wanted to give you an update on Michael Easton. You said you thought he might be behind the damage to your car the other night.'

I thought? Alice thinks. Aren't you supposed to be the detective?

'Okay . . .' she says.

'Well, we got in touch with Michael and he was in Barcelona the night your car was scratched. And he has witnesses to prove it.'

Alice takes a moment to let the news sink in.

'Has there been any other communication from Michael at all?' the detective asks. 'Emails, texts, notes. Anything at all?'

'No. Nothing since the Facebook message warning me off Simon.'

'That was the one that ended . . .' Alice hears the sound of a mouse being clicked ' . . ."Who is Michael?" Right?'

'Yeah.'

'Is there anyone else who could be behind this, Alice? Anyone you've fallen out with? Friends? Family? Former employees?'

The face of the last person Alice sacked surfaces in her mind – a nineteen-year-old called Jenna who shouted 'you can stick your stupid fucking job up your saggy fucking arse' as she stormed out of the shop. But that was fourteen months ago and, other than a near miss when she spotted Jenna in the cinema queue one night and waited round the corner until she'd bought her ticket, she's hasn't seen her once.

'Not really no,' she says. 'Although . . .'

'Although what?'

'Simon, the guy I'm seeing, he mentioned something to me about an ex-fiancée who he didn't part on best terms with. Her name's Flora. I don't know her last name.'

'Did he mention where she lives?'

'No. I'm guessing she's in Bristol but I'm not sure.'

'Right. Well, we're keeping an open mind at the moment, Alice, about who might be behind all this. But I don't think you need to worry about Michael. When I spoke to him yesterday he said he'd be in Barcelona for at least the next six weeks. He said he was staying with a friend. The implication was that he was doing a bit of soul-searching.'

'Oh.' The tight knot in Alice's stomach doesn't loosen. It's the unpredictability of it all that's the scariest thing. 'So what do I do now?' she asks DC Mitchell.

'I'm not sure I know what you mean.'

'I don't feel safe. I don't know who's doing this or what they'll do next.'

'You're scared. I understand that, and if you ever feel in any way vulnerable or worried you can give me a call. Or ring 999 if you are in any kind of danger. I could also arrange for a crime reduction officer to review your home security and provide you with a personal alarm.'

'That's it?'

'Well, obviously avoid going anywhere alone and park in well-lit spots. I'm here if you need me and the local units are aware of your situation. They'll keep an eye on your house and car whenever possible.'

'Thanks,' Alice says, but the knot in her stomach remains.

When DC Mitchell hangs up, Alice taps on the messages icon on her phone and sends a text to Simon:

Just spoke to DC Mitchell. Michael has an alibi! Could your ex be the one that scratched my car?

She puts the phone down, then opens her crisps. She shovels them into her mouth.

Simon's busy, she tells herself when he doesn't reply immediately. He's probably on the phone to a customer about a claim.

Truthfully she doesn't have the slightest idea what Simon does all day. He might not even talk to clients for all she knows. Whenever she's pressed him to tell her more about his job he's swiftly moved the conversation on with an: 'Honestly, I'd bore myself just telling you about it. Let's talk about something more interesting.'

Crisps finished, she folds the packet into a little triangle and drops it into the bin before picking up her phone and texting Simon again.

Are you still on for the cinema tonight?

It sounds needy, double-checking when they made the date only yesterday, but she can't think what else to text. He didn't reply to her chirpy *Morning! How are you?* that she sent on the bus to work. I'm not needy, she reassures herself. I just want to hear back from him, to check he's okay.

The door opens as she frowns at her phone.

'Man trouble?'

She looks up. 'Sorry?'

Lynne strolls across the room and takes the seat next to her. 'I've seen that look on your face before and it only means one thing.'

'What? No. Everything's fine.'

'So why are you gripping your phone like it's a grenade?'

'I'm not.' She puts the phone down and gives it a nudge then changes the subject, 'Everything okay on the shop floor?'

'Fine.' Lynne gets up, crosses the room to the minute fridge in the corner, and takes out a blue Tupperware tub. 'Quiet.' She glances back at her. 'Heard anything from the police about your car?'

'Yeah, they just rang. Michael didn't do it. He's got an alibi.'

'Seriously?' Lynne sits down and peels back the lid.

'There's no CCTV and they didn't send anyone out to finger-print the car or look for DNA.'

'You're kidding me?'

'I wish I was.' She casts a glance at her phone. The screen is dark. No new messages.

Lynne catches her looking. 'Has he dumped you?'

'No! What makes you think that?'

'Nothing you just . . .' Lynne stabs her fork into her boiled egg and chicken salad. 'You looked worried when I walked in, that's all.'

'Wouldn't you be if someone was sending you creepy messages and keyed your car and the police have no idea who's behind it?'

'True.' Lynne shrugs agreeably. 'How's Emily?'

Alice leans back in her chair and rubs her hands over her face. 'I'm worried about her. Adam's been disappearing at night, staying up late after she's gone to bed, and then going out.'

'I thought she stayed at yours during the week.'

'She was but she's been staying over at his more often; keeping an eye on him, probably.'

'Where's he been going?'

'He says the pub with friends but Emily thinks he's been cheating on her. She's been stalking his social media to find proof.'

Lynne chases an errant piece of egg around the tub then stabs it with her fork and pops it into her mouth. 'She needs to dump him.'

'Try telling her that.'

'She needs to work it out for herself. When I was her age I thought I knew bloody everything.'

As Lynne continues to share her wisdom, Alice mentally drifts off. She's stressing about Simon. There, she's admitted it to herself. Other than the handful of texts they exchanged yesterday about what film to see and what time, she hasn't heard a peep from him. He didn't reply to any of the texts she sent last night or the one she sent that morning and now she's annoyed with herself. She's being needy, looking to him for reassurance, but she's been feeling unnerved ever since Lynne sowed seeds of doubt about him being some kind of scam artist. It was a ridiculous suggestion, but he did leave the restaurant to make a phone call after she showed him the Facebook message from Ann Friend, and he was very odd after the car scratching.

'Who needs men!' Lynne's voice cuts through her thoughts. 'We should all go away together – me, you and Emily. Have you made plans for the summer yet? I've always fancied the Greek islands. What do you think?'

'Sorry, what—' Alice is distracted as the staffroom door creaks open. A thin young woman with short blonde hair and a nose piercing walks in with Larry following behind, one hand on her shoulder, his other hand clutching a black holdall with a load of new stock spilling out of the top.

'Caught her in the act.' He gestures for the woman to continue through the staffroom to Alice's office.

She scowls, then tries to twist out of his grasp. 'Fuck off, you old perv.'

Alice jumps out of her seat and hurries into her office, sweeping her desk for any potential weapons. She doesn't take any chances with shoplifters, not since one snatched up her stapler and threw it at her head before making a break for the door.

Chapter 23

@onthecliffedge:
Any update on the Harbourside murderer?

@DiddleyBopDee:
What do you mean? Has someone else disappeared?

@realmadwife:
My husband might if he doesn't put the bloody bins out on time this week.

@onthecliffedge:
Are the police looking into it?

@refrigeratorcar:
Nope. They said no foul play suspected.

@onthecliffedge:
But the bodies of the two men who disappeared haven't been found yet, have they?

@MotobkeBob:
Nope, that's because they're buried in the garden of someone who has loads of cats.

@refrigeratorcar:
What have cats got to do with it?

@MotobkeBob:
People who have loads of cats are weirdos.

@gemzy9:
OI! I'VE GOT FOUR CATS.

@MotobkeBob:
Point proved.

Chapter 24

Ursula

Ursula shoves the last piece of toast into her mouth then washes up her plate and puts it back in the cupboard. She sniffs the air. The musky smell she noticed the first time Edward showed her the kitchen has grown stronger. It's at its most pungent by the basement door. She tries the handle again. Still locked. She hasn't once seen Edward go down there since she moved in. Not that they're in the house together very often – other than when they ran into each other the other lunchtime it's only first thing in the morning and last thing in the evening. They're like ships that pass in the night.

'What are you up to, Edward?' she mutters as she drifts from room to room, opening drawers and lifting sofa cushions before dropping down to her knees to peer under pieces of furniture. She's on a later shift today and Edward has already left for work. She was already awake when he got up, and listened from the safety of her bed, the chain drawn across her bedroom door, as the floorboard on the landing creaked then the bathroom door clicked shut. She wasn't going to confront him about the newspaper clipping he stole back because she knew he'd only lie. Who was it? A relative? An ex-lover? She's pretty sure Edward isn't gay. When she moved her things in he was so taken by an attractive blonde walking past the house that Ursula had to ask him three times to move out of the doorway so she could bring in her suitcase.

Besides, what gay man would have a dartboard on the wall of his living room? She runs a hand along the top of the sideboard, the wood cool and smooth under her fingertips until she reaches the neat line of three darts. She taps at the flight, flipping it to the left, then the right then, completely without thinking, closes her hand around it and puts it in the pocket of her coat and glances at her watch. The van's loaded with parcels but if she doesn't get a move on she'll be late.

There's no light on in the window of number six, no baby sitting on the carpet in a sea of plastic toys, and no television flickering in the corner of the room. The window – the one she normally passes parcels through – is closed and the curtains in the bedroom above are still pulled. Has the owner gone out, Ursula wonders, her agoraphobia magically cured? She crouches down and peers through the letter box. There's a buggy, propped up against the hallway wall, and a pair of small, blue children's shoes beneath a tiny jacket on a coat rack. They're in. She feels sure of it.

'Hello!' she shouts. 'Courier!'

She listens for a response – for the wail of a child or a female voice – but the house is completely silent.

'Helloooo!' She shouts louder this time. 'Is there anyone home?'

There's a startled yelp in response and a pair of bare female feet appear at the top of the stairs. As the woman gets closer

Ursula sees that she's carrying the toddler, who is naked apart from the towel around her waist. As the woman reaches the last step her gaze flicks from the mottled glass panel of the front door to the letter box and her eyes meet Ursula's. She makes a strange strangled sound and her whole body jolts. Her heel slips on the edge of the step and she falls, landing with a thump, half on the bottom stair, half on the floor, the child tipped sideways in her arms.

'Oh my God!' Ursula grabs at the door handle. She turns it and pulls. Locked.

She crouches back down and peers through the letter box. The woman's still on her bum. She groans loudly as she awkwardly sets the wailing child onto her feet.

'Are you all right?' Ursula asks. The child has started crying, plucking at her mother, trying to get back into her arms. 'I'm so sorry. This is my fault. I shouldn't have shouted. I gave you a shock.'

The woman doesn't reply. Instead she closes her eyes as the child scrambles around her legs, her pudgy little hands grabbing at her mother's shirt, her chest and her hair.

'Have you hurt your back? Can you move?' Ursula whips her mobile phone out of her pouch. 'I'm going to call an ambulance.'

'No!' The woman's eyes fly open and she winces as she uses her arms to push herself back into a sitting position. 'No, don't!'

'You might have broken something.'

'I'm fine.' Her voice breaks on the last word and tears spill down her cheeks.

The fear and guilt Ursula feels is unbearable. She clutches the door handle again, as though her desperation might magically have released it, but it's still locked. She glances around the cramped hallway. There's a set of keys hanging on a hook to the right of the child's coat. 'Can you unlock the door? I could . . . I could . . .' She tails off. She has no idea what she could do but she feels completely useless stuck on the other side of the door.

'No.' The woman grasps the banister and slowly, agonisingly drags herself to her feet, bent double like an old lady. When she tries to right herself she yelps with pain, one hand clutching her back, and sinks down to the floor.

'What's your husband's number?' Ursula asks desperately as the child throws herself at the curled shape of her mother. 'He needs to come home and look after you.'

The woman stares at her for the longest time – a raw, desperate look in her eyes.

'Let me help,' Ursula says. 'Please, just tell me how.'

'No.' Her face hardens. 'Fuck off. Just fuck off and leave us alone.'

Chapter 25

Gareth

Gareth parks up outside his house and turns off the engine but, instead of opening the door and marching up the path to the front door, he remains in his seat, his hands lying loosely in his lap. Beyond the windscreen the world continues as normal: a ginger tom slinks down the street unperturbed by a lone jogger, face flushed red, speeding along the pavement in the opposite direction. Gareth is barely aware of his surroundings. Fear hasn't just rendered him myopic, it's completely paralysed him.

Twenty-five years he's been a security guard, six as a supervisor, and tomorrow it could all be over. He didn't tell Whiting on the phone why he wanted a meeting with him and Liam. He wants to explain what happened face to face. There's a part of him that's desperately hoping his boss will hear him out and, taking his exemplary record into account, let him off with a written warning, but the bigger part knows that what he's done is a sackable offence, written into the contract. He can already imagine the look of delight on Whiting's face. He just hopes the man asks Liam to leave the room before he officially lets him go. Seeing Liam's smug grin would be the final kick in the teeth.

Gareth's stomach growls with hunger. He couldn't face making a trip to McDonald's after he called his boss; just the smell of food would have made him retch. But it's after seven now and his mum will need dinner. And so will he if he's to stand any chance of getting a good night's sleep.

'Mum!' Gareth glances up at the newly installed CCTV camera as he walks into his house. 'I'm home.'

He shrugs off his jacket then unties his boots and takes them off. He frowns as he stands up again. The house is too quiet. Something's not right.

'Mum?' He walks into the living room. She's not in her chair, the television is off and her glasses case is missing from the side table.

'MUM!' He powers up the stairs, his arms pumping, his feet pounding the worn carpet runner. 'Mum, where are—' The word catches in his throat as he pushes at the door to her bedroom. 'What are you doing?'

Standing at the end of the bed, dressed in her best church coat, a small veiled hat he's never seen before and what looks suspiciously like half a fox around her neck, is his mother.

'What do you think I'm doing?' she says brightly as she bends over the open suitcase in front of her. 'I'm packing to go on holiday.'

'What?'

'I'm going on holiday, Gareth. It is allowed you know.'

'Where? With who?' As the relief at finding her alive and well wears off, his mind switches itself back on. He stands up straighter and takes a step towards the bed. The contents of his mother's suitcase make him want to cry. As well as packing socks and underwear she's added a framed photo of his father, a spatula, the TV remote control, a bottle of toilet bleach, an ornamental frog, the silver cup he won for cross-country when he was fourteen, a blue paperweight and a dinner plate.

'Mum,' he says again. 'Where are you going and who with?'

She doesn't look up from the pair of socks she's repeatedly balling and unballing. 'I'm going to the seaside.'

Gareth's mouth opens but he swallows back the truth that would break her heart. 'Who with?'

'Your dad.' The bright smile reappears on her lips. 'It's a surprise, but Ruth let it slip.'

It's been so long since that name was said aloud that it takes Gareth a couple of seconds to register who his mum is talking about. Ruth Cotter, the auntie he's never met. He's not entirely sure why the two sisters fell out – his mum said it was because she was left more money in their father's will. Whereas Uncle Tony, his mum's brother, once drunkenly claimed that the sisters fell out when Ruth spotted John at a dance and told her sister that was the man she was going to marry, only for Joan to accept his invitation to dance. But that was over fifty years ago. His aunt went on to marry someone else and have three children, cousins Gareth has never met.

He scans the room, taking in the open wardrobe doors, the chest of drawers with clothes spilling out, the odds and ends from every room in the house piled up on the bed, but he can't find what he's looking for. 'Did Ruth come round or did she send you a postcard?'

His mum smiles. 'Of course I'll send you a postcard, Gareth.'

He takes his mother's tremoring hands in his. 'Did any post arrive today?'

She looks at him blankly, confusion sucking the colour from her skin.

'Post,' he says again. 'Letters? Postcards? Maybe Sally or Yvonne put them somewhere. Can you remember?'

As she shakes her head he catches the panic in her eyes and the rigid set of her shoulders. She's on the verge of a meltdown, a sudden outburst of anger and frustration that will traumatise them both.

'Are you hungry?' he asks. 'Shall we go downstairs and I'll get you some toast and soup?'

'I want a cheese sandwich.'

'Okay.' He offers her the crook of his elbow. 'I'll make you one. Shall we go?'

While his mother watches TV, taking tiny mouse-like nibbles of her cheese sandwich, Gareth checks the box under her bed. The bundle of cash inside still contains £140. He pushes it back into place, then texts her carers, asking if anyone visited that day. When they both confirm that there weren't any visitors, he returns to the living room and fires up his laptop. The CCTV will reveal whether there were any unwelcome guests between shifts. His Auntie Ruth. Or someone pretending to be her?

The software that comes with the CCTV is nothing like the kit he uses at work. The interface is clunky and unintuitive and it takes him forever to retrieve the files he needs, then an age for them to load. His laptop is at least five years old and the fan whirrs noisily as the processor struggles with the size of the footage.

Please, he prays, as the screen freezes, please don't crash.

Something flashes white on the screen then row upon row off of black and white cells appear. He presses play and watches himself leaving the house at 8 a.m. The resolution is terrible – he looks like a faded, grainy image of himself, his goatee a grey smudge on his chin, but he's identifiable. If anyone he knows arrives or leaves the house he'll be able to recognise them. He presses play again, then fast-forward. For what seems like an age there's nothing but a doorstep, a patch of pathway and a small triangle of grass on the screen, then a figure darts into the house and disappears. He rewinds the footage, then sighs as he recognises the short, round shape of Sally, his mother's carer. He checks the time stamp in the corner – 8.30 a.m., the exact time he'd expect her to arrive. He speeds up the footage again. One minute passes, two, five and it's still just a shot of the step, the path and the garden with the occasional tiny black blur as an insect zooms in and out of the frame. He hits pause as a figure appears on the step and speeds down the path, but it's just Sally leaving. Then Yvonne arrives and, later, leaves too. He blinks several times; his eyeballs are drying from staring so intently at the screen, but he keeps watching, silently praying that someone, anyone, will appear. But the only person who does interrupt the monotony of the black-and-white footage is him, arriving home from work.

Sighing, he sits back in his seat and folds his arms over his chest. The TV's still blaring but his mum's fallen asleep in her chair, her temple against the headrest, mouth slightly open and a small piece of cheese sandwich crust hanging loosely from her fingers. There's no sign of a postcard anywhere. He searched his mum's room after he gave her the sandwich, then combed the ground floor of the house, even turning out the kitchen bin.

Think, Gareth. Think. If you wanted to get a message to someone how would you do it?

He looks around the room, his gaze flicking from his mother to the windows, sideboard and . . . phone! He carefully moves the laptop onto the floor and gets up. Did Ruth ring his mum on the landline? They might not have been in touch for years but his mum's lived in this house since he was born and she's registered on the electoral roll. It wouldn't take a genius to get in touch. But why ring after so long?

Gareth keys 1471 into the phone and waits as the call connects.

'You were called today at 16:41,' says the recorded voice, 'by 0161 . . .'

Manchester? Who do they know in Manchester? He takes his mobile out of his pocket, then listens to the message again, keying the digits into Google. He sighs as the search engine returns its results. It's a bloody PPI company and there's no way of finding out who might have rung before them. Taking another look at his mum to check she's still asleep, he walks into the kitchen with his mobile phone. Ruth's not the only one with detective skills. If she could find his mum then he can find her.

Chapter 26

Alice

'Alice!' Simon half-walks, half-jogs towards Alice as she steps through the doors of Showcase Cinema feeling self-conscious in the blue pencil skirt that hugs her hips.

He pulls her into a tight hug. She returns the embrace, then moves her hands from his back to his chest and gently pushes him away.

He looks down at her, concern wrinkling his brow. 'Are you okay?'

'Not really.'

'Why?' He rests a hand on her arm.

'I've been stressed out all day and . . . Simon, why didn't you reply to my WhatsApp messages?'

'What?'

'I sent you a few, including one that was quite important, and you didn't reply.'

He takes his phone out of his back pocket and looks through

it. 'Oh, God. I'm so sorry. I meant to and then . . . I guess I got distracted and forgot. I'm sorry. Are you really pissed off?'

'I . . . I . .' She doesn't know what to say. She wants to be honest with him but she doesn't want to come across as needy either. 'I thought you'd understand,' she says, 'about how much the car thing freaked me out. If Michael didn't do it, I don't know who did.'

'Can we talk about it later?' He runs a hand through his hair. 'I've had a lot on my mind recently and . . . it's no excuse, I know. But I do care, honestly.'

'Forget it, it's fine.'

But it's not fine, not in Alice's mind anyway, and as they walk to the concession stand, side by side rather than hand in hand, she can't shake the feeling that something's not right.

They settle into their seats, the box of popcorn propped up on the armrest between them, and Alice tries to relax as the trailers begin. It's a film she's wanted to see for a while and, unlike Peter who always decided what they'd watch, Simon was more than happy to go along with her choice. The rest of the audience are obviously keen to see it too because the screening's packed: there can't be more than twenty empty seats. She glances across at Simon as she takes a handful of popcorn, but he's too fascinated by the fight scene playing out on the screen to return her smile.

As the trailer ends and a new one starts she angles her body towards him. 'Who do you think did it then?'

'Sorry?'

'Who do you think scratched my car if it wasn't Michael? Could it have been Flora?'

'I don't know. No, I wouldn't have thought so.' His eyes flick back towards the screen.

'So who was it? I can't think of anyone who'd—'

The man in front turns around. 'Excuse me, but the film's about to start.'

When he turns back Simon whispers in Alice's ear, 'I feel like a kid told off in assembly.' He tips the popcorn box towards her so she can take another handful.

Alice settles back in her seat. She needs to chill out and try and enjoy the film. They can finish their conversation about her stalker afterwards. They'll both be more relaxed once they're in the pub and they've had a glass of wine or two. As the curtains roll back and the name of the film appears on screen, a latecomer makes their way across the front row, striding confidently through the gloom with a mobile phone torch app lighting their way. Alice frowns as the statuesque figure reaches the bottom of the stairs to her right. There's something about the broadness of the shoulders and the width of the hips that's familiar.

Oh my God, it's her!

As the film starts, flooding the first few rows with light, she catches a glimpse of the woman's face as she takes the steps two at a time – the square set jaw, the broad nose and the fine, wispy fringe. It's the shoplifter Lynne pointed out a few days ago, the one she called Godzilla. Alice sinks into her seat, but it's too late, the other woman must have felt her gaze. Their eyes meet for a split second and Alice glances hurriedly away. It's irritating, being in the same room as someone who's been stealing her stock and pushing down her targets. She probably flogged the skirt she stole on Monday and used the cash to buy a cinema ticket. That's if she didn't steal that too.

As the thundering soundtrack fills the screening room, Alice glances back at Simon, her gaze travelling from his face to his chest to his hands, gripping his thighs just above his knees. She barely knows the man but she's never seen him look so tense. Her instinct is to reach over and take his hand but the armrest and popcorn are in the way and she's worried about rejection. What if he doesn't weave his fingers through hers and instead lets his hand lie limply under the weight of her palm? Or worse, gives her hand a quick squeeze, then returns it to her own lap? No, she decides, pulling her handbag a little closer so she can wrap her arms around it, if Simon's stressed it's not her job to make him feel better. They're dating. She's not his girlfriend.

As the main character appears on screen and sprints through a dark street as bullets bounce off walls, skips and cars, Alice senses movement out of the corner of her eye. The shoplifter, three rows in front and half a dozen seats to the right, has twisted round in her seat. Alice averts her eyes, her body stiffening under the weight of the other woman's gaze. She tries to block her out, to lose herself in the action on screen, but she can *feel* that she's still being watched. She turns sharply, prepared to stare the other woman out until she's so uncomfortable she has to look away, but the shoplifter has turned back around. Sighing, Alice settles back and focuses again on the film. Twenty minutes later and she's completely absorbed. Forty minutes later she feels Simon shift in his seat. He's got his mobile in his hand, angled away from her, the screen casting a grey-blue light onto his skin. What could be so urgent that he needs to use his phone in the middle of a film? Before she can ask him what's wrong he twists round sharply, knocking the tub of popcorn to the floor.

Alice sits forward to pick it up, but Simon grabs her hand and hisses something in her ear.

'What?' She looks at him, his face all hollows and shadows in the darkened room.

'We need to leave.'

'Now?'

The man in front turns at the sound of her raised voice and tuts.

'Now,' Simon says.

'But the . . .' She gestures at the screen.

'Please, Alice. We have to go.'

She snatches up her bag and coat and, apologising repeatedly, makes her way past the knees of the other cinemagoers until she reaches the end of the row. She's vaguely aware of the shoplifter staring as Simon gestures towards the exit but she's too anxious to give her a second thought.

'What's the matter?' Alice asks as they step into the brightly lit foyer. 'Is it bad news?'

Simon pushes his hands into his jacket pockets and shifts his weight from one foot to the other, his gaze fixed on the double doors that lead out into the heart of Cabot Circus shopping centre. 'I, um . . . I can't really explain right now. Let's just get to the taxi rank.'

'I thought we were going to the pub.'

'I can't now, sorry.'

'What is it?' She puts a hand on his arm. 'Has something bad happened?'

'I . . . I really don't want to talk about it. I'm sorry.'

A myriad of explanations flood Alice's mind: there's been a death in the family, a fire, a terrible accident. It has to be serious to explain how pale he's become.

'So where are we going?' she asks.

'Home.'

'Okay but I might need to pop back to mine to get a few things first. I'm at work tomorrow and I haven't got my—'

'Sorry, Alice. I've confused you. I'm getting a cab back to mine and you're going . . .' He tails off but the implication is clear.

*

Alice stares out of the cab window, her mind so muddled she can't separate one thought from the next as the taxi ferries her out of the heart of Bristol towards Kingswood. Why was Simon so keen to bundle her into a cab? Why not suggest she watch the rest of the film alone? On the walk from the cinema to the taxi rank he'd looped an arm around her shoulders and they'd walked side by side. He didn't speak the whole way, but she felt comforted by his fingers on the top of her arm and his body bumping against hers; it was the most intimate they'd been all evening. There was a protectiveness to the embrace that made her feel safe.

Safe. She hugs her handbag tighter to her body as one thought rises out of the maelstrom. What if the text that Simon received hadn't been bad news at all?

Simon, her thumbs fly over her phone's keypad as she taps out a message. *If the text was from my stalker we need to tell the police. Please, ring me. We need to talk about this.*

She hits send then rests her hand on her lap, the phone still clutched between her fingers.

She forces herself to look out of the window as graffitied walls and buildings flash past. Simon's not going to reply, she tells herself. I'm going to have to ring him but not here, not with the taxi driver listening in. I'll get home, pour a glass of wine and then—

Her phone vibrates in her hand and she nearly drops it in her haste to check it.

I'm really sorry, Alice, Simon has written, *but I can't do this any more. We can't see each other again.*

Chapter 27

Gareth

'Damn it.' Gareth hangs up, cutting off the automated voicemail message mid-sentence, and runs a hand over the back of his neck.

It would have been a rare stroke of luck to get through to his uncle on the first try. Tony, his mum and Ruth's brother, is an alcoholic who spends his retirement splitting his time between the bookies and the pub. He's younger than his sisters, early seventies, and a nice enough bloke, jovial with a strong line in dirty jokes that had Gareth in fits of laughter as a teen. But he's as unreliable as they come and goes underground for long periods of time, only resurfacing when he wants something or he's run out of money. Not that Gareth's mum minds. On the rare occasions he pops round to say hello he's so witty and attentive that her mood is lifted for hours after he leaves.

Getting hold of him is going to be tricky though. He's rarely at home to answer his landline, never checks his answerphone and doesn't own a mobile. If Gareth's got any hope of finding out where Ruth is he's going to have to pop into the Dog and Duck and talk to Tony in person. He checks his watch. 8.20 p.m. Too late to ask Kath if she'd sit with his mum for an hour? She did say she'd be happy to help out.

Kath, dressed in navy jogging bottoms and a grey T-shirt with 'Mama' picked out in black sequins, shoos Gareth out of his house, still dressed in his security trousers but with a jumper pulled over his shirt.

'Go on, have fun with your uncle. Your mum will be fine.'

He glances back towards the living room, the blare of the television filling the house. 'It's not her I'm worried about.'

'I'll be fine too. Besides, I like watching *Great British Menu* at full volume. Clears my ears out.'

He laughs. 'And Georgia's okay on her own next door?'

'She's thirteen. She's probably relieved to have the house to herself.'

'Okay, well, I won't be more than an hour, hour and a half tops.'

Kath touches a hand to his arm. 'You take as long as you want.'

Gareth pushes open the door to the Dog and Duck, the first pub he had a drink in (illegally, with fake ID), and a flood of memories hit him as he inhales the musty tobacco tang still clinging to the walls, the sour scent of the beer/lager mix in the slop trays and the whiff of warm bodies. The pub's so busy it takes him a while to spot Tony sitting on a stool at the far end of the bar, partly hidden by two men and a woman, all laughing raucously. He winds his way towards his uncle then clamps a hand to his shoulder, making him jump. The indignation on his uncle's face swiftly morphs into pleasure.

'Well if it isn't my favourite nephew!' He reaches out an arm and squeezes Gareth firmly on the shoulder. 'What are you drinking? Lager, isn't it?'

Before Gareth can object, Tony fishes into his back pocket for his wallet and flicks through a wodge of tenners. Someone's done well at the bookies today.

'Cheers.' They clink glasses, then Gareth settles himself on a stool.

'Mum all right?' Tony asks.

'Pretty much the same.'

'Still remember who you are?'

'Yeah.'

'Still remember who I am?'

'Mostly.'

'Well that's the important thing.' Tony grins, exposing crooked yellow teeth. Back in the day he'd been a bit of a ladies' man, 'a right looker' Gareth heard someone describe him once, but the years have taken their toll and now he's got the spider veins, pockmarks and swollen nose of a heavy drinker. Gareth's wondered more than once how he's managed to live to such a ripe old age. 'He's pickled his inner organs,' his mum told him once. 'He'll probably outlive us all.'

'It's been a while . . .' Gareth ventures.

His uncle raises a wiry eyebrow. 'You tellin' me off, lad?'

'Just wondered how you've been.'

'You know, bit of this, bit of that.'

'Send any postcards recently?' It's a bit of long shot but he can't resist.

'Eh?' Tony gives him a look.

As Gareth opens his mouth to explain, he's distracted by a vibration in his trouser pocket. His first thought is that it's Mark Whiting, telling him there's no need to come in for a meeting with Liam tomorrow because he's done some investigating and

Gareth's off the hook. His second, less optimistic thought is that Liam's got in there first and Mark's texting to tell him not to come in for the meeting because he's got the sack. But the text isn't either of those things. It's from his mobile phone provider telling him that his next bill is available to view online. He reaches into his other pocket for his antacids and pops one in his mouth as his chest begins to burn. He's not going to be able to buy food if he gets the sack tomorrow, never mind cover a phone bill.

'What's up?' Tony asks. 'Girlfriend dumped you, has she?'

The comment smarts almost as much as the heartburn. Gareth's last relationship ended nearly two years ago when Susannah, his girlfriend at the time, told him that she was going to have to end things because she was thirty-eight and wanted to have children. She couldn't do that, she said, with a man who lived with his mother and was never going to move out. Gareth pleaded with her, telling her they could find a way to make it work, but she was resolute. Either he put his mum in a home or they were over. He had no choice but to end things.

'No, Tony,' he says now. 'Something weird's happened.'

'Weird how?' His uncle shifts on his stool, his curiosity piqued.

'Mum received a postcard the other day . . .' He pauses. 'From Dad.'

The last word takes a couple of seconds to register, then Tony's eyebrows shoot upwards. 'You what?'

'Two postcards, actually, in his handwriting; the first saying he loved her, the second saying he was going to see her very soon. That one was hand-delivered but the first one was posted. I don't know where it was sent from because the postmark was smudged.'

'Can I see?' Tony holds out a dry, red palm.

'Sure.' He hands them across and watches his uncle's face as he reads both messages then flips the cards over.

'Maybe they're old. Your mum's always been a bit of a hoarder.'

'No. They're new. Look.' Gareth taps the unsmudged part of the postmark on the first card. 'You can see the date stamp.'

'Have you rung the police?'

'I rang them after the first postcard arrived, to see if there was an update on Dad, but they said that no new information had been added to Dad's missing person case for years, so . . .' He shrugs. 'I told them about the postcard but the bloke I spoke to seemed like he couldn't have cared less. There's something else. I thought I spotted Dad in the Meads.'

'Seriously?'

'Yeah, on the CCTV, or at least I think it was him. I went after him but . . .' he shakes his head ' . . . by the time I got there he was gone. Logically I know it couldn't be him, but what if it was?'

Tony takes a sip of his pint then sets it down on the bar. 'I suppose there's a small chance your dad could still be alive. People have secrets, reasons why they disappear. I wouldn't have put John down as one of them, but you only know what people want you to know, not what they don't.'

'But why now? Why get in touch with Mum after all these years? Why the postcards? Why not just knock on the door?'

'Maybe he's ill . . . dying and doesn't want her to see him . . .' He gives Gareth a long look. 'Or maybe he's got regrets.'

'That's what I thought, but why not just ring? We've got the same phone number we had when he disappeared. And the second card was hand-delivered. If Dad is alive he's nearly eighty.'

'Doesn't mean he can't walk.'

'Well yeah, he might have walked into the Meads but . . . I dunno, maybe it was wishful thinking, me spotting him like that. I've been thinking about him a lot and maybe I saw what I wanted to see. I'd rather the postcards were down to him rather than William Mackesy trying to wheedle his way into Mum's will.'

'The psychic?' Tony laughs. 'The dead talk to me too – mostly asking me why I was such an arsehole to them while they were alive.' His smile remains fixed but something shifts in his eyes, a shadow behind the bright blue irises. Tony takes a long swig of his pint, then sets it down on the bar. 'You got any other suspects?

'Well, that's why I'm here, really. When I got back from work earlier Mum was packing to go on holiday. We're not going on holiday,' he adds hastily as Tony's eyes widen. 'Neither's she. The thing is, when I asked her who she was going with she said Dad and that Ruth had told her it was a surprise.'

'Ruth? Our Ruth?'

'I don't know any others.'

Sadness fills Tony's eyes. 'God, dementia's a bitch. Your mum and Ruth haven't spoken in . . . must be forty, fifty years.'

'I know. That's why I've come to see you. Either Mum . . . you know, went back in time and was reliving a previous holiday, or Ruth's been in touch.'

Tony shakes his head. 'What, with the offer of a holiday? Mate, I just told you. They don't like each other. Never have. They'll go to their graves without speaking.'

'But what if Dad's been in touch with Ruth?'

'Why would he do that?'

'I don't know.' Gareth suddenly feels incredibly stupid. It's a ridiculous theory – that his dad would track down a woman his mum fell out with forty-odd years ago.

'Does she still live in Wales?' he asks, despondence flattening his voice.

'Used to. She's in Keynsham now.'

'Keynsham!' Only a twenty-minute drive from Bristol.

'Yeah. Do you want her number?'

'Course I do. Have you seen her? Since she moved down, I mean.'

'Once. It was a while back, mind. Must be at least . . . I dunno . . . eighteen, twenty months ago. Something like that.' Tony scratches the back of his neck. 'You know what I'm like. I flit about.'

That's one way of describing his lifestyle, Gareth thinks as he picks up his pint and drains a third of it in one quick gulp. He glances round the pub as he wipes his mouth with the back of his hand. Everywhere he looks, people are laughing, chatting and smiling. There are two blokes playing pool, shouting obscenities at each other to try and ruin the shot, a man and a woman kissing at the other end of the bar, and groups of friends crowded around tables so small their knees knock. As Gareth surveys the joyful bubble of life that surrounds him he feels a sharp jab in his chest that's got nothing to do with heartburn. This used to be his world – down the pub every Friday and Saturday night, pub quiz on Tuesday and darts on Thursday – but he can't remember the last time he saw his old mates Barry, Alan, Dai and Doug. There were quiet patches when the others got married, and again when they had kids, but it has to be five years at least since they were all in the same room.

He looks back at Tony with his bulbous red nose, the spidery red veins on his cheeks and the slight tremor to his hand when he sets down his pint. That could be him in twenty-five years if he's not careful. As he takes a sip of his pint he thinks about Kath, sitting in his living room in her sweatpants with a cup of tea in her hands, and his heart aches with longing and regret. He can chase down a shoplifter but he can't work up the courage to ask his neighbour on a date. Why? What's he so afraid of? The worst that can happen is she says no and things are a bit awkward for a while.

He sets his pint down on the bar. It lands heavily, making Tony raise an eyebrow.

'Everything okay, Gar?'

Gareth grins at him. 'It's going to be.'

He's made a decision. He's going to stop second-guessing himself and tomorrow, in his break, he's going to buy a bunch of flowers. After work he'll take them round to Kath's. He'll thank her for looking after his mum then he'll ask her out for dinner. What's the worst that can happen?

Chapter 28

Ursula

Friday

You . . . you . . . you . . . you . . . you . . .

Ursula swears under her breath and presses the eject button on the van's CD player. She's tried breathing on the CD and rubbing it on her sweatshirt, but no matter how hard Whitney Houston tries, she can't get past that one word of 'I Will Always Love You'. The CD is scratched and no amount of breathing, spitting or rubbing it is going to bring it back to life. Poor CD, poor Whitney, Ursula thinks as she takes the silver disc out of the player and lays it on the seat beside her, both of them dead. With all her other CDs scattered in the footwell of the passenger side it's either the radio or silence and Ursula's had enough silence to last her a lifetime. She presses the preset button for Radio 2 then immediately clicks away as Jeremy Vine announces, 'On today's programme we'll be talking about loss and—'

165

'Sorry, Jeremy,' Ursula says as she presses another button. 'Not today.'

George Michael's dulcet tones fill the cab and Ursula smiles: 'Don't Let The Sun Go Down on Me', one of her favourites. She sings along, one arm resting on the rolled-down window, one hand on the steering wheel. She passes a primary school where children are filing into the playground hand in hand with their parents, and feels a tight twinge of regret. She loved teaching, she was good at it, but she couldn't go back, not after she'd scared her class so terribly. What happened that day was a big part of why she'd moved in with Charlotte. She couldn't continue to live in the house she'd shared with Nathan and she couldn't drive past her school without thirty small, frightened faces looming up in her mind.

As she passes the school an image pops into her head from the film she saw at the cinema the night before, of the main character sitting on top of a mountain as the sun sets and he wrestles with the decision he has to make. It was a good film, a thriller with loads of action and a hero you really rooted for. Even so, Ursula had ummed and ahhed about going. It was over thirteen pounds for a ticket – that was a lot of tins of baked beans – but she needed to get out of the house. It was either that or sit alone in her room in an empty building, thinking about the poor woman at number six. Ursula hadn't taken offence when she'd screamed at her to fuck off and leave her alone. That wasn't anger she'd heard in the woman's voice, it was fear. She wasn't agoraphobic and she hadn't locked herself in, of that Ursula was sure.

She rang the police as soon as she was out of sight of the house and reported her suspicion that a woman and her child were being kept prisoner in their own home. Ursula was nervous as she spoke but was reassured by how seriously the female officer took her allegation. Later, as she finished her shift she felt sure she'd done the right thing. But that surety hadn't lasted. The moment she put her keys in the door of number fifteen William Street, doubt began to creep in. What if she'd got it wrong? What if the woman really was mentally ill and a police visit pushed her over the edge? Even if she'd got it right the woman could still be in danger. If the husband found out the police had been round he might beat up his wife, or worse. The thought made Ursula feel sick. She couldn't live with herself if someone died because of something she'd done. Not again.

The thought propelled her out of the house and back into her van. She needed to steal something, to relieve the tight feeling in her chest. She was halfway to the Meads when she realised that all the shops would be shut, so she parked up in the centre of town and walked the streets until a bus stop film poster caught her eye. A trip to the cinema meant one hundred and twenty minutes when she wouldn't have to think.

The film had distracted her, but not in the way she'd imagined. She'd walked in late, then caught a glimpse of a man she thought she recognised, cast in shadow, several seats back. When she turned round to take a second look the woman sitting next to him had glared at her like she was the scum of the earth. She knew immediately who she was – the red-haired manager of Mirage Fashions who'd stalked the racks the last time she'd been in. What was it she'd nicked that time? She couldn't even remember. Her initial reaction was to get up and leave, but then she decided that she had as much right to be in the cinema as anyone else and stayed in her seat.

As George Michael's dulcet tones fade away a newsreader's voice fills the cab.

'Thirty-two-year-old mother of one Kerry Wilson was stabbed to death in her home in South Bristol last night. A man has been arrested and is being held in custody.'

Wilson. An image of a brown parcel with a white label. Wilson.

It was on a parcel she loaded into her van that morning. She goes cold all over. Paul Wilson. The man from number six.

'Move! Move! Move!' Ursula presses her palm to the horn, sounding it repeatedly at the bin lorry that's blocking the road. One of the bin men appears and gestures for her to back up.

'We're not going anywhere for a while, love!' he shouts, but she's already put the van in reverse. It takes her two, maybe three minutes tops to navigate an alternate route but every second feels like a lifetime and as she turns the corner into The Crest her heart is beating in the base of her throat. She's not sure what she expects to see outside number six – police tape, officers, maybe men in white suits, *something* to alert her to the fact that a crime's been committed. But the house, and the surrounding area, looks exactly as it did the previous day.

She runs up the steps and thumps on the door, then peers through the living room window. No child, and no woman. She bangs on the door again and is just about to crouch down to peer through the letter box when the door swings away from her. It only opens a couple of inches, constrained by a gold safety chain, but it's enough for her to see who's on the other side.

'You're alive!'

The woman doesn't reply. She stares at Ursula blankly, her face – or at least the tiny sliver of it that's visible – is impassive.

Relief so powerful it almost makes her cry surges through Ursula's body. 'You're not Kerry Wilson.'

The woman gives the tiniest shake of her head.

'It was on the radio . . . a Kerry Wilson was killed by her husband and I . . . I thought it was you. I thought that you might . . . I was worried that you might be dead.'

The other woman's lips curl, but it's not a smile of amusement. It's not sadness either; it's wistfulness. Ursula stares at her in alarm. She wishes she were dead.

'Sorry?' Ursula says as the other woman says something so softly she doesn't catch it. 'Sorry, what was that?'

'You shouldn't have called the police.'

'They were here? They came?'

The woman nods.

'Did they speak to your husband?'

The woman's breathing becomes quick and shallow. She's not maintaining eye contact any more. Her pale blue eyes are flicking back and forth, scanning the street below.

Ursula turns sharply but there's no one there. 'What's your name?' she asks as she turns back.

'Nicki.'

'Did the police tell him not to lock you in any more? Is that why you can open the door?'

'You need to go.'

'Is he due back? He's not normally here at this time of day.'

'Please. You have to go.'

'Wait!' Ursula shouts as the door begins to close. 'Let me give you my number. I want to help you.'

'I can't . . . you can't . . .'

'Please. One second.' Ursula puts the parcel she's holding on the low wall beside her and frantically digs around in the pockets of her hoody for a pen and a piece of paper. She rips a 'sorry you were out' slip from the pad, scribbles down her name, number and address and just manages to shove it into the gap before Nicki closes the door in her face.

'Wait!' She snatches up the parcel. 'You forgot this.' As she raises her hand to tap on the door she senses someone watching her and swings round.

There's a man at the bottom of the steps. He's tall, but not as tall as Ursula. He's clean-cut and attractive, dressed in a smart navy suit with a white shirt and paisley tie, with dark hair that's short at the sides and longer on top, swept back with gel. He's the husband; Ursula can tell from the proprietorial way his gaze flicks from the front door to her. She keeps very still as his eyes travel the length of her body and then return, dismissively, to her face. She's endured a similar sweep from men before, more times than she can count: curiosity swiftly followed by an analysis of her heavy breasts, thick waist and sturdy legs – ('Would I?') and then they scan her face ('God, no. Definitely not'). But there's something different about the way Paul Wilson is looking at her. He's studying her the way a man might look at another man when they're looking for a fight ('Can I take him? Can I not?').

'Can I help you?' His whole demeanour changes when he smiles. There's light in his eyes and an easy, friendly smile that would be utterly disarming if Ursula hadn't just watched him give her the once-over.

He walks up the steps towards her and holds out a hand. 'I take it that's for me.'

For a split second she has no idea what he's talking about.

'The parcel,' he says, as though she's slow.

'You're not normally here at this time.'

'Am I not?' He makes a big show of glancing at his watch, pushing back the sleeve of his suit jacket and holding his arm further away than is necessary so he can look down his nose at the time. 'I suppose you're right. Are you keeping track of my movements?'

'I'm sorry?'

'It was a joke.' He squeezes her arm. His fingers tighten around her bicep and remain there for one second, two, before he lets go.

In the distance she can hear a child crying, a dog barking and the faint squeal of an ambulance going by. The street is still deserted. It's just her, Paul Wilson, and Nicki, hiding behind the door.

'You knew I'd be here,' she says steadily. 'That's why you ordered a parcel, isn't it?'

The man's gaze flicks towards the upstairs window of his neighbour's house. Checking whether there are any witnesses, Ursula thinks. He might terrify his wife but she's standing firm.

'Are you criticising my shopping habits?'

'Of course not.' She forces a smile onto her face. Two can play at this nicey nicey charade.

'I don't think our paths will cross again,' Paul Wilson says. He reaches, again, for the parcel. 'If I could just . . .'

Irritation is starting to show on his face, in the tight set of his jaw and the twitch of his nostrils, but Ursula doesn't move her hand from her side.

'Possessions are so important, aren't they?' she says. 'That's why we like to keep them safe.'

'Aren't we the philosopher?'

'Just making conversation.'

'You like a chat, don't you? No, wait. That's wrong, isn't it? It's *gossip* you enjoy.'

'I don't know what you mean.'

'I think you do. I think you know exactly what I'm talking about.' And there it is again, the full beam of his grin: friendly, unassuming and warm. It's terrifying, Ursula thinks, how easily he can flick the switch. Is that why Nicki's still scared? Because Paul charmed the police? Did he tell them that his wife was agoraphobic, that she was mentally unstable, that the well-meaning courier had it all wrong? 'My parcel, if you please.'

This time Ursula raises her hand, but as Paul's fingers close around the package she has to force herself to let go.

'Come here again,' she hears his voice calling softly after her as she walks down the steps to the pavement, 'and it'll be the last thing you do.'

Chapter 29

Alice

Lynne doesn't sound convinced when Alice explains on the phone that she's not feeling well. 'Came on overnight, did it?' she asks. 'This terrible cold?'

Alice coughs pathetically, then picks up the length of kitchen roll she's laid out on the counter and noisily blows her nose. 'My throat was all scratchy when I went to bed and when I woke up this morning . . . it was all I could do to get up.' Her voice sounds feeble, even to her own ears, but in a fake rather than a convincing way. But there's no way she's going to work today, not after Simon dropped his bombshell last night.

'Want me to pop round later?' Lynne asks. 'I could pick up some stuff from the chemist in my lunchbreak.'

'No, no. That's very kind but Emily's looking after me.'

'She's home, is she? Not at work?'

Alice coughs again, clearing her throat for the lie. 'She's got a day off. She's on her way to the corner shop right now to get me some Lemsip.'

'Aw.' Lynne sighs. 'Well I'm glad someone's looking after you. Get lots of rest, sleep and drink lots of water. Hopefully see you tomorrow.'

Alice sniffs. 'Yes, I'm pretty sure it's just a twenty-four-hour thing.'

There's a pause. Lynne doesn't believe her, she can feel it, but she doesn't want to tell her the real reason why she's not coming into work. Lynne would want a complete rundown of exactly what happened the night before and who said what, and she just can't face it. Not yet.

'Hope you feel better soon,' Lynne says tersely. 'Look after yourself, bye.'

Cringing, Alice sets her mobile down on the kitchen table and stands up, stretching her arms out to the side. She went straight back to work after Michael assaulted her and it's utterly pathetic, calling in sick because she got dumped. It's not as though she's heartbroken – she and Simon only had two dates, three if you counted lunch, and they hadn't even slept together, but it's the not knowing that kept her up all night. She'd texted him back, as soon as she got out of the taxi:

I understand if you don't want to see me again, but could you let me know why?

Seconds ticked into minutes and when he still hadn't replied half an hour later she texted him again.

Please, just let me know why. I can take it. Was it because I had a go at you about you not texting (yes, I can see the irony there . . .) or is there another reason? I can't stop thinking about how urgently we had to leave the cinema? Was it to do with that? Or the weird messages I've been getting? Whatever the reason I can take it, Simon.

She told herself she'd wait a full hour before contacting him again, telling herself that maybe he was dealing with whatever emergency had called him out of the cinema, but she cracked after ten minutes and rang him. Her call went straight to voicemail and she hung up. There was nothing to say that she hadn't already said in her text.

She tried to watch TV but couldn't concentrate. She made herself soup and toast for lunch but found she couldn't eat more than a mouthful. She tried putting her phone in her bedroom so she wouldn't obsessively check it but ended up pacing the room instead. She turned to Google, searching for answers:

Why did my boyfriend suddenly dump me?

Why do men blow hot and cold?

My stalker scared off my boyfriend

She read some interesting theories – that maybe her boyfriend had been feeling that something was wrong for a while, that he wasn't 'that into her' or she was too keen. The last explanation rang bells. She *had* come across as needy with all the unanswered text messages, and then confronting him about them, but that didn't explain why he'd suddenly decided to leave the film part way through. No matter which way Alice looks at what happened, and she's examined it from every conceivable angle, Simon's sudden decision to dump her *had* to be down to the text message he received in the cinema. Everything he'd done since they'd met – running after her with her purse, bringing her flowers, offering to speak to the police, accompanying her home after her car was scratched – suggested that he was a decent, honourable man. Had Flora threatened her in some way? Had he dumped her to protect her? It was the only theory that made sense.

She scrolls through her phone, pausing over DC Mitchell's number, then swipes past it. She's got nothing new to report to the police. There's no text she can show the detective, no evidence of abuse. A slow rage builds as Alice strides around the kitchen, phone in hand. Whoever's been stalking her has won. They got what they wanted when Simon messaged her to say it was over.

She looks at her phone again and scrolls through her Facebook messages until she finds the one from Ann Friend.

I hope you're happy, she types back. *He's split up with me because of you. You won. Well done.*

Her thumb hovers over the send button. Should she send it or not? If they reply they might say something that gives her a clue to their identity. But what if they don't? She doesn't think she could bear the smugness of their silence.

She deletes the message. Her stalker has only won if she lets them. If she gives up. She didn't fight for her marriage when Peter told her he was seeing someone else. She let him walk away. She didn't have the energy, or the inclination, to work out why he'd cheated on her. There was a conversation to be had about what had gone wrong in their marriage but she didn't want to pick over the bones of their relationship so, rather than find closure, she chose to shut down emotionally instead. But this is different. This isn't about infidelity or a failure to communicate. It's about control, and she's going to take it back.

Why, Alice asks herself, head in hands, did she never think to ask Simon his surname? She had so many opportunities – in the cafe, over dinner and during their many text marathons. How had it never come up? Or maybe it had? She can vaguely remember asking him his surname, so why doesn't she know it? He must have changed the subject or distracted her with a joke.

She types *Simon Insurance Bristol* into Google and looks at the results. There's a Simon James, a Simon Lancaster, a Simon Perkins and a Simon Kelly but they're mostly company owners or in very senior roles and, more importantly, they're not the Simon she's looking for.

She enters a new search *Insurance Company Bristol* and raises her eyebrows as she scrolls through the results. One hundred, there are exactly *one hundred* insurance companies listed in Bristol. She'd had a half-baked idea that there might be thirty, forty tops, and she could spend the day ringing them to ask if they employed a Simon. But a hundred? She'd have to book time off work to get through them all. And that's assuming a receptionist would share employee information with a complete stranger. If anyone rang her at work to ask who she employed she'd tell them that was confidential and give them short shrift.

She texts her daughter: *Emily, if you were trying to track someone down on the internet where would you look? I've already googled Simon + insurance companies in Bristol but there are a hundred results. How can I narrow it down?*

A few seconds later her phone pings with a response: *WHAT . . . ARE . . . YOU . . . DOING . . . THAT . . . FOR?*

Alice texts back: *I'm trying to find out who sent me the weird text messages on Facebook and scratched my car and I can't do that unless Simon talks to me.*

So ring him.

I can't. He won't answer my calls.

Why? What have you done?

Nothing as far as I know. He dumped me last night.

There's a pause then: *Oh, sorry to hear that, Mum. I know you liked him.*

So? How do I track him down?

You don't. You let it go.

What about the weird Facebook messages?

Have you had any new ones?

Not since he dumped me.

Well then. Forget about it, Mum. He's obviously got a psycho ex-girlfriend – and you don't want to be a part of that. If anything else happens, contact the police.

Do you think anything else will happen?

NO! Now step away from Google and forget about that loser. You're getting obsessed.

But Alice can't step away from Google. She has to find out the truth, or at least try.

She searches her brain for the tiniest sliver of information that will aid her. She doesn't know Simon's surname or where he works but he did tell her he lives in a three-bedroom house in St George's. But surprise, surprise, he didn't mention the name of the street. What else? He was engaged to a woman called Flora, an actress.

Alice tries imdb.com. That's where all actors and actresses seem to be registered. If she can't find Simon then maybe contacting Flora is her next best bet. A few results are returned but the women are either too old or too young. Maybe Flora isn't successful enough to be on IMDb or, like a lot of people in the profession, she's got a different stage name. Alice searches Facebook next, looking for Floras in Bristol and dozens of tiny Flora profile photos fill her screen.

She discounts any that are too old or too young to match the woman she's looking for, then clicks on the first possible match and hits the message button.

Hello, my name is Alice Fletcher. Are you an actress and were you ever engaged to someone called Simon? If so I need to talk to you. Please message me back.

'Urgh.' She runs her hands over her face as she copies and pastes the message into the next profile. It's going to take her hours to contact them all. It's almost as though Simon deliberately withheld any facts that would help her track him down. But why? What was he trying to hide?

Chapter 30

Gareth

Gareth shifts his weight in the hard-backed plastic chair, putting his hands on the arms so he sits up taller. He looks across at the clock on the wall and taps the soles of his leather shoes on the floor: left foot, right foot, left foot, right foot. Mark Whiting looks up from his computer screen.

'Do you mind?'

'Sorry.' Gareth presses his feet into the floor. It's 1.42 p.m. The meeting was scheduled for 1.30 p.m. and Liam Dunford is twelve minutes late. Maybe he's ill, Gareth thinks. Really ill. So ill he couldn't ring in that morning to explain why he wasn't coming to work. Maybe, an evil little voice whispers in the back of his head, maybe he's dead.

'Well.' His boss stops his one-fingered typing and sits back in his chair. 'It's not looking hopeful, is it?'

For one terrifying moment Gareth thinks he's talking about his job prospects but then Mark adds, 'I think he's a no-show, don't you?'

'Yeah.' Gareth moves to stand up then slumps back as his boss waggles his hand, indicating that he should stay where he is.

'So are you going to tell me what this is about? This *urgent* meeting that you requested?'

Gareth rubs his palms together. 'Liam's not said anything to you?'

Mark sits forward, elbows on the desk and his chin on his hands and fixes Gareth with an enquiring look. He's a good ten years younger, all designer suits, shiny shoes, gelled hair, tanned skin and eyebrows that are suspiciously tamed. 'Liam's not said anything. I sent him a text yesterday, reminding him about the meeting. He replied saying he'd be here but I haven't heard anything since.'

Interesting that Liam didn't get in first with his version of events. Gareth had assumed he would.

'You did ring him when he didn't show up this morning, didn't you?' Mark adds.

'Of course I did but there was no answer on his mobile or his landline. I assumed he'd been out drinking and slept through his alarm again . . .' He pauses, letting that little nugget of information sink in. 'I rang him again an hour later and there was still no answer.'

'And you're not going to tell me what all this is about?'

'I um . . . no. I'd rather wait until we're both in the same room, if that's all right with you?'

Mark nods his head wearily. 'Look, whatever this is about I'm not going to pursue it unless Liam can be bothered to turn up. Give me a ring or send me an email when he's back in work. And when he does come in, tell him he's got a verbal warning for not ringing in.'

Gareth coughs into his hand to hide his smile. 'Yes, boss, of course.'

Chapter 31

Ursula

'I'm not going to steal anything,' Ursula tells herself as she strides across the Meads landing, sweating under her thick woollen coat as she heads for Mirage Fashions. 'I'm just going to look.'

It was all she could do not to head straight there after she'd walked back to her van, feeling Paul Wilson's eyes burning into her spine. She hadn't though, she'd forced herself to finish her round, trying and failing to push the desperate expression on Nicki's face out of her mind. She'd thought she was helping her by calling the police to report a suspected domestic abuse situation but she'd only made things worse.

She keeps an eye out for the security guard as she walks through the entrance of Mirage Fashions but surprise, surprise, he's nowhere near the doors. He's hovering by the checkout, watching the shop assistants as they work. He's definitely the laziest security guard in the whole mall. Unlike some of the others, who trail after her everywhere, the old bloke at Mirage

Fashions seems to be counting down the days to retirement. Ursula heads for the back of the shop. She doesn't slump or move furtively. At six foot three she's visible whatever she does and to try and shrink herself down would only draw unnecessary attention. Instead she walks confidently, shoulders back, as though she's got a wad of cash in her pocket and a burning desire to spend it. Her eye is drawn by a rail of pretty, multi-coloured skirts. They'd be mid-calf on most women and knee-length on her but she could carry one off with the right top and her favourite boots. She runs a hand up and down the material then plucks at the elasticated waistband. They only go up to a size twenty and she's a twenty-four but there's enough give in the cloth that it might actually fit. She keeps her eyes on the security guard on the other side of the room as she unclips the skirt from the hanger and swiftly folds it up. The flatter she can make it the less likely she'll be noticed once she shoves it under her top. Her gaze flits to the CCTV cameras on the ceiling. She's standing so close to the rail there's no way they can pick up what she's doing. Her heart beats faster as she pulls at the elastic at the bottom of her sweatshirt. Two, three minutes tops and she'll be out of the shopping centre and well on her way to the van.

'Careful. That rail's really loose. If you flick through the clothes too fast it collapses.'

Ursula jolts as a woman, dressed in the store uniform, appears to her left. She's young, barely out of her teens. Her gaze flicks to Ursula's waistline and the size twenty skirt in her hands. Where did you pop up from? Ursula thinks as she frantically tries to decide what to do. She really wants the skirt but making a break for it would be too risky. But she doesn't want to leave without it. The dark cloud she's spent the last two years running from will descend the second she makes it back to the van and she can't let that happen, she won't.

She looks at the shop assistant and smiles brightly. 'Could you point me in the direction of the changing rooms? I'd like to try this on.'

Ursula glances at her reflection in the changing room mirror, the skirt hooked over her arm. Her cheeks are flushed, there are dark circles under her eyes and her damp fringe is clinging to her forehead. She hastily looks away, peeling off her coat and hanging it on a hook on the wall. She plucks at the hem of her sweatshirt and moves it back and forth to try and get some air to her clammy skin. She wants to sit down to catch her breath but there's no chair in the cubicle so she sinks onto the floor instead and gathers her knees up to her chest. The sound of voices, and clothes being arranged on rails, drifts from beneath the swing door. The young sales assistant is chatting to a colleague at the entrance to the changing rooms.

'You know someone else has gone missing? Another man.'

'No!'

'Yeah. Last seen heading for the Harbourside at about three in the morning. I heard from Kaisha who heard from someone who works in Costa that he was one of the security guards that works here.'

'Not Larry!'

'No! He's out there, you massive twat.'

The sound of laughter rings through the cubicles.

'God, that's really scary. His poor family. That's the second bloke to disappear on the Harbourside in how many weeks?'

'Actually it's three now. I had a look on the internet and there's been two go missing, a month between them, and then this guy. And the police are still claiming that there's no Harbourside Murderer.'

'But if someone is pushing them into the river how come they haven't found their bodies yet? Surely they'd wash up eventually.'

'Who says they went into the water? There's no CCTV there, that's why the police have got no leads. They could have been bundled into a van then chopped up and buried in Leigh Woods for all we know.'

The young woman gasps. 'Don't say that.'

'I'm just saying what other people are thinking, that's all. Just promise me you'll stay with your friends on a night out. Don't get any stupid ideas about walking home alone.'

'Okay, okay. Jeez. Thanks for that, Lynne. I'm not going to be able to sleep tonight now!'

As the voices drift away Ursula slowly gets to her feet, the conversation she just overheard still ringing in her ears. She looks down at the skirt in her hands and makes a decision. With no one manning the rack at the end of the cubicles she'll be able to walk straight out with it. She can easily get to the exit without being caught.

'Seriously? You let her use the changing rooms!' She jumps at the sound of a raised voice and hurried footsteps on the lino flooring. 'Kaisha, she's a bloody shoplifter. Her face is on the staffroom wall!'

'You!' The door to her cubicle is yanked open and a pink-cheeked woman with a short brown bob glares up at her. The grey-haired security guard appears beside her, swiftly followed by the younger shop assistant. Before Ursula can say a word, the skirt is snatched from her hands. 'I'll take that, thank you very much.'

'I'm sorry, miss.' The security guard steps forward and takes Ursula by the elbow. 'But you're going to have to leave. You're banned.'

'I don't know what I'm supposed to have done,' Ursula protests as she's frog-marched along the line of cubicles and onto the shop floor, 'but you've got it all wrong. This is my favourite shop.'

The security guard laughs. 'Course it is, you haven't been caught before.'

As he walks her through the entrance and onto the concourse, Ursula tries to turn back but his grip on her elbow is surprisingly strong.

'Wait! I've forgotten my coat. It's still in the cubicle. Please, just let me go back and get it.'

'Nice try, love.' Before she can say another word, she's propelled out of the shop. 'Now get on your way or I'll call the police.'

'Shit,' Ursula says as she opens and closes the cupboard doors in the galley kitchen. 'Shit, shit, shit.'

Tears trickle down her cheeks as she takes out the last tin of beans from her cupboard and drops two pieces of bread into the toaster. It was a shock, being bundled out of Mirage Fashions like that. Humiliating, too. She's never been caught shoplifting before and, for once, she hadn't actually stolen anything. The expression on the shop assistant's face as she snatched the skirt from her hands is burnt onto Ursula's brain – anger and revulsion, like she was the lowest type of scum.

Nathan bought the coat she was forced to leave behind. He'd known she'd been eyeing it up in Evans for weeks but couldn't justify the eighty-pound price tag. He'd popped in to buy it on his lunch break one day and hung it up on the coat rack at home for her to find. She hadn't immediately spotted it when she came in. She was tired after eight hours spent wrangling five-year olds and all she wanted to do was get out of her clothes and lie in the bath with a book. But as she climbed the stairs Nathan shouted up to her, asking her to help him get the food shopping in from the car. A complaint formed on her lips but she swallowed it back. He was tired too. When he told her to put on her coat she automatically reached for the thin mac she'd chucked over the banister at the bottom of the stairs, only for Nath to point at the rack.

'No, not that one,' he said. 'Your other coat.'

He'd helped her put it on, standing behind her on tiptoes as she slipped her arms into the soft wool mix. When she stooped to kiss him she didn't think she'd ever felt happier. It was the greatest gift she'd ever been given. Not the coat. Him.

Now, as she stirs the baked beans in the pan, she swipes the back of her hands over her cheeks and tries to blink away the tears. Rain is beating at the glass panel of the back door and the garden beyond is a blur of green and brown and grey.

Let it go. She hears Nathan's voice in her head. *It's just a coat, Albi. It's not me.*

But I haven't got you either, have I? And that coat was—

Movement in the garden makes her turn sharply.

There's a cat crouched under the tree, holding something small and feathery in its mouth. 'Hey!' She bangs on the glass, then turns the key in the lock and pulls the door open. 'Hey! Shoo! Leave it alone.'

The cat looks at her, a tiny fledgling clamped within its jaws.

'Shoo!' Ursula claps her hands together, then stoops down, picks up a small stone, and hurls it across the lawn. It doesn't hit the cat but the motion startles it. The bird falls from its mouth and it springs away, jumping from the grass to the wall.

'Shoo!' Ursula shouts again as the cat vanishes from the top of the wall, disappearing into the next garden or the alleyway beyond. She runs back into the hallway and slips her feet into her battered trainers and grabs the nearest coat. She doesn't give a thought to the fact that Edward will bollock her for using his things as she slips her arms into it and pulls the hood over her head. She just wants to get back to the bird before the cat does.

But there's no cat in the garden as she hurries through the rain, her trainers slapping against the wet patio then trampling on the grass. Out of the corner of her eye she sees a small white-washed window poking out of the pebbles at the base of the house but she doesn't stop to examine it. She has to rescue the bird.

'Please be alive,' she prays as she scoops up the tiny, still, feathered body. 'Please, please, please be alive.'

Chapter 32

Gareth

After his meeting with Mark Whiting, Gareth has one of the busiest afternoons in the Meads that he can remember. He breaks up a fight outside Costa between two blokes in their early fifties, then chases and apprehends two shoplifters. After this he moves to the control room and deals with a three-year-old girl going missing (eventually located in Claire's Accessories, pulling all the jewellery off a display) and calls in the cleaners after a shopper drops a tin of hot chocolate that explodes over the floor. Over the last couple of hours he's barely had time to pee, never mind anything else, but he did make sure he bought a bunch of flowers for Kath during his break.

Now, as Raj arrives to start his shift in the control room, Gareth nips into the toilets then makes his way down to the first floor. There's an hour to go until the end of his shift and as he patrols the walkways and common areas of the shopping mall he sorts through his thoughts. Last night in the pub, after he made his decision to ask Kath out, Tony gave him Auntie Ruth's number. Gareth was feeling so buoyed up he decided to bite the bullet and give his aunt a ring there and then. The pub was at full volume so he went outside. Someone called Maureen answered the phone. She told him that Ruth had been hospitalised for a stroke a week earlier and they didn't know when she'd be back. They chatted for a while, discovered they were cousins, and Maureen promised to ring if there was any news. Afterwards, when Gareth returned home, it was all he could do not to beckon Kath into the kitchen and tell her everything. But when he walked into the living room, she jumped out of her armchair and slipped her feet back into her slippers. She was obviously keen to get back to Georgia and he didn't want to keep her. Later, after he put his mum to bed and turned in himself, Gareth couldn't sleep. Should he tell his mum or not? There was a very real chance that the news about Auntie Ruth's stroke would upset her, regardless of their estrangement. It might also confuse her if she was having one of her episodes trapped in the past. At one in the morning he made his decision. He'd tell her. Then it was up to her if she wanted to see Ruth.

Now, Gareth strolls along the walkway, scanning the level for any unusual activity. The number of shoppers has thinned out now the mall is so near to closing and those that are left are darting from shop to shop, their faces pinched with anxiety. Gareth watches them, trying to guess what they're so keen to get their hands on. The man speeding towards the jewellers is almost certainly grabbing a last minute present for his wife's birthday. The woman nipping into Claire's Accessories probably has a daughter who's lost her favourite hairband or needs to fill party bags for the weekend. And the old man walking towards Waterstones is—

Gareth's heart stills.

White-grey hair. Olive-green jacket. Rigid spine.

Go, Gareth's brain tells him, but he doesn't move an inch. It is as though someone has pressed pause in his brain. He can't move, he can't think, he can't feel. All he can do is watch. His heart restarts with a thump so powerful that his brain sparks back to life. Thoughts, dozens of them, flood his mind and now it's indecision that paralyses him. It's Dad. It's not Dad. I want to find out. I don't. I don't know if I could bear the disappointment. What if he rejects me? What if he doesn't? If he walks away, I'll never know.

He takes off, jogging after the man, catching up with him as he reaches the bookshop's glass double doors. He reaches out a hand and touches him on the shoulder. The man turns slowly, twisting at the waist as his neck follows suit. He raises a hand in self-defence. The skin is slack and lined, aged-spotted with bulbous, rope-like veins so prominent it's as though they've risen to the surface in an effort to escape. But Gareth doesn't see the man's hands. His eyes are trained on the back of his head, the sliver of face as he turns and then—

'I'm sorry.' Gareth takes a step backwards, his hands dropping to his side. 'I'm sorry. I thought you were someone else.'

Somehow Gareth manages to make it to the end of his shift. He locks his pain and disappointment in a box in the back of his head and marks it 'Do not open unless alone'. He keeps it there until all the doors are checked, all the shoppers have left and all the rotas for the next week have been completed, then he leaves the shopping centre, crosses the near-empty car park and lets himself into his car, then he puts his hands on the steering wheel and he sobs.

As Gareth walks up the path to his house, Kath's flowers hanging loosely from his hand, he doesn't so much as glance at the CCTV camera above the door. He doesn't care who's been sending his mum the postcards. He doesn't even care if Mackesy has been trying to extort money. And he hasn't got the energy to ask Kath out. He's tired, so damned tired. All he wants to do is say hello to his mum, change his clothes and then watch TV so loud that it blocks out his thoughts.

'Mum!' He puts the flowers on the sideboard, slips off his jacket, then pauses as he crouches to remove his shoes. Something's not right. The house is too quiet. The TV's not on. Oh God, she's not packing for a holiday again, is she?

'Mum?' He pops his head into the living room then does the same in the kitchen and heads up the stairs. 'Mum?'

He pushes open the door to her bedroom. The room's exactly as it was when he left that morning, curtains pulled, the suitcase on top of the wardrobe and the bed neatly made. His heart lurches as he heads for the small bathroom. He knocks on the door and waits.

A second passes, then two, three. He turns the handle. 'Mum, are you in there?'

But there's no one sitting on the avocado-coloured toilet or standing in the shower. There's only one room left to check but when he walks into his bedroom it's as empty as every other room in the house.

'Shit. Shit.' He flies down the stairs, grabbing hold of the banister as his feet slip out from beneath him on the second to last step. In an instant he's up again. He grabs his keys from the wooden bowl by the front door then he's out of the house, down the path and sprinting down the street. He runs all the way to the corner shop and grips the counter, sweat pouring off him and his wet socks clinging to his feet.

'Have you seen my mum?' He takes three shallow breaths. 'Joan. My mum. Has she been in?'

Fred, the man who's owned the shop for as long as Gareth can remember, slowly shakes his head. 'I've not seen her in weeks. Is she okay?'

Gareth doesn't answer. He bursts back out again and pushes at the door to the post office. Locked. They've already closed up for the day. The only other shops on the small stretch of street are a boarded-up hairdresser and a Chinese takeaway. He doesn't bother going in there. It only opened six months earlier and he's pretty sure his mum's never been in.

Panting and panicked, he desperately tries to work out where she might have gone. Did she decide to take herself off to the doctor or the dentist's? She'd normally go with Sally or Yvonne but if they'd already left and she'd had some kind of accident then . . .

Kath! He's told his mum over and over again that if anything happens she needs to go next door and ask Kath for help. He's pinned a note to the side of the front door, saying the same.

He sets off at a sprint, then slows as a stitch gnaws at his side. He should never have left his mother alone. He's been telling her for months that she should move into a care home where she'd get better help, but she's always refused. On a good day she's lucid enough to argue with him. On a bad day she bursts into tears or looks at him confused, telling him that she promised 'until death do us part' and she's not going anywhere without her John.

'Kath!' He hammers on the door with his fist. 'Kath! Kath!'

He sees a shadow move behind the thin living room curtains then the light in the hall goes on and the front door opens.

'Is she here?' he asks before his astonished neighbour can speak. 'My mum, is she here?'

There's a split second as Kath's lips part when he thinks everything's going to be okay, that's she's going to tell him that his mum's in her living room, watching telly at top whack. But then her eyes fill with concern and she shakes her head.

'Mum's not at home.' Gareth grips the door frame. 'She's not anywhere. She's completely disappeared.'

Chapter 33

Alice

Alice lifts her glass and chinks it against Emily's and Lynne's. 'Thanks for coming out, both of you. I would have gone mental if I'd spent another minute at home.'

'Oh cheers!' Her daughter laughs. 'Glad I was such great company. I'd have stayed the night at Adam's if I'd known.'

'You know what I mean.' Alice takes a sip of her wine. 'Thanks for putting up with me, both of you.'

'I'm just glad you're okay,' Lynne says. 'I knew something was up when you rang in sick this morning but I didn't want to pry.'

'I've said it before and I'll say it again. Simon's a shit.' Emily sits back hard in her chair. 'I know you didn't want to play games but—'

'Ems.' Alice holds up a hand. 'It's not about that. Didn't you listen to a word I just said?'

'I did. But personally I think he's totally gutless and you're

192

better off without him.' Her daughter looks from her to Lynne, who shrugs.

'He could have been more supportive,' Lynne says. 'Sorry, Alice, I know that's not what you want to hear but I think maybe you're reading too much into that text.'

'Exactly.' Emily sits forward again. 'Let's say it was Flora who texted him. If she threatened you, why didn't he call the police? Or even better, talk to you about it!'

'Emily. Not so loud.' Alice turns her head. There's a man sitting alone at the next table. He's staring down at his phone but he's close enough to hear every word. She lowers her voice. 'Maybe he just panicked. Or . . . I don't know. Maybe he dumped me to protect me.'

Emily snorts into her hand. 'Really?'

Indignation bubbles in Alice's chest. 'Lynne, help me out here. You don't think I'm being ridiculous, do you?'

'No.' Her best friend shakes her head. 'I don't, but honestly, Alice, I think you're better off out of it. Someone didn't want you around him and maybe it's safer that you're not.'

'But what if he's not safe?'

'Then he should go to the police.'

'He's not your problem, Mum,' Emily pipes up. 'Not any more.'

Alice reaches for her wine. They both have a point. She probably is safer without him. Whoever scratched her car hasn't been in touch since. But it feels wrong, forgetting about Simon and carrying on like they'd never met.

'Excuse me a minute.' She pushes her chair away from the table. 'I'm just going to go to the loo.'

The toilets are towards the rear of the pub, near the back door. Outside there are steps that lead down to a heated patio, with a box of blankets for anyone still feeling the effect of the cold night's air. Alice pauses as she comes out from the loo, distracted by the laughter drifting up from below, the low rumble of a man's amusement and the high-pitched squeal of a woman having fun. It reminds her of the time she had lunch with Simon in the cafe when the conversation naturally bounced between them as though they'd known each other for years. It wasn't like that in the restaurant when she quizzed him about his ex-girlfriend and he hurried outside to take a call.

As more laughter creeps under the back door, curiosity prompts her to turn the handle and step outside onto the narrow platform at the top of the metal stairs. It takes her eyes a moment to adjust to the dark but then she spots them, the couple on a bench beneath the only heater that's not casting a hazy orange glow. They're wrapped in each other, totally lost to the world, the blanket around their shoulders falling away as they kiss. She thinks of the way Simon smiled at her in the restaurant and the warmth of his coat against her fingers as she took his arm. She continues to stare, lost in the memory, as the couple break apart and the man reaches across the bench for a pack of cigarettes. He holds one out to the woman, then pops one into his mouth and sparks his lighter. Alice inhales sharply as his face is illuminated. She takes a step back, catching her heel on the wooden door frame. As she overbalances she feels a hand in the centre of her back, stopping her fall.

'I was wondering where you'd got to.' There's amusement in her daughter's voice. 'I told Lynne I thought you'd probably gone for a poo. Why are you outside? I thought you gave up smoking years ago?' Alice feels her daughter attempt to squeeze past her to get a better look and she twists round sharply, blocking her view.

'Let's go back in. It's freezing out there.'

'Mum, what are you doing? You look weird. What are you hiding?' As Emily pushes past, Alice watches warily as her daughter reaches the railings and looks down. She can't see her expression but from the way her spine stiffens she knows she's spotted the couple below.

'What the fuck?' Emily's howl reverberates around the small courtyard and then she's off, heels clacking on the metal steps.

'Emily, stop!' Alice hurries after. 'Emily! He's not worth it. Come back in!'

But her daughter's already reached the bench where Adam has cast off the blanket and is clambering to his feet. As she gets closer he holds out a hand to ward her off. 'It's not what you—'

Emily's outstretched hand connects with the side of his head. She hits him again, the blow glancing off his shoulder as she tries to claw the nails of her other hand into his cheek.

'Stop!' Alice shouts as Adam's shock wears off and he grips Emily's wrists. He holds her at arm's length as she twists and writhes and kicks. Laila, standing to one side, watches with her hands cupped over her mouth.

'Emily, stop it!' Alice shouts but her daughter has given up fighting and now she's screaming obscenities into her boyfriend's face.

'I can explain!' Adam shouts back. 'If you'd just fucking calm down.'

Alice steps towards him. 'Don't you swear at my daughter. Get your hands off her. Now!'

There's something in her tone that must remind him of his own mum because he immediately lets go of Emily's wrists and steps away.

'Take her home. She's embarrassing herself.'

Alice snaps round at the sound of Laila's voice but before she can respond, Emily launches herself across the courtyard. Alice throws herself at her daughter, wrapping her arms around her waist and pulling her away before her outstretched hands can tear clumps out of Laila's long, black hair extensions.

195

'You're a fucking bitch!' Emily screams as Alice hauls her away. 'You'll pay for this. I swear it. You'll both pay for this. You're a pair of cheating, lying—'

'Stop it!' Alice hisses in her ear. 'Don't stoop to their level. Walk away. You're better than this.'

Her daughter continues to shout and scream as Alice marches her up the stairs, twisting and gesturing and fighting every step they take. She's still shouting when Alice pushes her towards the door of the pub, but the moment it closes behind them she howls and bursts into tears.

They half-guide, half-carry Emily down the street, Lynne on one side and Alice on the other. It breaks Alice's heart, hearing her daughter sob so desperately. It makes her angry too, the callous way Adam spoke to her, even though he was in the wrong. There's a part of Alice that's proud of Emily for reacting the way she did. Not of the screeching and swearing, but because she let her anger erupt rather than holding it in. It couldn't have been more different to her own reaction to Peter's infidelity. When he broke the news that he was moving out because he'd met someone else she simply stared at him from the sofa, too shocked to move and too numb to speak. She made her feelings known later, ringing him up at all times of the day and night, telling him how much she hated him, demanding that he tell her the name of the woman he'd left her for, or else crying and begging him to come back. Peter being Peter, he simply ignored her calls, relaying a request to stop through their daughter instead. Emily took Alice's side of course. She told Peter that she didn't want to meet his girlfriend and never would (she finally relented after six months).

Alice meanwhile turned to wine to ease her through the pain and spent night after night searching the internet for clues as to her rival's identity, torturing herself with comparisons that she had no way of knowing were true. Peter's new love would be tall, blonde, slim and unlined. She'd be funny and witty and the best sex he'd ever had. When she did eventually work out who she was through surreptitious searches on LinkedIn and Facebook, she stared in shock at the photo of the middle-aged woman staring out from the screen. She was slimmer than Alice, that much was true, but there was nothing smooth about her face, and her hair rather than being the long, wavy blonde tresses of Alice's imagination was a short, wiry elfin cut. She'd stared at that face for a very long time, then she'd closed the laptop and knocked back the last of her wine. She didn't bother to look again.

As Emily sobs on her shoulder, she wishes she could take her daughter's pain away. She wants to tell her that it won't hurt as much as it does right now and that, one day, she'll think about Adam and not feel a thing. But not now, not today. Today all she can do is listen as her daughter asks why, over and over again, and hold her close and let her cry.

As they continue to walk down the street, drawing closer and closer to their flat, she glances across at Lynne. While the drama was playing out on the pub patio she remained at their table, guarding their things, wondering where the hell they'd both gone. She took one look at Emily's tear-stained face as they crossed the pub, scooped up the bags and coats and headed straight for the door. And she's been full of sympathetic noises and reassuring platitudes ever since. As Alice smiles at her friend there's a clattering sound behind them, like a can being kicked down the street. She turns sharply as someone, or something, darts behind a car.

'Did you hear that?'

Lynne nods, unconcerned. 'Probably a cat.'

'Someone's following us.'

They all stop walking. Even Emily stops crying and turns to

look. Alice stares at the car, heart pounding, willing a cat to slink out from behind.

'Do you—' Lynne begins but Alice silences her with a 'Sssh.'

'Mum?' Emily whispers. 'What is it? What did you see?'

Alice takes a step off the pavement and into the road. She's not going to walk directly up to the car. She's going to try and catch a glimpse of whoever's hiding behind it from the other side of the street.

'Alice!' Lynne hisses. 'What are you doing?'

Alice holds up a hand, telling her to stay where she is.

There's no one there, she tells herself as she nears the centre of the road, her gaze still fixed on the car. No one's going to hurt you. There's no one—

The vibration of her phone in her handbag makes her heart leap into her throat but before she can steady herself she spots a car travelling down the road towards her, its headlights on full beam.

'Mum!' Emily shouts. 'Get out of the road.'

But Alice is already sprinting towards her. She makes it to the pavement a good three or four seconds before—

'Stupid bitch!' Laila shouts from the passenger window as the car zooms past.

It isn't until Emily is safely tucked up in bed and Lynne's in a taxi home that Alice thinks to look at her phone. She puts down the glass of wine she's been drinking and pulls her handbag onto her lap. A new Facebook message from Ann Friend appears as she taps at the screen.

Flora can't help you, Alice. Leave Simon alone.

Chapter 34

@onthecliffedge:
I hear the Harbourside Murderer has struck again.

@MotobkeBob:
You mean someone else has got pissed and fallen into the Avon.

@onthecliffedge:
Apparently this time the victim was a security guard from the Meads shopping centre.

@DiddleyBopDee:
Maybe a shoplifter pushed him in. lol.

@lisaharte101:
That's someone's child/dad/brother you're talking about. Imagine if someone you loved went missing?

@DiddleyBopDee:
Jeez. Can't you make a joke on Twitter any more without someone jumping down your throat?

@realmadwife:
If my kid doesn't stop asking me to buy Robux EVERY SINGLE TIME he logs onto the Xbox I might disappear too. Can you swim to France from Bristol?

@refrigeratorcar:
Actually, that's an interesting thought. What if none of these men are dead and they just decided to vanish? You know, made it look like they drowned and secretly started another life somewhere else?

@MotobkeBob:
Come to think of it there's a phone box on that corner. I think it's got TARDIS written on the side.

@refrigeratorcar:
Everyone's a comedian.

@onthecliffedge:
Apart from Bob. He's just a knob.

Chapter 35

Ursula

Saturday

As usual there's no sign of Edward when Ursula gets up but there's evidence that he returned home after she went to bed: his toothbrush is damp to the touch, as is the nail brush (some days earlier she figured out that's how he knew she'd used it). And when she walks downstairs to make breakfast she can see that his wax jacket has been added to the coat rack in the hall. Stomach rumbling, she wanders into the kitchen and makes her breakfast. Out of the corner of her eye she sees a black-and-white cat slinking across the garden.

'Ha!' she says. 'No baby bird for you.'

She wasn't sure if she'd done the right thing, taking the fledgling to the animal rescue centre. She'd read all sorts on her phone about returning it to the nest or putting it somewhere out of harm's way. But Jessie, a member of staff in a green sweatshirt, took one look at the bird's manky bloodied eye and declared that Ursula had done the right thing and it would probably pull through. She'd driven back home feeling really quite happy. But as the sky outside her bedroom window began to darken, so did her mood. She couldn't get the image of Paul Wilson's face out of her mind, or the frightened look in his wife's eyes. What if he'd hurt her once he entered the house? The thought worried Ursula so much she felt sick. But what could she do? She'd rung the police and she'd given the woman her contact details.

You can't save everyone. Nath's voice was in her head when she pulled the duvet up around her chin, closed her eyes and tried to sleep.

No, but I could have saved you.

Now, toast finished, coffee drunk and everything washed up and put away, Ursula glances at her watch. It's 6.42 a.m. and there's been no knock at the door. Her parcels are normally delivered bang on time – 6.30 a.m., or near enough. They've never taken this long before. She walks to the front door, opens it and looks up and down the street. No sign of Bob's van. She remains in the doorway for another few minutes, hands crossed over her chest and rubbing her arms, shivering in the cool morning air, then steps back inside. She looks longingly at Ed's tweed jacket. She hasn't got a spare coat and the temperature's not going to creep above five degrees according to the radio. She touches the thick material, then shakes her head. It's not worth it for the amount of grief he'd give her. She'll put another sweatshirt on instead.

Five minutes later she jogs back down the stairs and takes another look outside. Still no sign of Bob and it's 6.49 a.m. She'd normally be shutting up her van and setting off by now. She takes her phone out of the pouch, considers whether or not to ring the depot, then tucks it away again. Bob's probably been caught in traffic and she doesn't want to get him into trouble. He's a nice bloke, if a bit slow.

At 7.07 a.m. she hears Ed leave his room and the sound of the shower running and reluctantly takes out her phone. Something's obviously gone wrong.

'Hello,' she says after the call connects and her boss announces her name. 'It's Ursula Andrews. Bob hasn't showed up and I'm not sure what to do. Should I come into the depot to collect today's parcels?'

There's a pause then a long, slow exhale. 'Oh,' Jackie Clowes says. 'I'm so sorry, Ursula. I meant to ring you yesterday but it completely went out of my head. Could you come in?'

'To the depot? Sure. I'll just—'

'To my office, please. We need to have a little chat.'

Now it's Ursula's turn to pause. 'We need to have a little chat' sounds ominous. Whatever Jackie needs to tell her it's not going to be good news.

'What's it about?' she asks, her heart fluttering uncomfortably in her chest.

'I'll tell you when you get here. I'll see you in half an hour or so, that sound okay?'

As offices go, Jackie Clowes's is about as bland as they get. There's a company calendar on one wall with an image of a man hiking on a mountain, a spider plant bursting out of a tiny pot and a desk with a chair on either side.

Jackie looks up at Ursula and smiles tightly.

'Thanks for coming in so quickly.' She gestures at the free chair. 'Have a seat.'

Ursula sits down, resting her feet on the floor and clasping her hands in her lap. As Jackie glances back at her computer screen Ursula shifts position, pulling her feet behind her and crossing them at the ankles, then she changes position again and crosses her legs.

'Right, so.' Jackie looks across at her. 'We haven't had a catch-up for a while. How's everything going?'

Ursula clears her throat. There's so much she could say but she doesn't think her boss would be interested in the fact that her ex-best friend threw her out for stealing, her new landlord's a weirdo and she's worried about a customer's wife who may or may not be the victim of domestic abuse. Instead she says, 'Not bad, still enjoying the job.'

'Good, good.' Jackie nods but, if she's pleased, her pleasure doesn't register on her face. 'No . . . um . . . difficult experiences or . . . customers?'

Ursula frowns. 'I'm not sure what you mean.'

'We've had . . . I've had . . . a complaint.'

'About me?'

'Afraid so. And it's quite serious. They say you've been harassing them.'

'What?' Ursula's mouth falls open.

'Obviously I'm not at liberty to disclose who the complaint came from but they mentioned that you refused to hand over a parcel and you also attempted illegal entry into their property.'

Ursula sits up straighter in her seat as the penny drops. It's come from Paul Wilson.

'It was a man, wasn't it?' she says.

'Actually it was a woman. She was quite distressed.'

'That's because her husband forced her to make the phone call. Jackie, I'm pretty sure she's a victim of domestic abuse. I even rang the police. I know I probably should have told you about it but—'

Jackie Clowes holds up a hand. 'I know about the police allegation. I also know that it didn't come to anything. It was all part of your campaign of harassment, the woman said. She also said she's been receiving unwanted phone calls from you and you've been sending taxis to her address at all times of the day and night which has caused her a great deal of distress.'

'That's not true! Check my phone. He's made her say that, the husband. Honestly, Jackie, you need to believe me. I haven't done anything wrong.'

Jackie presses her lips together and gives her a look that says, 'I really don't want to do this but . . .'

'Please, Jackie,' Ursula begs. 'Give me a different round or . . . or . . . I'll do Bath or Keynsham. I can get up earlier. I need this job. Please.'

'I'm sorry, Ursula. If this were the only complaint then I'd let it go, or at least give you a different route. But there was a second complaint, a different customer who said his parcels arrived damaged or thrown behind his wheelie bin.'

'That's not true! I've never done that. It must be Paul Wilson. He must have asked a friend to ring and—'

Jackie holds up a hand. 'I'm so sorry, Ursula. It's out of my hands.'

'It's not, though. You're the boss. You can—'

'It's in the regs.' Jackie touches a bound booklet to her left. 'Obviously your van is your own but I'm going to need your lanyard and pass.'

Ursula stares at her boss's open palm. This can't be happening. Almost every penny she had she spent on the deposit and first month's rent, and she's only got three weeks left until Edward asks for more. There's no way she can get another delivery job. Even if she got through the interview it would only take one phone call to Jackie to make them change their minds. She's going to have to join an agency and hope to God there's a job she can start straight away.

She removes the lanyard from her neck and places it into Jackie's outstretched palm without making eye contact.

*

Ursula is halfway to the Meads shopping centre when she remembers that she's been banned. With a heavy heart she takes a right rather than a left at the roundabout and heads back to South Bristol. She can't risk a trip to Mirage Fashions, not with staff and the security guard on the alert. If she's caught and they call the police, she'll end up with a fine that she won't be able to pay. Although, she thinks ruefully, if she was given a prison sentence instead at least she'd be fed three times a day and have a roof over her head.

Ten minutes later, and back in the kitchen of number fifteen William Street, she miserably surveys the contents of her food cupboard as the DJ on the radio warbles on about the latest Bristol City match and asks fans to phone in. She went food shopping the other day but there's not much to choose from: half a loaf of bread, some Heinz tomato soup, most of a packet of pasta, a KitKat, a few dry crackers and a can of corned beef. She picks up the corned beef, umming and ahhing as she turns it over in her hand. At two pounds it wasn't cheap and she had planned to buy some potatoes and onions to make a hash but sod it, she's had a shit day and if she can't go shopping to relieve her stress then a corned beef sandwich, a bowl of soup and a KitKat will have to do.

As she stands up she sniffs at the air. There's been an odd smell in the kitchen ever since she moved in. At the time she put it down to damp – Charlotte's house was riddled with it – but this is different. It's a musty, uriney smell. She opens the door to the garden to let some air in, then fits the key onto the tab of metal on the side of the can. She turns it until the lid opens to reveal the slab of processed meat, then grabs a chopping board and squeezes the tin. The corned beef doesn't budge. Sighing, she reaches for a knife from the wooden block but her favourite, the one with a long, thin blade, isn't there. She looks for it on the draining board and then in the sink but the kitchen is as pristine as normal. Other than the missing knife there isn't a single thing out of place. The knife isn't in any of the drawers or the cupboards. It can't have broken; Edward once told her how indestructible these particular knives are. He must have taken it, although God knows why. She reaches for another knife instead and slips it in between the slab of corned beef and the tin and wiggles it until the meat slips free. As she carefully slices it, making each sliver as thin as she can, the DJ stops speaking and the first notes of a song, picked out on a guitar, start to play.

Whoa, whoa, whoa, whoa.

Ursula slams her hand onto the radio as the drums kicks in and the room falls silent before Jon Bon Jovi has the chance to sing. She presses her palms onto the counter, heart pounding, breath coming in short, sharp bursts, eyes shut. But it's too late, the song's already in her head, 'Livin' on a Prayer', going round and round on a loop.

'No!' she says as faces appear behind her closed eyelids: laughing and mocking, leering at her. 'No!'

She opens her eyes again and stares out into the garden, desperately trying to remember the grounding technique that Charlotte tried to teach her the last time she had a panic attack.

'Five things,' Ursula says aloud. 'Five things I can see. I can see a patio. I can see grass. I can see a tree. I can see a cat. I can see a wall. Four . . . four things I can feel. I can feel the counter under my fingers. I can feel the tiles under my feet. I can feel air on my lips. I can feel the cold.' Her breathing slows as she slowly reconnects with her surroundings. 'Three. Three things I can hear. I can hear birdsong. I can hear a drill in the distance. I can hear . . .' She pauses, frowning as she tries to make out the third sound. 'I can hear scratching.' She turns sharply. 'I can hear scratching coming from the basement door.'

Chapter 36

Gareth

It's after 8.30 a.m. when Gareth finally picks up the phone to call his boss. He should have done so an hour ago but whenever he picked up his mobile the thought of what he was about to say made him put it back down again. But he's going to have to make the call now. If he leaves it any longer he won't have a job to return to. He sits down in his armchair, his stomach twisting at the sight of his mother's empty chair.

'Hello, Mark Whiting.' His boss's clipped tones bite at his ear.

'Hi, Mark, it's Gareth.' The words come out in a rush. 'I'm afraid I won't be in today. My mum's gone missing.'

There's a pause then, 'Oh dear. I'm really sorry to hear that. Have you been in touch with the police?'

'Yes. I rang them straight away.'

He'd rung everyone he could think of before he rang the police – Sally, Yvonne, Uncle Tony, his cousin Maureen and the hospitals – then he'd checked the landline to see if there were any missed calls (there weren't). He was sitting in the warmth of Kath's kitchen, his voice becoming more and more strained with each call. When there were no other avenues to explore he rang 999. The operator was as calm as he was anxious and asked him question after question – how old was his mum, what had happened, what was her name and date of birth, had she ever gone missing before and was the behaviour out of character? There were more questions, about what she'd been wearing, her medical condition, and where he was calling from. He'd expected the call handler to pass him on to a police station. Instead she told him that she'd circulate the details to his local unit and someone would come round.

The next hour, as he returned to his house and Kath made him umpteen cups of tea, squeezing his shoulders whenever she passed, was one of the worst of his life. Every fibre in his being told him to get up from the table and go and look for his mum but he'd been told to stay where he was in case she came back. Finally, there was a knock on the door. Two uniformed police officers introduced themselves, then ran over the questions he'd already answered on the phone. They also requested a few recent photos of his mum and then asked if they could search the house. When he asked why and was told they needed to check if his mum was hiding, it was all he could do not to cry.

When they returned to the living room carrying his mum's hairbrush ('In case we need a DNA sample,' the female officer explained) he showed them the mystery postcards and Kath, standing beside him, had gasped softly when he'd explained about his dead dad. He showed the police the CCTV footage next, pausing as Sally, then Yvonne entered and left the house, then froze the screen as his mum appeared in the frame. She was carrying a black handbag and was dressed in grey slip-on shoes, a brown dress and her best M&S red wool coat. It was for best, she'd tell him, refusing to wear it if he ever tried to get her into it for a visit to the doctor's.

The female officer took a screenshot of the image of his mum on the CCTV and reassured him that all available officers would look for her. 'Where might she have gone?' she asked. 'Any favourite places? Any relatives? Anywhere with any significance? Old addresses? Places she loved when she was younger?'

Gareth's mind went blank. It was so long since his mum had gone anywhere other than the corner shop and the post office that he couldn't think of a single place she might be. He silently remonstrated with himself. Why hadn't he talked to her more about her past while he still had the chance? He'd been so wrapped up in the day-to-day challenges of caring for her that he hadn't taken the time to just talk. It was only when the male officer discovered the memory box that he even remembered that it existed. They took it with them when they left, promising that someone would be in touch. Shortly afterwards Kath gently explained that she needed to get back to Georgia to check she was okay, apologising for leaving him alone. Then it was just Gareth, his thoughts, the silent television and the dip in his mum's favourite chair.

'Gareth? Gareth, are you still there?' The rough tones of his boss's voice snap him back into the living room and he grips the armrest, anchoring himself to the chair.

'Yes, sorry. What was that?'

'I don't suppose you've heard from Liam Dunford.'

'I'm sorry?'

'Liam. You know he's been reported as missing? The police came to see me last night.'

In the split second Gareth takes before replying he feels a rush of emotion – incredulity, frustration and, most powerfully of all, rage. How dare Mark Whiting mention Dunford in the same breath as his mother? Does he have any idea what Gareth's been through in the last thirteen hours? How terrified he was when the last of the light faded away and the world outside his window turned black? There was no way his mum would stay out after dark, no way at all. Why hadn't she come home? Was she lost? Walking in circles or heading in completely the wrong direction? Had she fallen? Was she lying somewhere unable to get up, somewhere no one could see? Whiting doesn't give a shit about any of that; he just wants to make sure his rota is filled.

'Seriously?' He takes a sharp, raggedy breath. 'I ring you to tell you that my mum's disappeared, that she's been missing all night and you ask me about that bastard?'

'I'm sorry?'

'He could be at the bottom of a lake for all I care.'

'Gareth,' Mark says slowly. 'I'm not sure I like your tone.'

'Well I don't like your tone either. My mum could be . . . she could be . . .' He presses a hand to his chest, unable to speak. But it's not acid burning beneath his ribs, it's fear.

Gareth sits at the kitchen table with his head in his hands and a rapidly cooling cup of tea in front of him. He's screwed it now, totally screwed it, not just his career but his entire life. The mortgage might be paid on the house but his mum's rapidly dwindling savings are almost gone thanks to the government deciding that anyone with more than a certain amount of money has to pay for their own carers. That just leaves him and the pitiful salary he gets as a security supervisor. Or rather, he got. He wouldn't be surprised if when the post arrives tomorrow it includes his P45.

'Oh God.' He sits back in his chair and stares at the ceiling. At some point, preferably sooner rather than later, he's going to have to ring Mark Whiting back and apologise. But not now. Whiting would enjoy hearing him grovel and he can't deal with that level of smugness, not until he's calmed down a bit.

It seems he's not the only one to lose his rag; from the high-pitched screeching coming from next door it sounds like Kath is having a battle of her own.

'I don't want to go to school!' Georgia's voice drifts through the wall swiftly followed by Kath's, 'Well you're going whether you like it or not.'

'I want to join the search for Joan.'

'You can do that when you get back from school.'

'I want to go now!'

'Stop making excuses and go to school!'

'I hate you. I hate you so much!'

Gareth raises his eyebrows. He'd never have got away with screaming at his mum like that when he was a kid. He'd have suffered a swift clip round the head followed by, 'Wait till your father gets home.'

He sits forward in his chair. Is that where his mum's gone – to look for his dad? He used to work at WD and HO Wills, a cigarette manufacturing plant in Hartcliffe, after he left the navy until it closed in 1990. Then, somewhat ironically, he worked as a hospital porter in St Michael's until he retired in 1998. But there's no factory in Hartcliffe any more. It was flattened years ago and now it's Imperial Retail Park. It's in South Bristol, a good hour's walk from the Meads and two miles from Gareth's house. It's not somewhere he's ever worked and he can't remember taking his mum there for years but, in theory, she could walk there. He stands up, phone in one hand, the small, white card the police officer gave him in the other. He should call and tell them what he's remembered. But what if the police can't get over there for another hour? It could be too late. If his mum is in the retail park she'll be confused and upset and he needs to be the one to find her, not a stranger in a uniform.

Chapter 37

Alice

Are you watching me? Alice stands at the glass double doors of the store, searching for her stalker, scanning the walkway for anyone who isn't striding around the shops. Anyone watching her is likely to be stationary, resting up against a wall or a column or sitting on a bench. She's been a nervous wreck all day. When one of the clothes racks collapsed at the start of her shift she shrieked so loudly that Lynne came running.

She still feels shaky, but not as much as she did last night when she read Ann Friend's message about Flora. Unsure what to do, she rang Lynne. Ten minutes later her best friend was at the front door.

They talked for hours, reading and rereading the messages, trying to work out who could be behind them. They drew up a list of suspects beginning with people who might hold a grudge against her: Peter, his new girlfriend, Jenna who she'd sacked, Michael, and Adam. Then they spread the net wider, writing down anyone Alice had ever had a disagreement with: the hair-dresser she'd complained about, the manager of the rival fashion chain who'd once accused her of luring away her staff, even her grumpy 'mail-stealing' neighbour on the first floor. Then they wrote down all the people that might have a problem with Simon. There were only two names on that list: Flora and the woman from Costa. With Simon refusing to answer his phone there was no way of knowing if there were more.

On Lynne's prompting Alice texted him, telling him about the latest message. She'd expected silence but he'd replied almost immediately:

Whatever you're doing, stop. It's over. Forget you ever met me.

She tried calling but he didn't pick up and when she got voicemail six times in a row she had to admit defeat.

'He must care about me,' she said to Lynne, 'or he wouldn't have replied to the text.'

'If he cared he'd pick up the fucking phone and tell you what's going on.'

By this point in the conversation it was nearly two o'clock in the morning and neither of them could see straight for tired-ness and red wine so they decided to call it a night. They argued about who should take the sofa and who should take the bed but Lynne won out and Alice dragged herself off to her room. When she got up five hours later she rang DC Mitchell to tell her what had happened the previous night but the call went to voicemail. It's nearly six hours later and she still hasn't heard back.

'Hey!' Lynne nudges her elbow, then immediately apologises as Alice jumps out of her skin. 'Sorry, but I was just wondering what to do with this?'

Alice looks at the thick winter coat she's holding towards her and shakes her head. It's not a coat they have in stock. 'What is it?'

'That shoplifter, you know Godzilla, she left it in the changing room last night. Kaisha hung it up in the staff changing room when she checked the cubicles but I'm wondering if we should just chuck it?'

'No, she might come back for it and if we've binned it she'll kick off. I can't deal with that at the moment. Could you, um . . . could you just tuck it under one of the counters? We'll keep it for a week and chuck it if she doesn't come back.'

'All right.' Lynne doesn't look convinced but she tosses the coat over her arm. 'Fancy grabbing some lunch?'

'I, um . . . I thought I might go out and get some air. Wander round a little bit.'

'Great idea. I'll just go and grab my bag.'

'No, don't. I just . . . I just need a bit of time alone.'

'I thought you didn't want to be on your own.'

'I don't, not at home, anyway. But I'm just going window-shopping. There's loads of people about. I'll be fine.'

'Yeah, and your stalker could be one of them.'

'Cheers!'

'No . . . I mean . . . I just want you to be safe.'

'I will be.' She touches a hand to Lynne's arm. 'Whoever's behind this wants me to be scared and lock myself away. But I'm not going to do that. If I want to go out, I will.'

Lynne doesn't look convinced and when Alice walks out of the shop, coat on, handbag slung across her body, her silence follows her.

As Alice walks down Broad Street she can't help but feel bad about Lynne. She doesn't like lying but if she told her where she's actually going she'd have disapproved. Both Lynne and Emily have told her over and over again that she's got to let this thing with Simon go. And maybe she should. Trying to work out what the hell's going on has given her sleepless nights and made her feel more stressed than she has in a very long time. But it's not even about Simon any more. Any feelings she had for him vanished when he chose to dump her rather than explain what was going on. No, this is about her anonymous messenger. She doesn't like the fact that someone is pulling the strings of her life. She's going to find out who they are and take back control.

The barman at the Evening Star looks up as she walks in, then reluctantly puts away his phone as she approaches the bar.

'What can I get you?'

'A gin and tonic, please.' Screw not drinking at lunchtime. She's going to need all the Dutch courage she can get.

'Anything else?' He gestures at a red-backed menu lying on the bar. 'Any food? We've got a new chef.'

'No thank you.' She's already decided that she'll grab a sandwich from Sainsbury's on her way back to work.

As the barman tips a measure of gin into a glass Alice takes her phone out of her bag. No missed calls from DC Mitchell. And no texts or messages, other than one from Emily, thanking her for looking after her last night. When her daughter got up that morning Alice took one look at her puffy eyes and pallid skin and asked if she was going to ring in sick. Emily looked appalled. 'Just because Adam's a fuckwit doesn't mean I have to miss a day's pay. I'll let him stew. Silence is the best weapon, Mum.'

She wondered if that was true. She'd been doing the opposite with Simon and it hadn't got her very far. As the barman plonks a gin and tonic in front of her, Alice pays, then carries it across to an empty table. It feels weird coming back to the bar where she first saw him but it's the nearest pub to work. Quiet too. She's not going to be overheard.

She knocks back half her drink, but the inside of her mouth dries as she taps at her phone then holds it to her ear. *He probably won't reply,* she thinks.

'Hello?' a male voice says. There's a pause, as though he's about to say something else but he falls silent instead.

'Michael, it's Alice.'

Another pause, and doubt starts to creep in. There's almost no chance he'll be able to help her, but she can't just dismiss Lynne's theory that he and Simon set this whole thing up. It's no more unreasonable than the idea that Flora would stalk her, or Peter's pregnant girlfriend suddenly decided to try and ruin her life.

'Hi,' Michael says and Alice's heart twists in her chest.

'Where are you?' she asks.

'Sorry?'

'Are you still in Spain?'

'Why? What's this about? If it's about your car I already told the police I was in Barcelona and I've got friends who—'

'I know. They told me.'

'So why are you calling?'

'Do know anyone called Simon?'

'Who?'

'Simon. He picked up my purse after . . . after you attacked me in the pub . . .'

'I'm sorry.' The words come up in a rush. 'I've got to stop you there, Alice, to say how sorry I am. I'm . . . I'm really fucking sorry. Honestly I . . . I've never, never hurt a woman in my life. I just . . . I'd been drinking since I woke up and . . . there's no excuse. I'm an alcoholic and I'm getting help. I've got some friends out here who've booked me into a place where . . . you don't need to know all the ins and outs and I'm rambling. I'm just so sorry. Really. I would have apologised earlier but the . . . the police said I should leave you alone.'

Alice says nothing as his words sink in. Instead she stares past the bar towards the corridor where Michael elbowed her at the base of her throat and then tried to kiss her. The memory, the spit glistening on his lips and the pink peak of his tongue, makes her feel sick, but she can't reconcile that lurching, aggressive man with the bumbling, apologetic voice in her ear. It's as though Michael was wearing someone else's skin that day and what happened stripped it away, revealing a stuttering mouse of man.

'I forgive you,' she says and as the words leave her mouth she feels a weight drop from her shoulders. 'Do you know him, or where he is?' she adds quickly. 'Simon? The blond-haired man who picked up my purse?'

'Simon . . . Simon . . .' Michael deliberates over the name. 'No, that's not ringing any bells. If I'm honest my memory of what happened is a bit hazy anyway but I'm pretty sure I don't know a Simon.'

'Right. Okay.' She doesn't know whether to feel disappointed or relived.

'I really am sorry.'

'I know you are.' She pauses, unsure how to end the call then simply says, 'Goodbye,' and takes the phone from her ear. She taps the screen to end the call, then reaches for her glass.

The barman coughs lightly as she takes a sip. He coughs again, louder this time.

'Sorry to eavesdrop,' he says as she glances across at him, 'but, um . . . quiet pub and all that.' He shrugs. 'Anyway, I remember you. You were here a few days ago, weren't you?'

Alice sits up straighter. 'Yes, I was.'

'The Simon you're looking for . . . was he the blonde bloke who was sitting over there with a laptop?' He points across the pub to an empty table.

'Yes, that's him.'

'Then you need to try Radio Bristol.'

'Radio Bristol?'

'On Whiteladies Road.' He spreads his hands wide on the bar.

STRANGERS

'He's called Simon Hamilton, the bloke who was sitting there. Radio Bristol DJ. Comes in occasionally to work on his stuff for his show, pranks and that. I don't think it's funny.' He shrugs again. 'But some people must do.'

Chapter 38

Ursula

Ursula walks slowly across the kitchen, her feet soundless on the tiled floor.

Scritch, scritch, scritch, scritch. The sound, like a nail being repeatedly dragged against wood, is coming from the bottom of the basement door. Ursula's knees click as she crouches down to listen. There's a pause in the scratching then, *scritch, scritch, scritch,* the noise starts up again. Pressing one hand against the wall for balance, she peers through the keyhole but it's so dark on the other side of the door that she can't see a thing.

It's just a rat, she tells herself as she backs away from the door. She looks back at the slab of corned beef lying on the chopping board and shudders. If there are rats in the basement they might be in the kitchen too. She's going to have to call Edward and ask him to get vermin control in. If the rat makes it up to her bedroom she'll . . . well, she has no idea what she'll do. Stick it out or sleep in her van; that's about as far as her options go.

Scritch, scritch, scritch.

She looks back at the door, weighing up the noise. That's no rat. There's no way little claws could make a sound that loud.

'Go away!' She stamps up and down, then grabs the knife and bangs the handle on the counter.

The scratching stops, for a second or two, then suddenly starts up again.

She turns on the radio and the chirpy, cheery voice of the presenter immediately blocks out the sound. She turns the radio off and there it is again, the continuous scratching and scraping. She stands very still, staring at the bottom of the basement door, her mind whirring. She assumed Edward had insisted on the radio being on at all times because he's one of those people who can't stand returning to a quiet house but now she's not so sure. She sniffs the air. The horrible musky smell has definitely grown stronger.

A cold chill lifts all the hairs on her forearms. A locked door. A bad smell. A missing knife. A newspaper clipping. A landlord obsessed with keeping his nails clean, who doesn't get home until late. And a radio kept on 24 hours a day to block out the noise.

No, she tells herself firmly, that would be ridiculous. There's no way Edward is keeping anyone locked in the basement, no way at all. She takes her phone out of her pocket and looks on BBC news for coverage of the three Harbourside disappearances.

There they are, the three missing men. She tries to match their photos with the black-and-white image she saw on the newspaper clipping but none of them look familiar. What if . . . her mind whirs . . . what if the photo she saw wasn't of someone that Edward had kidnapped but someone who was next on his list?

No, she tells herself firmly. There's no way Edward would have advertised for a lodger if he was keeping people prisoner in the basement. Unless . . . a shiver runs down her spine . . . unless they were previous tenants. No, no, not possible. All the missing men were walking by the harbour when they disappeared. If Edward abducted them he would have had to smuggle them into the house while she was fast asleep in her bed. It doesn't seem possible, although, looking at the dates on the website, one of the men disappeared before she moved in.

Feeling vaguely ridiculous she gets down on her hands and knees, then flattens herself against the kitchen floor, her mouth inches from the basement door.

'Hello? Can you hear me?'

The scratching stops, making her catch her breath.

'Are you . . .' She pauses. She was going to ask 'are you human?' but that's stupid. What's a rat going to do, squeak no? 'If you're imprisoned against your will, scratch the door.'

There's a beat then a *scratch, scratch, scratch* against the wood.

'Oh shit.' She breathes heavily. 'Do you need food and drink?'

Silence, then a strange *ugh, ugh* sound like someone smothering a sneeze. Ursula backs away from the door, heart pounding in her throat. That has to be a person. She's never heard an animal make a noise like that in her life.

'Shit. Shit. Shit.' She moves her thumb over the keypad of her phone.

9 – 9 –

She deliberates. What if she's wrong? What if the police come round and there isn't a man tied up in the basement? What if she's got it stupidly, ridiculously wrong and when they barge down the door they discover a rat? She'd never live it down and she's had quite enough people laugh at her in her life. She could ring the RSPCA or pest control instead? No, she can't because she's got no way of letting them into the basement. But it can't be a rat behind the locked door. And she's never heard a dog or a cat go *ugh, ugh*.

She needs to find out what's going on in the basement and she needs to do it alone. If she could just peek through the keyhole or under the door. Or—

A memory flashes in her mind as she looks towards the kitchen door. She saw a window yesterday, when she went outside to rescue the bird. It was half-hidden in the gravel against the wall of the house, the glass obscured with white paint.

Ursula kneels on the pebbles at the back of the house, a large rock that she found at the back of the garden on the ground beside her.

'Hello!' she says. 'I'm going to break the window and get you out.'

She feels stupid even as she says it; the window's sealed shut and she's pretty certain that whoever, or whatever, is in the basement won't be able to hear a thing.

'Right.' She sits back on her heels and picks up the rock. She holds it to her chest like a netball. The glass looks thick and she's going to have to throw it with some force. 'Here we go.'

Before she loses her nerve, she says, 'Three, two, one,' and then throws.

There's an almighty crash as the rock disappears through the glass, then a boom as it hits the floor. Ursula listens for a scream or a shriek or a moan. When none comes she snatches up the wooden spoon she took from the kitchen and stabs at the sharp shards of glass still embedded in the window. When the most lethal-looking pieces have fallen away she places oven gloves on both hands, carefully grips the frame and eases her head through the gap.

'Hello?' Her voice echoes around the basement. 'Hello, is there anyone there?'

It takes a while for her eyes to adjust to the gloom and at first all she can see are the stone stairs that lead up to the kitchen and a ton of cardboard boxes and then . . . she inhales sharply.

'Oh holy fuck.'

Chapter 39

Gareth

'Mum! Mum!' Gareth stands in the middle of the near-empty car park, turning in a slow, tight circle. 'Where are you?'

He remembers making the same frantic cry when he became separated from his parents during their yearly holiday to Barry Island, a seaside resort in South Wales. They were on a mission to get fish and chips, striding across the pleasure park with a distant stand in their sights. He'd jogged behind, three years old, struggling to keep up. He'd stopped in his tracks when he spotted the 'get the ball in the bottle' stall adorned with huge cuddly teddy bears, soft toy bananas and brightly coloured buckets and spades hanging in a row. He stood to one side, watching open-mouthed as another young boy tried, and failed, to land a single ping-pong ball in the wide necks of the clustered green bottles but was rewarded with a keyring anyway. Gareth turned, ready to shout to his mum for a go. Only there was no sign of his mum in her flowery summer dress and best M&S sandals, nor his dad in his knee-length navy shorts and open-necked shirt. There were just legs, so many legs. When he craned his neck to examine the faces all he saw were curious or indifferent eyes. Fear hollowed his belly as he ran, pushing through the crowds, shouting for his mum. When he saw her, in her lovely summer dress, he pulled at her skirt. A woman he didn't know turned and looked down. She had soft, kind eyes but the disappointment made Gareth burst into tears. He was eventually reunited with his parents ten or fifteen minutes later, when they burst into the lost children shack after hearing a tannoy appeal. It felt like a lifetime to three-year-old Gareth. He thought he had lost them for good.

It's 3.34 p.m. now, nearly thirty-one hours since he last saw his mum, and nearly twenty-four hours since she walked out of the house. He's looked everywhere. He's been into every shop and asked every cashier and shop assistant he could find if they've seen her. He's thrust 'Missing' posters that he knocked up on his laptop into the hands of every shopper he saw. But there's no sign of her, not in the retail park and not in the surrounding area. He ran until his lungs burned, stopped to walk, then ran again, always calling her name, alternating between 'Mum!' and 'Joan!' In three hours it will start to get dark. His mum's already been missing for one night. He can't bear the thought of her being gone for two. His only hope is that she's found some kind of shelter – an outbuilding, garage or shed. The nights have been so cold recently, dropping down to minus five. He'd struggle to sleep outside in this weather, even in a warm coat, and his mum's seventy-nine years old.

He looks at his watch again. It's 3.35 p.m. Every minute feels like an hour. He wants to keep searching. When he's driving or running or handing out flyers he feels like he's helping, that he's one street corner, one person closer to finding his mum; there's hope mixed in with his desperation. But when he's sitting at home alone, waiting, the only thing that he feels is fear.

The house is a tip. Gareth has left no drawer unopened, no wardrobe unemptied and no pocket unchecked. He started in his mum's room, searching through her possessions for something, anything, that might be a clue. But there were no answers to be found in her jewellery box, her dressing table, her wardrobe, her chest of drawers or even under the bed. There was nothing to explain where she'd gone, and as he stands in the doorway surveying the mountain of clothes on the bed, his mother's possessions scattered around the room and the two postcards lying side by side on her beside table, it's all he can do not to cry.

Was another postcard delivered? Did it tell her to go somewhere? Has she got it with her, tucked in her favourite leather handbag? But how could a postcard arrive? He checked the CCTV and no one unusual approached or entered the house. Might Sally or Yvonne be lying? Did whoever wrote the postcards cajole or blackmail one of them into bringing a third message into the house? He dismisses the thought as quickly as it pops into his mind. But *someone* convinced his mum to leave, of that he's sure.

He received a phone call from the police shortly after he returned home. The woman he spoke to said her name was Lisa Read from Avon and Somerset Constabulary, one of the sergeants on duty today. She told him that all available officers were trying to track his mum down. There was a possibility, she said, that his mum had got onto a bus and she needed Gareth to confirm if a captured CCTV image was in fact Joan. He leapt to his feet, ready to drive to the station, but Sgt Read told him that she could text him the image instead. When his phone vibrated with a new message his heart was in his throat.

'Yes,' he told her on speaker phone as he gazed down at the blurry image. 'Yes, the lady in the red coat with white hair is my mum.'

Sgt Read went on to tell him that they also had CCTV footage of his mum getting off the bus on Park Street and walking up the hill, passing several shops. But then she'd turned a corner into a street with no CCTV and disappeared. 'We're looking,' she told him. 'Right now. We're doing everything we can to find her.'

When she ended the call, Gareth fought the urge to ring her back. Why hadn't he asked her more questions – how many officers were out looking for his mum? What was the name of the street where she'd disappeared? How were they looking for her and what more could they do? The grainy image of his mum showing her bus pass to the driver had completely thrown him. It was years since she'd last got on a public bus; he drove her everywhere she needed to go, mostly to the doctor's and the dentist's for the last few years as well as the odd day trip. He didn't even know where her bus pass was; he'd never had to look for it. It had probably been in her handbag, along with the other bits and bobs that she hadn't used for years.

He closes the door to her bedroom. He'll tidy everything up after he's had a cup of tea. As he heads into the kitchen a loud rapping on the front door makes him clutch the counter in alarm. It's the police. They've found something. He heads into the hallway with his heart in his mouth.

But it's not a pair of police officers standing on the path beyond his front door. It's Kath, holding a Pyrex dish, with Georgia behind her, red-eyed and kicking at the ground. The food smells of mince and there's melted cheese and slices of tomato on top. Gareth's stomach rumbles. He can't remember the last time he had something to eat.

'Can we come in?' Kath asks, her bright tone a stark contrast to her daughter's expression. 'I've brought dinner. It's lasagne. I don't imagine you've been eating well.'

'Thank you. That's very kind.' He stands back to let her in. Georgia doesn't so much as look at him as she trails behind her mum, clutching a bag of salad, but she mutters, 'thanks', under her breath as she passes.

A few minutes later they're all congregated around the small kitchen table with plates, knives and forks and glasses of water in front of them; Gareth's apologised for the lack of soft drinks.

Kath looks across at him, wielding a serving spoon. 'Big portion, Gareth?' As their eyes meet she sniggers. 'Sorry.'

'Mum, that's gross,' Georgia mutters, her face stony.

Gareth smiles, for what feels like the first time in days. 'I'd love a large portion please, Kath.'

She ladles a hefty slice of lasagne onto a plate then gestures to the bowl of salad in the centre of the table. 'Help yourself. Georgia, how much do you want?'

'I'm not hungry.' Her daughter pulls the sleeves of her jumper over her hands, then buries them in her lap.

'Come on. You need to eat something. Just a little bit, and some of that salad.' Kath hands her a plate. 'Right, that's me done. Enjoy folks!'

Gareth gratefully forks a mouthful of meat and pasta into his mouth. He tries not to stare at Georgia, who's sullenly pushing a piece of lettuce around her plate with her fork.

'Ignore her,' Kath mouths across the table. 'Bullies.'

Gareth nods then eats another mouthful of lasagne. It's really quite good.

'So,' Kath says. 'Any updates?'

Her eyes soften as she listens to his reply. She rests her fork on the side of her plate as he tells her about the last phone called he received from Sgt Read.

'Well that's good, isn't it?' she says. 'That they know where she got off the bus? It'll help narrow down the search.'

'Yeah,' he says wishing he could match her hopeful smile. Beyond the kitchen window the sun is starting to sink in the sky. In another hour or so it'll be gone.

Kath catches him looking. 'They'll find her. Someone's bound to have seen her. Her photo's all over social media.'

'Is it? I didn't know.'

'Excuse me.' Georgia's chair scrapes against the floor tiles as she pushes herself back from the table. 'I'm just going to the toilet.'

Neither Gareth nor Kath say a word as she leaves the room. Kath waits until the stairs stop creaking then gets up and shuts the kitchen door.

'I don't know what to do,' she says, taking her seat again. 'Things at her school are unbearable. I spoke to her form tutor today and she says there's a rumour going around that a group of girls – the bullies – are trying to get Georgia to bunk off after registration to go on the rob.'

Gareth can't imagine a group of teenaged girls breaking into people's houses. He's completely lost touch with the world.

'Shoplifting,' Kath clarifies. 'At the Meads, where you work.'

'Right.' He sits up taller in his chair. He can't do anything to help Kath and Georgia with school matters but if these kids are trawling round the Meads he could. 'Have you got photos of them? These girls? I could keep an eye out the next time I'm monitoring the CCTV.'

'No, I haven't. I've asked Georgia to tell me their Instagram handles but she won't. And I can't look through hers either because it's private.'

'Ah. The teacher didn't tell you their names?'

'I wish. It's all "the other parties" this and "certain individuals" that. I don't know what they think I'd do if they gave me their names. It's not like I'm going to cosh them over the back of the heads when they leave school for the day.' She laughs dryly. 'As much as I'd like to!'

'Could you take her out of school?'

'What? And have her moping around all day, popping her head into my beauty room whenever she gets bored? Mum can I have a tenner? Mum can I buy this app? Mum, can I use your fake tan? I wouldn't mind if she actually wanted to talk to me about stuff but it's like she thinks I've got limitless funds. Sorry,' she says, 'I didn't mean to come over here to have a moan.'

'It's fine.' Gareth reaches across the table to touch the back of her hand then thinks better of it and turns the movement into a strange, sideways bend instead. 'We all need to talk.'

His words sound empty, even as he says them. He looks back towards the kitchen window and the darkening sky and sighs, the voice of his three-year-old self echoing around his head.

Chapter 40

Alice

Alice has never known an afternoon at work to go as slowly as this one. The shop was busy when she returned from the pub but there was no way she could face serving on the tills, smiling sweetly and asking customers if they'd found everything they wanted. Lynne, folding a customer's jumper and sliding it into a bag, spotted her walk in. Alice gave her a tight smile and a nod hello, but instead of going over for a chat, slipped past the counter and went into the staff changing room out the back. She hung up her coat then went into her office, pulled down the blinds and took out her phone. She read all the texts Simon had sent her, then read them again with a keener eye. There was nothing in what he's written to suggest that their relationship, as brief as it was, was a practical joke. What kind of sick joke would that be anyway, leading a woman on, then scaring her half out of her mind? She's certain he's not behind the creepy Facebook messages – he'd have to be a complete sociopath to do something like that – but he did lie to her about his job. She looked him up on the BBC Radio Bristol website while she was in the pub and there he was, all blonde hair, wonky face and beaming smile. No wonder he'd responded, 'I've heard that before,' when she told him in Costa that he had a nice voice. Whatever he was up to he wasn't working as a DJ now, not according to the note at the bottom of the webpage:

Simon Hamilton is currently taking a break from presenting. Everyone at BBC Radio Bristol wishes him well.

What else has he lied to her about? Did Flora even exist?

A sharp knock on the office door makes Alice hurriedly drop her phone into her lap. She angles herself in front of her computer screen, then says, 'Yes. Come in!'

'Just me.' Lynne pops her head round the door. 'We've cashed up, shutters are down and Larry's gone home. You coming?'

'Yeah. Just give me a second.' As she shuts down her computer she can feel her friend studying her face. She forces herself to smile and looks across at her. 'Are you okay?'

Lynne steps into her office, pulling the door shut behind her. 'I was going to ask you the same thing. Did something happen at lunchtime? You've been hiding away in here all afternoon.'

'Look at this.' Alice unlocks her phone and hands it to her.

'What is— Oh!' Lynne raises her eyebrows. 'Is that . . . is that your Simon?'

Alice nods.

'I thought he told you he worked in insurance.'

'He did.'

'So he lied?'

'Yep.'

'Maybe he was sacked from the radio station and had to take another job?'

'In insurance?'

'Good point. But why would he take a break from presenting?'

233

'Maybe he's ill.' The thought suddenly occurs to her. It would explain a lot. Maybe he lied to her about what he did for a living because he was battling cancer and didn't want her sympathy. Maybe the text message in the cinema had something to do with that? But it was late at night and she can't imagine any doctor breaking bad news via text. Her first thought when Simon pulled her out of the cinema was that it was a family emergency. Maybe he was caring for a sick relative or he'd suffered a bereavement? Whatever it was he could have told her. She's not a child.

'What are you going to do?' Lynne asks.

Alice meets her friend's eyes. 'I'm going to find out the truth.'

'Just be careful. I don't think it's a coincidence that whenever you try and get in touch with Simon, something horrible happens.'

Alice doesn't make the call to Simon with Lynne in the office. Instead she waits until all her staff have left through the back door, then she locks up and takes the stairs to the car park. It's almost empty and her heels click-clack on the concrete, the sound echoing off the walls. She walks quickly, scanning the dozen or so parked cars, checking they're all empty, Lynne's warning still ringing in her ears.

By the time she reaches her car she's breathing in short, sharp bursts. She does one final sweep of the car park before she opens her door and gets in. No one's followed her and no one's watching. No one she's spotted anyway.

Keeping one eye on the rear-view mirror she takes out her phone and calls Simon's number. It goes straight to voicemail. Surprise, surprise.

'Simon, it's Alice again. I know you told me not to ring you or contact you again but we need to talk. I know you don't work in insurance. I know you're a radio presenter. I know why you've taken time off work.' She pauses after the lie. 'Do you know the Red Lion, the gastropub in Kingswood? I'll be waiting there for you at eight o'clock tonight. Meet me and I promise once we've spoken I'll never contact you again.'

Alice fidgets in her seat, rising to smooth her skirt over her bottom before she sits down again. She reaches for her lemonade, takes a sip, then sets it back down. It's 8.32 p.m. and she's on her second glass. She would have switched to the jug of tap water after she finished the first but when the waiter came over to ask if anyone would be joining her she felt so flustered she ordered a second. Simon still hasn't replied to her voicemail and embarrassment and regret are setting in. She shouldn't have come. When she got home Emily was sitting at the kitchen table, still in her work clothes, with an open bottle of wine in front of her, one glass already gone.

'I've saved you some,' she said. 'I thought we could order a pizza and watch that film on Netflix everyone's been talking about. I just wanted to say thanks for looking after me last night.'

Alice felt torn. Her daughter needed her. Emily would never say as much but it was there: in the forced enthusiasm in her voice and the tightness of her smile. If she went out Emily would finish the whole bottle, stalk Adam and Laila on social media and do something she regretted. Either that or cry herself to sleep. Sod Simon, Alice thought as she gave her daughter a hug. She'd already wasted too much of her life trying to figure him out and she was done with the weird messages and subtle threats. Did it *really* matter if she never found out who'd sent them? Let the freak who scratched her car think they'd won.

As she changed out of her uniform in her room she found herself looking forward to a night in front of the TV with a pizza and a bottle of wine. It was months since she'd done that with Emily – long before Michael and Simon had entered her life and Adam had slid into her daughter's DMs. The only drama of the evening would be in the film they watched and that was perfectly okay with her. When she walked back out of her bedroom, phone in hand ready to order the pizza, she found Emily in the hallway, pulling on her boots.

'You don't mind if we do film night another night? Amy just texted asking if I wanted to go to the pub with her and Jo. It's been ages since I saw them and—' She screwed up her face in apology. 'Sorry, Mum. Do you mind?'

Of course Alice didn't mind. She was pleased that Emily was going to spend time with her friends. She might just have a pizza and wine night all by herself. That was something she hadn't done in a while either. But after Emily left, and she scrolled through the options on the pizza app, her thoughts drifted back to Simon. What if he showed up at the Red Lion and she wasn't there? She might miss out on her only chance to find out what was going on. She wrestled with herself for a few moments, then made a decision. She'd go to the pub to meet him. And if he wasn't there, she'd never contact him again.

It's 8.36 p.m. and there's still no sign of Simon. Alice opens her purse and takes out enough money to pay for the lemonade. She's hungry and she's pissed off and she's going home. She scans the room for the waiter to ask for the bill, then inhales sharply as the door opens and Simon steps into the pub.

'Alice?' He walks up to her table, his hands in his pockets and a wary expression on his face.

'You made it then.' The steely tone in her voice surprises her. She'd expected to feel relieved to see him, maybe even pleased, but all she feels is a sharp stab of irritation as he pulls out a chair and sits down.

'Yeah. I'm sorry I'm late.'

'I can't say I'm surprised.'

'I'm sorry.' He meets her eyes. He's got a good three or four days of stubble on his chin and his skin looks patchy and dry. 'For everything. I'm guessing someone at the station told you what's been going on.'

'Yes,' she lies.

'I was only ever trying to protect you.'

'Protect me!' She's surprised to hear herself laugh.

'They were threatening to hurt you, Alice. If I ever saw you again.'

'They?'

'Whoever's been stalking me.'

'It's not your ex then?'

'No.' He shakes his head. 'It's got nothing to do with Flora.'

She stares at him open-mouthed. 'Then why mention her when I asked you over dinner if there was anyone who'd try to put me off you?'

'Because . . .' His gaze drifts to the table. 'Because she's the only person I've ever really hurt.'

'But it's not her?'

'No.'

'Then who's stalking you?'

He raises his eyes to look at her. 'It could be half of Bristol for all I know.'

Alice listens intently, elbows on the table, leaning towards Simon as he tells her in hushed tones about his old job as a radio presenter and the pranks he used to play – ringing up Subway to say he was trapped on the tube, ringing hotels to say he was on the toilet in room 211 and didn't have any toilet paper, ringing random numbers and pretending to be a mobile phone operator testing the volume levels on their phone by making them say increasingly nonsensical phrases.

'It was all light-hearted stuff,' he says. 'The listeners loved it. They were always emailing to tell me how much it made them laugh or to give me new ideas. Of course, I'd get the odd email telling me I was cruel, but they were in the minority.'

'And then what happened?' Alice asks.

'And then . . . then someone tried to destroy my life.'

He tells her about the stalker who has made his life a misery for the last three months; about the anonymous letters he received at the station telling him that he's not the big man he thinks he is; the Twitter abuse; the photos of him going about his day-to-day business posted on social media; the texts telling him to kill himself; and the emails to the radio station manager accusing him of paedophilia and rape and demanding his job. He tells her how, after one particularly vicious text, he was too scared to leave his house for three days. When Alice asks whether he contacted the police he smiles tightly and reels off the same advice she was given by DC Mitchell after she reported the damage to her car: keep a record of everything, vary your routine, tell friends and family what's going on etc., etc. The police are actively investigating, he tells her, but they've got no leads.

'That's why you freaked out, isn't it?' she says. 'When that woman recognised you in Costa. You thought she was your stalker?'

'Yeah. Being on the radio not many people recognise me and when she launched herself at me like that I . . .' He tails off and shrugs.

'Why didn't you tell me any of this?'

'I didn't want to scare you.' Simon rubs his hands over his face. 'I know, I know . . . it was the wrong thing to do.'

'The wrong thing? Simon, you let me believe that I had a stalker but it was *you* they were after. Why the hell didn't you tell me? We had so many conversations – in person and on the phone.'

'Yes,' he says, 'yes we did. But I didn't want to come across as a victim. I didn't want to be that person any more. I liked how I felt when I was with you. I felt like the old me. I felt . . . normal.'

'Great, bully for you. So you let me freak out instead? Wow. You're . . . you're quite something.'

'I'm sorry, Alice. I know apologising isn't enough but—'

'Who did you ring in the restaurant?' she snaps. 'After I showed you the Facebook messages?'

He sighs. 'The detective in charge of my case.'

'And you didn't think to tell me then? Or after we found my car?'

'I know. I know.' He rubs the back of his neck, unable to meet her eyes. 'I just . . . I dunno. I thought it would scare you off.'

She stares at him incredulously. She could have been – still could be – in danger and Simon still didn't tell her about his stalker. Not because he was protecting her, but because *he* didn't want to feel like a victim any more.

'I realised,' he says, 'that I had to stop seeing you when I got the message in the cinema. I know . . . I should have told you about it but I didn't want you to be scared. I thought the best thing to do was to cut off all contact so the stalker would leave you alone.'

'What did it say? The message?'

He sits back in his chair, craning his neck to look at the diners. When he turns back to Alice there's fear in his eyes. 'I don't even know who I'm looking for. They could be old, young, male or female, and the police are as clueless as me.'

Alice shifts in her seat, suddenly aware of an elderly couple at the next table looking at her and Simon and whispering between themselves.

'Simon! What did the text say?'

He shakes his head. 'It wasn't a text. It was a Facebook message.'

'Tell me what it said!'

'You really want to know?'

'Yes.' She glances at his mobile on the table in front of him. 'Yes, I do.'

'Okay.' He unlocks the phone, then slides it towards her.

She looks at him, searching his grey eyes, then glances down at the screen. Same blank profile photo. Same name, Ann Friend.

Are you enjoying the film, Simon? Nice blue skirt your girlfriend is wearing tonight. Her hair looks lovely. It smells great too.

Chapter 41

Ursula

Ursula is lying on her bed, staring at the ceiling, her fingers interlocked behind her head. Whenever she closes her eyes she sees ferrets, dozens of them, twisting and jumping around the cellar, zipping in and out of plastic tubes and digging into pieces of old carpet. When the glass in the basement window smashed they all darted from sight, scurrying backwards and hiding in tubes, squeaking and shrieking in fright. As she watched through the broken pane they slowly crept out again and resumed their play, neatly avoiding the shards of glass scattered all over the floor.

Ferrets. Why hadn't Ed told her instead of being all mysterious about the locked basement door? She can't stop thinking about the glass, scattered over the ferrets' play area. It would only take one of them scooting frantically backwards to end up with a shard in its foot. There was no way she could sweep it out of their way; a broom wouldn't reach down that far, she couldn't fit through the small window, and with the basement door locked there was no other way in. As she tried to decide what to do, a white ferret, larger than the others, darted up the stone steps and scratched at the bottom of the kitchen door.

Bloody ferrets. She would have understood if Ed had told her about his pets. Why on earth didn't he just say?

A sharp knock at her bedroom door makes her sit up sharply.

'Coming,' she says, heart thumping as she swings her legs off the bed.

Ed is every bit as angry as she expected him to be. His face is flushed red, from his cheeks to the base of his neck.

'I take it that was you,' he says. 'The smashed basement window.'

Ursula drops her gaze, a muscle twitching in her cheek. 'I'm sorry, I—'

'What the hell were you thinking?'

A droplet of spittle lands on her chin and she raises a hand to wipe it away. 'I heard a noise, in the basement and—'

'So you thought you'd smash your way in? Jesus Christ, what's wrong with you? Ever heard of one of these?' He raises his mobile and thrusts it towards her face.

'I . . . I . . .' She doesn't know what to say. I thought you had men locked down there?

'You could have killed them! I've had some of those ferrets for nearly ten years. Do you think I like keeping them in the basement like that? If I had my way they'd have the run of the house, but for some reason this country has fucked-up, arcane rules about keeping pets in rental properties so instead I have keep them hidden away in case the landlord drops in. It's not good for them, being deprived of sunlight like that.'

'You should have told me. Then I wouldn't—'

Ed lifts his hand and, for one horrible moment, she thinks he's going to hit her. Instead he runs it through his hair. 'Why couldn't you just do what I told you? Three rules, that's all you had to keep. Three . . . little . . . rules.'

'I'm sorry,' Ursula says again. 'Please, Ed. Let me make it up to you. I'll, um . . . I'll tidy up. I'll make you dinner for a week. I'll—'

'Make it up to me?' He laughs in her face. 'How? By rooting through the drawers? By using my things? By damaging the fixtures and fittings?' He presses a hand to the door frame and the latch she installed. 'Oh, and I'd like my dart back please, the one you stole from downstairs.'

'I haven't got it. I . . . I did but it was in my coat pocket and I've lost it. My coat I mean. I lost my coat.'

'And now you've lost your room.'

'What?'

'You heard me. I want you out on Monday. You can pack tomorrow.'

'But I've got nowhere to go. I've got no money. And I lost my job this morning.'

'Not my problem. And don't even think about reporting me to the letting agency for subletting or keeping pets because I'm moving on too. My ferrets aren't safe in the basement any more. I've had to lock them in their cage.'

Ursula's lips part but no sound comes out. There's no point arguing or begging for her deposit back. She's massively screwed up. Again. It's as simple as that.

It's just after 1 a.m. and Ursula is sitting on her bed, looking around her room. When, she wonders, did her life become so small? *Why*, she keeps asking herself. *Why* does she keep fucking up? She had a nice home with Charlotte but she screwed that up by stealing and now she's going to have to move out of Ed's

243

place too because she couldn't leave well enough alone. She's got no money, no job and, after tonight, nowhere to sleep. She's also got nowhere to turn. Her dad's dead and her mum lives in Spain with the stepdad she can't stand. There was a time, when Ursula was at university studying to become a primary school teacher, when there were loads of people she could have turned to, but they've all fallen away over the years. How does that happen, she wonders. How does someone's world shrink until there are only a handful of people left in it? She had Nathan. She had Charlotte. And that was enough for her. She loved them and they loved her. But Nathan is gone and Charlotte hasn't responded to any of the texts Ursula has sent apologising for what happened and begging to meet up.

She looks down at the framed photograph in her hands and runs a finger over Nathan's cheek.

'Help me,' she says. 'Tell me what to do.'

She waits for his voice, for those familiar warm, loving tones that she holds in her head, but all she can hear is the panicky beat of her pulse in her ears. It was the same sound she heard when she thought someone was trying to get out of the basement, the same frantic pounding she felt in her throat when Nicki fell down the stairs. It was the same sound . . .

She squeezes her eyes shut as the memory consumes her and in an instant she's walking towards the exit of the Wellington pub in the centre of Bristol, hand in hand with Nathan. It's Friday night, the barman has called last orders but the speakers are still pumping out music – Bon Jovi's 'Livin' on a Prayer'. She and Nath are both pleasantly drunk. They're chatting about which kebab shop to visit before they go home and Nathan's reaching for the door handle. It's hot in the pub and Ursula's already imagining the sweet relief of the cool night air on her face.

'Taking your kid for a walk are you?' The words cut through

the pounding music and Ursula feels Nathan's hand tighten in hers. She turns her head. There's a large group of lads sitting at a table to their right.

'Ignore them,' she hisses.

'What was that?' Nathan turns towards the lads.

'I was talking to your bird.' A bald bloke, early thirties with tattoos poking out of the sleeves of his polo shirt, raises his chin in Ursula's direction. 'Who's wearing the heels? You or her?'

There's a chorus of laughter and two of the men reach across the table to high-five each other. Ursula pulls on Nathan's hand again. They've heard every possible comment about their height difference since they got together and normally her boyfriend would ignore them or shrug them off, but he's had a hard day at work. One of the kids he was looking after in the paediatric unit at St Michael's developed an infection and had a cardiac arrest and died. It's taken her the best part of three hours to lighten his mood.

'Who's wearing the heels, mate?' Nathan asks. 'Your missus was – when I bent her over your kitchen table.'

There's a flurry of movement as the bald bloke jumps to his feet, knocking the table and showering his mates with beer. 'Say that again!' he roars. 'Say it again, you little runt.'

The barman shouts something about calming down but all Ursula can hear is the blood pounding in her ears as she tugs at the door handle and pulls her boyfriend after her. 'Nathan, come on!'

Somehow she manages to get him out of the door but then she feels his grip loosen and his hand fall away.

'Nathan!' She pulls on his arm as the bald bloke and his four mates pile out of the pub but Nathan doesn't move an inch.

'I'm not running,' he says.

'Please!' She pulls on his arm again. 'Please! They're not worth it.'

She's never seen him like this before, rigid with anger, clenching his teeth. He's not a fighter. He's never shown the slightest hint of aggression, towards her or anyone else.

The bald bloke gets the first punch in. It connects with Nathan's jaw and he reels backwards. Ursula screams but Nathan doesn't hit the floor. Instead he regains his balance and swings round, landing a blow on the bald lad's cheek. There's a pause, a split second where Ursula sucks in the cold night air, and she prays that it's over, that two punches are enough, but then one of the other lads leaps forwards, smacking Nathan on the side of the head. Then there's no time to think or hope or pray because the others leap in too and there's arms and fists and blood and rage and Nathan's dark head disappears as he's punched and kicked and thumped to the ground. And now Ursula's scream fills her ears as she launches herself at the mass of torsos and limbs, shoving and pushing, desperately searching for Nathan's hand or foot, his shoulder or his leg, anything she can latch onto to pull him away. She doesn't see it coming, the blow that lands on the side of her head, that makes her brain rattle in her skull and her ear explode. Then she's toppling and dropping, palms scraping against the hard concrete of the pavement, her bare knees taking the brunt of the fall. She feels rough hands in her hair, yanking her back up, then Nathan shouting, screaming at her to go. And she twists and she fights and she claws at the man that's holding her and when she's finally free she scrabbles to her feet and she runs.

Chapter 42

Gareth

Sunday

Gareth is on his third cup of coffee of the morning when there's a sharp double rap on the front door. He jumps, slopping coffee onto the kitchen table and hurries out into the hall. As he gets closer to the front door he sees two shapes beyond the mottled glass and his heart leaps into his throat. If the police want to speak to him face to face it has to be bad news.

He yanks open the front door and searches the faces of the man and woman standing on his front step. He doesn't recognise either of them. The tightness in his belly increases as they stare expressionlessly back.

'Is it . . . is it Mum?' he asks.

The man on the left, dressed in slacks and a navy-blue jumper with a white shirt collar peeking beneath the neckline, flashes a badge at him. 'DC Forbes from Avon and Somerset Constabulary. This is DC Merriott. Are you Gareth Filer?'

'I am, yes.'

'We'd like you to come into the station for a chat please.'

Gareth goes cold. He'd rather they just broke the news. He doesn't want to sit in a police car for ten or fifteen minutes, fearing the worst. 'Just tell me.'

The detective looks puzzled. 'Tell you what?'

'My mum. You've found her, haven't you? Is she dead? Is that why you're here?'

The detective still appears to have no idea what he's talking about.

'My mum's name is Joan Filer,' Gareth clarifies. 'She's a vulnerable missing person. She's been missing since Friday afternoon. Lisa Read is the officer I've been in touch with.'

The detective glances at his colleague, who frowns and lightly shakes her head. Neither of them have the slightest idea what he's on about.

'Right.' DC Forbes regains his composure with a quick clear of his throat. 'I see. I'm very sorry to hear that, but we're here about a different matter. Liam Dunford has gone missing and our enquiries suggest that you know something about his disappearance. We would like you to come to the police station with us so that we can interview you formally. You're not being arrested but you can have a solicitor during the interview if you want one. Your attendance at the station is purely voluntary.'

Gareth stares at him, a thousand thoughts whirling through his head as he tries to make sense of what he just heard.

'I, um . . . I . . . Okay, but I can't be long.'

'You do not have to say anything but it may harm your defence if you do not mention when questioned something which you later rely on in court. Anything you do say may be given in evidence.'

Gareth stares at the detective, feeling progressively more scared the longer he speaks.

'Am I . . . am I under arrest?'

The detective shakes his head. 'As we explained back at your house you're here voluntarily to answer some questions. You are free to leave and stop the interview at any time. You may also have a solicitor present if you wish.'

'Then why say all that? All the stuff about evidence if I'm not under arrest?'

'It's part of the interview.'

'I'm definitely not under arrest?'

'No, you're not.' The female detective sitting on the right of DC Forbes gives Gareth a look like he's missing a few brain cells.

Gareth feels like a fool. He's watched hours of police dramas on the TV but now he's the one in the small, grey room with a black digital device recording every word he says, he feels completely wrong-footed. Worse than that, he feels like a criminal and he hasn't done anything wrong. In a different universe he'd be the one sitting on the other side of the table, the one asking the questions, the one in control.

'Is it too late to ask for a solicitor?' he asks, then instantly regrets it when he catches the look exchanged between the two detectives.

DC Merriott puts her pen to her notepad and looks up at him from under her thick blonde fringe. 'Sure. We can delay the interview until he turns up. Name and number?'

'I haven't got one. I've . . . I've never needed one, apart from when Mum drew up her will.' His cheeks start to burn with shame. They're looking at him like he's an idiot and he's not. He's just a normal bloke. He's never broken the law in his life.

'We could get a duty solicitor in for you,' DC Merriott says.

'How long would that take?'

'Maybe half an hour, maybe more.'

'Then no.' Gareth shakes his head decisively. 'I don't want one. I want this over as quickly as possible. My mum's missing. I need to get home.'

'Okay then.' DC Forbes glances down at his pad. 'So, tell us about your relationship with Liam Dunford.'

'We're colleagues. Well, I'm his superior, but I didn't recruit him. Mark Whiting did that.'

'You're security guards, is that right? At the Meads shopping centre in Bristol.'

'Security officers,' Gareth corrects him. 'But basically, yeah. That's right.'

'And how would you describe your relationship?'

Gareth considers the question. 'Professional,' he says, after a pause.

'Professional, right.' DC Forbes scribbles something on his pad, then glances up. 'Any issues, arguments, that sort of thing?'

Gareth sits very still. He knows his body language is being scrutinised for any sign of discomfort or guilt and, despite the overwhelming urge to rub the back of his neck, he doesn't move a muscle.

'No more than with anyone else,' he says.

'So there were disagreements then? It's normal, isn't it, in a work environment? We can't get on with everyone we meet.' DC Merriott smiles encouragingly at him.

'As I said, no more than with anyone else.'

'Right.' DC Forbes presses his lips together. 'Then why would you say to your boss, Mark Whiting, and I quote, "He could be at the bottom of a lake for all I care"?'

Gareth sits forward in his seat, resting his elbows on the table, then remembers his decision not to move a muscle and sits back sharply again. 'Because my mum had just disappeared and Mark was asking where Liam was. Right then I couldn't have given two shits.'

'Understandable. Totally understandable.'

Gareth watches the detective's hand move over his pad. He can't read a word he's writing and they still haven't told him what's happened to Liam, other than the fact that he's missing. Is he dead? Do they think someone murdered him? His heart beats fast. Do they think he did it? Do they think he killed him and dumped him in a lake?

'So,' the female detective says, 'tell me, Gareth, why would Liam tell his friends that he was blackmailing you?'

Gareth's jaw drops and his mind goes completely blank. 'I'm . . . s . . . sorry what?' he stutters.

'When interviewed about his disappearance, Liam's friends told us that he said . . .' she glances down at her notes ' . . . he had you wrapped around his little finger. Those were their exact words. Why would he say something like that, do you think?'

'He . . .' The word catches in Gareth's dry throat. He wets his lips with his tongue, then reaches for the plastic cup of water on the table and takes a sip. As he drinks he weighs up the question. If he denies that Liam was blackmailing him they'll know he's lying. If he tells them the truth they'll have the motive they need.

'Is he dead?' He sets his cup back down, his gaze flitting between the detectives. This time it's their body language he's trying to read.

The detectives exchange a glance, then DC Forbes meets his steady stare.

'Why don't you tell us?'

Gareth leaves the police station on shaky legs, his back slick with sweat. He glances over his shoulder as he descends the concrete steps. He can't shake the feeling that, at any moment, Detective Sergeants Forbes and Merriott will come flying out of the black, glossy door and haul him back in. There was a point in his interview, as he explained why Liam was blackmailing him, where he felt certain he was never going to leave that claustrophobic grey room ever again, a belief that was reinforced when DC Forbes asked him where he'd been between 2 a.m. and 4 a.m. on Thursday 28th March. He was at home asleep, he told them, his throat desert dry. No, he admitted when asked, there was no one who could confirm his alibi but the CCTV above the front door would show that he hadn't left the house. DC Forbes raised an eyebrow. 'Not via the front door, anyway.'

When DC Merriott announced there would be no further questions for now and turned off the digital recorder it was all Gareth could do not to slump over the table and cry. Instead he sat rigidly in his seat, his hands on his thighs, and asked if he could leave. He followed the two police officers through the labyrinthine corridors in a daze, feeling as though he'd been transported into another world. Was Liam dead? He still didn't know. All he wanted was to get the hell out of that building and run all the way home.

But he doesn't run. Instead he walks slowly out of the shadow of the station and into the weak March sunshine. He walks on autopilot, crossing the road, turning left, turning right, not knowing or caring where he's going. Only when the police station is no longer in sight do his legs give way. He sinks down onto a low wall outside a chip shop and slumps forwards, his elbows on his knees. Then he rests his head in his hands and he closes his eyes.

Chapter 43

Alice

Monday

Wherever Alice goes in the store, and whatever she does, she can feel the weight of Lynne's gaze resting on her shoulders.

It was Lynne she turned to on Saturday, after she said goodbye to Simon in the car park of the Red Lion. It was an awkward parting. A lot of the anger she'd felt earlier in the evening, when she'd had a go at him for not telling her about his stalker, had dissipated but she couldn't bring herself to give him a hug. She had too much she needed to process. Instead, as they hovered outside the pub door, she raised a hand and pointed across the car park towards her VW Golf and said, 'That's my car. I'll be in touch.'

As she sat in the car and watched Simon drive away she deliberated about who to ring. She didn't want to worry Emily, not when she was on a night out with her friends trying to forget what a bastard Adam had been, and Lynne, being Lynne, was only too happy to chat. She drove to her house and they sat in the lounge, clutching mugs of tea, Lynne listening intently as Alice told her everything that had happened. When she got to the bit about the cinema Lynne clamped one hand to her mouth and stared at her with disbelieving eyes.

'They didn't . . . the stalker . . . they didn't really sniff your hair?'

Alice shook her head. 'There were a couple of young girls sitting behind us. We're pretty sure it had nothing to do with them. But it freaked Simon out so much he thought we should leave.'

'And that's why he dumped you? Because he thought his stalker was going to hurt you?'

'That's what he said.'

'Aren't the police doing anything?'

'He's reported it but they haven't got a clue who's behind it. Whoever's been stalking him has been careful to cover their tracks.'

'Shit.' Lynne put down her cup and rubbed at her arms, her gaze drifting towards the closed curtains at the windows. 'That's scary.'

'I've freaked you out.'

'No, it's not that. It's just . . . it's one thing to be stalked by someone you know, but to have no idea at all . . . it could be anyone, anyone you meet on the street.'

'Exactly. I think that was part of the reason he was so cagey with me when I asked him about his job. For all he knew the stalker could have been me.'

'So what are you going to do?'

Alice gave her a long look. 'I'm going to help him find out who's doing this. We're going to set a trap.'

Now, as she unpacks the new stock in the back room and hangs the dresses, shirts and jumpers on a rail, she mentally rehearses the plan to catch Simon's stalker. When she left Lynne's and arrived home a little after midnight Emily was curled up on the sofa under a blanket watching *Gogglebox* on demand.

She laughed as Alice walked in, then peeled back the blanket so she could sit down. 'Dirty stop-out! I got home over an hour ago. What time do you call this?'

For the second time that evening Alice recounted her conversation with Simon, her daughter's eyes growing bigger and bigger as she told her about the plan that they'd made.

'I can't believe he's letting you go along with that. It could be dangerous, Mum.'

'How is it dangerous? We'll be in a public restaurant.'

'What if the stalker's got a knife? They could do way worse than sniff your hair.'

To be fair to Simon, he said no, straight away, when Alice suggested laying a trap. It was too dangerous, he said, and there was no way he was going to agree to her setting herself up as bait. She explained that it wasn't just about him any more. Now she was going to be looking over her shoulder too, regardless of whether she saw him again. If either of them were ever going to move on with their lives they had to find out who the stalker was. Her plan was for Simon to reactivate his social media with a tweet saying he was taking his date to a certain restaurant in town. Alice would arrive early, sit at the back and take photos of everyone who walked in. When Simon arrived, she'd be able to show him the photos to see if he recognised anyone.

'That's a shit plan,' Emily said. 'Whoever spotted you going into the cinema and knew you were wearing a blue skirt, could have been anywhere. They could have been on a bench or in the car park, or they might have been in the lounge area of the cinema drinking coffee. Same when your car was scratched. They weren't necessarily in the restaurant, were they? But they knew where you'd parked.'

'Oh.' Alice felt deflated. 'Lynne thought it was a good plan.'

'Lynne agrees with everything you say, Mum.'

'So? What's the alternative?'

'Look, if you were right and someone was following us home from the pub the other night then he, or she, knows where we live. And that's where we lure them. Simon should put a post on his Twitter account saying he's looking forward to a romantic dinner at his girlfriend's house. I'll go and speak to Helen across the street, explain what's going on, and ask if I can camp out in their front bedroom for the night. If anyone does hang around our house or park up their car I'll take photos with my phone. Then we show them to Simon, and if he doesn't recognise them, we take them to the police.'

'What if the stalker tries to break in?'

'Into our flat? Good luck with that on the second floor!'

'Okay then, what if they don't show up at all and just send another message?'

Emily grinned. 'They'll come, because Simon's going to tweet something that will really wind them up.'

Now Alice glances at her watch. Seven hours until he comes to the shop to pick her up. She wonders if their hello will be as awkward as their goodbye was last night. She's not angry with him any more, not like she was in the pub. She understands why he cut off all contact with her, but her feelings have definitely shifted. She wants to help him, not rip off his clothes and drag him to bed. As she hangs another pale pink jumper on the rack and pulls off the plastic dust jacket, she wonders what they'll talk about in her house and whether it would be a better idea to put on a film instead.

Nothing violent, she thinks as she reaches into the cardboard box for another pink jumper. Something funny. Something that won't make them jump out of their skins if they hear a noise.

Chapter 44

Ursula

Ursula barely recognises the woman staring back at her from the mirror: her eyes are so swollen they look like two hard-boiled eggs, covered with a red, shiny skin. She spent all of Sunday hidden away in her room, packing and crying. The force of her grief for Nathan, and the life that they'd shared, was as raw and as powerful as the day she'd sat with Barry and Pearl in a pastel-painted room, clutching hands, barely breathing as they waited for news. The brain damage Nathan had suffered as a result of the attack was irreversible, the consultant told them. His battered body was being kept alive with machines and tubes and he would never regain consciousness. Never open his eyes. Never speak. Never smile. The man she'd loved was gone, and no matter how much she prayed, bargained or raged, he was never coming back.

She remembers kissing Nathan on the lips, she remembers the rough callous on the side of his thumb, she remembers Pearl's soft sob and then . . . nothing, no memory at all. It is as though the grief that raged through her scorched her neurons, as well as her heart. Her brain would not remember, it wouldn't make her live through that kind of pain again. Somehow she made it to the funeral, with Charlotte beside her, pale-faced and red-eyed as they walked hand in hand up the aisle, the grief-etched faces around them a blur. When Nathan's coffin was brought in, Ursula doubled over, a fist pressed to her solar plexus as the air left her lungs. She felt Charlotte's hand around her waist and a soft shushing sound and then . . . then . . . her brain shut down again. As the congregation sat and stood, listened and sung, she kept her eyes fixed on one single shiny brass handle on the coffin that held the man she loved.

It's not real.

She stared at the shiny brass handle.

Albi it is.

You're not in there.

I am.

Push the lid off. Get out.

Albi, I love you.

She stared at the shiny brass handle.

This isn't happening. It's not real.

Afterwards, as she followed Nathan's coffin out of the church, she'd trailed a hand along the slim table near the door. She ran her fingertips over the soft leather of hymn books and orders of service, the words embossed in gold. She stroked pamphlets and booklets and A4 sheets advertising fayres and bring and buy sales. Then her fingers moved over something different, something solid and jewelled rather than smooth and cool. It was a broken brooch in the shape of a flower, one petal snapped off. It had been abandoned by its owner, maybe because it was broken, or perhaps a cleaner had found it by a prayer cushion and put it on the side. Either way Ursula closed her hand around it and carried it, the first thing she'd ever stolen, out of the dark chapel and into the cool brightness of the churchyard. She transferred it to her pocket as the procession moved to Nathan's plot and, as the coffin was lowered, she pressed her thumb pad into the sharp brooch pin. Then she pressed it again and again and again.

A soft, tinging sound snaps Ursula away from her reflection and she hurries out of the bathroom and back to her room. Is it Charlotte? She texted her late last night begging for her room back. There was no reply by the time she passed out, but maybe Charlotte was asleep or she wanted some time to think.

Ursula snatches her phone up from the bed. Missed call from a Bristol number, but not one she recognises. Jackie? she thinks hopefully. Maybe they're busy and she wants her to come back to work. She hits the button to call voicemail then presses the phone to her ear.

It isn't Jackie's voice that speaks breathily into her ear.

'I'm sorry,' the woman gasps between sobs. 'I'm so sorry. He made me do it. I couldn't say no. He threatened to hurt . . . he said he'd hurt Bess if I didn't. But he . . . he . . . please . . . I don't know who else to call . . . please, I'm sorry. Please help me before he comes back.'

As the call ends, Ursula is already halfway down the stairs with her keys in her hand.

All the curtains are drawn at the windows of number six The Crest but when Ursula taps lightly on the glass, one of them is yanked back so sharply she jumps. Nicki stares out at her but it's not the same pale, wan face Ursula saw the day before. This face is a riot of colours: mottled red on the cheekbones, one eye, squeezed shut, a deep black and purple, a yellow bloom across the bridge of the nose.

Ursula presses a hand to her mouth as she looks from the woman to the child in her arms. Dressed in a nappy and clinging to her mother's neck, the child's back is exposed. Dotted on either side of her spine are dozens of dark bruises and there's a deep red bite mark at the top of her thigh.

'Open the window!' Ursula slaps a hand against the glass, then instantly regrets it as Nicki's face pinches with fear and she backs away, disappearing into the gloom of the darkened room.

Ursula tries the door handle but it's locked. 'Nicki, can you open the door? Have you got the key?'

Nicki shakes her head but she's not looking at Ursula, she's looking beyond her, her eyes darting this way and that. Ursula snaps round, arms raised, muscles tensed. If this is another trap she's not going to let Paul intimidate her again. But there's no one behind her and when she runs back down the steps to the gate there are no men in any of the parked cars.

'I'm going to ring the police.' She takes her phone out of her back pocket as she returns to the house, but before she can get it to her ear, Nicki slams a hand against the glass. 'No,' she mouths. 'No, no, no.'

Ursula's heart is pounding so hard she feels like her chest might burst. 'Hospital,' she says.

Nicki shakes her head and waggles her hand frantically, signalling for Ursula to leave. Whatever drove her to beg for help has been replaced with a fear so powerful she can't move.

Ursula points at the baby. 'Hospital,' she says again.

Nicki's demeanour changes. If fear made her rigid then love collapses her and she folds herself around the child and buries her face in Bess's dark, curly hair.

Ursula taps gently on the base of the window, then waggles a forefinger at the handle on the other side of the glass.

Nicki glances at it.

You can do this, Ursula urges. You can escape.

She can see Nicki wrestling with the decision, looking from the child to the window, looking back into the house and then outside. The last time Ursula came to this house, the front door was open. Nicki could have slid back the security chain and walked straight out but she didn't because it's not a door or a window holding her prisoner. It's something far stronger than either of those things.

Ursula wants to look over her shoulder, to check that Paul Wilson isn't silently sneaking up behind her. She resists the urge. She knows instinctively that if she shows the slightest hint of fear Nicki will snatch back the curtain and never come out.

'Nicki.' She touches the glass again. 'Nicki open the window.'

For one terrible second, as Nicki bends at the waist, Ursula thinks she's going to pull the curtain closed. Instead she whips a blanket off the sofa and wraps it around the child. She shifts the baby further up her shoulder, reaches for the handle and pushes the window open.

As she drives, Ursula snatches glances at Nicki, sitting in the passenger seat with the baby in her arms. Nicki hasn't said a word in the last ten minutes. There was a moment, after she passed the child through the open living room window, when Ursula worried that she was going to remain inside. But then she hooked a leg over the sill and clambered out.

'Are you okay, Nicki?' she asks.

She nods but the terrified look on her face remains.

'Have you got anywhere you can go?' Ursula asks. 'After you've seen a doctor?'

A small, sharp shake of the head.

'No family, friends?'

'No.'

'Me neither,' Ursula says. 'I'd let you stay with me but I'm being kicked out today.'

'How come?'

'It's a long story. Basically I fucked up.'

There's a pause, a shift of the atmosphere but Nicki doesn't say a word and Ursula keeps her eyes on the road as she navigates her way through the mess of roadworks and fused traffic lanes in the centre of Bristol.

'I fucked up too,' Nicki says as Ursula swings the van off the roundabout onto Victoria Street.

'How come?'

'I let him talk me into leaving Gloucester after Bess was born.'

A pause hangs in the air as Ursula ponders what to say next. Every question she thinks of feels loaded. She needs to be careful. One wrong word and she'll frighten her passenger into running the moment she parks up. She's got to get her to a doctor. Her and the child. She couldn't live with herself if Nicki lost her nerve and went back to Paul.

'Do you have family there?' she asks. 'In Gloucester?'

'My mum and my sister.' The tension at the edges of Nicki's eyes softens, just the tiniest bit. 'Bess doesn't even know who they are.'

Regret diffuses through the cab like perfume. It's a scent Ursula knows only too well.

'There's someone I care for,' Ursula says softly as they cross Bristol Bridge, 'that I haven't seen in a very long time.'

'How come?' Nicki asks as the child in her arms squirms and moans. The little girl is still dressed in a nappy and blanket. Neither Nicki nor Ursula wanted to waste time at the house looking for clothes.

Ursula rolls down her window and inhales a deep lungful of cold, traffic-fumed air. No one ever asked her why she ran back into the pub. Not the landlord. Not the police. Not Pearl. Nathan was on the floor outside, being kicked and punched to death – of course she'd go to get help, that's what everyone thought.

But what if she'd stayed? What if she'd remained outside and fought? Some of the blows rained down on Nathan would have been turned on her instead. Twelve. Ten. Six. Four. One. What if one blow was the difference between life and death? What if the kick that shook his brain from his skull had been aimed at her instead?

She loved Nathan's mum Pearl. She was the kind of mum that Ursula had always longed for – supportive, kind, complimentary and loving. She'd been grateful to sit beside her in the family room in the hospital and later, at Nathan's funeral. Not because she gained any comfort from the physical proximity but because it meant she didn't have to look her in the eye. If Ursula had just been braver her son might not be dead. As much as she wishes she could rewind time, she can't. But she can help Nicki and Bess now.

Chapter 45

Gareth

Gareth is hanging his mum's clothes back up in the wardrobe when his phone rings. He snatches it up from the bed, registers a Bristol number that he doesn't recognise, and presses the mobile to his ear.

'Hello? Who is this?'

There's a pause then he hears a deep, rattling cough. 'It's Tony. Has there been any word on your mum?"

Gareth drops down onto the bed then relays the latest police update about her getting the bus to Park Street. 'Can you think of anywhere nearby she might have been heading?' he asks. 'Anywhere with special significance to her or Dad?'

As Tony considers the question, Gareth stares at his mum's slippers, tucked under the wardrobe, and mentally urges his uncle to remember something, anything, that might help.

'No, sorry, mate.' There's a sag in his uncle's voice. 'I haven't got the first clue, but your auntie Ruth might.'

'Ruth? I thought she was in the hospital.'

'She is. There's where I'm at now. She's not well – paralaysed down her right side and having trouble talking and eating and whatnot, but your cousin Maureen says you're welcome to pop in and see her. Don't tell Ruth that Joanie's missing though; Maureen doesn't want her upset.'

As Gareth scans the faces of the largely elderly patients on the Acute Stroke Ward he realises that he doesn't have the first clue what Auntie Ruth looks like, or his cousin Maureen. After what feels like an age, he spots an old bloke with a ruddy face waving at him from the corner of the room and hurries over.

Tony presses a finger to his lips as Gareth begins to say hello. An old lady with a mop of white curly hair and heavily lined cheeks is fast asleep in the bed.

'She's sleeping,' Tony whispers. 'I said I'd sit with her for a bit while Maureen goes to get a cup of tea.'

'Okay, no worries.' Gareth slips into the seat beside him and casts his eyes over the aunt he's never met. He can't tell if Ruth shares his mum's cornflower-blue eyes but there's a similarity in the shape of their noses and the hue of their skin. Neither woman is very tall but his mum is weightier, carrying her fat around her belly and under her chin.

Tony taps him on the back of the hand. 'You doing okay?'

'Yes,' he says instinctively, then shakes his head. 'No. I'm not. I'm worried sick.'

'How long's it been now?'

'Too long.'

'She'll be okay. We Halpins are made of stern stuff.'

He considers whether or not to tell Tony what happened at the police station earlier. He still can't quite believe that he was interviewed under caution about Liam's disappearance. Couldn't you hate a bloke's guts without wanting him dead?

He sits back in his plastic chair and crosses his arms over his chest. No, he decides, he won't share what happened. Tony's a gossip and it'll spread through South Bristol before he even gets home. Gareth shifts in his chair, sitting forward with his hands on his knees. It's as though his body has completely forgotten how to be at rest. He sneaks another look at his auntie Ruth. Would it be out of order to feign a coughing fit to wake her up?

He stands up, ignoring Uncle Tony's questioning look. He needs a walk, to stretch his legs while he waits. Was it a David Attenborough documentary he once saw that said sharks have to keep moving or they die? At least if he's moving he won't feel like he's completely wasting his time. He strolls down to the end of the ward then, aware of a nurse watching him, strolls all the way back. He stands at the end of Ruth's bed, arms crossed over his chest. He's just about to ask Tony how long she's been asleep when he spots something on the side table at the top of the bed.

There are two silver-framed photos angled towards Ruth. Gareth picks one up, holds it out at arm's length and squints. It's some kind of bright party scene with balloons and banners. 'Is this her family?' he asks Tony.

'That was taken at Ruth and Martin's 40th wedding anniversary. That's them with the kids – Maureen, Grant and Keith. Don't bother asking what the grandkids are called. I haven't got a clue.'

Gareth puts it back down and reaches for the other photo, of three kids playing in a garden. Unlike the multicoloured party photo this one is sepia-toned and faded. He can make out a weeping willow and a greenhouse in the corner of the photo, but when he tries to focus in on the faded faces of the kids his long-sightedness gives him three little beige blobs instead.

'Tony.' He walks back to his uncle and holds out a hand. 'I don't suppose you've got any reading glasses?'

'Sure.' His uncle fumbles in his inside pocket then snaps open a glasses case.

Gareth puts on the specs then looks back down at the photo. He blinks, his brain struggling to process what he's seeing. There's a girl sitting cross-legged on the grass playing with a doll, but that's not the child he can't stop staring at. He's transfixed by the taller girl with the blonde hair, pushing a wheelbarrow holding a dark-haired little boy.

'Georgia?'

He hears the creak of Tony's chair as he stands up, then feels the weight of his uncle's body pressing into him as he looks over his shoulder at the photo.

'Who's Georgia? That's your mum there, with the dolly.' Tony traces a bitten fingernail over the glass. 'And that's me in the wheelbarrow. And that tall one with the long blonde hair, that's our Ruth.'

As Gareth stares at the photo he hears DC Forbes's voice ringing in his ears: 'Not via the front door, anyway.'

The second postcard wasn't posted through the letter box. It came through the unlocked back door.

'Gareth!' Kath calls as he jogs down the path to the school gates where she's waiting for him. 'Gareth what's going on?'

He touches a hand to her elbow and angles her towards the reception of Pero's Academy. The playground is deserted and his voice rings out on the quiet South Bristol street. 'We need to find Georgia.'

She shakes him off. 'Not until you tell me what's going on.'

He stares at her, trying to work out why she's so angry. All he said when he rang was, 'Where's Georgia?' After she told him she was at drama club at school he stuttered, 'I'll meet you there,' and hung up. Maybe it's because he didn't answer the phone when she rang him back. He could hear his mobile ringing in his coat pocket as he sprinted down the corridors of the hospital and out into the car park, but he didn't stop to answer it. He didn't have time to talk; he had to get across town.

'Gareth!' Kath says again. 'What's going on? I thought Georgia had been in an accident or something. You scared me half to death. She's fine by the way. She sent me a text.'

'I need to talk to her.'

'Why? What's going on?'

'I worked it out,' he gasps. 'When you came round with the lasagne yesterday, Georgia knew where our toilet was without asking but she's never been in our house before. At least that's what I thought.'

'What?'

'I think she's been coming round to see Mum after school, climbing over your fence and going in the back door. Georgia looks just like my auntie Ruth when she was a little girl and . . . Kath, we need to find your daughter. I think she knows where Mum's gone.'

'Could you sit down please and let me speak to Georgia's mum.'

Jane, the woman behind the counter in the school office shoots Gareth daggers and points to three royal-blue padded chairs on the other side of the room. Reluctantly, Gareth does as he's told. He's already tried twice to explain why it's imperative that Georgia Curwen is taken out of drama club immediately. And twice he's been told to sit down.

He sits forward in his seat, forearms on his knees, all his attention focused on Kath in her black beautician's tunic and white slacks, but he can't hear a word she's saying. As he watches, Kath gestures several times towards the door to their right, a door that leads into the school, and to Georgia. Only one person – a teacher probably, from the lanyard around her neck – has walked through it in the last five minutes.

STRANGERS

The school office woman shakes her head and points a finger at her screen. Whatever Kath just asked her, the answer is no. Gareth takes his phone out of his pocket. No texts or emails from Sgt Read and no update about his mum on the Avon and Somerset Constabulary Facebook page either. His thumb hovers over Sgt Read's contact number. If the police turned up he's pretty certain they'd get him into the school.

He turns his head as the locked door opens and a woman and a small figure in an oversized navy uniform walk into reception. But the girl, chin down, fingers fiddling with the hem of her blazer, isn't Georgia. He's never seen her before.

He moves to stand up, then slumps back as Kath shoots him a look. She speaks to the woman for several minutes, then crouches so her eyeline is the same as the girl's and asks her a question. Gareth strains to listen but Jane is banging away at her keyboard, making it hard for him to hear.

'What?' Kath's sharp tone cut through the noise. 'She's gone where?'

As the girl shrinks even further into herself, Kath stands up and glares at the women in the school office. 'If anything's happened to my daughter . . . This is a school, for God's sake. You're supposed to keep her safe!'

Chapter 46

Ursula

Ursula stares at her belongings, piled up against one wall of her bedroom. She's not thinking about how many trips up and down the stairs it will take her to load them into her van or where she'll go once she's all packed up. She's thinking about Nicki, sitting on the hard plastic chair in the curtain-lined hospital cubicle with Bess on her knee. She's thinking about the grave face of the doctor as she removed the blanket from the child's shoulders. She's thinking about the way Nicki crumpled when Bess was taken out of her arms and the tears that squeezed through her blue-black eyes.

'Please don't take her off me. Please, please.'

Ursula crouched beside her, one arm round her shoulder, as the doctor gently explained that she wasn't taking Bess anywhere, she just needed to examine her.

'I should have . . . I should have . . .' Nicki didn't take her eyes off her daughter for one second as the doctor laid her on the bed and ran her fingers over the child's arms, legs and spine. 'He could have killed her and I . . . I . . .'

Ursula squeezed Nicki's hand as she rocked back and forth on the chair. 'It wasn't your fault. Nicki, look at me. It wasn't your fault. She's safe now. They're going to look after her. It's over. You're both safe.'

She stayed with Nicki and Bess until a uniformed police officer and a woman called Laura from Social Services turned up. Ursula spoke to them outside the curtained cubicle and told them all she knew. All the while, her mobile was buzzing in her pocket. When she finally checked it, when Laura was talking to Nicki alone, there were five text messages from Ed:

Please don't leave any food stuff in the kitchen.

Please ensure you take your possessions only.

Any theft or additional damage done to the property will be reported to the police.

After you leave, lock the front door and post the keys through the letter box.

I want you out by the time I get back at 7p.m. If you're not out by then you'll find your stuff in the front garden.

Seven o'clock. That was in less than two hours' time. She didn't know what to do. She wanted to stay with Nicki but everything she owned was in the back bedroom of number fifteen William Street and she knew Ed would make good on his threat. She was going to have to go. When she broke the news to Nicki she braced herself for tears, or worse, but Nicki simply nodded.

'Thank you,' she said, 'for everything.'

A look passed between the two women. No more words were needed. Nicki's soft smile said more than enough.

Now, Ursula wipes the tears from her cheeks with the heels of her hands and forces herself up and off her bed. Nicki's safe. Bess is safe. Now she's got to look after herself. She reaches for one of the black bags lying against the wall and hauls it over her shoulder, then grabs a suitcase with her free hand. She makes it halfway across the room when the doorbell rings.

'Bollocks.' She drops her things and hurries down the stairs. The postman hasn't delivered a single thing for her since she moved in and if a charity collector is expecting her to give them money she'll laugh in their face.

'Hel—' The second half of the word catches in her throat as she opens the door and Paul Wilson stares back.

'Where is she?'

One moment Ursula is standing by the front door, the next she's stumbling backwards down the hall as she's shoved hard in the chest. She puts a hand out to the wall to stop herself from falling and feels a sharp pain in her ring finger as her fingernail catches and rips clean off.

'Where are they?' Paul kicks the door shut behind him. 'Where's Nicki? Where's my kid?'

'They're not here.' Her heel catches against the bottom step of the stairs and she falls, her cocyx grazing the hard wooden step. In a heartbeat she's moving again, frantically scrabbling backwards, socks slipping against the carpet as she tries to get back on her feet. As she half-runs, half-crawls up the stairs she can hear Paul behind her, breathing heavily, each step a weighty creak.

She makes it through the door of her bedroom, then something – a hand or a fist – hits her squarely between the shoulder blades and she's knocked clean off her feet. Her fingertips graze her mattress, then her knees hit the carpet with a thud.

'Where is she, Ursula?' His hand wraps around her face and something papery is pressed into her eyes and her nose. 'I found your little note by the phone.'

His hand releases her and she opens her eyes. The piece of

paper she gave Nicki with her name, phone number and address is lying crumpled on top of the mattress. Less than six inches away from it is her mobile.

'Oh no you don't.' Her head jerks back as Paul yanks at her hair and when she glances back at the mattress her phone is gone. 'Where's . . . my . . . fucking . . . family?'

He shoves the back of her head so she's bent over the bed, her face pressed into the rough, dusty mattress. She twists and she flails, palms pressed against the bed as she tries to lever herself away from him, to get her head from under his hand, but his fingers are threaded through her hair and no matter which way she moves, she can't escape.

'Where'd you take them? The police station? Her mum's? To a fucking *shelter*?'

Ursula tries to think of something, anything, she can say to stop him from repeatedly bashing her face into the mattress but the waves of pain coursing from her scalp to her shoulders have paralysed her brain and all she can do is screw her eyes tightly shut and wait for it to end.

'Or are they here?'

His fingers loosen in her hair and the pressure on the back of her head suddenly lifts.

'Is that why you're not talking? Have you hidden them away?'

She hears the creak of a floorboard but she remains bent over the bed, her nose pressed into the grubby cotton. He's playing with her. If she speaks or turns or moves, he'll attack her again. She begins to count in her head:

One.

Two.

Three.

She hears another creak, then another, then the clack of a leather-soled shoe hitting wooden boards. He's left the bedroom. He's walking along the landing, whistling softly to himself.

She jumps at the sound of a door slamming open. He's reached the bathroom. He's looking inside.

She slowly lifts her face from the mattress, her skin pulsing and throbbing. She's got two options: lock herself in the bedroom, or run for it. But the padlock is on the other side of the door and she's doesn't trust the thin safety catch to keep her safe. Run, then. If Paul's passed the bathroom she could make it. She could slip out of her room before he can catch her, peg it down the stairs and out the front door. She needs to go now, while she still can.

She grips the mattress and slowly, slowly rocks back from her knees to her feet. She eases herself up, teeth gritted as she pulls herself up to her full height. She listens, all the muscles in her body tight, primed, ready to run.

Silence.

She pivots slowly so she's facing the open bedroom door.

Why has Paul stopped walking? Where is he? She holds herself very still, listening, trying to work out where he is. She can feel him, sense him in the shallow air she's sucking into her lungs. He's still on the top floor of the house, he's not far away.

The muscles in the back of her knees loosen as she stares through the open doorway to the top of the stairs and she feels herself sag. What if she doesn't get away? What if he grabs her as she leaves the room? What if he pushes her down the stairs? She looks back at the window. She could get there before him. She might even be able to open it and scream. But then what? He could kill her before anyone had time to get help.

'You.' She turns sharply to find Paul in the doorway with a knife in his right hand. He crooks the index finger of his other hand. 'Come with me.'

'Last chance,' Paul says as Ursula crouches down where she's been told to sit, in the small gap between the doorway to

Edward's room and the banister that runs along the landing. 'Where's the key?'

She shakes her head. 'It's not my room, I told you.'

He takes a step back, hands raised. 'We'll see.'

Ursula squeezes her elbows closer to her waist, presses her chin into her chest and cradles her head in her hands. She braces herself for impact.

SMACK!

Paul's foot makes contact with Ed's bedroom door. She feels the wall shake behind her, but the door holds.

SMACK!

Paul kicks it again.

SMACK!

SMACK!

SMACK!

She hears the sound of wood splintering and wonders if the noise is carrying out to the street. Even if it does, she can't imagine anyone calling the police.

As Paul continues to kick at Ed's bedroom door she tries to work out what to do. Once he's in he'll realise that Nicki and Bess aren't there and he'll turn his attention back to her. There's no way she's going to tell him that she took them to the hospital. Should she lie? Tell him she took them to a shelter? No, he'd want her to take him there. The police, she decides, she should tell him she took them to a police station instead.

SMACK!

SMACK!

SMACK!

She sees one of Paul's black shoes move towards her through the crook of her elbow. He's stopped kicking and he's breathing heavily, puffing through his nose. When he grunts she looks up sharply and her arms fall away from her knees as she prepares to defend herself. But Paul's not interested in her. He's pressed up against the door, one arm reaching through a gap in the splintered wood, the other hand hanging loosely by his side, still clutching the knife. It's close enough that Ursula could reach up and grab it. But then what? Even if she could get it out from his fingers she's pinned between the banister and his legs.

'Fucking yes.' There's the clicking sound of a lock being turned and Ursula puts her hands on the floorboards, ready to scrabble to her feet.

Paul steps away from her as he pushes open the door to Ed's room. There's one second, two seconds, three seconds of silence then.

'What the fucking hell is that?'

As Paul steps inside Edward's bedroom, Ursula slowly uncurls. She could run. If she takes off now she might be able to make it down the stairs and to the front door before he caught up with her, but she might not. And he's still got the knife. The door to her bedroom is ajar. She might be able to cross the landing to her room before Paul caught up with her, but then what? Even if she put the safety chain across he'd kick his way in. She stands up slowly, tensing as the floorboards creak under her weight, then risks a glance to her right, into Ed's room. She can see a window, a chest of drawers and Paul, standing in the centre of the room with the knife hanging limp in his right hand. He's staring, mouth agape, at something on the wall. Something she can't see.

Paul senses her watching and turns his head sharply. Ursula tenses, preparing to run, but then she sees the expression on his face. His eyes flick back towards the wall, but not for more than a split second before his gaze returns to her face. Whatever is on that wall has unnerved him.

'Who are you?' he asks.

STRANGERS

When Ursula doesn't immediately reply, Paul wipes his palms on his suit trousers then drags his gaze away from her and turns on the spot, slowly surveying Ed's room.

'What is it?' he asks. 'Some kind of undercover operation? Surveillance?'

The urge to step into the room and discover for herself what's on the wall is more than Ursula can bear but she doesn't move a muscle. She doesn't trust what she's seeing, this sudden emotional switch. He's faking fear. He's trying to lure her into Edward's room so he can hurt her. There's no way he's going to leave the house until she's told him where Nikki and Bess are.

'Is it all a ruse?' Paul asks. 'The courier thing?'

A small frown buries itself between Ursula's eyebrows as she tries to follow his line of thought. What does he think is going on in Edward's bedroom and who does he think she is?

'Why aren't you saying anything?' Paul says. He moves over to the window and looks outside. 'You got backup coming or something? The rest of your team?'

And *then* Ursula understands. He thinks the house is a front for an undercover operation. That's why he's sweating and rubbing his hands together. He thinks he just assaulted a police officer. He's absolutely shitting himself. Things could go two ways now. He'll either kill her – if she's dead she can't 'report him' – or he'll run. Her gut instinct tells her that he'll run – he's a coward at heart – but what if she's wrong?

She doesn't give herself time for second guesses. Instead she pulls up to her full six foot three and takes a step into the room, her heart thundering in her chest. As she does she catches a glimpse of the wall and a gasp catches in her throat. She smothers it with a cough and Paul, still at the window, turns.

'Paul Wilson,' Ursula says, 'I am arresting you on suspicion of actual bodily harm. You do not have to say anything but—'

She doesn't get to finish the rest of the sentence. As Paul rushes towards her she takes a step to her left, giving him just enough space to get through the doorway, then she turns and watches as he sprints across the landing, down the stairs and through the open front door.

Chapter 47

Alice

Alice has given up trying to hide the fact that she's using her phone. Since Lynne came into the stockroom earlier she's had Kaisha and Lauren both wander in too. Kaisha wanted to ask about holiday entitlement and Lauren had a query about a skirt a customer had seen online. Even Larry the security guard popped in to tell her that the area manager had arrived – he was 'in the area and wanted a chat' apparently – and he'd shown him to her office.

Since lunch Alice has received three texts: one from Emily telling her that Helen opposite has agreed to let her camp out in her front bedroom for the evening and she's looking forward to playing detective while enjoying a nice bottle of wine, and two texts from Simon. One saying he'd meet her at the shop at closing time, the other saying he'd reinstated his Twitter account. She checked it immediately and found his most recent tweet pinned at the top:

Looking forward to a lovely night in at my girlfriend's house. And if anyone thinks I'm doing anything else THEY'RE NOT LISTENING.

The last part of the tweet took Alice aback. It was Emily's idea, to get a reaction out of the stalker. Hardly subtle. But subtle wasn't the point. The point was to drive Simon's stalker out of the darkness and she was pretty sure the tweet was going to do just that.

It had certainly garnered some attention. There were already tons of replies – most of them expressing relief that he was still alive or tweeting they were glad he was back, a good half-dozen asking who his girlfriend was and one or two telling him not to shout. Alice went through every profile and took a screenshot. She was pretty sure Simon's stalker wouldn't bother to comment publicly, but actually doing something rather than speculating wildly helped dampen her nerves.

It's been five minutes since Larry popped in but if their area manager, James Malone, is going to turn up so late in the day and couldn't be bothered to give her advance notice then he can bloody well wait. He'll probably tell her it's a 'courtesy call' when what he's actually doing is turning up unannounced to try and catch her out. Well, her store's running like clockwork – almost all of the new stock is out, the shop floor is tidy, profits are up and staff absences are down. With any luck Lynne will have made him a coffee. She might deny it, but Alice knows she's always had a crush on the man.

She looks at her watch. Simon's due any minute. There's only a couple of minutes until the shutters need to come down at the front of the shop and she still needs to check the store's empty and the cashing up's been done. As Alice leaves the store-room and steps out onto the shop floor she frowns. There's no sign of Lynne. Probably in her office, batting her eyelashes at James Malone and hanging onto his every word.

'Is it all right if I go?' Kaisha steps out from behind the counter. 'Lauren's already gone and it's my mum's birthday today and I told my sister I'd be round at hers straight after work.'

'Course.' Alice waves a hand towards the back of the store. 'Go out the back entrance, would you, though? I'm about to close up.'

'No worries.' Kaisha flashes her a smile and scurries off as Alice heads over to Larry, who's standing by the glass doors with his hands clasped behind his back.

'You can get off too.'

'You sure?' He glances up at the metal shutters. They've been lowered to the top of the door to dissuade any stragglers from popping in.

'Yeah. Course. See you tomorrow.'

She remains by the door as Larry shuffles off towards the back of the shop. She scans the foyer outside for Simon. He's really cutting it fine and her area manager is still waiting patiently for her to join him in the back office. She reaches into her pocket to check her phone just in case Simon's sent a last minute text but her mobile's not there. She must have left it in the back room. Sighing, she casts an eye over the shop. Lynne's obviously been through all the racks because everything looks neat and tidy, although that bloody broken rail is still hanging on for its life. She'd have chucked it weeks ago but head office still haven't sent her a replacement. Actually, that's something she's going to have a word with James Malone about. He'd be the first one to point a finger if it injured a customer so he can bloody well get on the case.

'Excuse me?' Alice nearly jumps out of her skin as someone taps her on the shoulder.

'Jesus Christ!' She stares up at the hefty woman in a sweat-stained top standing beside her. Where the hell did she come from?

'I was sitting over there, waiting for you,' the woman says, as though reading her mind. She points across the store to where the shoe racks and padded poufs are hidden behind racks of clothes. 'I need to talk to you about something.'

Alice takes a step back. There's something about the intense look in the woman's eyes that's unsettling. She's staring at her as though—

'Oh, for God's sake. It's you.' She runs a hand through her hair as she places the woman's face. It's the shoplifter who was staring at her in the cinema. What the hell was Larry thinking, letting her in?

'Right, I know why you're here.' Alice stalks over to the sales counter, ducks down, then pulls a large bag from underneath it. She thrusts it at the woman. 'There's your coat. You can go now.'

The woman frowns as she looks into the bag and pulls out the contents. 'Thanks, but that's . . . that's not why—'

The sound of trainers squealing on tiles makes Alice look towards the foyer. But it's not Simon that comes hightailing it round the corner. It's a short man with a goatee beard and a blonde woman in a beautician's uniform.

'Don't shut the shop!' the man shouts as they draw closer. 'Gareth Filer, security. You need to let us in.'

'Woah!' Alice reaches the door before he does and holds up a hand. He doesn't look like a security guard in his white trainers, blue jeans and navy jumper but there's something familiar about him that makes her pause.

'My daughter!' the beautician says, slapping a hand against the glass wall of the shop as she gasps for breath. 'Is she in there?'

'There's no one else here,' says a voice from behind her. 'I'm the only customer left.'

Alice glares at the shoplifter, pulling on her coat. She's going to have words with Larry tomorrow. It's his job to check there there's no one left in the shop before he closes the shutters. Retirement or no retirement, she's seriously considering letting him go. 'You all need to leave. I'm locking up.'

And I *really* need to go and talk to James Malone, she thinks.

'Please.' The woman in the beautician's outfit pushes at the door, angling to get in. 'She's missing. Please. Let me just look.'

The man adds his weight to the door, forcing Alice to let go of the handle. 'I checked the CCTV. She definitely went into your shop. And she hasn't come out.'

'Fine.' Alice locks the double doors, then slaps at the shutter button on the wall. It creaks back into action and slowly begins to slide down over the glass. 'Come in. But you're going to have to leave via the back entrance.'

She's so flustered as the couple push their way in that she doesn't notice Simon strolling along the foyer with his hands in his pockets until he's almost right up against the glass. She makes frantic hand movements for him to hurry then unlocks the doors and ushers him in. As she locks the doors for the second time, the shoplifter comes rushing over and clutches Simon's arm.

'Oh my God! It's you.'

Simon pales and takes a step away from her, but she continues to hang onto his arm. Height-wise there's not much between them and she's staring straight at him, her eyes roaming his face.

'Simon?' Alice says, but he doesn't reply. He's staring at the woman as though he's about to be sick.

It's his stalker, it has to be. She's the one who's been sending Alice all the Facebook messages, who scratched *You're Not Listening* along the side of her car. She jolts as someone touches her on the shoulder. It's Gareth, the security guard with the goatee.

'Not now.' She tries to pull away but he sidesteps her so he's right in her face.

'Please. It's important. I need you to check the female changing rooms. A thirteen-year-old girl has gone missing and we're pretty certain she's hiding in your shop.'

'There's no one else here. The changing rooms will have been checked.' Behind him, the shoplifter has let go of Simon's arm and is rummaging around in her bag. He doesn't look as though he's about to be sick any more but there's confusion on his face.

'Georgia!' The shout fills the store. The beautician's given up waiting. She's hurrying in and out of the racks of clothes, screaming at the top of her voice.

'Alice.' The security guard glances at her name badge. 'Please. The changing rooms. We need to check them now.'

'Simon?' Alice says. 'Is it her? Is it the stalker?'

As the tall woman gawps at her, Simon shakes his head sharply. 'No,' he says. 'But she knows—'

'The changing rooms,' Gareth interrupts and the bubble of irritation that's been building in Alice's chest finally bursts.

'Fine,' she snaps. She just wants him to stop talking and go away. 'Changing rooms. Come on.'

As she stalks across the shop floor, the security guard hurries along beside her, muttering something about his mum and someone called Georgia. Alice lets the words wash over her. The sooner she shows him that there's no one in the changing rooms, the sooner she can get back to Simon and the shoplifter and find out what the hell is going on.

She sighs loudly as they reach the cubicles. Rejected clothes are still on the railing and none of the curtains have been pulled back and checked. No wonder Kaisha shot off as fast as she did. She knew Alice would get her to sort out this mess.

'Right.' Alice pulls back the first curtain to reveal a small cubicle containing a mirror and a dress hanging up on a hook.

She takes the dress and loops it over her arm. Something else she's going to have to put away before she can leave. She glances at Gareth, who's moving down the row of cubicles, crouching to peer under the curtains.

'No one here.' Alice pulls back the next curtain. 'No one here. No one here. No one—'

She lets out a gasp of surprise. Sitting in the corner of the cubicle, dressed in school uniform, her arms wrapped around her knees, is a short, blonde teenage girl.

Chapter 48

Gareth

Gareth takes one look at Georgia's tear-stained face and his heart leaps.

'Kath!' He shouts. 'Kath! Kath, she's here.'

For several seconds no one says a word, not him, not Georgia curled up on the floor and not Alice standing beside him with dresses hooked over her arm. Then Kath arrives, wide-eyed and breathless and starts shouting at her daughter.

'Stop!' Gareth yells through the crying, berating, apologising and confusion. 'Everyone please just stop.'

There's a lull in the noise, then Kath says, 'What the hell do you think you're playing at, Georgia? You scared me half to death,' and it all starts up again.

'Kath, please.' Gareth puts a hand on her shoulder. 'Please, this is important. Please just let her explain.'

He crouches down and looks at Georgia, still gripping her knees. 'You're not in trouble, but I need your help. We need to find Joan, my mum, and I think you know where she is.'

Georgia lets out a loud sob and buries her face in her arms.

'We know why you're here . . .' he glances up at Kath, who's got her hands pressed to her cheeks. 'Amy told us, your friend. She said some girls from school have been bullying you and they told you that if you stole stuff for them it would stop.'

Georgia shakes her head.

'You didn't want to,' Gareth says softly. 'Did you?'

Georgia doesn't move.

'You should have told me,' Kath says and her daughter lets out a loud sob. 'Why didn't you tell me about it, love?'

There's a soft murmuring from between Georgia's arms.

'What's that?' Kath crouches down beside Gareth. 'What's that, love?'

'You were always busy.' Georgia lifts her chin but keeps her eyes covered. 'You told me off if I wanted to talk and you had a client in.'

'That's not—' Kath starts, but Gareth silences her with a finger to his lips.

'Did you come round to ours instead?' he asks.

Georgia doesn't reply.

'Did Joan wave at you from the window, maybe? When you got home from school? Or talk to you in the back garden? Did she invite you in for a cup of tea and you climbed over the fence?'

Another loud sob escapes the young girl's folded arms.

'Did she show you her memory box? Did you see the postcards from my dad?'

There's a further sob, then an anguished cry that sounds like, 'I was only trying to help.'

Gareth doesn't speak. He continues to crouch, his thigh muscles burning as he waits for her to say more. If he pushes her too hard she'll clam up. If he gives her space she might talk.

She's the missing piece in the puzzle of his mum's disappearance. He can't believe it took him so long to figure it out.

'She was so kind to me.' Georgia's voice is a whisper; any louder and it would break. 'I wanted to do something nice.'

'You sent her a postcard. You copied my dad's handwriting.'

'She missed him. I thought it would make her happy.'

'And you talked about going on holiday?'

'She wanted to go to the seaside. I knew she couldn't, not in real life, and she'd forget all about it the next time I saw her, but she was so excited. She called me Ruth and I didn't know who that was. I thought . . . I thought . . . it was just make-believe.'

'It's okay, Georgia,' Kath says softly. 'It's all right, love.'

'Do you know where she's gone?' Gareth asks.

The question hangs in the air. He's holding himself so still he can't breathe.

The silence is punctuated by a sob, then seven words that make his heart sink: 'I wish I did but I don't.'

Chapter 49

Ursula

It's so strange, staring into the face of a man she first saw printed on a tiny scrap of newspaper, but it's definitely him, the man standing next to her. Simon Hamilton is the man plastered all over Edward's bedroom wall.

'A shrine?' Simon says, his grey eyes searching hers.

'Well.' Ursula shrugs uncomfortably. 'That's one word for it.'

She's not sure how to describe what she saw when she walked into Edward's room but 'shrine' is too innocuous. One wall was plastered with photos of Simon – newspaper clippings, computer printouts. There were other things too, handwritten notes saying 'smug bastard,' 'pride comes before a fall' and 'he who laughs last laughs longest', maps, red wool, coloured tacks, photos of BBC Radio Bristol and a couple of printouts of houses and streets. There were printouts from Facebook too, with faces circled.

After Paul made his escape, Ursula moved to the window and

watched as he jumped into his car and pulled away. She needed to call the police, warn them that Paul Wilson was a domestic abuser who was hunting for his wife and child, but he'd taken her mobile with him and there was no landline in the house. She'd have to find a payphone. She looked back at Edward's wall. It was like something from a serial killer film with all the photos and the threats and maps and the wool. Who was this man that he was so obsessed with? She cast a glance back towards the hallway, torn between leaving to call the police and staying to find out more. An email, pinned to the wall, caught her eye. Several sentences were picked out in neon yellow high-lighter pen:

Please stop contacting me.
Some people have better things to do with their time.
Don't be a troll all your life.

The email was signed Simon Hamilton, Presenter, BBC Radio Bristol, but it was written to someone called Ann Friend. Edward hadn't told her not to change the channel on the kitchen radio because he was trying to mask the sound of his pets; he was waiting for Simon Hamilton to start broadcasting again.

It wasn't until Ursula turned to leave that she spotted another set of photos. Pinned up on the right hand of the door were printouts of a woman. In one she was sitting at a table in a cafe with Simon. In another she was walking down a road alone. Then there was one, quite close up, of the same woman in an outfit that Ursula recognised: it was the bright pink blouse the staff wore at Mirage Fashions with 'Alice' picked out in black on a white badge. She was gazing above the line of the camera, at the person who'd secretly taken her photo, her brow creased into a frown. Underneath, Ed had written: *Who's laughing now?*

'Shit,' Simon says, his hands shaking as Ursula hands him the photo of Alice. He glances towards the back of the shop where the sound of crying and raised voices has dropped to a low murmur. 'Does she know?'

Ursula shakes her head. 'I drove here to warn her but I couldn't see her anywhere. I heard one of the other women telling a customer she was out the back so I thought I'd wait.'

'Why didn't you just call the police?'

'I did. I called them from a phone box and told them after . . . after I spoke to them about something else. They said they'd send someone round but I couldn't stay there, not in that house. What if Ed had turned up?'

Simon exhales noisily through his nose. 'This has gone on long enough. We need to go to the police station – you, me and Alice. We need to show them all this . . . all this stuff . . . and tell them everything.'

'Tell the police what?' Alice asks as she walks towards them.

Simon shoves the printout into his pocket. 'Ursula here has discovered who my stalker is.'

Alice gawps at him, then at Ursula.

'Who is it?' she asks.

'My housemate,' Ursula says. 'It's a long story but basically—'

'Is it a woman? Is she called Flora?'

Ursula shakes her head. 'No. His name's Edward.'

'Edward who?'

'Bennett,' Ursula says, remembering the name she saw on the tenancy agreement.

Alice looks at her blankly. The name's not ringing any bells.

'Who is he?' she asks Simon.

He shakes his head. 'I've got absolutely no idea.'

'And you trust her?' She gestures towards Ursula. 'You know she's a shoplifter? I wouldn't trust a word she says.'

'Can we just go?' Simon looks pained. 'Please? She's got evidence. We need to take it to the police.' He points at the shutters. They're all the way down. 'How do we get those things open again?'

'We don't,' Alice says. 'We leave through the back. Come on, I'll show you.'

'Right,' Alice says as they reach the back door to the shop. 'I'll let you two out but I'm going to need another five to ten minutes to tell Lynne she can go, get rid of the three people in the changing rooms and explain to my area manager that I need to leave urgently.' She takes a breath. Her brain is whirling at a hundred miles an hour. It's torture, having to wait to find out more about the man who's been making her life a misery for the last week, but she can't just abandon the shop. She needs to do her job. 'Wait for me in the car park, by my car.' She looks at Simon. 'White VW Golf?'

He nods.

'Great.' She pulls on the handle to the back door, then swears under her breath. 'Sorry. It's locked. The keys are in the office. Wait here for a sec.'

Ursula waits with Simon for all of two or three seconds, then hurries after Alice. She obviously doesn't like or trust her and she wants to talk to Alice before they go to the police station, to apologise for stealing from her shop.

'Alice! Alice!' she calls softly as she jogs round the corner, sweating under the weight of her winter coat, one hand clutching her ribs. But Alice is way ahead of her. She's already at the other end of what looks like a staff changing room and approaching a small office with a closed door and Venetian blinds at the window.

'Alice!' she says again but her shout is lost in Alice's scream.

It all happens so quickly. One minute Ursula is watching Alice step into the room and the next she's gone, yanked inside by an arm that appears from behind the door and hooks itself around her throat. Before Ursula can react, before her stunned brain can process what she just saw, a man steps into the doorway with Alice in his grip.

Ursula blinks, then blinks again. The man standing about four metres from her is holding a knife in his right hand. He's small and slight with little round specs that make his eyes seem bigger than they are.

Ed.

His eyebrows flash upwards in surprise as he meets her gaze, but then his face is a blank again. The muscles in Ursula's thighs twitch and her heart pounds in her chest. She needs to get out, to get help, to—

'Stay where you are.' Edward casually moves the knife to the base of Alice's neck. 'Or I'll cut her throat. You can come out now!' he shouts to someone standing out of sight.

A woman with a dark bob wearing a pink Mirage blouse stumbles out of the office on shaking legs. Ursula's seen her before. It's Lynne, the woman who chucked her out of the changing room the other day.

'Sit!' Ed orders, gesturing at the ground at his feet.

A sob catches in Lynne's throat as she does as she's told. 'Alice, I'm sorry. He locked me in the office when I went in with a coffee. He wouldn't let me leave.'

'Enough.' Ed's gaze flicks towards Ursula. 'You need to sit down too.'

He smiles as she walks towards him on unsteady legs and lowers herself onto the cold lino and gathers her knees to her chest. 'Right then, Alice. I think it's time your boyfriend joined us. Don't you?'

Chapter 50

Alice

When Ed tells Alice to shout Simon's name she doesn't say a word. Not because she doesn't want to, but because she physically can't speak. The crook of his elbow is pulled so tightly around her throat she's struggling to breathe. Her fingers are gripping his arm but she's given up trying to yank it away because it makes him tighten his grip and tip the point of the knife into her cheek. He's a short man but taller than her and she can hear his breath in her ear and feel his body pressed up against her back.

'Shout Simon's name,' Ed says again.

'She can't,' Ursula says from the floor. She and Lynne are sitting cross-legged in front of Alice. Lynne's head is bowed and she's weeping quietly. But Ursula's not afraid to look Ed in the eye, even though he's told them both that if they speak they die. 'You're holding her too tightly.'

'When I want your opinion I'll ask for it,' Ed snaps, but he releases his grip on Alice's neck the tiniest amount. 'Don't try anything,' he hisses. 'Don't shout anything apart from "Simon! I need a word." If you say anything else I will slash your throat and then your friends'. Do we understand each other?'

She nods, or as much as she can.

'Go on then,' he urges. 'Shout for your boyfriend.'

Alice's first shout is little more than a shrill squeak. Fear has closed her voicebox and she feels light-headed and hot.

'Again,' Ed says, releasing his grip a little more. 'Louder this time.'

'Simon!' Alice shouts, her voice breaking as she says his name. 'I need a word.'

A hush falls over the small room as they listen for a response. Even Lynne stops weeping. Alice feels sick with fear as she stares at the doorway, waiting for Simon to appear. What's Ed going to do when he does show up? Slit her throat then turn the knife on him? She thinks of Emily, sitting in Helen's front bedroom, sipping wine as she watches the street. She imagines her checking her watch, wondering where her mum has got to. She's probably already texted to check that the plan is still in place. But Alice's phone has been turned off. Ed made her do it while he watched, the knife tip pressing into her cheek. She had to turn Lynne's phone off too.

Who will tell Emily that she's dead? A police officer? Peter? Or will social media break the news first? She can't die. She can't leave Emily. She doesn't want her daughter to deal with that kind of pain alone. A tear rolls down her cheek and she closes her eyes.

The sound of trainers squeaking on lino makes her open them again and she gasps as Simon appears in the doorway. His eyes flit from her to Ed and he stumbles backwards, his hands held away from his body, as though he's trying to push away what he's seeing.

'You run and she dies,' Ed says and Lynne lets out a terrified sob.

Simon freezes, his hands still outstretched.

'Call the police and she dies,' Ed says. 'Do anything other than what I tell you and she dies.'

Simon swallows, then nods mutely.

'Come into the room and sit down on the floor.'

As Simon steps forward on shaky legs, his arms now raised in surrender, Edward pulls Alice closer, his arm pressing against the cartilage of her windpipe, causing a wave of panic to flood her body. She claws desperately at his arm.

'Is there anyone else in the shop?' Ed asks her.

He releases his grip, just enough to let her talk and she gulps down air.

He increases the pressure again. 'I said, is there anyone else in the shop?'

This time, when he loosens his hold she releases all the air in her lungs to say, 'No.'

As the word leaves her mouth she believes it. She genuinely believes there isn't anyone else in the building, but then she remembers Gareth the security guard, the beautician, and the teenager that she left in the customer changing cubicle and her fingers tremble against Edward's arm. What if they walk into the room next? Will Ed kill her for lying? Please, she prays as Simon sits on the floor beside Lynne, please stay wherever you are.

'You.' Edward kicks out at Lynne, making her screech with fear. 'There's tape and nail scissors in my bag. Use them to bind the hands of the other two.'

'Whatever this is about,' Simon says, 'I'm sure we can—'

The words are knocked out of his mouth as Edward's boot connects with the side of his head. The kick makes the arm around Alice's throat tense and for two or three terrifying seconds, she can't breathe.

'I will tell you when you can speak,' Ed barks at Simon as Alice lifts her chin, gulping for air. 'You!' He points the knife at Lynne, who's holding a roll of black duct tape and some rounded nail scissors. 'Do his hands first.'

Fresh tears roll down Alice's cheeks as Lynne binds Simon's hands, then Ursula's. When Simon first appeared in the doorway she felt a flurry of hope. He was bigger than the man with the knife to her cheek. He could overpower him. He could make it all stop. But he didn't. He walked into the room like a lamb and sat down on the floor. And now his wrists are bound and there's nothing he can do to help her.

'Alice's next,' Ed orders and Alice holds out her hands for her friend to bind.

'I'm sorry,' Lynne whispers. As their eyes meet, Alice sees the terror she feels reflected back at her.

'You will be if you keep talking,' Ed snaps as Lynne finishes hacking at the tape with the nail scissors. 'Right. Your turn.'

He shoves Alice roughly to the ground. With her hands bound, she hits the floor elbow first, but she doesn't groan or scream. She swallows the pain and twists into a sitting position. Simon, beside her, nudges her gently but she doesn't turn to look at him. All her attention is focused on the knife Edward has just put on the table to her right so he can bind Lynne's hands. Although Alice's wrists are taped together, her hands are still free. If she could just get hold of that knife then Ed will be defenceless. Four against one. They should be able to overpower him.

As Ed winds the black tape around Lynne's wrists, Alice looks to her left. She makes eye contact with Ursula first, swivels her eyes towards the knife, then looks back and raises her eyebrows. Ursula raises her eyebrows too and gives the smallest of nods. Alice nudges Simon, who's been watching the exchange. He looks over at the knife and frowns. He seems conflicted, but

Alice hasn't got time for him to make up his mind. Edward has nearly finished cutting through the duct tape with the nail scissors. If she doesn't make a grab for the knife now it's going to be too late.

Her heart thumps against her ribs as she shuffles on the floor, moving from a cross-legged position to knees bent, feet to one side. She freezes as Ed stops cutting the tape and glances at her. She bows her head, eyes fixed on the ground, waiting for a kick or a blow. When none comes she risks a sideways glance. To get to the knife she's going to have to get onto her knees and lunge, arms outstretched. If she can knock the knife off they can rush at Ed as he tries to pick it up. She steels herself. She's got to do it, *now*.

In an instant she's up on her knees and throwing herself at the table but she underestimated how far away it is and her bound hands land six inches from the knife. She frantically shuffles forward but, as her fingers graze the edge of the blade, it's snatched away from her and Ed's angry roar fills her ears.

'Stupid bitch!' The knife curves through the air, then slices through the thin material of her blouse and cuts into her skin.

Chapter 51

Gareth

Gareth is crouched in the cubicle with a finger to his lips when he hears the scream. Georgia, still curled in the corner, shrieks with fear, then makes a strange gulping sound as her mum smothers the sound with her hand.

'Ssssh,' Kath whispers. 'Georgia, ssssh.'

Gareth doesn't think his heart has ever beaten as quickly as it is right now. He's been trained for all sorts of situations over the years – fires, terrorist attacks, natural disasters – but never anything like this. He never dreamed there'd be a hostage situation in the Meads. He's not sure what it was exactly that made him realise something dodgy was going on. Maybe it was his training or some kind of sixth sense. Earlier, when Kath was trying to get Georgia to open up about what had happened, he caught snippets of a conversation as three people, a man and two women, passed the cubicles. Something about a stalker and taking evidence to the police. He left Kath and her daughter in

299

the cubicle. telling them to stay where they were, and peered between the clothing racks at the end of the stalls, watching as the red-haired shop manager led a very tall woman and a blonde-haired man towards the back of the shop. If everyone was leaving, he needed to remind Alice to let them out too.

But no one left. Instead he heard someone double back, heading to the staff changing room and a woman calling Alice's name. It went quiet for a few minutes, then a different female voice shouted, 'Simon.' There was something about the strangled way she called the name that made the hairs stand up on Gareth's arms. Something was wrong. Very, very wrong. He crept out from behind the racks of clothes and stepped quietly through the back of the shop, keeping against the wall. He froze when he heard weighty footsteps, trainers slapping against the ground. Simon, running after hearing his name? Gareth waited a few seconds, then set off again. As he drew closer to the staff changing rooms he heard a new voice – male, clipped, posh – saying, 'Do anything other than what I tell you and she dies.'

Instinctively Gareth clutched at the radio, clipped to his belt. But it wasn't there. He wasn't on duty and wearing his uniform. He had no weapon and no way of radioing for help. Unless . . . in his mind he sees Kath clutching her phone in the car, repeatedly dialling Georgia's number. If she still had battery left he could call the police.

Now, with the scream still ringing in his ears, he presses 999 on Kath's phone and holds it to his ear. It connects almost instantly.

'Emergency, which service do you require?' the operator asks. 'Fire, Police or Ambulance?'

'Police,' Gareth says.

'Connecting you now.'

Gareth stares at the cubicle curtain as the call connects. It's the only thing separating him from whatever madman is holed up in the staff changing rooms. He's standing now, with Kath and Georgia crouched behind him, both breathing hard.

'What is the telephone number you are calling from?' the police operator asks him.

'I don't know,' he hisses. 'And I haven't got time to talk. There's a potential hostage situation in the —'

He gasps as two things happen at once. The curtain is yanked aside and Alice stares in at him with terrified eyes, the sleeve of her blouse slashed, her arm drenched with blood. There's a man standing behind her with an arm around her throat and a knife pressed to her cheek. His eyes meet Gareth's. 'End the call.'

Chapter 52

Ursula

There was a moment, after Ed locked Ursula, Simon and Lynne in the office so he and Alice could search the shop for stragglers, when Ursula thought they might be able to escape. There was no laptop or landline in the cramped room because Ed made Lynne remove them before he locked them inside. He also gathered up everyone's bags and mobile phones. He called Ursula a liar when she told him hers had been stolen by a man who'd barged into their house searching for his wife and child. It was only when she described the inside of Ed's room that his expression changed.

'You can pat me down if you don't believe me,' she said, raising her bound arms above her head.

He grimaced – 'I'd rather not' – and ordered her into the office.

As the lock turned outside she and Simon headed straight for the narrow window. They were two storeys up and there were people milling around on the pavement below. If they could just open it, they could shout for help.

'Don't bother,' Lynne said miserably as Ursula pulled at the handle. 'He made me lock it. He's got the key.'

Simon suggested they try and smash the glass with the office chair but his hands were bound and it took him forever just to pick it up. Even when he did manage to lift it, his awkward throw was so feeble the chair bounced off the pane. They tried hitting the glass then, smashing their fists against it and shouting, but it was double glazed and the people on the street below didn't so much as glance up.

They were still trying to decide what to do when the key turned in the lock and a terrified-looking woman in a beautician's uniform told them to come out. For one wonderful second Ursula thought they'd been rescued, but then she noticed that the woman's hands were bound too. As she filed out of the office with Simon and Lynne she saw a short man with a goatee standing beside a crying young girl. They both had their hands tied with tape.

Standing at the far side of the staff changing room, with one arm around Alice's throat and the knife pressed into her cheek, was Edward.

'It turns out Alice was lying,' he announced to the room. 'Which is a shame . . . for her. Now that we're all assembled, let's make our way out on to the shop floor. The show is about to begin.'

Ursula, sitting cross-legged against a wall, has Gareth on one side of her and Simon on the other. Sitting beside Simon is Lynne with her head in her hands, then Kath with her daughter weeping beside her. Standing between the racks of clothes, with one arm still around Alice's neck and the knife pressed under her jaw like some kind of macabre puppeteer, is Ed.

His gaze rests on Simon.

'You're not the big man now, are you, eh?'

Ursula feels Simon stiffen.

'Nothing to say? Cat got your tongue? Or maybe you only talk shit when you're on the radio? Or is Twitter your new favourite way to express yourself? You're fucking *listening* now, though, aren't you?'

When Simon still doesn't respond, Ed tilts the knife so the tip of the blade presses into the soft flesh under Alice's chin, making her shriek. The right arm of her blouse is drenched in blood and her face is pale and clammy. She looks on the verge of passing out.

'Stop!' Gareth says, making Ursula jump. 'Ed. That's your name, right? Whatever your problem is with Simon we can sort it out without anyone getting hurt.'

'Ha.' Ed laughs dryly. 'Trained in hostage negotiation, are you? When I want a washed-up security guard to speak I'll ask you. You'll keep your mouth shut if you've got any sense.' His gaze flicks back towards Simon. 'And you'd better start talking if you want this to end.'

'Okay . . . okay. I'm talking.' Simon's shoulder knocks against Ursula's as he shifts position. 'What is it you want?'

'I want you to stand up, open the window behind you and jump.'

'Why?'

'Please,' Kath says from the end of the row. 'Just let my daughter go. She's got nothing to do with this and you're really scaring—'

'We can all go home once Simon does what he's told,' Ed snaps. 'What's it to be then, Si?'

'I . . . you can't . . . I don't know why you're doing this. I don't know what I'm supposed to have done.'

'Don't you?' Ed snorts. 'That doesn't surprise me. How many

people's lives have you ruined, Simon? How many people have killed themselves because of your practical jokes? Any idea? One? Ten? Fifty? Any idea, or don't you care?'

Ursula sneaks a sideways glance at Simon. His blond hair is slicked with sweat at the temples and a tendon is pulsing in his cheek.

'I . . . I . . . I don't know . . . I don't know of any. I never . . . I never meant to hurt anyone. I didn't—'

'I'd say one was enough, wouldn't you?'

Ursula sees Alice's horrified eyes flick towards Simon.

'I'm sorry,' Simon says. 'Whatever it is you think I've done . . . if I'd have known . . . if someone had told me I'd—'

'You'd have done what? Invented a time machine? Rewound time so my brother didn't kill himself? So you didn't ring him on your show to claim you found rat droppings in your soup?'

Simon's expression changes.

'Ah, so you do remember. In which case you'll also remember that he lost his shit with you down the phone. He told you you'd find worse than rat droppings in your soup if you ever visited the restaurant again. That it wouldn't be the first time he'd got his revenge on a customer by—'

'I didn't . . . I wouldn't—'

'Don't interrupt me! Any idea how much trade dropped off after that? How rumours went around Bristol to avoid the Fattened Calf because they had a poor hygiene record? How my brother was sacked when he was just on the verge of getting a Michelin star? How he couldn't get a job anywhere else so he had to work in a fucking service station kitchen? How he couldn't even bring himself to cook at home any more? Do you have any idea what that did to him? Do you? Of course not. You didn't give it a second thought because, to you, it was just a *prank*. Ha fucking ha.'

As Ed continues to rant, Ursula watches with horror as his

grip tightens around Alice's neck. She's lost so much blood she's gone limp in his arms. Ursula feels a wave of panic course through her. Ed's not going to let any of them out of there until he gets what he wants.

'I know what it feels like to lose someone,' she says.

Ed's gaze swivels from Simon to her, his eyes small and dark beyond the glint of his glasses. 'Did I ask you to speak?'

'No.' She shifts position, from her bum to her knees, her bound hands held out in front of her. 'No, you didn't. But I understand . . . Ed, I know how much it hurts to lose someone you love.'

'Sit down,' Ed snaps as she struggles to her feet. Ursula ignores him. A strange, tense silence falls on the rest of the group as though they're all holding their breath.

'I lost the love of my life,' she says as she slowly steps towards her housemate. 'He was beaten to death and instead of helping him fight, I ran away.'

Ed shrugs, unmoved.

'No, you don't care, do you?' Ursula says. 'But you cared about your brother. That's what all this is about, isn't it?' She's less than a metre away from him now, her palms are sticky and she's sweating beneath her thick coat. 'You want Simon to hurt as much as you hurt. But it won't help you. I looked the men who killed Nathan in the eye. I testified against them and helped them get sent to prison for a very long time. I thought it would help. I thought I'd feel better. But it didn't. Nathan's still dead and he's never coming back.'

'Sit down.'

A bead of sweat rolls down Ursula's back as she holds out her bound hands. 'Give me the knife.' The sharp crack of Edward's laughter makes her jump, but she keeps her hand outstretched.

'Killing Simon isn't going to bring your brother back.'

'No, but at least Simon will be dead.'

306

'I'm sorry,' Ursula says. 'I'm sorry you lost your brother. I'm sorry you're in so much pain.'

For several seconds Ed doesn't say a word. His eyes grow soft and misty beneath the hard sheen of his glasses and the tension in Ursula's chest eases. She's getting through to him. All he needed was for someone to tell him that they understood.

'Is it Nick?' she asks. 'Your brother? His name's carved into the windowsill in my room.'

Ed nods.

'He wouldn't want you to do this. He wouldn't want Simon to die or for you to go to prison.'

'How do you . . .' Ed's voice breaks and he swallows '. . . how do you know?'

'Because he sounds like he was a good person.'

Ed says nothing, but his eyes don't leave hers. She's getting through to him, she can feel it.

'Give me the knife, Ed,' she says softly. 'Please. For Nick.'

Edward stifles a sob and, as he lowers the knife from Alice's throat, Ursula's heart leaps. He's going to do it. He's going to give her the knife. She leans towards him, reaching for it, the muscles in her arms tensed and straining.

'You're doing the right thing,' she whispers.

The force of Ed's laughter is like a punch to the gut and she recoils, her hands pressed to her belly.

'Really, Ursula? Really? I'm sorry. I can't keep it up. It's too funny.'

'But . . .' she stares at him, unable to reconcile the twisted smile on his face with the look of utter devastation she witnessed just seconds ago ' . . . but what about your brother?'

Edward laughs again as he returns the blade of the knife to Alice's throat. 'Nick was the arsehole who squatted in my spare room. You put two and two together and made "doesn't actually exist". There is no brother. There was no suicide.'

'What?'

'I made it all up. I thought it would be fun to see who'd feel sorry for me, and you fell for it. Honestly, Ursula, I thought you were cleverer than that.'

Ursula stares down at him, too shocked to speak. He's completely lost the plot. 'I don't. I don't understand.'

'There is no brother. I'm the chef Simon rang, you stupid bint. Now, sit down. You're spoiling my fun. Sit . . . down,' Ed says again and she retreats, stepping backwards, her eyes not leaving his face until someone touches the back of her calf and guides her back to her spot on the floor. She told him about Nathan. She opened her heart and he laughed in her face.

Simon, beside her, sits up taller. As he moves, something sharp digs into Ursula's side. 'So it was you,' he says to Edward. 'You were the head chef at the Fattened Calf that I rang. Or is that bullshit too?'

'What was bullshit was what you did to me. You ruined my career. In one single phone call you destroyed everything I'd worked for since I was sixteen and you did it all in the name of entertainment. And you never apologised. Not you, not the station. No one. You couldn't have given two shits. But I'm done talking. On with the show. Seeing as Simon is such a reluctant player it seems as though I'm going to have to add to the cast.'

Ursula hears the note of warning in Ed's voice and looks up.

'You.' He points to Kath. 'Get your kid to open the window above Simon. If she even thinks about shouting for help I'll push her out myself.'

'No. Not Georgia.' Kath tightens her grip on her daughter, pulling her head into her shoulder. 'I'll do it.'

'Are you going to make me repeat myself?'

'It's too high. She won't be able to reach.'

'There are stools over there.' Ed inclines his head towards the shoe racks. 'Use one.'

'No.' Georgia starts to cry. 'No, Mum, I don't want to. Mum, please, I'm scared.'

As Edward shouts at her to shut up, Ursula runs her hand over the sharp object that jabbed itself into her as Simon shifted position. There's something in the pocket of her coat. Something hard and sharp that she stole from her landlord a few days ago. Gareth glances at her as she twists to one side, wincing as she wriggles her bound hands into her pocket. Her fingers close around the dart and she awkwardly eases it out. He nudges her.

'Give it to me.'

Ursula shakes her head and clumsily slides the dart behind her to the small patch of flooring between her bum and the wall.

'Please,' Gareth hisses as Georgia slowly walks past them, a clothes rail wobbling under the weight of her footsteps as she heads for the stools. 'I can do this.'

Ursula shakes her head again, but Gareth reaches behind her before she can stop him, and when she feels for the dart it's gone.

No one says a word as a sobbing Georgia clambers onto the stool and reaches for the catch at the base of the window. When the frame swings out Ursula holds her breath, willing the girl not to speak. Distant sounds drift into the shop – sirens, traffic horns and the rumble of a bus or truck – but Georgia doesn't say a word as she steps down and runs straight back to her mum.

Edward nods at Simon. 'Off you go.'

A muscle pulses in Simon's jaw as he slowly gets to his feet.

'Simon!' Alice gasps. 'Simon, no!'

Ursula glances at Gareth, her palms sticky on the cold wooden floor. If he attacks Edward with the dart now, with the blade of the knife held under Alice's chin, she could be dead before he even gets close. She coughs lightly to try and get Gareth's attention but he doesn't so much as flinch. There's only one person everyone's focused on and that's the man with the knife in his hand.

'Time to jump, to entertain the plebs for the last time.' Edward stares at Simon and tilts his head in the direction of the window. 'What's a little public humiliation between friends?'

'No,' Simon says. 'I'm not going anywhere.'

A wry smile plays on Edward's lips. 'You mustn't have heard me. I told you to jump.'

Simon opens his arms wide. 'You've got the knife. If you want me dead I'm here. Or do you always hide behind women?'

Edward's laughter rings out in the room. 'You must think I'm stupid. Get on that fucking stool.'

'No.'

Ursula holds her breath as he takes a step towards Edward. Simon's an arsehole. It's Alice's life he's playing with, not his.

'Stay where you are,' Ed says, 'or I'll cut her throat.'

'You're not going to do that. You want me dead, not her.'

'Doesn't matter to me either way. She's a liar like you.' Ed's eyes glitter behind the circular frames of his glasses. He presses the knife deeper into Alice's chin, which makes her groan and tip back her head. 'If she dies you'll spend the rest of your life blaming yourself. And if you die then . . .' He shrugs. 'Either way, I win.'

'Don't do it, Simon,' Alice says, her voice little more than a whisper.

'No?' Ed tilts his head to one side. 'Are you sure about that Alice? Because if he jumps I'll let you have your mobile phone back. You can ring your daughter, warn her not to drink the bottle of wine I left on your doorstep. '

Simon frowns. 'What bottle of wine?'

'My little back-up plan, in case you didn't show up here. Well, when I say "wine" it's ninety-eight percent wine. The other two per cent isn't going to give you a headache when you wake up the next morning. Mostly because you won't wake up at all.'

'Emily!' Alice cries as she struggles to get out of Edward's grip, her bloodied fingers striping the skin of his forearm. 'She'll drink it! Simon, she'll drink it!'

'Still think he shouldn't jump?' Edward asks, pressing the tip of the knife back into her cheek. 'If he does I'll give you your phone back. You can ring her, or 999. Either way it's not too late. Not yet anyway.'

Alice suddenly becomes very still, her gaze fixed on Simon's face.

'Who do you choose?' Ed asks. 'Your daughter or your boyfriend?'

'No.' She shakes her head lightly. 'No, no.'

'Your daughter or your boyfriend. Who's going to die?'

'It's okay, Alice,' Simon says softly. 'It's okay.'

Ed's smile widens. 'Are you going to choose for her then?'

As Simon falters, Ursula becomes aware of Alice staring at her. Alice blinks slowly and deliberately then her gaze flicks towards Ursula's feet and she blinks again. Her eyes travel to the broken clothes rail. Another blink. The dart in Gareth's clenched hand. Blink. A sideways glance towards Ed's stomach. As she blinks for the fifth time Ursula inhales sharply. She understands what she's telling her to do.

Ursula gently nudges Gareth, indicating with her eyes that he should look at Alice.

As his eyes swivel towards her, Alice does it again. She looks at Ursula's feet, blinks, the clothes rail, blinks, Gareth's hand, blinks and then Edward's stomach. Gareth's brow wrinkles with confusion then he raises his eyebrows as what he's seeing sinks in.

'No?' Ed says, still focused on Simon. 'You're not going to

311

do the valiant thing? Ah, fuck it. I'll choose. Sorry, Alice. You and your daughter are both dead.'

Everything happens in the blink of an eye. Ursula kicks out at the clothes rail, Ed loosens his grip on Alice's neck as it crashes to the ground, and Gareth barrels towards him, head down and arms spread wide. As he buries the dart under Ed's ribs, Alice twists free. A split second later the two men tumble to the ground. Gareth's on top, his knees either side of Ed's hips. He leans his weight into Ed's left shoulder and reaches for the knife in his outstretched right hand. Ursula holds her breath as Gareth's fingers creep nearer and nearer her landlord's wrist. Just a few more centimetres and he'll smash Ed's hand against the floor and release the knife. Gareth grunts in frustration. He can't quite get there. He's heavier than Ed but they're similar heights and Ed's more supple. He's holding the knife just out of reach. Gareth shifts to his left, gritting his teeth as his fingers slide along Ed's right arm. As he inches closer he has no choice but to release the pressure on Edward's left shoulder.

BAM! The heel of Ed's hand smashes into Gareth's chin. He reels back, arms whirling, but he doesn't move from Ed's hips. As Gareth shakes his head sharply, still reeling from the blow, Ed sits up, the knife glinting as he angles it towards Gareth's chest. Screams fill the shop as Gareth grabs Edward's wrist then the two men tip to the side as they wrestle for control of the knife. There's a tangle of arms and legs as they twist and thrash and pant and grunt, the blade hidden between their locked bodies. Then there's blood. More blood than Ursula has ever seen.

Chapter 53

Joan

Movement in the corner of her eye makes Joan turn her head. A robin is hopping around in the undergrowth, a little red and brown dumpling of a bird, his feathers puffed out to keep warm. Joan smiles. She's always loved robins. There's something about their beady little black eyes, sweet little chirp and the curious cock of their heads that makes her think they're cleverer than other birds. Braver too. John managed to tame one in their garden. He had it eating seeds out of the palm of his hand.

Joan shivers in her best M&S coat and hitches her handbag over her shoulder. It's getting dark on Brandon Hill and she needs to get home. It's the strangest thing but she's not entirely sure what she's doing standing there or how she arrived. She glances to her right, craning her neck to gaze up at Cabot Tower. It looms over the park, its red sandstone body and cream Bath Stone ornamentation faded to grey in the dark. As a child she thought of it as Rapunzel's tower with its jutting balconies, flying buttresses and the winged figure sitting on the top. It was where John proposed to her, back in 1962. She hadn't wanted to move after their lovely picnic lunch but he'd insisted they climb the tower and admire the view. After some needling she'd finally relented and when they reached the top she was pink-cheeked and puffing with her hair clinging to the back of her neck. She'd barely got her breath back when John dropped to one knee. She heard a gasp of surprise from a lady to her right, a giggle from someone to her left, and then it was as though everyone was holding their breath and all she could hear was John's voice and the faint whistle of the wind.

Is it their anniversary? Is that why she's here? For years they marked their special day with a pilgrimage to Cabot Tower, just the two of them at first, then later with Gareth in their arms. Where is Gareth? She looks around for her son but there's no one else there. Just her and the robin, still hopping and observing, keeping an eye on her, never straying very far away.

Joan presses a hand to her mouth as she yawns. She's very tired. She can't remember ever being as tired as this. She wants to lie down, just for a moment. She needs to close her eyes and catch her breath.

The robin hops away from her, deeper into the undergrowth. It turns, looks at her with its little beady eye and tilts it head.

'This way,' it seems to say. 'Follow me.'

Joan reaches under her body to dislodge a pebble from her hip, then she places her handbag beneath her head and pulls her coat over her shoulders like a blanket. The cold ground is a long way from the comfy bed she shares with John but it will do, for now. She reaches out a hand from the coat and touches the soil. Still hard, but there are bulbs beneath it, daffodils, crocuses and tulips, all waiting for the spring. It's amazing really, she thinks as she closes her eyes; all that life, just waiting to burst through.

Her mind drifts as her breathing slows. There's Ruth with her lovely long blonde hair, crouched beside her, pressing a postcard into her hands. And there's Gareth, crawling around on the rug. And there's John, walking down the path with his hands in his pockets and his best hat on. He looks happy. He must have had a good day at work. She's ever so pleased. She's been waiting for him to come home. He's been gone a long time and she's missed him. Hello, love. She opens the door and she smiles.

Chapter 54

Alice

Alice holds up a hand to her eyes, shielding them from the bright, cool sunshine as she steps out of the crematorium with her arm looped through Gareth's. The dark clouds that were gathering when she woke up that morning have disappeared and there's a hint of spring in the air. There's a small group of men huddled outside the building, Gareth's friends, she presumes. One of them raises his hand.

'We'll see you in the pub then, mate!'

'See you there, Doug,' Gareth calls back.

'It was a lovely service,' Ursula says from Gareth's other side. Like Alice, she's holding his arm.

'Yes.' He forces a smile but Alice can see the sadness in his eyes. It's been ten days since Joan's body was found curled up in bushes on Brandon Hill. Ten days since Gareth wrestled the knife away from Edward Bennett and, in the tussle that followed, drove the blade into the other man's body. They gathered around the dead man, not knowing what to do or how to feel. It felt like forever but it couldn't have been more than a few minutes. Then, as the police pounded on the shuttered doors, Alice dragged her way into the back room, dripping blood all over the floor, and retrieved her phone from the pile on the table, turned it on and called her daughter. When Emily answered and told her there was no bottle of wine on the doorstep Alice sobbed hysterically. She was still crying when the paramedics arrived and stretchered her out to the waiting ambulance.

They're going to have to relive what happened when the case goes to trial but, for now, they're all trying to look after each other, particularly Gareth. He was informed of his mother's death in a police interview room. He was released within twenty-four hours, but the prospect of a murder trial still hangs over him, over them all, like a dark cloud. His defence says there's a very good chance he'll get off because the CCTV and witnesses all attest to the fact Edward was fatally wounded by accident. But how Gareth's still standing Alice has no idea. She and Ursula take turns popping round but Kath's pretty much a fixture in Gareth's house these days. She's not sure when Gareth and Kath became a couple, or even if they are, and she's too discreet to ask, but there's a closeness between them that wasn't there the last time she was with them both.

'Gareth!' Kath comes rushing around the crematorium and reaches out a hand to touch the side of his face. 'Are you okay? I'm so sorry I didn't stay for the whole thing.'

'You had to look after Georgia.' He unloops his arm from Alice's and rests his hand on Kath's, holding her hand to his cheek. They gaze at each other, neither one saying a word, and it's such a tender, private moment that Alice takes a few steps away and averts her gaze. Ursula, on Gareth's other side, does the same.

After a beat Gareth says, 'How's she doing?'

Standing some distance away, in the crematorium garden with her arms wrapped around her body, is Kath's daughter. She'd cried all the way through the service and had to leave twice. The second time she and Kath didn't return.

'I'm worried about her,' Gareth tells Kath. 'I've told her over and over again that it wasn't her fault but she's still blaming herself.'

'The funeral was always going to be the hardest bit,' Kath says softly. 'Her counsellor told her as much. She'll be okay. I think she misses your mum more than anything else.'

'We all do.'

Out of the corner of her eye, Alice sees them hug tightly then Kath says something about getting back to Georgia and seeing him later, at the wake. As she hurries across the garden towards her daughter, an older man with ruddy cheeks and a bulbous nose steps forward and clasps Gareth's hand in his.

'It was a good service. You did her proud.'

Gareth nods. 'Thanks, Tony.'

'Your dad would be proud of you too, for what you did the other week and for looking after your mum all these years. You did them both proud.'

Tears shine in Gareth's eyes but he blinks them away before they can fall. 'Thank you. That means a lot.'

'Your cousins are over there.' Tony points across the gardens to where a middle-aged woman and two men are sitting on a wooden bench. 'They'd love to see you.'

'Of course. Mum would have been touched that they came.'

'We're family, we stick together. Well, we do now.' Tony smiles tightly, his lips pressed together, then squeezes Gareth's arm. 'I'll see you in the pub.'

As he wanders away, Ursula says, 'Want us to meet you in the pub too, Gareth, so you can chat to your cousins alone?'

'No, no.' He holds out his elbows for Alice and Ursula to take. 'You can meet them. I've only met Maureen before and she's great.'

Alice shoots Ursula a smile as they both take Gareth's arms again. She's seen a lot of the tall, warm-hearted woman since that terrible night in Mirage Fashions. After the emergency services arrived they both sat in the back of an ambulance as paramedics looked them over. A cheery man called Steve tended to Alice's shoulder wound while Ursula removed her sweatshirt and T-shirt, exposing violent bruises on her shoulders, ribs and on either side of her neck. Alice was so horrified she gasped. Ursula must have been in unbearable pain after Paul Wilson attacked her, but instead of taking herself off to hospital, she'd driven to the Meads to warn her about Ed.

Later, after they'd spoken to the police and been discharged from hospital following a series of X-rays and scans revealed that neither of them had sustained any lasting damage, it was into Ursula's arms that she fell. Alice had walked up to the automatic glass doors of the hospital, phone in hand, asking Emily where she was parked outside, then found she wasn't able to breathe. It came from nowhere, the panic attack that made her heart beat so violently she felt certain she was going to die. When her legs turned to jelly, Ursula caught her and half-dragged, half-carried her back inside to the nearest empty chair. She stayed with her, talking her out of her panic attack, telling her to name five things she could see, four things she could feel, until Alice's pulse gradually slowed and she no longer felt like she was drowning. Eventually a doctor checked her over, confirmed it was a panic attack, and Emily drove her, and Ursula, back to their flat.

Ursula stayed with them that night, sitting round the kitchen table with Alice, Emily and Lynne as they drank wine to numb the shock of what had happened, trying to make sense of it all.

At one point in the evening, when Emily went to the corner shop to get more to drink and Lynne popped out for a smoke, Ursula apologised to Alice for stealing from her shop. She told her about Nathan, the funeral and the brooch, the first thing she'd ever stolen. She cried as she explained how dead she'd felt inside after Nathan's death, how invisible, and how shop-lifting made her feel more alive. It became a habit she couldn't stop, she'd even stolen from a friend, and she hated herself for doing it. When she finally stopped speaking, Alice was crying too.

At some point Emily must have put Alice to bed – she can't remember – but when she got up the next day she was relieved to find Ursula asleep on the sofa, her long limbs hanging over the arms. That first day was like nothing she'd ever known. The phone didn't stop ringing. What had happened in the Meads had made the national news and every journalist in town – and beyond – wanted to speak to them both. In the midst of all the furore there was one phone call that knocked Ursula sideways. A softly spoken woman rang Alice's landline and asked 'to speak to Ursula Andrews please'. Ursula took the phone into the bathroom with her and when she emerged half an hour later her face was wet with tears.

'That was Nathan's mum,' she said. 'She heard on the news that I'm staying with you and looked you up in the phone book. She wanted to check I'm okay.'

There were more calls, for both of them, and when they logged onto Alice's laptop to check social media they stared at the screen open-mouthed. It was as though everyone they'd ever met in their lives wanted to check that they were okay. When Ursula checked her Facebook messages there was one from someone called Charlotte saying how sorry she was for being such a terrible friend and how responsible she felt for what had happened to Ursula afterwards.

'How's it going living with two blokes?' Alice asks Ursula now.

'Good.' She beams across at her. One of the messages they read together was from two of Nathan's friends telling Ursula to ring them. They had a spare room in their shared house and it was hers if she wanted it. 'Last night I forced them to watch *Mamma Mia 2*.'

'And have you heard from Nicki?'

'Yep.' Ursula nods. 'She and Bess are back with her family in Gloucester. I'm going to visit them next week after I've . . . um . . . after I've seen my counsellor. We're going to talk about the possibility of me returning to teaching. She said we've got a lot to work through but she . . .' she smiles cautiously ' . . . she seems hopeful.'

'That's good. Really good news.'

'Have you . . .' Ursula pauses. 'Have you heard from Simon?'

Out of the corner of her eye, Alice sees Gareth shake his head. He's got no time for the bloke. Like Ursula he thinks Simon put her in danger by playing up to Ed.

'No,' Alice says. 'Not for a while.' She glances back at Gareth. 'And I'm happy for it to stay that way.'

And she is. She doesn't hate Simon. She doesn't bear him any kind of ill will. In fact she almost understands why he did the things he did, but he's not the man she thought he was. One thing she's learned recently is that she shouldn't make snap judgements about people. She never would have guessed that she'd become so fond of a short, goateed security guard and a tall, sweaty shoplifter.

Gareth swears under his breath and she follows his line of sight, expecting to see a tall, blonde man lolloping their way. But it's not Simon strolling across the garden towards them in a smart black suit and tie. It's someone she's never seen before, an older man with a comb-over and walnut-coloured skin.

321

'Gareth!' The man draws closer and holds out his hand.

'William.' Gareth unloops his arm from Alice's to give his hand a perfunctory shake.

'I'm so sorry I missed the service. I would have got here earlier but there was a bit of a situation at home.'

'Spirits was it? Causing trouble?' One side of Gareth's mouth twitches into a smile.

'The only spirits involved were in Sheila's lunchtime gin.' There's a fake ring to the older man's laugh. 'No, seriously, your mother was a wonderful woman and I'm so very sorry for your loss.'

'Thank you. If you'd excuse me,' Gareth points across at his cousins, chatting on a bench nearby. 'There are a few people I still need to say hello to.'

'Of course. Of course.'

Alice links her arm back through Gareth's as he sets off towards them. 'Who was that?'

'William Mackesy. Calls himself a spiritual leader when really he's a cold-reader masquerading as a psychic. My mum was sucked in by it, though. She made a donation to his church.'

Alice grimaces. 'Ouch.'

'It gets better. You know those three men who went missing on the Harbourside?'

'Yeah.'

'My uncle Tony told me Mackesy went to the police about them. Apparently their spirits told him they were buried in Leigh Woods.'

'I thought their bodies had washed up under the floating harbour?' Ursula says.

'Exactly. By all accounts they were drunk and fell into the river. All of the Harbourside Murderer stuff was people scare-mongering.' Gareth pauses. 'I knew one of the men who died. Did I tell you? Liam Dunford.'

'God.' Alice looks across at him in alarm. 'I'm so sorry. I didn't know.'

'It's fine. We weren't friends, but he didn't deserve to die.'

They lapse into silence and Alice finds herself thinking about Lynne. She was such a terrible friend to her while all the Simon stuff was going on and she's been trying to compensate. They went to the cinema last night and she's joining Alice, Ursula and Gareth for a curry at hers tonight.

'Albi . . . or Abi!'

Alice turns to see who's shouting. Gareth and Ursula do the same. William Mackesy is walking towards them, his brow furrowed and one hand pressed to the side of his head.

'Oh God, here we go,' Gareth mutters under his breath. 'He's probably going to tell me that an older woman is talking to him and her name begins with J.'

'I've got . . .' William Mackesy screws his eyes tightly shut. 'I've got a man here . . . a young man. His name . . . I'm struggling to catch it but he's trying to tell me something.'

'William,' Gareth says. 'This really isn't appropriate.'

'He's telling me . . . he's saying . . . he's saying, "I love you, Abi." Is one of you Abi? No? Annie maybe? It definitely begins with A. He's very insistent that I talk to you. He says I have to tell you that it wasn't your fault.'

Alice glances at Ursula. All the colour has drained from her cheeks. Gareth notices too. He pulls on her arm and turns her in the other direction. 'Come on, let's go.'

As they march across the lawn towards the three figures on the bench, Ursula looks over Gareth's head to Alice. 'What was the first name he said? Albi or Abi?'

'Albi,' Alice says. 'What does that even mean?'

'It's short for Albatross.'

'Aren't they supposed to be unlucky?'

'Only if you kill them,' Ursula says and raises an eyebrow.

As they continue on down the path, past dozens of low granite memorials, Alice sees something twinkling out of the corner of her eye. It's a tiny metal windmill ornament that someone has placed on one of the graves and surrounded with blue, white and green pieces of sea glass. Ursula spots it too. She drifts away from Alice and gently runs her fingers over the glass, then pauses as she touches the windmill.

'It's lovely,' Ursula says, her empty hand falling back to her side. She turns to look at Alice and Gareth and she smiles.

Chapter 55

Larry

THREE MONTHS LATER

Larry thinks the river Avon is at its most beautiful at night, with tethered boats rocking gently and the lights of the dockside reflecting on the inky black water. At 3 a.m. most of the city is asleep with just a few stragglers making their way home from nightclubs and bars. A few months ago, Larry would have been tucked up in bed too. He always used to be a good sleeper – a hard day's work, a good meal and then he'd be out the moment his head hit the pillow – but something strange has happened to his brain. It doesn't turn off the way it used to. It waits until dark, then bombards him with questions. Who will he be when he's not a security guard any more? Is his cough bronchitis or lung cancer? Why didn't he ask out Linda Bailey in 1973? That's why he walks, so late at night, to drive the questions out of his head.

He's pretty sure it's his impending retirement that's stealing his sleep. As a young man he dreamed of empty days with nothing to do, telling himself that his last day at work was his first day of freedom. Now that date is within touching distance he feels unsettled and unbalanced, as though the ground is shaking beneath his feet. He doesn't want to be one of those old blokes who spend every day in the bookies or the pub. He's got no interest in travelling and the thought of joining a club makes him feel sick. For all its faults, at least people know who he is at work. He's Larry Woolley, security guard, and he's treated with respect.

He screwed up letting that lunatic Edward Bennett into the shop, but how was he to know that he wasn't the new area manager? He said he was, although he hadn't given his real name. Alice never told Larry anything about staff changes, and besides, with his smart suit, briefcase and nerdy glasses Edward was certainly dressed the part. It still rankles Larry that he left before it all kicked off. He'd have sorted it quick sharp. Although fair play to Gareth for stabbing the bloke. Lunatics like that have to be stopped. Another wrong 'un was on the radio news that morning. Some bloke called Paul Wilson jailed for seven and a half years for beating up his wife and kid. A shocking sentence. They should have strung him up by his neck. But the country hadn't completely gone to the dogs. At least the murder charge against Gareth had been dropped. Good thing too.

Larry turns his head sharply as a swaying figure emerges from a side street about twenty metres away. Pissed. Lost. Stumbling around, trying to find his way home. Larry grinds his teeth as the man starts to sing. It's a tuneless rendition of Queen's 'We Are the Champions'. As the man stumbles towards the river, Larry maintains his gentle, ambling pace but his breathing begins to quicken and his hands twitch at his sides. Larry doesn't like singers, especially young, drunk ones. The last bloke that insulted him was so drunk he couldn't walk in a straight line. He was shouting lyrics at the top of his voice and as Larry passed him he told him to keep it down because people were trying to sleep.

'Fuck off, granddad,' the bloke slurred.

Larry turned. 'What did you just say?'

'Something wrong with your hearing?' He rolled his eyes, then took a sudden, unbalanced step to his left, straying towards the edge of the path and the sharp drop to the river below. 'I told you to fuck off. Mind your own business you miserable—'

'Have some respect.'

'Respect?' His face twisted into a sneer. 'For you? I could fucking flatten you. Piss off back to the old folks' home you waste of space.'

Larry's pulse quickened. 'Come here and say that.'

'Nah.' The young bloke waved a dismissive hand through the air and turned to go. 'I don't fight old men.'

Larry ran at him and pushed him hard in the chest, the force enough to knock him clean off his feet. His arms windmilled desperately as he fell and then *splash*; the river swallowed him whole. Larry rushed to the edge of the path and watched him flailing around in the dark water, gasping and spluttering as his coat billowed around him, pressing up round his head. There was a moment – a good two or three seconds – when Larry considered diving in after him. Nah. He shook his head decisively. Fuck him. If he was such a big man he could get himself out.

That night he slept better than he had in months.

His second victim didn't see the shove coming. Larry had trailed him for a while after spotting him arguing with a girl on the steps of the amphitheatre where he'd called her all sorts of horrible names. She'd run off crying and the bloke – a miserable excuse for a man – had set off for a wander, a bottle of vodka in his hand. After he disappeared under the water, Larry didn't stick around.

He decided not to do it again. To get away with it once was lucky, twice was a fluke, but then he heard that little weasel, Liam Dunford, blackmailing Gareth and the injustice of it all made his blood boil. He was only popping up to the changing room to get something out of his bag. Alice didn't like him sharing the shop changing room with the sales girls. She said it made some of them feel uncomfortable. Larry wasn't bothered. He thought the world had gone unisex mad and besides, he likes the camaraderie of being around the other security guards even if the only thing he has in common with most of them is the job. He was rounding the first set of stairs when he heard Liam's whiny demands. Horrible little runt. He knew Gareth's mum wasn't well, they all did, and there he was, blackmailing the bloke, trying to steal his hard-earned cash.

Now Larry allows himself a brief little smile of satisfaction as the gap closes between him and the drunk singing and stumbling towards him. It turns out he might have decided how to spend his retirement after all.

Acknowledgements

Strangers is set in Bristol and, while a lot of the locations are actual places, some have been invented to suit the plot. The Meads is a fictional shopping centre. It was named by Johanet Sloan who won a competition on my Facebook author page. Thank you to the readers who offered their surnames for some of the characters in this book, and to my Twitter followers who let me use their handles. The conversations they have in this book are fictional and don't reflect their personalities or views.

Strangers wouldn't be the book it is without input from my amazing editor Helen Huthwaite. She pushes me to make my books the best they can be, responds to my emails with lightning speed and never, ever drops the ball. She's also a genuinely lovely person. A huge thank you to Phoebe Morgan for stepping into Helen's shoes as she goes on maternity leave. My book couldn't be in safer hands and I couldn't ask for a nicer person to work with.

Grateful thanks as always to my superstar agent Madeleine Milburn who has been with me every step of the way over the last eleven years of my career and continues to be the best agent on the planet. And a big thank you to Hayley Steed and Liane-Louise Smith for working their magic with TV options and foreign rights.

If you've read about this book in a magazine or heard me talk about it at an event or on the radio that's down to the high priestess of publicity, Sabah Khan. Thank you for your PR voodoo (I still can't believe you got me on The Sara Cox Show!). A huge thank you to marketing maestros Hannah O'Brien and Ellie Pilcher for their innovation, creativity and hard work. Big smooches to Anna Derkacz for making me laugh over boozy lunches (and being a sales superstar) and to everyone at Avon and HarperCollins who work so hard on my books. Thanks also to John Rickards for doing a superb job on the copyedits. For anyone looking for a freelance editor/copyeditor John is your man!

I would have struggled to research this book without the following people who answered my endless questions: Tony Kent and Neil White for legal expertise, Stuart Gibbon for police procedural help, and Scott James who talked me through his experience of working as a security guard.

My family and friends are the people who keep me going when doubt sets in, deadlines loom and my stress levels rise. Big love to my parents Jenny and Reg Taylor who have supported me every step of the way (and foist my books onto everyone they know), my sister Bec Taylor who is my biggest cheerleader and my brother Dave Taylor who shares each and every one of my social media posts. Lots of love to Lou Foley, Sami, Frazer and Oliver Eaton, Sophie, Rose and Mia Taylor, Ana Hall, James Loach, Angela Hall, and Steve and Guinevere Hall. And ALL my love to Chris and Seth – my little family and my everything.

Thank you and kitty kisses to Rowan Coleman, Julie Cohen, Kate Harrison, Tamsyn Murray and Miranda Dickinson for holding my hand every step of the way. Drunken fist bumps to my criminally good friends for entertaining me and making me laugh. Massive hugs to the friends who support and put up with me, you know who you are.

Finally, a huge thank you to the publishers, booksellers, retailers, reviewers, book bloggers, librarians and readers who acquire, stock, recommend, lend, borrow and buy my books. I am hugely grateful.

And thank YOU for choosing to read my book. I hope you enjoyed it.

To keep in touch with me on social media please follow me on:
Facebook: http://www.facebook.com/CallyTaylorAuthor
Twitter: http://www.twitter.com/CallyTaylor
Instagram: http://www.instagram.com/CLTaylorAuthor
And if you'd like to receive quarterly updates with all my book news then do join the free C.L. Taylor Book Club. You'll receive THE LODGER for free, just for signing up.

https://cltaylorauthor.com/newsletter/

Reading Group Questions

1. At certain times of the book, we see the response to events on social media in the form of Twitter posts. What do you think this adds to the novel? Do you like it?

2. *Strangers* focuses on three main characters – Alice, Ursula, and Gareth. Who did you feel most connected to, and why?

3. Towards the start of the book, Alice has an unpleasant date with Michael. Do you think she handles this interaction in the best way? How did this scene make you feel?

4. Whereas many crime books focus on the idea that a crime is always committed by someone you know, this novel focuses on the notion that strangers are the ones to watch out for. Do you agree with this? Which idea is most frightening to you – the idea of being hurt by a stranger, or by somebody close to you?

5. What did you think of the way things ended for Joan? Are you glad her story ended where it did?

6. How important do you think the shopping centre setting is as a pivotal place in the novel? Why do you think the author chose a shopping centre for this key scene?

7. Ed behaves badly in this book – but how far does what happened in the past go towards excusing what he does?

8. The central theme of the book is loneliness. How successfully do you think the author explored this theme?

9. Do you think Ursula was right to get involved in Nikki's situation? Why do you think she responded the way she did?